E S S

Praise for J.G. Farrell and *The Hill Station*

J.G. Farrell was born in Liverpool in 1935 and spent a good deal of his life abroad, including periods in France and North America, and then settled in London where he wrote most of his novels. Among his novels, *Troubles* won the Geoffrey Faber Memorial Prize in 1971 and *The Siege of Krishnapur* won the Booker Prize in 1973. In April 1979 he went to live in County Cork, where only four months later he was drowned in a fishing accident.

In 2010 the public chose *Troubles* from a shortlist of six contenders as the Winner of the Lost Man Booker Prize of 1970, as no titles published that year were ever considered for the prize due to a change in submission rules.

The Hill Station

and an Indian Diary

J.G. FARRELL

edited by John Spurling

W&N
ESSENTIALS

First published in Great Britain in 1981 by Weidenfeld & Nicolson
Published in paperback in 1993 by Phoenix
This paperback edition published in 2021 by Weidenfeld & Nicolson,
an imprint of The Orion Publishing Group Ltd
Carmelite House, 50 Victoria Embankment
London EC4Y 0DZ

An Hachette UK Company

1 3 5 7 9 10 8 6 4 2

A CIP catalogue record for this book is
available from the British Library.

ISBN (Mass Market Paperback) 978 1 4746 1395 8
ISBN (eBook) 978 0 2978 6620 6

Printed and bound in Great Britain by Clays Ltd, Elcograf, S.p.A

www.weidenfeldandnicolson.co.uk
www.orionbooks.co.uk

Contents

Foreword

The Hill Station is roughly half a novel. It consists of nineteen chapters, about fifty thousand words. The day before his sudden death in August 1979 Jim Farrell wrote a postcard to Rosemary Legge, his editor at Weidenfeld, saying that he hoped to deliver the completed novel of eighty to a hundred thousand words by the end of that year, as arranged. The rough notes he made for the novel (most of them on the backs of old Weidenfeld envelopes) contain enough material for at least another nineteen chapters. The content of these notes overlaps a good deal and they were obviously jotted down at different stages in the novel's preparation, but they are not of course dated. However, there is one set of notes which, because it mentions none of the material already used in the half-completed novel, may well be the layout of the unwritten half; and it is arranged in sixteen sections which look very much like chapter summaries. By this stage Jim had apparently dropped his original idea of bringing in Madame Blavatsky.

His method of writing a novel, so far as I remember, was to make a complete draft in typescript and then do a second, revised version. Another friend of his insists that he only ever wrote one version, but against this is the fact that in the margins of the typescript for *The Hill Station* are various minor additions and reworkings in handwriting. Rosemary Legge remembers no such handwritten additions to the completed typescripts of *The Siege of Krishnapur* or *The Singapore Grip*. We can assume then, I think, that *The Hill Station* is a first draft. The title, incidentally, is not Jim's, or at least no more than his working identification. He often referred to his 'novel about the hill station'. However, when he wrote his last postcard to Rosemary Legge he had still not decided on a title. Added to the margin at the top of chapter 16 of the typescript is what looks like a possibility for one: 'The Doctor of Confusion'.

I am not at all sure that Jim would have approved of his last novel being published in its unrevised and uncompleted state. Yet, like all the other relations and friends (with one exception) who read it, I very much wanted it published. Why? First, because it's a curious and gripping story; secondly, because it has at least three unforgettable characters (Dr McNab, the Rev. Kingston and the Bishop) who seemed, like Pirandello's Six, to demand to be given life; thirdly, because it powerfully evokes Victorian Simla; fourthly, because Jim was cut off in his prime not only as a man but as a novelist. His art was developing vigorously and consistently. *The Hill Station*, although it was intended to be a 'small' novel compared with the previous three, clearly represents a further consolidation and advance of his powers. It may not be complete but, without it, one's understanding of him and his work is not complete either.

The text as published incorporates most of his marginal additions. Jim did not always indicate exactly where they fitted, so I have had to make a few guesses. Occasionally the marginalia were simply direct quotes from source material or reminders to himself of material which he had not quite decided how to place: these have been omitted. I have also smoothed out the odd bit of clumsy grammar in the typescript, but have worked on the principle of leaving anything rough that could be left without badly jolting the reader; it seemed best to avoid being drawn towards 'improvement' and even such a minor inconsistency as that of Mrs Cloreworthy on page 96 becoming Mrs Claworth on page 136 has been allowed to stand. The worst jolt of all, of course, is the abrupt breaking-off of the text *in medias res*. I have suggested elsewhere in this volume, towards the end of my essay on Jim's work, how the story would probably have continued and ended, so as to spare the reader at least some of the feelings of sadness and disappointment which came over me when I first finished reading the typescript. But those feelings are inevitable, just because, as Malcolm Dean reminds us in his personal memoir, Jim was such a good storyteller. The only antidote is to be warned in advance and to enjoy what there is of the journey without expecting any proper destination.

The Indian Diary was written while Jim was travelling in

India in 1971, researching *Krishnapur*. Like the notes on the backs of envelopes it was a typically modest affair, kept in a small triplicate book with the carbon removed, so that the numbering of the original's pages is rather confusing, page1 being followed by two further page1s and so on. There was rather more doubt about publishing this diary than about the novel. I felt strongly that it should be published, because although, apart from the train journeys, it has no direct bearing on *The Hill Station* – Jim went to Mussoorie but not to Simla, which he meant to see in the autumn of 1979 – it gives a remarkable account of his immediate reactions to India. The descriptive passages, especially those about Indian funeral rites, carry as strong a sense of the country as any I have read. Then his response to the people he met is characteristic of his approach to the characters in his novels as well as being – in the one case I can vouch for, that of my great-uncle, Edmund Gibson – sharply lifelike. Finally, the whole diary seems to me to reveal a lot about Jim himself at that crucial period in his life when his whole view of the world and how he could render it in fictional form was beginning to shift and expand. This is perhaps slightly to overstate the matter. The diary is not obviously confessional or self-analysing, but it does convey very distinctly Jim's ambivalence about himself, his class and race and their ex-Empire. Out of that ambivalence he created all his best work, including what there is of *The Hill Station*. Here in the diary one can see him in life being the liberal outsider and reluctant sahib, whose sympathies and antipathies, self-doubts, hesitations and moments of atavistic impatience are so sensitively and humorously explored in fictional characters like the Major in *Troubles*, Fleury in *Krishnapur*, Matthew in *Singapore* and McNab in *The Hill Station*.

I have put a few brief notes to the diary, simply to explain, where I could, who the proper names belong to, and I have corrected the spelling of one or two place-names. I have also left out a superfluous second reference to my uncle's driver's wife's suicide, suppressed two illegible words, supplied one that was missing, and occasionally paragraphed. Otherwise nothing in the diary has been tampered with.

The rest of this volume consists of essays by three of Jim's friends. Malcolm Dean knew him better and for longer than either Margaret Drabble or I did and has contributed a personal memoir; Margaret Drabble has concentrated on the central elements of his mature work and I have tried to set *The Hill Station* in the context of his six preceding novels. This book is not intended as a tribute, still less as a memorial, but as the best that can be done in the circumstances to keep open a particular dialogue with the contemporary world which ought to have continued for a long while yet. Elizabeth Bowen, reviewing *Troubles*, wrote that it was 'not a "period piece"; it is yesterday reflected in today's consciousness. The ironies, the disparities, the dismay, the sense of unavailingness are contemporary.' All three of us allude to Jim's political views, without pinning them down. He had not pinned them down himself, they were still evolving. He was a writer who, during the last ten years of his life, found himself arriving in the course of working on each fresh novel at a new point in his relationship with reality. The experience is fairly common, its vivid articulation rare. For that reason above all Jim's work will live and for that reason the diary – which marks one such point – and the half-finished, untitled last novel – which marks another – are essential parts of it.

I would like to thank Jim's mother and his brother Richard, his friend Bridget O'Toole, and John Curtis and Rosemary Legge at Weidenfeld for their help in preparing this book.

John Spurling

The Hill Station

I

Nowadays the railway goes all the way up to Simla, but before the turn of the century it stopped at Kalka. The rest of the journey, some fifty-eight miles of it up into the hills, still had to be accomplished in a two-wheeled cart drawn by a couple of vigorous Kabul ponies under the auspices of the Mountain Car Company, as it was called . . . a devastating last lap of your journey if you were coming to Simla to repair your health. The best that could be said for it was that this two-pony vehicle, the tonga, was itself an improvement on the sedan chairs and litters that had been the invalid's lot in yet earlier days before the building of the road.

There was a hotel at Kalka, however, where you could rest before you began the climb, owned also, as it happened, by the enterprising proprietor of the Mountain Car Company, a certain Mr Lowrie, a plump, bright-eyed fellow with curling moustaches who liked to pretend that he knew everything about everything in the hills and in the plains, or, as he put it, 'between Heaven and earth'. He owned another hotel, too, on the Mall in Simla which was no doubt a help in the matter of keeping himself informed. He was always either up there or down here and sometimes it was hard to believe that he was not in both places at the same time, such was his energy and ubiquity. Yes, if he did not know all your secrets by the time you left Kalka he would most certainly learn them when you reached Simla. But he was a sympathetic individual and so why should you keep anything from him? True, he could be a little indiscreet on occasion, but that was only because he found your affairs so fascinating the he could not resist sharing them with others.

It was Mr Lowrie's custom to meet the trains arriving in Kalka whenever he had the opportunity and over the years regular visitors came to expect to see him there at the railway-station, standing sun-helmet in hand in front of a carefully marshalled regiment of hotel bearers and coolies. His wife, a motherly lady in a cotton dress, as a rule stood beside him with smelling salts and eau de cologne in case of emergency, for sometimes it happened that people left their escape from the burning plains too late, or almost too late. Indeed it was for this reason that Mr Lowrie found train-arrivals so intensely interesting: his experienced eye would pass swiftly over the passengers descending from the train and within a few moments he would have the entire train-load classified. There would probably be a party of boisterous young officers on their way to Simla for a few weeks of sport and flirtation, each one of them armed with a highly questionable sick-certificate when, most likely, he had no worse malady to complain of than boredom at some remote station on the plains. There would be Government officials, too, perhaps accompanied by their wives: many of them he would know already by sight, having seen them in preceding years, and soon he would come to know them even better by hearsay as news of their doings during the cold season in Calcutta, Delhi and Bombay gradually filtered through to the Himalayan foothills. These people were engaging enough, certainly, but there were usually other travellers whom Mr Lowrie found even more interesting. These were the invalids.

It seldom took him more than a moment to pick out their pale travel-stained faces. The dust that accompanies almost every human endeavour in India during the hot weather would have cast a dull veil over them in the afternoon sunlight, turning them into ghostly figures, coughing some of them, others leaning with weary gestures on sticks or on the arms of the bearers they had brought with them on their journey. These invalids very often spent a night or two in Kalka before moving onwards and upwards . . . the sickly children, the recently pregnant young women hoping for delivery in the hills, the men whose health had been shattered by malaria or dysentery or simply by working too hard in a climate to which they were not accustomed. Poor ghosts! They gathered here under Mr Lowrie's sparkling eye, as on the bank of a dark river, waiting to be ferried to the other side. With practice Mr Lowrie had grown skilful at telling which of them would not return.

There were three cemeteries in Simla (well, four, if you counted the 'Nun's Graveyard' belonging to the Convent of Jesus and Mary at Chota Simla) but of these three, two were already full and the third was filling rapidly. Sometimes Mr Lowrie wondered whether it might not be a good idea to start one in Kalka, too, in order to spare his ponies so many unnecessary journeys. There was, as it happened, already a small cemetery in Kalka but it was ill-tended and poorly patronized. Could something not be done with it? Mr Lowrie, who also managed to be a churchwarden 'up there' as well as an hotelier, took naturally more than a passing interest in graveyards and their occupants. Of course, as Mr Lowrie well knew, people preferred burial at a higher altitude where it was cooler and where the countryside reminded them of home, and he was not the man to argue with the whims of his clients. But still, looking at the ghostly passengers assembling on the railway platform to be ferried onwards by the Mountain Car Company he could not help but pick out those whom he would have liked to divert neatly into the cemetery at Kalka, thus sparing them and everybody else the nuisance and fatigue of their long climb into the hills. This pallid young woman, for instance, accompanied by a vigorous, impatient gentleman, her attempt to appear animated did not deceive Mr Lowrie. She was being ridden at her last fence, poor soul, and soon her life's steeplechase would be over. Would she not be better to end her days peacefully at Lowrie's Hotel in Kalka? Why, certainly she would! And yes . . . yes . . . he had thought as much! The Mountain Car Company would only be taking this poor soul on *part* of its journey upwards, the rest it would have to accomplish on its own. Or this old codger leaning on his stick to punt himself out of the stinging sunlight into the shade, *how*, short of breath as he was, would he survive at an altitude of seven thousand feet? Besides, there was not enough flesh on him to make a vulture's supper! He would be far better advised to make the cemetery at Kalka his final destination.

Yes, Mr Lowrie would shake his head sadly as he watched his 'ghosts' assemble on the platform. There was nothing to be done about it. He had once or twice ventured to propose to certain of them a somewhat longer stay in Kalka than they had evidently been considering. But whether or not they had altogether caught the drift of his remarks, it had been to no avail. He had been rebuffed. Still, he had taken it philosophically. He had, after all, only been trying to help. He was not a man to take offence. He had continued as before to provide the ferry-service the ghosts required of him, glancing at them searchingly and occasionally indicating to his wife some poor soul who would not be returning. It was, by the way, a profitable business the Mountain Car Company, there was always that to console him. As for his wife, she would turn pale herself and begin to tremble whenever Mr Lowrie pronounced sentence on somebody: she had never been able to get over the shock of it. She knew he was always right. However, once she had recovered herself, husband and wife would both step forward to greet the condemned person, smiling at him sympathetically, almost tenderly. Then they would gently help him towards the exit.

2

One day in March 1871, two ladies and a gentleman found themselves sitting in a railway carriage whose destination was Kalka and whose arrival there would be, no doubt about it, in due course supervised by Mr Lowrie. The gentleman was middle aged, reserved, and had a somewhat melancholy air. The ladies, one of whom was his wife and the other his niece, had taken seats opposite each other at one of the windows although for the moment there was nothing to be seen but a few feet of a platform at Delhi railway station. If Mr Lowrie had been present he might have had to look twice at the older couple to make sure they were not 'ghosts', so tired and drawn did they look, for they had both spent the day before on the railway, too, and the day before that, and the day before that . . . travelling to Bombay where they had been to meet the younger woman. She, at any rate, would not have caused Mr Lowrie a moment's hesitation for she was the very picture of health: her eyes were bright and her cheeks had the colour that only youth and a sea voyage can bestow.

Only if he had looked closely would he have noticed that one of her arms hung rather loosely at her side and ended in a hand whose shrinking tendons had drawn its fingers into a permanently clutching little fist. But Mr Lowrie could not be expected to notice everything. Besides, he was not a specialist in this field, being more interested in the illnesses themselves than in their after-effects.

'Are ye comfortable, Emily?' her uncle, who had seated himself beside her, enquired.

By way of reply she smiled and patted his hand with her good hand before turning with a little sigh of pleasure to gaze out of the window at the astonishing variety of Indian life to be glimpsed even on the little area of platform beside her. The older woman, who had pleasant grey eyes and an independent air, exchanged an amused glance with her husband at that little sigh but neither of them said anything. They had arrived several minutes too early and other passengers were still hurrying along the platform. One or two hesitated for a moment at the door to their compartment, peering inside, before moving on to another. The older woman leaned her head back against the corner seat and closed her eyes. A little while later she opened them again, aware of a slight commotion, for another passenger was being installed in the compartment by an excited coolie who was afraid that the train might depart before the passenger had time to reward his services. Indeed, the late-comer barely had time to settle with the coolie, raise his hat and say 'Good morning' to the occupants of the compartment and take his seat before the first booming explosions of steam echoed around the station. Almost imperceptibly the train began to move.

The newcomer was a clergyman in his late forties. He had taken a seat beside the far window and almost immediately produced a book from somewhere and began to read. This gave the other passengers the chance to study him with discretion. He had a long, thin, intelligent face, deeply lined about the mouth and a very high colour. There were many strands of silver in his

black hair and his cheekbones stood out sharply from his
fleshless face. But what made the strongest impression of all was
the fact that his eyes, though they were deeply sunk beneath
heavy brows, glistened with unusual brightness. He wore not
the clerical collar but the white neck-cloth of the old-fashioned
clergyman, and a long straight coat, which, when he was
standing, reached almost to his heels and somewhat resembled a
cassock. Both the coat and the high waist-coat he wore beneath
it were decidedly threadbare, the ladies noticed, and their eyes
moved up to the suitcase he had placed in the net above his head:
this, too, had been better days and appeared to be fastened by a
piece of rope passed around it and knotted at the handle. But
once they had taken this in there seemed to be nothing more to
be discovered from his appearance and they retired into their
own thoughts once more. The other gentleman, however,
continued to keep an eye on him, idly curious to see the title of
the book he was reading. When, presently, he did manage to
catch a glimpse of it he frowned slightly. It was Keble's *The
Christian Year*. The title stirred some faint memory from years
ago but he became drowsy and fell asleep before he could seize
it.

The train puffed steadily northwards over dusty glaring
plains of dried mud, with here and there a mud village, a well, a
field of sugar-cane, a few palms, a pair of yoked water-buffalo,
another mud village, a field of mustard improbably yellow, a
temple, a few banyan or peepul trees and so on and on until the
mind grew weary with the repetition. The old travellers had
barely given it a glance: they had seen it many times before. And
even the young woman by the window who was so interested in
everything eventually became hypnotized and stared out in a
trance at the fleeing scenery.

As the hours wore on it became very hot. Despite the dust the
windows had to be kept open and a fine white film collected on
hair, on clothes, on luggage. To refresh themselves the ladies
once or twice patted their brows with handkerchieves soaked in
cologne. Only the clergyman appeared unaffected by the heat,
although the high colour had drained away from his face and he
had become quite pale. He read on steadily, absorbed, looking

up for a moment now and then but with the air of someone who for the moment has forgotten where he is. On one such occasion the younger woman happened to meet his gaze and thought how gentle his eyes seemed.

Occasional sounds filtered through to them from the next compartment. Tenor voices sang a song, but muffled . . . they could not hear it well enough to make out the words. Later there was some bumping and banging and laughter, as if a wrestling match were going on. The two women smiled at each other interrogatively. A little later the younger woman touched the hand of her aunt, smiling, to draw her attention to something; and, turning, the older woman saw that a head had appeared outside the window, or really only half a head: some curly hair, a pair of bulging blue eyes, an upturned nose and a blond moustache. The owner of these features, wearing a lieutenant's uniform, had left one leg and one arm anchored in the window of the next compartment while he clung precariously to the outside of the speeding train with the other. A third arm, also in a uniformed sleeve, encircled his waist as a precaution.

'Don't encourage them, Emily dear. I fear they may kill themselves,' said the older woman, smiling.

Although she assumed an indifferent expression as best she could, Emily had the greatest difficulty avoiding those bulging blue eyes hurtling along outside the window. She did her best to concentrate on the clergyman reading his book on the other side of the compartment. As she watched him a drop of perspiration fell from his brow and splashed on the page, but he read on without noticing, his lips moving almost imperceptibly. After a little while Emily could not help snatching another quick glance out of the window and what she saw made her catch her breath. 'Oh, do look!'

The protective arm which had encircled the waist of the young man clinging to the outside of the train had been withdrawn and now the haft of a fishing-rod was poking out of the next window and tickling him in the ribs. He was obliged to remove the hand which had been gripping the gutter above their window in order to fight off the fishing-rod which continued to torment him. He hung there for a moment swaying dangerously with every lurch of the train and trying to kick someone inside the next compartment: his outside foot slipped or seemed to slip, then recovered itself. At last, somehow or other he managed to scramble back into the compartment disappearing from Emily's view.

'Gracious! I thought he would fall.'

The train puffed on over the plain. More thumping, banging and laughter was to be heard from next door. Another song was sung. An empty bottle was flung out of the window and rolled away down the verge, there were a few minutes of noisy argument, but at length the afternoon heat asserted itself and even the inhabitants of the next compartment were quelled. Emily's head, too, began to droop. Another hour passed. Her companions slept. Only the clergyman read on relentlessly.

After a while the train came to a halt, jolting them awake. Emily peered out sleepily at a long row of natives sitting on their heels with their backs to the station-house wall. Others were carrying their bundles and bedding towards the third-class carriages. A sign read SAHARANPUR. She raised her small hand to capture a yawn, longing at the same time to be alone so that she could scratch herself all over: the most that she could permit herself for the moment was to wriggle a little in her itching garments. Then she blinked, for into her field of vision there had suddenly crept an extraordinary sight. The young officers from next door had somewhere discovered a coolie's luggage-cart, two of them had seized its shafts and miming a prodigious effort were dragging it past Emily's window, heads bent, groaning as if they were slaves driven to exhaustion. On the cart itself stood a figure clad from head to foot in a white sheet, face whitened with chalk, a hand resting eloquently on his heart. He gazed straight into Emily's eyes, his mouth open with adoration. 'Surely all this can't be meant for *me*!' she thought, taken aback. But there was no doubt about it: the white-faced figure on the cart had the bulging blue eyes and curly hair of the young man who had earlier clung to the outside of the train. The apparition went trembling slowly by and disappeared. The natives sitting on their heels against the wall had watched it go by impassively and without any comment.

'Well, Emily,' said her uncle, 'you're in India only a couple of days and already it seems you have made a conquest!'

'Oh, I expect they are just silly boys,' she said, but looked rather pleased nevertheless. 'In Bath, you know, when my father took me to regimental balls, the younger officers sometimes paid me the most amazing compliments. You'd hardly believe the things they would say! I would have to make it quite plain that I was not interested in their foolishness. And sometimes even the older officers would have to put them in their places!'

'Is that so?' replied her uncle. 'Well, I wouldna worry this time. I doubt they are too serious.' And a faint smile lit up his melancholy features.

'Ah!' exclaimed the clergyman suddenly. The others glanced in his direction but it was not Emily's conquest which had caused that deep sigh but the book he was reading. He was slowly shaking his head over it and his eyes had filled with tears. The movement of his head caused another drop of perspiration to splash on the page, or perhaps even a tear, it was hard to say. He looked up then, with the surprised but glad air of someone waking from a deep sleep to find himself surrounded by friends, examining his fellow-passengers for the first time. He smiled at them. For a moment it seemed that he would say something, his mouth began to open ... but then his eyes dropped once more to the book on his lap.

'Oh look! They're coming back. How vexing!' murmured Emily and hurriedly averted her gaze. Her eyes shone, however, and it was evident to her uncle that she considered the young officers' antics a pleasant enough diversion for a long and tiring journey.

The coolie's cart creaked slowly along the platform once more. Out of the corner of her eye Emily saw that the blue-eyed officer had now sunk to his knees, one hand resting pathetically on the side of the cart, the other still clasped to his heart. In the meantime his comrades had discovered some soot or blacking and had added dark rings under his eyes and the most lugubrious mouth. Just as the cart was approaching Emily's window once again, however, there was a commotion which rather spoiled the effect. A whistle blew and at the same moment two late-coming passengers, a European woman wearing a hat and veil against the dust and a small boy, were escorted hurriedly across the platform to the nearest door, which happened to be the one beside Emily. As a result the cart's progress was checked, the two officers who had been dragging it both let go of the shafts simultaneously and sprinted for their own door afraid that the train was leaving. The shafts hit the platform with a bump, almost dislodging the blue-eyed officer who put his hands on his hips in a gesture that declared plainly how fed up he was to be so ill-treated. He looked so rueful and pathetic that Emily, though she could not see what happened next because by this time the veiled lady was standing on the step beside her and, while saying farewells to her escort who was insisting on kissing her hand copiously, was blocking Emily's view. The small boy had climbed on to the seat opposite her and was looking anxious. The lady climbed the step into the compartment. Her escort, a tall, grey-faced gentleman no longer young, raised his sun-helmet, revealing a bald head that glittered in the sunlight. The train began to move.

The young man was still in the cart although by now he was struggling to get out of it. 'Hey! wait for me!' he called to his friends, at the same time getting himself comically entangled in his improvised toga.

'He'll be left behind!' cried Emily, her hand to her mouth. But no, he had been exaggerating his difficulties. Though the train was by now gathering speed he jumped for the step and clung on without difficulty, making some laughing remark through the open window to his friends inside the compartment. Then he took hold of the gutter above his head and in one smooth movement, like a gymnast, raised his knees to his chin and swung himself feet first through the window. The hands and head were retrieved. Emily sat wondering at the grace of his movement.

The clergyman suddenly coughed convulsively over the pages of his book. With a visible effort he obliged himself to stop immediately, however, and continued reading. The lady who had just entered the compartment had taken a seat opposite him beside the window. She had lifted her veil to reveal a delicate little face surrounded by dark ringlets which she was now patting carefully into place, a task which required such concentration that the tip of a pink tongue had appeared in the perfect bow of her lips. She did not appear to be much older than Emily although, of course, she must be because the little boy, who was evidently her son, was at least six or seven years old. He was a pale and silent little fellow whose eyes were constantly on his mother. His nails, Emily could see, were badly bitten and she could not help comparing him with her own little brother who was about the same age and whom she had successfully trained out of the habit by dipping his little fingertips into a disagreeable-tasting ointment. He leaned over to his mother and whispered something in her ear but she continued patting her hair and idly gazing out of the window beside her. Presently, Emily caught his eye and smiled at him but he dropped his gaze immediately and stared at the floor. A strange new perfume stole through the dusty air of the carriage, stirring echoes of warmth and excitement. Emily breathed in deeply and her pulse quickened at the thought of the new life awaiting her in India. Even the clergyman perhaps noticed the perfume for he looked up suddenly at the lady opposite him, but then his features convulsed in a coughing fit. His shoulders heaved. Again he mastered himself and with a deep, shuddering breath he went on reading.

'Was that last station Saharanpur?' asked Emily. Her aunt, drowsing opposite her, opened her grey eyes sleepily, nodded, and closed them again.

'Well perhaps it will not be too long then before we arrive at Kalka,' mused Emily aloud. She wondered whether the train would halt again and if so whether anything more would be seen of the young officers. They had quietened down again: evidently the heat had once more got the better of them. Her uncle and aunt slept. The clergyman read on, his face so pale in the blue shadow of the compartment that it might have been ivory.

3

The railway was running alongside a road and now that the sun was lower in the sky there was a little traffic to be seen on it: a few natives clad from head to toe in white muslin who were carrying bundles on their heads, a boy herding water-buffalo, and a camel harnessed to a hay-cart, its lips puckering disagreeably as the train went by. The traffic increased and soon a temple, a mosque, and one or two mud hovels were to be seen, then a number of more substantial houses and a bazaar. The train slowed and came to a stop at a primitive platform of baked red earth; from the shade of the trees beside it there issued a ragged little army of hawkers: water-vendors with bulging water-skins on their backs, sellers of nuts and chapatis and fly-covered sweetmeats and oranges and bananas. Behind them hobbled a few emaciated beggars, holding out bony arms towards the train and mewing feebly.

Seeing her white face at the open window the hawkers crowded round Emily's window, trying to place their wares in her lap, but she would have none of it. Her aunt opened her eyes a little to see what all the fuss was about, then closed them again. Beside Emily her uncle slept: his half-open mouth increased the melancholy cast of his features. After a while the hawkers fell away, discouraged, and joined the circle round the next compartment. Here business was being done.

'If that's an orange, my friend, I say it's a damn rotten one,' came a loud English voice. An orange, hurled from the window, flashed across the bright platform and splattered against the station wall beneath a brilliant cascade of bougainvillea. Emily shook her head vigorously, for beggars had taken the place of the hawkers at the window, cupping skeletal fingers in front of her. Soon they, too, became discouraged and dropped away. The platform was quiet. 'The young men next door have forgotten about me,' Emily thought. But a moment later she heard the door of their compartment open, followed by some chuckling and whispered instructions. One of the officers came skipping out on to the platform carrying a small wooden box. He bowed to her, placed the box carefully on the platform beside her window and jumped on to it. He stood there on one leg in an artificial pose, one arm raised in front of him, the other flung out sideways. At the same time the blue-eyed officer came tripping along the platform like a ballet dancer, still swathed in the white sheet and with his face even more elaborately whitened than before. Now and then he would stoop as if to pick an invisible flower, would sniff at it and place it delicately with an invisible posy. The path he was following brought him nearer to her window. 'Get on with it, Teddy,' growled the officer standing on the box in an undertone. 'I can't stand on one leg for ever.'

The blue-eyed officer paid no attention, his eyes on the ground searching for invisible flowers. By now he was only a few feet from where Emily sat. Suddenly he looked up, straight into Emily's eyes, his mouth open in shock. His hands flew open, dropping the flowers. He stood there, transfixed. So unexpected did Emily find this that she, too, felt a shock. They stared at each other.

'About time, too,' grumbled the officer on the box and reaching over his shoulder drew an invisible arrow from an invisible quiver, fitted it to his invisible bow-string, bent the bow, aimed it at the chest of his companion, and released it. The blue-eyed officer shuddered visibly at the impact and, without for a moment removing his eyes from Emily's face, began to waltz drunkenly about the platform tugging with both hands at the arrow lodged in his chest. It was only then that Emily was at last able to turn away, aware that she was blushing.

She was relieved to see that her aunt and uncle were still asleep. The clergyman, too, was still bent over his book, but the lady opposite him had been watching with interest. She smiled sympathetically at Emily and said, nodding to the window beside her: 'It seems that we both have admirers.' It was only then that Emily noticed that there was yet another officer, somewhat older than the young men performing the charade on the platform, who was standing on the waste ground on the other side of the train and staring fixedly into their compartment.

'I believe that person is a Captain Hagan,' went on the lady with a laugh which revealed her little white teeth. 'He went to great lengths to have himself introduced to me at Annandale last season but of course I would have nothing to do with him. Nor *will* I have anything to do with him. He has the worst possible reputation. He may stand and stare as long as he likes, it will do him no good.'

The man who had been identified as Captain Hagan continued to stand there perfectly still with one hand on his hip in an arrogant pose, staring at the lady in the most peculiar way. How long he might have remained there is hard to say for at this moment the whistle blew, there was a jolt that echoed down the train from one carriage to another and very slowly they began to move again. A few seconds later and he had passed from Emily's view.

She turned back hurriedly to see how her own officers were getting on. Ignoring the fact that the train was creeping away the blue-eyed officer lay on his back on the platform while his friend went through a comic pantomime of dragging the invisible arrow out of his chest. But it would not come. With each tug the blue-eyed officer's back came up off the platform a few inches and then sank back again. Baffled, his companion scratched his head, then decided to place a foot on the blue-eyed officer's chest for leverage. He bent double for a supreme effort. His face contorted with the strain, he pulled and pulled until, suddenly, it came free and he sat back with a bump on the platform. Emily gasped. It all seemed so extraordinarily lifelike . . . it was as if there really had been an arrow lodged in the blue-eyed officer's chest. But now they both jumped up, laughing, and swung themselves aboard the train. Not a second too soon, either. As it was they had to work their way back along the outside of the train to their own compartment. One after the other they swung themselves in through the window and disappeared from view.

Emily felt bewildered and a little upset, wondering whether this could be the way that people often behaved in India: surely that could not be the case. The little boy was eyeing her surreptitiously and before he could look away she said to him: 'I have a little brother the same age as you at home called Tom. What's your name?' But the boy dropped his eyes and made no reply. As for his mother, she had become engrossed in rummaging in her handbag from which she presently produced a small mirror and a lace handkerchief.

The train had now left both the town and the road behind and was rattling out into the plain again. Emily stared in a trance at the horizon where a great bank of clouds was gathering beneath the rays of the late-afternoon sun. But after a while she realized that these were not clouds but mountains . . . indeed, the mountains of their destination, the western Himalayas. She looked around with excitement but her aunt and uncle were still asleep. The clergyman, though he had momentarily closed his book, was sitting with his head in his hands in a brown study, his lips working slightly as if reciting something to himself. Only the other lady had noticed Emily's excitement and the cause of it. She smiled condescendingly and said: 'Yes, we shall soon be at Kalka.' After a moment she added: 'Is this then your first visit to the hills?'

Not only to the hills, explained Emily, but to India herself. She had come out from England to visit her aunt and uncle. *They* had been living here for years and years, since before she was born, ages, twenty years at least, well, her uncle had, he had been married before to someone who had died, and so, of course, she had never seen him until she had got off the boat in Bombay and there they had been, and now here *she* was, she added laughing, and perhaps she should have introduced herself: her name was Emily . . . Emily Anderson. And Emily went on to add a few other interesting details about her family and about her voyage out by way of the wonderful new Suez Canal and one or two other matters, not necessarily relevant to the other subjects she had mentioned. The truth was, although she did not say so to her new friend, that although her aunt and uncle had turned out to be kindness itself and she had already grown deeply attached to them, if they had a fault it was that they were inclined to be taciturn. And not only did many of the conversations they had between themselves seem to consist mainly of a faint smile or a raised eyebrow (a grunt or a click of the tongue and they became positive chatterboxes!) but there was something about them which seemed to discourage unnecessary words in others . . . at least, Emily found it discouraged them in *her*. And this was too bad because she dearly loved to chatter and was already beginning to suffer a serious deprivation in that respect. She had even been beginning to wonder just how much longer she could keep up these faint smiles and raised eyebrows. This explains why Emily's confidences, although one would have expected only a trickle since they were made to a perfect stranger, looked like turning into a flood which would sweep the lady away as she sat there with mirror and lace handkerchief. She weathered them, however, without difficulty and even volunteered a few of her own, though her manner was inclined to be condescending for her husband, Mr Forester, was an important personage in the Irrigation Department, as she explained, and although she was tactful enough not to say so, it was plain as a pikestaff that Emily's uncle, sleeping with his mouth open, was not a person of the same rank, or of any importance at all to the Government of India. His profession was . . . ? she wondered. When Emily told her she nodded as if to say that she had feared as much and returned her gaze to her mirror. Still, Mrs Forester was a person who enjoyed a conversation herself and could see no real harm in befriending her inferiors, given the democratic circumstances of a railway journey. She even told Emily that she might call her Mary and explained that her husband, though he himself was detained by his duties in the plains for the hot weather, always insisted that she and her child should seek the cool solace of the hills.

While Mrs Forester was sharing this information with her, Emily's gaze had kept returning to the clergyman opposite her. He had opened his book again but before he could begin reading he was seized by yet another fit of coughing and this time a serious one. It caused him to snap his book shut immediately. The ladies eyed him with concern. He had raised a hand and hunched his shoulder in order that the sight of his convulsed and spluttering face should not give offence to them, at the same time lowering his head so that his forehead was almost touching

the dusty seat beside him. Once in this position he seemed
unable to recover, his coughing lips pressed against the material
that covered the seat. What could be seen of his face had turned a
startling greenish-white and around the rim of his hair drops of
perspiration glimmered and trickled together. The coughing
grew more and more laboured, the shrieking of his breath grew
more and more strident, the hush between each explosion of air
grew longer until it seemed that he must choke to death there
and then in the railway carriage.

'Can nothing be done?' cried Emily, leaning forward to take
him by the shoulder. But she was thrust aside a moment later by
her uncle who dragged the clergyman off his seat and forced him
to bend double, supporting him with one hand and using the
other to grip him by the back of the neck. With a supreme effort
the clergyman managed to drag in another long, whistling
inhalation of air, cough, inhale again more easily, cough again
and, finally, overcome his coughing. He sank back, exhausted,
murmuring: 'Thank you, thank you, forgive me,' through the
folds of a cotton handkerchief he had pressed to his lips. Emily's
uncle, meanwhile, had been rummaging in a suitcase from
which he now produced a flask and a cup. From one to the other
he poured a dose of amber liquid and held it out to the
clergyman. Seeing him hesitate, he added: 'Aye, go ahead. It'll
do ye no harm. I'm a physician. McNab's the name.'

The clergyman obediently drained the cup. A little colour had
come back into his cheeks and he looked from one to another of
his travelling companions with a rueful smile. In the confusion
the book he had been reading had fallen at Emily's feet. She
stooped to pick it up, wondering whether Mrs Forester had seen
what she herself had seen, or thought she had seen. The instant
before he had snapped the book shut at the beginning of his fit of
coughing it had seemed to her as if a tiny spot of scarlet had
appeared on it, bright as a poppy on the white page.

The clergyman's sudden choking-fit had done something to
break down the reserve which had hitherto stifled conversation
so Emily, in order not to miss anything, was obliged to look,
now out of the window at the startling cloud-formation of
mountains which drew ever nearer, saying to herself firmly:

'This is my first view of the Himalayas', now at the clergyman who was introducing himself as the Reverend William Kingston. He was on his way to Simla, he explained, not as a visitor but to return to his parish. He had been to Calcutta for an interview with the Metropolitan, he added, and had taken the opportunity of pursuing some further business in Delhi.

'Oh? Then you are at Christ Church?' enquired Mrs McNab. But the Reverend Kingston shook his head with a smile. 'I'm afraid it's nothing so grand, Mrs McNab. You might know Simla well and still not know my parish. I am the pastor of Saint Saviour's at Boileauganj. My congregation is made up largely of Native Christians and only partly of those English families unable to worship in Christ Church for want of space during the season. Sometimes, too, we get a few soldiers who come up to us from the barracks at Subáthu. And yet we like to think that our humble manner of prayer is no less acceptable to our Lord than that of the Viceroy and his staff in Christ Church,' he concluded with a hint of sarcasm. After a pause he went on: 'I shall be glad when we reach Simla. I have only one curate to assist me and he is elderly and infirm and so I am bound to worry a little about what has gone on in my absence. But you, Doctor? Are you and Mrs McNab frequent visitors to Simla?'

'Och, well, no . . . we aren't, I suppose,' replied McNab guardedly, darting a glance at his wife. 'It is some years since we last came this way.' His eyes once again strayed in his wife's direction. She gazed back at him with that faintly ironic air of hers: for a moment some kind of unheard, unseen intelligence passed between them, as if each knew precisely what the other was thinking. *This* was the sort of thing that Emily found so frustrating, the fact that her aunt and uncle were clearly having a conversation that she herself could not join in!

'I suppose your duties kept you in the plains?' suggested Kingston.

'Well,' began McNab. 'To tell the truth . . .'

'What my husband means is that he does not really care for Simla or its society,' broke in Mrs McNab, laughing. 'It is only to please Emily and myself that he has allowed himself to be dragged up here!'

'No, Miriam, you know that is not the case,' protested McNab, 'though it is true that I am no longer quite comfortable in such refined society,' he concluded with an ambivalent grimace.

Meanwhile, the Reverend Kingston was taken by another fit of coughing.

'That's a bad cough, Mr Kingston,' the Doctor went on conversationally. 'Have ye had it long?'

'It's nothing, Doctor,' replied the Reverend Kingston calmly, once he had recovered his breath. 'The dust, you know, and the dryness are inclined to excite one's throat at this season. Once in the cooler climate of the hills it will no longer be troublesome.'

'So you have had it for a little while?'

'On rising in the morning, yes, for a few days. But only a little . . . it is the dust, nothing more. It is terrible the way it finds its way everywhere once the cold season is over.' McNab nodded his agreement and Kingston turned to make a polite enquiry of Mrs Forester whether she was a frequent visitor to the hills.

'We have a bungalow, Mr Kingston, not far from Barnes Court. My husband, I'm afraid, rarely gets the chance to visit us there. He says it is the penalty he must pay for having a position of such heavy responsibility.' She hesitated, as if about to enlarge on her husband's position, but before she could do so Dr McNab casually asked the Reverend Kingston: 'You have noticed no other symptoms with that cough of yours? No headache, for example?'

'I have noticed nothing, Doctor.'

'Have you perhaps noticed that your voice has increased a little in resonance?'

'Yes, perhaps.'

McNab, exchanging another mute intelligence with his wife, now suddenly smiled. Emily was charmed, she found it so unexpected on her uncle's severe and melancholy face. McNab said to the Reverend Kingston: 'Miriam tells me it is a bad habit of mine to question chance acquaintances about their state of health. Is that not so, my dear?'

'Certainly,' replied Miriam, smiling too. 'Besides, you gave me a promise that you would leave your profession in the plains where it belongs and now I see you are already looking for a patient where none exists.' To their fellow-passengers she added: 'He excuses his tactless behaviour by saying that he is making observations for a treatise on Indian Medicine which he will one day write. Yet the years go by and still we have seen nothing of this treatise, although there are always big piles of notes and documents for the white ants to make their supper of. Well, John, it is true?'

'You're unkind,' sighed McNab, looking once more as if all the cares of the world rested on his shoulders, 'but, aye, it is true.'

'There!' said Miriam. 'You see he is penitent. But that will not stop him transgressing again when the opportunity next arises. My advice, Mr Kingston, is to decline to answer any further questions he may put to you.'

'I can assure you your husband's questions don't trouble me in the least,' replied the Reverend Kingston. 'On the contrary, I'm grateful for his interest, though I'm not ill enough to warrant it.'

'He would like us all a great deal better if we would kindly contract some rare disease to make a chapter in McNab's Indian Medicine, is that not so, my dear? And what is this! You are already beginning again!' For the Doctor had reached out a hand for Kingston's wrist and, his face thoughtful, was taking his pulse. However, he released the wrist again after a few moments and with a brief nod to the clergyman sat back without any further comment. Kingston for his part did not seem in the least perturbed. 'We are all in God's hands, Doctor,' he remarked cheerfully.

'Aye, that's true, I suppose,' agreed McNab with a sigh.

4

'Ah, Dr McNab!' called a plump little man with curling moustaches hurrying along the platform towards where Emily and her uncle and aunt were standing in a bright fog of dust. 'How are you, sir? It is good to see you back again after such a time. You see I never forget a face, sir, and I am still taking the pills. Yes, indeed! All is ready for you, sir. And Mrs McNab has come, too, for a breath of air in the hills. No doubt you found it already becoming too hot, Madam, in Krishnapur?'

Even at the best of times the arrival of an Indian train at its destination presents a scene of bustle and confusion, but this was Kalka, the railhead for Simla and the season was only just beginning. Emily had been unable to prevent herself wondering whether her eye might not fall on two or three cheerful young officers during this last fragment of her journey before their way and hers parted for ever and she had decided, if her eye *did* fall on them, that she might permit herself just the hint of a smile, to show that she had not been altogether unamused by their play-acting. But once she was on the platform it fell not on two or three but on scores of young officers. This came as a shock, particularly as in the dust and confusion she was quite unable to tell *her* officers from the rest. Moreover, in addition to the officers swarming everywhere there were the other passengers, too, all of whom seemed to have brought their personal bearers and attendants with them in some other less salubrious part of the train and were now attempting to reunite with them, groping and shouting in the dust. There were Government officials being greeted by other Government officials and at the same time shouting at the *babus* brought along to organize their papers and lend them an air of consequence: these naturally had *khitmutghars* and bearers and baggage-coolies, not to mention a great deal of furniture and household paraphernalia into the bargain. Then there were the ladies, European ladies who also appeared to come by the dozen (to whom they belonged it was not easy to say) and their *ayahs*, every last one of them chattering like a parakeet. Then there were the folk who belonged to the non-official world, of whom the best that could be said was that they, too, were human beings, owners of stores and tailoring and catering establishments in Simla and these people, like it or not, though they might not appear on the Government House List, still had to have their retinues of servants, not to mention agents and clerks and middlemen of various shapes and kinds. All these men and women, whether native or English, were baying and howling at each other in the fog of dust and sunlight. In addition, dogs, chickens, goats and children shrilled their support. Horses whinnied and stamped and rolled their eyes, because certain enterprising officers had brought their own mounts with a view to distinguishing themselves at the Simla races and these poor brutes had not unnaturally mistaken Kalka railway station for a shambles which would presently reduce them to beefsteaks.

Given the crush and the din, the only sensible policy was to stand one's ground and wait for matters to improve. The Reverend Kingston and Mrs Forester evidently thought so, too. Mrs Forester had come to stand beside Emily and was telling her with the confidence of the old hand that this was always the most disagreeable part of the journey but that Emily should not worry, order would soon be restored. The Reverend Kingston stood a little way from them and seemed unable to get out of the stream of traffic: he was barged this way and that by vigorous people dragging suitcases and to tell the truth he was beginning to look rather agonized: he did not seem accustomed to crowds. At one moment it seemed as if he might even go under the hooves of a snorting, bridling racehorse, but he escaped and came to a safer haven a little nearer Emily and Mrs Forester in the lee of a pile of suitcases. There he mopped his brow with a grey cotton handkerchief.

Despite the competing noise from all around, the plump little man who had just now struggled up to the McNabs continued nevertheless to shout deferential remarks. Neither the Doctor nor Miriam made any reply but they both listened, somewhat warily, to what he had to say. While this fellow was bellowing his polite conversation into the McNabs' ears his eyes did not cease to rove with excitement over the new arrivals on the platform. Emily felt them come to rest on her. A moment later and they moved on to Mrs Forester at her side and then, well, they positively shone with interest. Their owner began to bow rapidly and a groan of pleasure escaped his lips. His remarks to the McNabs dried up in mid-sentence. Still bowing and touching the brim of his sun-helmet with the side of his index finger, he approached the two ladies. 'Would you be requiring accommodation, Mrs Forester, if you please?' he enquired, snatching off his hat and holding it in both hands. 'Lowrie's Hotel is ever at your service, Madam, should you be requiring same.'

As if they only had a second for their work his eyes feasted themselves on Mrs Forester's pretty face and then dropped to the hat in his hands. Mrs Forester shrugged and nodded, her eyes on some distant point, plainly settling a matter of no importance with a person of no importance.

'Madam will find a vehicle awaiting her convenience outside the station hall,' said the plump individual, placing the sun-helmet back on his head and again tapping its rim with the side of his finger. 'And perhaps this young lady is travelling with Madam?' he went on, his eyes now on Emily but at the same time taking two steps backwards to signify the end of his interview with Mrs Forester.

'Emily, this is Mr Lowrie,' said Dr McNab. 'We will spend tonight at his hotel here and go up tomorrow. Mr Lowrie, this is Miss Anderson . . . and the Reverend Kingston who will, I expect, also be in need of lodgings for the night but it would be as well if you ask him yourself.'

The Reverend Kingston in the meantime had sat down, extenuated, on a cabin trunk and had until now avoided being spotted by Mr Lowrie. At the mention of the clergyman's name he looked quite taken aback.

'Do you mean to say that Kingston has returned, Doctor?' he asked in disbelief, scanning the platform for a second time but still failing to see Kingston behind his barrier of suitcases.

'Surely that cannot be so!' But following the direction of McNab's gaze and moving a little to the right he saw that it was indeed the case, Kingston was sitting there. For a moment he looked quite upset. 'Well, well, well,' he muttered as if to himself, 'that is a surprise, quite a surprise! So the fellow has come back, has he? Well, well, well. It will do him no good, either, I should think . . . but we shall see, I expect, in due course.'

'What do you think, Doctor?' Mr Lowrie went on, resuming his conversational tone. 'The Reverend Kingston does not look in the best of health, perhaps a longer stay in Kalka might suit him? What is the purpose, I often wonder, of carrying sick bones up into the hills when they would do as well down here? Yes, he looks a sick man and it is a tiring journey up the hill.'

'Rubbish, man,' replied Dr McNab curtly.

Mr Lowrie bowed mutely.

Some of the crush and din around them was by now beginning to dissipate. Of the healthy and vigorous young officers and officials the majority had already made their way accompanied by their ladies and servants through the glittering fog to the shade of the awning which to Emily appeared blue-black in the surrounding brilliance, almost like a solid object. She, too, longed to be somewhere cool.

A few young officers had remained to assist the elderly and infirm passengers and unescorted ladies with whom they had been travelling, their gallantry aroused by a pretty face that could be seen here and there among those lagging behind. Mr Lowrie's eye was on a man in his fifties, very thin, whose clothes appeared several sizes too large for him and hung from him as from a clothes horse; whether this was for the sake of coolness or on account of a sudden loss of weight it was hard to say. Emily was startled to hear Mr Lowrie mutter: 'Look at that! Not a pick on him! Not enough to make a hyena's luncheon!' and chortle grimly to himself. 'And see those children, as sickly and spindly a pair as I ever set eyes on, poor things,' he went on with relish, adding after a moment with more decorum, 'but perhaps they will do better in the cool of the hills.'

Dr McNab, who had turned away to give instructions to the coolies for the removal of their luggage, now reappeared to take Miriam by the arm.

'I expect you all just happened to find yourselves travelling in the same compartment and then became acquainted?' said Mr Lowrie falling into step beside them. But the Doctor did not reply. He looked weary himself after the day in the train, Emily thought. She herself was tired and longing for a bath, but excited nevertheless to arrive in this strange town.

'Of course, Doctor, it could be that more than one of your fellow-passengers arranged in advance for you to accompany them?' muttered Mr Lowrie. 'I must say, they could hardly be in better hands.'

Dr McNab had removed a handkerchief from one of his pockets and was mopping his brow with it. 'Miss Anderson is my niece,' he said reluctantly, pausing to glance back at Mrs Forester and the Reverend Kingston who were following them. 'My sister's girl,' he added rather grimly, his eyes on Mrs Forester.

'I believe, Doctor, that the Reverend Kingston's condition would hardly permit him to resume his, hm, sacerdotal duties? Of course, a spell in the hills does sometimes work wonders (though not perhaps as often as is commonly supposed) . . .'

'Nonsense, Lowrie. He is in the best of health.'

Again, Mr Lowrie bowed mutely. He opened the palms of his hands for a moment, inspected them, and then carefully closed them once more.

Emily's view had been momentarily blocked by the brown skeleton of a coolie and the burden that weighed him down, a great roll of bedding that he was carrying for a portly Indian gentleman puffing alongside him, but now she could see why her uncle had paused to look back. Mr Lowrie, too, glanced back and another involuntary groan escaped him. Several officers had been helping an elderly lady some way behind them and now one of them had left this group and advanced on Mrs Forester. Emily recognized him at once as the man she had seen earlier standing with his hand on his hip and watching Mrs Forester through the train window. He raised his sun-helmet and said: 'Permit me to re-introduce myself, Madam. We met last season. Captain Hagan, at your service.'

Mrs Forester gazed at him blankly, however, and showed no sign of wanting his company or assistance; nor did she need it, for Dr McNab had made arrangements for her luggage to be conveyed to Lowrie's Hotel with the rest and she was carrying nothing but a light parasol. In the violet-blue shadow of the parasol her face seemed pale and mysterious. Captain Hagan ventured to raise a hand, saying: 'Allow me, please.' Since she was carrying nothing but the parasol he attempted to take that from her. She showed no sign of wanting to release it, however, and he was obliged to unpick her small, gloved fingers one by one from the handle before he could gain possession of it. She smiled faintly when he had done so.

Dr McNab took Miriam's arm again, saying mildly: 'Let us find some shade without delay.' Captain Hagan and Mrs Forester moved forward, too. He continued to hold the parasol so that its blue shade fell neatly, like a cage, over her head and shoulders. After a few steps Emily noticed her raise a hand and take his arm, allowing her wrist to lie loosely in the crook of his elbow. There was something a little shocking about this tiny gesture of surrender. Her little boy followed in the arms of his bearer, though there appeared to be no good reason why he should not walk for himself.

But where, Emily was wondering, have *my* officers got to? It was unfair that Mary Forester's officer who, after all, had done nothing more throughout the entire journey than stare at her insolently through the window with his hand on his hip should now be holding her parasol for her while his comrades who had put on a veritable theatre display for *her*, Emily, should have slipped away without even giving her the chance to smile at them . . . not that she would have, probably, but at least they might have given her the opportunity.

Meanwhile, Mr Lowrie, occasionally raising his hat deferentially to people he glimpsed even at a great distance and who paid no attention to him, had fallen into step beside her as they made their way towards the distant awning. 'And so you and Mrs Forester are just chance acquaintances, Miss Anderson?' he was saying. 'And where, if I may beg to ask, did she join your delightful little . . . hm . . . No! Saharanpur! But that is no distance at all! I wonder why she should board the train there . . . How interesting! I expect, since she is travelling unescorted by a . . . by a . . . that she was not seen off at Saharanpur by any . . . by . . . Gracious! A tall gentleman, you say, older than herself! Who could he be? With a grey face? Well, Miss Anderson, not *grey*, surely. Oh? Greyish, I see. I see. Well, upon my word . . . And so she means to brazen it out *up there*, does she?' he added to himself in a vehement undertone. 'Gracious me!' Noticing that Emily had overheard this last remark he added hastily: 'Oh, nothing of importance, Miss Anderson, a mere . . . a mere . . . *entanglement* . . . common enough *up there*, you'll find, yes. It's the colder climate, you know. Blankets, you know. As for us, mosquito nets, that's our lot down here! This Captain . . . hm . . . Hagan .·. . was, of course, also travelling in your compartment and there made the acquaintance of . . . of . . . La Forester . . . that is, of Mrs Forester . . . No! You mean, they perhaps had already . . .? Merciful heavens! And I would not say that she looks to be altogether in the best of . . . not that *that* is so surprising . . . But now the reverend gentleman *he* was travelling . . . I see, of course . . . as was natural, only natural, and he mentioned perhaps in conversation his pastorate at Saint Saviour's where I, too, have the honour of, in a humble degree, officiating as . . . hm . . . churchwarden . . . that is to say, the fellow-members of the parish have done me the honour of . . . a charge heavy with responsibility but one which, nevertheless . . . in short . . .' Mr Lowrie winked at Emily. 'In short, the Vestry Committee . . . need I say more?'

Emily gazed at him, quite bewildered.

'But he was summoned, was he not, by the Metropolitan to account for himself . . . He did not, I suppose, mention . . . no, well, never mind, we shall find out soon enough . . . Ah, the elderly curate, is it? That's what was on his mind, was it? Forsythe? Ha! That old dodderer should have been put out to grass ten years ago, my dear young lady. As it is everyone knows *up there* that the old fool is less of a curate than a sorcerer's apprentice and will shortly . . . I give you my word . . . I vouch

for it . . . will shortly go to his Maker!' And Mr Lowrie chortled,
touching the rim of his sun-helmet deferentially for no apparent
reason.

'But you yourself, Miss Anderson, look in the best of health,
if I may be permitted to say so . . . those rosy cheeks, it does the
heart good to see such a . . . such a . . . such youth and beauty; my
dear Miss . . . they do not last long out here in India, I can assure
you . . . Why, I've seen enough fair "ghosts", as I call 'em, pass
through Kalka who just the season before had been healthy and,
ah . . . if you permit me to say so . . . ah, voluptuous girls.
"Ghosts" . . . that's the private word I have for 'em . . . It just
occurred to me one day, Miss Anderson, like a nickname you
might say, and ever since, when I see them pass by, that's the
word I say to m'self . . . "Ghosts". Dear me! What a country!
What a place we have chosen for ourselves! I expect your father
and mother sent you out here to look for a . . . to find a . . . yes, of
course, to stay with your aunt and uncle, quite so.' And Mr
Lowrie bowed and saluted as he led the way at last into the shade
of the awning.

Here in the deep-aubergine shade several other travellers who
had just stepped out of the sunlight stood blinking while they
waited for Mr Lowrie, blind as puppies in the sudden darkness;
others had been rounded up by his wife, Mrs Lowrie, who was
standing in front of a platoon of hotel bearers clad in smart white
tunics with scarlet cummerbunds round their waists and gold-
feathered *pagris* on their heads. The truth was that, although the
premier hotel in Kalka, Lowrie's was by no means the only one.
Sometimes it happened that ignorant or unworldly passengers
allowed themselves to be snared by touts from one of the other
establishments: for this reason a significant display was mounted
by the Lowries in the station hall.

Now there was another delay while Mr Lowrie made a few
arrangements and hurried over to whisper something to his
wife: this gave Emily a chance to look around chastely and
wonder again where her officers had got to. The only officer in
sight was Captain Hagan. Even in the shade of the station hall he
continued to hold the parasol protectively over the head of his
companion. His face was expressionless. Mrs Forester stood

beside him with a petulant air. Her little boy had been set down by his bearer and clung listlessly to his hand. The Reverend Kingston stood nearby; his battered suitcase was now in the charge of a native bearer at his elbow: extremely tall and round-shouldered, with the face of an imbecile, this man towered over the clergyman most incongruously and added to his air of bewilderment. He smiled at Emily and came over to her; the tall native shambled uncertainly after him, holding Kingston's suitcase in both hands as if he did not know what he was expected to do with it.

'Travelling in India can sometimes prove an ordeal, Miss Anderson,' he said with a weary smile. 'I would have liked to continue my journey up the mountainside this evening but Mr Lowrie tells me it is impossible. Of course, none but the vehicles belonging to the postal service are allowed on the road during the hours of darkness. No doubt that is the reason Lowrie will not agree to it.'

Emily nodded sympathetically, aware that the Reverend Kingston was merely worrying aloud, as anxious travellers will when their plans go astray.

'You see,' he added fretfully, 'I fear that my presence may be urgently required at Saint Saviour's. But still, there is nothing to be done about it. It takes six hours by tonga even to reach the dak bungalow at Solon and the sun is already low in the sky.'

At last, with a graceful sweep of his sun-helmet, Mr Lowrie was ushering the passengers out to the rickshaws which had drawn up in the forecourt. But even out here there was still some worry and delay: certain of those who had to be installed in rickshaws were infirm, or downright invalids, and the rickshaws themselves had assembled higgledy-piggledy and facing in all directions: Mr Lowrie's *khitmutghar* was doing his best to unpick this intricate muddle of shafts and spoked wheels.

It somehow happened that the Reverend Kingston was one of the first away. He had difficulty getting his suitcase away from the tall native who had been carrying it. This man had at last surrendered it but now went loping away beside Mr Kingston's rickshaw, grinning and twisting his neck in an odd sort of way.

Almost immediately, and before they were out of sight of the station, he accidentally ran in front of the rickshaw, obstructing it and almost causing it to overturn. The rickshaw-coolie shouted angrily at him, but Kingston did not seem upset. He said something to the man in a gentle tone, pointing to a place behind the rickshaw. They set off once more and this time the native went shambling after the vehicle in the place allotted to him. A moment later they had vanished in a cloud of dust. Mr Lowrie had paused to watch this little incident, chuckling derisively and shaking his head. A little later he edged over to Emily and said in a low, almost confidential tone: 'Yes, Miss Anderson, as I was saying earlier, I've seen 'em come and go in my time, healthy young creatures, lovely persons going down to the plains in the prime of life . . . and then, why, in just a few months they creep back as skeletons asking me to ferry them back *up there* again before it's too late. Fair skeletons! Ah, what a pity it is to see 'em so!'

'That'll do, Lowrie,' said Dr McNab sharply. He had evidently overheard the hotelier's remarks.

Mr Lowrie bowed mutely and took a step back.

'It's time these ladies were away. Kindly look to it.'

Dr McNab moved to the assistance of a lady climbing into a rickshaw nearby, leaving Emily and her aunt together. Miriam took Emily's hand and gave it a reassuring squeeze.

It was at this moment that Emily, looking up, at last saw two of her three officers: the blue-eyed one she had heard called Teddy and the one who had stepped on to the wooden box on the platform at Saharanpur. They were wheeling a very elderly wizened, white-haired person down the sloping path which led from the platform through a thick grove of bamboo. This person, it was hard to tell whether it was a man or a woman, was curled up knee to chin in a basket chair mounted on small wheels and seemed to be asleep. Evidently the two officers had had some difficulty unloading basket and occupant from the train and were only now catching up with the other passengers. But here they came at last, the blue-eyed Teddy pushing the chair while his friend sauntered along beside it with a wry expression on his face and looking somewhat out of sorts. Their path led them quite close to Emily. She decided that if they noticed her she might give them a half-smile.

She thought at first, so busy were they with their charge, that neither of them *would* notice her, but then, just as they seemed about to pass her by, Teddy happened to look up. He gazed at her blankly for a moment, then recognized her. He took his hands off the chair and began to tug at an invisible arrow lodged in his chest, smiling at her as he did so. But almost immediately the basket chair began to run away down the slope, chattering on its little iron wheels. The wizened little skeleton in the careering chair opened one hooded lizard's eye which fixed itself on Emily, then closed it again as Teddy, bounding after the chair, managed to recapture it before it overturned on the path.

'Teddy, you are an ass!' drawled his companion. 'What on earth do you think you're doing?'

Once he had a firm grasp on the chair again Teddy turned to look back at Emily and mimed the mopping of his brow, as if to say: 'That was a near thing!' She gave him her faint smile and turned away. Her uncle was beckoning her to install herself in a rickshaw. Then she found herself sitting there as she was pulled through the dusty, crowded streets of Kalka, watching bemused the glistening skin of the coolie's back where muscles glinted and faded like fish gently rising to feed at the surface of a pond.

Later, tired though she was by her journey, she knelt by her bedside.

> This night I lay me down to sleep,
> And give my soul to Christ to keep;
> Sleep I now: wake I never,
> I give my soul to Christ for ever.

And she continued to kneel for a little while with her elbows resting on her bed, comforted by this verse which she had been in the habit of reciting since her earliest childhood. For a few moments she thought of her mother and father and brother and felt lonely.

And oddly enough it was not so much the clear blue eye of

Teddy that remained in her mind as that other eye, the lizard's eye, lying like a jewel deep in folds and tresses of skin. And she thought: 'How strange that one could not say whether it was a man or a woman it belonged to!'

5

Emily and the McNabs breakfasted early in the hope of making their escape from the plains before the day grew too hot, and they did so on the deep veranda which fronted the hotel, a delightfully cool and green place shaded by palms and decked with fresh flowers brought down by the tongas of the Mountain Car Company from the more temperate regions above. Emily had been hoping to see again some of the people she had seen the day before but, apart from Mr Lowrie who bustled about cheerfully giving orders and exchanging an occasional word with his clients, the only face she recognized was that of the tall, gangling native who had attached himself the day before to the Reverend Kingston: this man, grinning or grimacing to himself, was walking about aimlessly in the compound, occasionally even breaking into a run for a few steps though he plainly had no destination. Once, for no apparent reason, he uttered a strangled shout and rubbed his face with a bony hand.

Mr Lowrie approached with a bow and said: 'I trust that Madam slept well . . . and you, too, Madam.'

The ladies reassured him.

'There was coughing, I'm afraid, Doctor, in a room not too far from your own.'

'Heard nothing, thank you, Lowrie,' replied McNab reaching for a piece of toast.

'I fear it came from Mr Kingston's room and as a churchwarden of Saint Saviour's I naturally take an interest in the health of . . . of . . . Ah, you may not have heard, Doctor, that they have been kind enough to elect me to the Vestry Committee of that church . . .'

'No, I don't believe I have heard that,' replied McNab in a tone that was far from encouraging.

'And you would not have heard either,' pursued Mr Lowrie, refusing to be discouraged and even leaning forward confidentially the better to funnel his report into the Doctor's ear, 'that there have been certain . . . ah . . . difficulties at Saint Saviour's in the past few weeks. The parishioners have been upset by certain rituals of what one would have to call . . . ah . . . a Puseyite cast, quite unknown to our Protestant traditions. Kingston is thought to be . . . ah . . . going "over the Tiber" . . . Do I make myself clear?'

'"Over the Tiber"? What nonsense is this?'

'I mean going over to Rome! The Bishop of Simla, as you know, sir, has a summer residence up above and is but lately installed. It appears that he is quite worried by what has been going on . . . Yes, the Bishop is quite definitely worried, sir.'

'Nothing I can do about that, I'm afraid, Lowrie. If it were a broken leg that ailed the Bishop now I might be able to help.'

'I know for a fact, Doctor, that His Grace's secretary has been wondering whether the Reverend Kingston's health . . . ah, whether it might not be better if Kingston agreed to retire as incumbent on account of his health . . . which does seem to be, poor fellow . . . which does appear . . .'

'His health is as sound as yours, Mr Lowrie.'

Mr Lowrie bowed mutely and retreated, looking taken aback. When he had gone Miriam said to her husband: 'But Mr Kingston is ill, is he not?'

McNab gazed back across the table at her for so long that it seemed to Emily that he was not going to reply at all. But at long last he said reluctantly: 'Perhaps.'

'So? You decline to tell us what you learned about Mr Kingston because you have a lack of regard for the intelligence of women.'

'You are unjust. I have heard the man cough and I have taken his pulse. What do you expect me to have learned from that?' (McNab, as it happened, believed that he could tell quite a lot from the pulse.)

'Well then? You just told a lie to poor Mr Lowrie. Emily, you are my witness! Your uncle is guilty of speaking untruthfully!'

'Not at all,' replied McNab calmly, a smile at last lighting up his austere features. 'I said merely that his health is as sound as Mr Lowrie's. I didna say I considered Lowrie's health to be sound. On the contrary, I believe Lowrie to be suffering from a condition of the heart which with his delight in exciting himself about other people's affairs might very well carry him off at any moment.'

'Nonsense!' laughed Miriam. 'Emily, when you pick a husband you must make sure he will tell you the truth.'

'I shall do my best to remember, certainly,' smiled Emily.

'And while we are about it why don't you sometimes show some warmth and affection to Emily and me?'

'Och, it is not the way of a Scot.'

'Oh, indeed? And why don't you sometimes tell us we're intelligent and pretty and what beautiful dresses we are wearing?'

'I wouldna want to encourage ye to vanity. Besides, ye're too intelligent to require compliments,' replied McNab innocently. The women eyed him suspiciously.

One by one the tongas of the Mountain Car Company drew up in the compound, some to depart again immediately with those who had risen and breakfasted early, others to wait the late-comers. The Reverend Kingston, as it happened, was again one of the first to leave, pausing only to exchange a few words with the McNabs who were awaiting their luggage. He had lost the pallor of the day before and looked restored after his night's rest. While she was watching the clergyman's departure Mr Lowrie approached Emily with a note from Mary Forester inviting her, if her uncle agreed, to make part of the journey up to Simla with her in her landau, which would be, perhaps, 'a more comfortable introduction to the hills'. The uncomfortable alternative, now in front of Emily's eyes, was a tonga such as the Reverend Kingston was now climbing aboard. This time he sat back to back with the tall, gangling native to whom he had once again surrendered his battered suitcase.

'What a pair they make, Miss Anderson, what a pair! If you ask me, one is as mad as the other . . . Did you see his suitcase? He would perhaps have felt more at home with such a suitcase at a Hindu Lodge than here at Lowrie's Hotel!' Mr Lowrie was beside himself with glee and even Emily had to smile a little, so incongruous did the two men appear sitting there as the tonga rattled away.

People of wealth or position in Simla society, as Dr McNab was aware, seldom had recourse to Mr Lowrie's tongas but kept landaus instead for use on the road to the plains, even though they were not permitted to use them in Simla itself where only the Viceroy was allowed to circulate in a carriage. Given the rigid caste system among the British in Simla which prevented social contact between the official and non-official worlds, he found it surprising that Mrs Forester should invite his niece to accompany her but he could think of no reason why Emily should not do so if she wanted to. But Emily could not decide for a while whether she wanted to or not. The answer was that she half-wanted to. And so it was decided in the end that she should ride in the landau as far as the dak bungalow at Solon and continue the journey by tonga with the McNabs.

The sunlight was already growing too sharp for comfort when the landau emerged from the drive of Lowrie's Hotel into the streets of Kalka and the crowds that Emily had noticed the previous evening had melted back into the shadows. Now only a few white-clad shopkeepers were to be seen reclining in the shade of stalls or lurking in the dim interiors of their open-fronted shops. A few women, swathed from head to foot in white or black muslin, sat on their heels beside a well in the shade of an awning of rush matting, chattering among themselves. Emily just caught a glimpse of hennaed fingers raised in protest or derision as the landau slipped by, then the houses and bazaar dropped away and they were on the road to Simla.

Almost immediately they began to climb into a maze of low hills. For a while the roofs of Kalka remained visible below, but then the folds of two hills closed together like curtains and they were seen no more. The road, which was little more than a cart-track, wound this way and that hugging the side of one hill after another, dipping occasionally but then continuing its gradual ascent once more. In no time Emily had lost all sense of direction, one hill looked so much like the next. The mountain ranges she had seen from the train were no longer visible and the only signs of cultivation were a few terraced plots on the bare ridges. Nor were there any trees to be seen, indeed nothing but interminable red slopes of rock and shingle covered with scrub burned brown or yellow by the sun. Emily had been expecting lofty pines and cedars and had to struggle not to feel disappointed.

Mary Forester had greeted Emily in a friendly way and had made a little polite conversation with the McNabs before setting out, but once they were on the road she had sunk into her own thoughts. Once she had touched Emily's hand and pointed, smiling. Emily had looked, shielding her eyes, and would rather not have seen what she did see, an eagle with a baby rabbit in its talons rising as if without effort from a ridge at a little distance. Mrs Forester's little boy, Jack, saw this, too, and looked so distressed that Emily wanted to reach out and comfort him but felt unable to do so in the presence of his mother. Mrs Forester appeared somnolent but her face beneath the wide-brimmed hat she was wearing looked prettier than ever. Emily herself felt drowsy: although they continued to climb it grew no cooler. She fell into a trance, dazed by the brightness all around and hypnotized by the black shadow of the leather hood crawling now this way, now that, over the floor of the landau and by the steadily ticking wheel beside her. From time to time they paused at a wayside hut to change ponies, then they went on again immediately.

But at last they became aware of a smell of warm pines and the air grew a little fresher. Presently signs of green foliage appeared and an occasional clump of trees. On several occasions a tonga or bullock cart passed them going down towards Kalka but empty of passengers or baggage and once Mrs Forester remarked that at this time of the year almost all travellers would be going in the same direction as themselves; only in September and October would the downward traffic begin. Emily gazed out over the steeply sloping countryside where far below them the road they had already travelled could be seen, a white ribbon

passing back and forth across the hillside as it descended. Down
there one of the tongas which had passed them earlier could be
seen as a dark speck dragging behind it a curtain of white dust
many times its own size; soon it met four even smaller specks of
men on horseback setting up a dust-cloud of their own as they
climbed: then each party disappeared for a few moments into the
dust stirred up by the other. Emily could see no sign of an
ascending tonga that might be the McNabs, however.

At noon the landau turned off the road into the shade of a
little valley of pines which unexpectedly clung there like an oasis
in those bleak hills. The *sais* and the boy's bearer who rode
beside him dismounted and one handed baskets and hampers
down to the other. There was a pretty glade at this spot,
explained Mrs Forester, well known to travellers between Simla
and the plains, where it was pleasant to stop and take some
refreshment. 'Let us take a stroll while the bearer is unpacking,'
said Mrs Forester and, holding her parasol in one hand and
taking Emily's arm with the other, she led her towards a path
which disappeared into the pines, pausing only to inspect on the
way a tonga drawn up in the shade but deserted except for its
sais. 'It appears that someone has had the same idea as ourselves.'

After a little way the ground on one side of the path fell away
steeply, so steeply that quite without expecting it Emily
suddenly found herself looking down on the tops of the pines. A
murmur of water was to be heard from somewhere near at hand.
It grew louder as they proceeded along the path. Putting her
finger to her lips Mrs Forester indicated to Emily that she should
stay where she was; she herself tiptoed delicately forward
holding up her skirts in one hand. She beckoned to Emily.

'It is only the poor gentleman with the cough.'

The path led into a delightful glade dappled with sunlight. At
its head a waterfall cascaded from some overhanging rocks into
a dark pool surrounded by ferns and rhododendrons. There,
sitting side by side on a moss-covered log, were the Reverend
Kingston and his bearer. Mrs Forester, smiling, cupped a hand
to Emily's ear. 'But why, I wonder, is he sitting with his bearer?'

While the ladies watched, the bearer fumbled in a bundle of
cloth and produced what appeared to be a chapati, offering it to

the clergyman with a shaking hand. Kingston, lost in thought, gazing at the tumbling white water, for a moment did not notice it . . . then he took it, examined it for a moment and placed it on a large flat stone a few feet away. Then he sank to his knees in front of it, lifting his joined hands in prayer and calling out in a penetrating voice words which Emily could not make out because of the splashing of the water. But while the clergyman prayed, arms now outstretched with upturned palms, his white face almost radiant against the dark green of the ferns and rhododendrons, the bearer gazed with longing at the chapati on the rock, bowing and shaking his head rapidly in his excitement, even uttering groans from his dribbling mouth. At Emily's side Mrs Forester was shaking with suppressed hilarity at this curious sight. Emily herself felt ashamed to be watching it. And because it seemed as if they might go on like that for ever, the clergyman in an ecstasy of prayer, the bearer writhing and dribbling with anticipation, she detached herself from Mrs Forester's hand and retreated softly back down the path they had come.

6

From where they had left the landau at the edge of the pines a considerable stretch of the road they had just travelled could be seen and now Emily could make out the four horsemen she had seen earlier as tiny specks much further down the hillside. They were approaching at no great distance. Mrs Forester's brows gathered in a pretty frown when she saw them and she glanced at Emily but made no comment. A little later she looked at them again, smiling to herself, but still said nothing, merely indicating to the bearer where he should spread the rugs on the soft bed of moss and pine-needles. Emily continued to keep a watchful eye on them as they grew larger, partly because it soon became clear that this was a party of young officers and there was something about them, even at a distance, which suggested that they could possibly be *her* officers, but mainly because they made an astonishing sight, covered from head to foot as they were in white dust, both horses and riders. It was almost, it seemed, as if four equestrian statues of white marble had ridden off their pedestals.

Emily saw them hesitate and exchange a few quick words as they approached the landau which was plainly visible from the road. Then one of them left the road and trotted forward into the pines, followed at a walk by his companions. Mrs Forester still showed no sign of being aware of his approach and perhaps had not even noticed it. Emily watched, intrigued by the white marble horse whose moist brilliant eye looked as out of place in that white head as if it were a real eye set in a statue. The rider she had by now recognized as Captain Hagan.

'Good afternoon, Mrs Forester,' he said, ignoring Emily. He had dismounted and cast the reins aside and was now walking forward rather stiffly; the horse, nodding its head, followed meekly at his heels as if it were a dog.

'Captain Hagan! Why, what a pleasant surprise!' exclaimed Mrs Forester throwing her hands up in a theatrical gesture of astonishment. 'How strange that we should meet again so soon.'

'But since we both have the same destination it is hardly . . .'

'Do you know Miss Anderson?' asked Mrs Forester without waiting for him to finish.

'I was saying,' repeated Hagan, looking put out, 'it is hardly so . . .'

'We are travelling companions,' said Mrs Forester, interrupting him again. 'Is that not so, Emily? We have decided to be friends, Emily and I, because we find men to be such coarse brutes, so lacking in refinement, is that not so, Emily? Why, Captain Hagan, I have just introduced you to this pretty young lady and you have yet to notice her presence.'

Hagan bowed to Emily, looking somewhat baffled by Mrs Forester's banter. He half-turned and raised an arm to indicate his companions who had meanwhile dismounted a few yards away and were making a great game of banging the dust from each other's clothes.

'Let me introduce my friends, Lieutenants Potter, Woodleigh

and Arkwright, all at your service. Step forward, lads, and meet
Mrs Forester and Miss Anderson.'

The young men did so, still laughing. By now they had
removed their sun-helmets and wiped some of the dust from
their faces and Emily could see that these were indeed *her*
officers. For a moment she wondered how she would discover
which name went with which officer, but as each bowed over
her outstretched hand he spoke his name in clear tenor or
baritone . . . Charles Woodleigh, Walter Arkwright, Edward
Potter. As this last officer, Lieutenant Potter, bowed with
exaggerated gallantry to kiss her hand Emily was confronted by
a mass of tight blond curls, still rather dusty from the road, and
then, as he raised his head again, by two blue eyes, one of which
winked at her. Emily did her best not to appear flustered.

'Teddy Potter altogether at your service, Miss Anderson,' he
murmured, as if for her ears alone.

'If you would care to share our refreshment you are most
welcome to do so,' said Mrs Forester who had noted with a smile
the elaborate attentions that Potter had been paying to Emily's
hand. And she continued to smile to herself as Captain Hagan
and his younger friends were protesting that no, they could not
possibly presume to . . . that they had had no intention of . . .
though it was true that if they were to tiff at the dak bungalow as
they planned they would have to wait *as usual* while their tiffin
was chased squawking over the hillside . . . in short, if the ladies
did not mind they would first go and take a quick plunge in the
pool and then come back and . . . but only provided they weren't
imposing.

While Mrs Forester summoned Emily and little Jack to sit
beside her on the rug that had been spread out on the ground
and nodded to the bearer who was waiting to serve them with
patties and cold meats and hard-boiled eggs from the dishes
which he had set out in their absence, the younger men retired in
the direction of the pool, Potter and Woodleigh shouting that
they were going to give Arkwright a ducking, he needed it, he
was getting above himself, indeed he was! Arkwright was the
one of Emily's officers who had taken least part in the play-
acting on the train the day before and who had not made much

impression on her; his manner was more reserved than that of
the others. Reserved or not, he now had to run for his life down
the path, Potter and Woodleigh pelting after him. Captain
Hagan, after a moment's hesitation, stalked rather pensively
after his younger companions.

It was very peaceful in this glade striped with the long blue
shadows of the pines and scented with their resin. Emily had
been keeping an eye out for the tonga conveying her aunt and
uncle which surely could not be very far behind. Presently, from
somewhere on the hillside below them they heard the sound of a
horn being blown and a little while later the McNabs' tonga
came into sight. Emily ran out into the road to meet them with
an invitation from Mrs Forester to join the picnic in the glade.
The McNabs readily accepted, smiling at Emily's enthusiasm,
and came to sit beside Mrs Forester and her son.

'Well, Jack,' said McNab to the little boy. 'Shall we climb a
tree later?'

The boy whispered something into the Doctor's ear and he
raised his eyebrows. 'Frightened? Well, we'll find an easy one
then. Aye, with a bird's nest in it, would that do?'

Captain Hagan now returned from the pool and was
introduced to the McNabs. He had contented himself with
washing his hands and face, he explained, but his younger
friends, careless of the Padre's susceptibilities or of who might
come upon them unexpectedly, had insisted on stripping naked
and plunging bodily into the pool, where he had left them
sporting like otters. Mrs Forester asked whether Mr Kingston
had taken offence.

'He did not appear to notice them at all,' replied Captain
Hagan, accepting a plate of ham and cold spiced beef from Mrs
Forester's bearer. He added something rapidly in Hindustani to
the bearer who nodded and hurried away, returning in a
moment with a bottle of beer and a glass.

'This feels damnably warm,' Hagan said as he took it. The
bearer looked concerned. Hagan waved him away, however.

Emily had been having a discreet look at Captain Hagan in an
effort to decide what to think of him and had come to the
conclusion that although she had to acknowledge that he was a

handsome man she did not altogether like his looks. It was not so much his features, which were manly and regular, as the expression they wore . . . an arrogant, supercilious expression, it seemed to her. And when he smiled, which she now saw him do for the first time as he conversed with Mrs Forester, a corner of his mouth lifted disagreeably to reveal some very white and very even teeth. But his tone was pleasant enough as he chatted with the ladies and Emily decided that perhaps he was not so bad after all.

'Ah, now here comes the Padre Sahib,' Hagan remarked presently.

'Will you ask Mr Kingston if he will come and eat something with us?' asked Mrs Forester.

Captain Hagan obediently got to his feet and went to meet the clergyman.

'I hope he does not feel that his bearer has been invited, too,' added Mrs Forester with a smile.

The bearer, indeed, showed every sign of being about to accompany the two men to where the others were sitting, but on a word from Kingston he halted in his tracks, hanging his head beneath his shoulder as if his neck were broken and grimacing. He then sank down to sit cross-legged on the very spot where he had halted. He did this in a way that was so odd that the ladies exchanged a smile.

'It is very kind of you, Mrs Forester,' Kingston said, taking a seat beside her on the trunk of a fallen tree which lay conveniently nearby, 'but I must only delay a little while. I'm anxious to continue beyond Solon if possible before dark.' And of the variety of food which Mrs Forester offered him he would accept only an apple. This, peeled and quartered with care, he ate with evident pleasure, discreetly patting his finely moulded lips with a handkerchief when he had finished. He had given up eating meat during Lent, he explained.

'You will certainly make yourself ill if you continue,' remarked McNab.

In the meantime cries were heard at a distance and Potter, Woodleigh and Arkwright reappeared, faces shining more like those of schoolboys than of officers and hair still wet from their swim. Potter's hair was darker, and more tightly curled than ever, Emily noticed; she was not sure that she liked men to have curly hair.

Hardly had they in turn joined the little party picnicking in the glade than their high spirits infected the others: the ladies chaffed them over the amount of food that each had piled on his plate, and even the Reverend Kingston laughed indulgently at their gluttony. Only Hagan seemed withdrawn, watching his younger companions in a sombre and detached sort of way. Now and again he turned to look over his shoulder at the clergyman's bearer who was still seated cross-legged on the ground at some distance; the fellow could be heard muttering incoherently and there was a long, glittering needle of saliva hanging from his chin.

'I think the poor brute is hungry,' said Hagan presently as if to himself.

Teddy Potter, meanwhile, was explaining to the ladies and especially to Emily that the road to Simla was positively infested with hostile tribesmen, with thugs and dacoits of every shape and description who were, moreover, particularly interested in making away with fair young English damsels . . . yes, it was jolly lucky that he and Woodleigh and Arkwright, under the 'awe-inspiring command' of the 'universally dreaded' Captain Hagan, should be on hand 'in the nick of time' to prevent Miss Anderson being carried off to become the unwilling bride of a hook-nosed Pathan chieftain with a dagger in his belt. Why, most likely the rascal was already watching them from behind those very trees!

'Wait!' cried Woodleigh in alarm. 'I believe I just saw a movement in yonder bushes . . . the glint of a blade, I think it was.'

'Or the glitter of cruel, eagle eyes watching their fair prey . . .'

'I do believe the brute is hungry,' remarked Hagan again.

'But there's no need to worry! We are here to protect you!' cried Potter, edging a little closer to Emily. 'No bandit chieftain will make you his bride unless . . .'

'Unless what?' asked Emily, laughing.

'Unless the wretched Arkwright falls asleep at his post while

Woodleigh and I are out fighting with our bare hands the tigers which I forgot to say roam these very woods in search of a dainty maid for tiffin.'

'But why are you fighting them with your bare hands?'

'Because our guns have missed fire, of course, as they always do according to *Blackwood's*.'

'When you have throttled the tigers and woken up Mr Arkwright then what will you do?' asked Emily, who was discovering that talking to strange young men was easier than she had thought.

'The brute must be fed,' declared Hagan sombrely and picking up Woodleigh's sabre, which the latter had just now stuck quivering in the ground at his side the better to defend Emily in case of attack, he leaned forward to hack off a piece from the side of spiced beef.

'We will set off to your rescue, of course, to the chieftain's lair deep in the mountains! But alas! We may arrive too late! We may find you with gold bangles round your pretty ankles and a hook-nosed baby in your arms!'

'Spitting betel juice at us for our pains . . .'

'I should certainly do nothing so disgusting,' said Emily stoutly, 'even as Mrs Bandit Chieftain. I find you most unkind.'

'Here, Woodleigh, let us give the fellow a sandwich,' said Hagan, folding the slice of spiced beef into a chapati and handing it to Woodleigh.

'At your service,' cried Woodleigh, springing to his feet and touching his forelock in a comical manner.

'No, wait a moment, please,' said Dr McNab, rising to his feet to detain Woodleigh. 'He must not eat that.'

'Ah? And why not, pray?' asked Hagan.

'The man is a Hindu and must not eat beef.'

'Still . . . let us see whether he will eat it.'

'That wouldna be right,' said McNab calmly but in a firm tone. Woodleigh hesitated, looking from one man to the other.

'He is an imbecile and will not notice,' pursued Hagan pleasantly.

'Nevertheless, it shouldna be done.'

Hagan hesitated and turned to the Reverend Kingston with a

smile. 'Well, Mr Kingston, what is it to be? Are we to feed the fellow a beef sandwich or are we to hold back out of respect for his superstitions?'

Potter had ceased his chatter to Emily and for a moment nobody else said a word while Kingston considered. It seemed that he had been contemplating other, perhaps more spiritual, matters. 'It is best that we do not give him the sandwich,' he said at last with a shrug to suggest that he did not consider it a matter of great importance.

Hagan sat down again and said, still smiling: 'Well then, we must let the brute go hungry.'

'He ate something but a little while ago,' Kingston reassured him.

'And behold, there is a melon. Let him eat that!' cried Potter in a facetious tone, pointing. And it was true, there on a moss-covered rock a few paces from where the native sat there was a melon, evidently ripe and in good condition, no doubt left there by some other traveller.

'Certainly, let him eat that and infect himself with cholera,' agreed Hagan, 'and that will put him swiftly out of his misery, which is the best solution of all.'

Nobody answered this assertion except the Doctor who made a wry grimace and shook his head. Emily whispered to Teddy Potter: 'Do melons have cholera in them?' And he whispered back: 'Yes, I'm afraid they do, Miss Anderson . . .' and he added in an even more confidential tone: 'If I had seen you raising a cool slice of melon to your pretty lips, why, I should have had to dash it from them. And do you know,' he went on, speaking almost into Emily's ear, 'I believe I should have dashed that slice of melon from your lips anyway . . . merely out of *jealousy*!'

Emily felt herself blushing hotly at this audacious confidence and could find no reply to it. She stared fixedly at the ground and tried to think of something ordinary.

'Will you take nothing with you then, Mr Kingston, for the rest of the journey?' asked Mrs Forester, for the clergyman was taking his leave, saying that he must really be on his way, he had not intended to delay so long. 'You still have a long road to travel.'

But Kingston declined with thanks. Emily had noticed that once or twice he had had to master a fit of coughing and he looked already very tired. His pale, bony face stood out sharply against the dark brown and green of the pine grove, giving the impression of the face of a saint painted on a medieval ikon. Mrs Forester rose to accompany him the few yards to his tonga: surprisingly, she had lost her superior air and seemed anxious to please him.

But before they had time to move away Captain Hagan remarked: 'Is it not odd that a man of the cloth should feel tenderness to such native prejudices?'

'It is not the matter of his eating beef or not eating it which concerns me, Captain Hagan, but the salvation of his soul. By the grace of God even this poor imbecile will have the chance to choose the True Way and enter into glory. While he is in ignorance it does not greatly matter what he eats.'

'Come now, Mr Kingston! By allowing him to do as he pleases do you not give support to the superstitions of an idolatrous faith?'

'I can assure you, Captain Hagan, that I give no support whatever to his idolatry,' replied Kingston calmly. With that he turned away and accompanied Mrs Forester to the waiting tonga. Seeing them approach, the bearer struggled to his feet and hurried towards the vehicle, his thin arms milling the air in his excitement. Soon he had installed himself on the forward seat beside the *sais*, cradling his master's pathetic suitcase in his arms. Having said goodbye to Mrs Forester the Reverend Kingston clambered up to sit back to back with his bearer. There was a cry from the *sais* and the crack of a whip. The two ponies pulled the tonga out on to the road and attacked the slope which here was at such an angle that the clergyman had to struggle to prevent himself being tipped out on to the road. He sat there holding on grimly with both hands to prevent himself slithering off the seat. Emily wondered how, weak as he was, he would ever have the strength to complete his journey without falling out of the back of the tonga. They heard the *sais* blow his horn as they approached the bend in the road; then the vehicle and its passengers had disappeared, but presently they heard, more faintly, the horn sound again at another bend higher up the mountain, and again, more faintly still, at another, and so for a little while they could chart Mr Kingston's progress.

Mrs Forester had not returned to where the others were sitting but had lingered on the far side of the glade watching her little boy. With his bearer crouching behind him Jack sat on the ground absorbed in building a delicate little house of twigs. Captain Hagan got to his feet and strolled over to join Mrs Forester; as he did so, Emily noticed Teddy Potter exchange a surreptitious wink with Woodleigh.

'It is time we were going, too, David,' Miriam said to McNab. He nodded but made no immediate move.

Hagan was saying something to Mrs Forester but she appeared out of sorts and suddenly turned her back on him. He tried to take her by the elbow to turn her towards him but she shook his hand away and spoke to him sharply, crossly; it was too far to make out the words. With a shrug he left her and sauntered back towards the centre of the glade, his face expressionless. On his way he passed the melon which earlier they had noticed some traveller had left there. Picking up Woodleigh's sabre Hagan began to slash at this melon, aimlessly at first but then more viciously. Red flesh and juice flew everywhere. In a few moments he had reduced it to pulp. The others watched him in silence.

'There's an end to its infection,' he said when he rejoined them. Nobody made any reply and after a while he said: 'All the same, Doctor, I'm surprised that you should want to defend these Hindu superstitions. The natives would do a damn sight better in my opinion if they ate some of these filthy cows that roam about everywhere.'

'It is a matter of common humanity,' replied McNab testily, 'that one shouldna impose upon an idiot that which he wouldna agree to if he were in his right mind. And that's all there is to be said about it.'

7

Darkness was falling by the time they at last reached the outskirts of Simla. Dr McNab was relieved to see the first lights glimmering above them in the trees. Not only was he tired himself, he was concerned for his wife and niece: for the past hour Miriam had been feeling faint, though it was probably nothing more serious than weariness combined with the rarefied air of the hills. In any case he had been obliged to hold her in her seat with an arm round her waist and one hand clutching her dust-coat while he used the other to keep them both from being jolted out of the tonga. Moreover, it had grown chilly as the sun declined and they had felt the need to huddle together. As for Emily she had made the journey sitting in front beside the Pathan *sais*. In this position she had been in less danger of being thrown out of the vehicle on steep slopes but exposed to the chilly evening air and with only one good arm to steady herself she, too, had clearly found the last few miles an ordeal.

Yet despite his weariness and concern McNab was at the same time aware of a feeling of contentment, subtle at first but gradually growing stronger as they climbed the last slopes towards the Simla ridge. The humid air brought back indistinct memories of his childhood as the road wound up through cedars and oaks. Rhododendrons crowded the banks on each side, their flowers glowing like lamps in the dusk and white roses nestled among the brambles and ferns. All this came as a pleasant shock to him, he had grown so accustomed to the plains during the thirty years he had spent in India. He had taken dislike to Simla on his last visit: the people had irritated him and he had felt he had no business there. But now he found himself looking forward to the few weeks he would spend there.

The McNabs had arranged for accommodation at Lowrie's Hotel on the Mall. This establishment was in many respects similar to the hotel in Kalka but with one distinct advantage over it, in McNab's view: its proprietor was less often to be seen on the premises. But during the season it was hard to find room anywhere in Simla and since Mr Lowrie considered himself indebted to the McNabs for some trifling treatment the Doctor had bestowed on him on their last visit it had seemed natural as a last resort to turn to him. The only alternative had been an expensive one, the renting of a bungalow. Having renewed acquaintance with his former patient McNab now wondered whether this might not have been a better plan, after all.

Presently, therefore, they found themselves installed in rooms at Lowrie's Hotel with such luggage as they had been able to bring with them in the tonga: their heavier trunks would follow them up from Kalka by bullock cart in three or four days' time. Miriam and Emily were barely able to eat any supper and retired to bed immediately afterwards. McNab, who suddenly felt quite exhausted himself, was about to follow them when a bearer approached with a message scrawled on a piece of paper which, he said, had just been delivered by some *badmash* from the bazaar. He had evidently spent some time trying to chase this man away before discovering his purpose. The messenger was waiting under a tree in the compound. The message was from the Reverend Kingston and begged the Doctor to come to 'the priest-house' without delay on account of 'a serious illness'. There was no further explanation.

'What! At this time of night!'

'Sahib?'

'Nothing, nothing. I was just grumbling to meself.'

And McNab, feeling thoroughly disgruntled and wearier than ever, went to fetch his bag. Miriam was already asleep so he did not disturb her. On his way out he caught a glimpse of his own grim, drawn face in a mirror and thought: 'It won't be long now before some younger fellow has to be doing this for you.' Seeing him come out the messenger, a ragged old cut-throat with a great sweeping moustache, stirred from his post and signalled to the Doctor; the two men fell into step without a word. 'Aye, but will he? What's the betting he'll stay warm in bed . . . as I would, too, if I had any sense.'

Saint Saviour's, McNab remembered, was on the fringes of

the Lower Bazaar; their way led along the Mall until they came to the Town Hall, then they turned off to the right and began the steep descent from one narrow evil-smelling passage to another. If you are already tired, as McNab was, it can be as taxing to make your way *down* a steep slope as up one: in no time his legs were aching and his head was spinning for lack of oxygen at that unaccustomed altitude. But his guide plunged onwards as if there were not a moment to lose, carrying a lantern in one hand and the Doctor's bag in the other. On they went, through doorways, over flat roofs, down crumbling staircases, even through hovels where McNab could just make out dark figures sleeping on charpoys wrapped in blankets. At last the slope evened out a little and they passed under a dark looming building surrounded by trees. Looking up McNab saw a cross silhouetted against the star-sprinkled sky. The priest-house lay a few yards further on, a dilapidated brick building of one storey surrounded by native hovels. There was an impressive door here, made of oak and studded with brass, but off its hinges and wedged permanently into place with boulders: the guide ignored it and led the way instead into the narrow passage between the priest-house and the next building. A stench of urine and curry met the Doctor's nose. His guide had stopped and was tugging at a bell-rope outside another door which this time came up only to McNab's chin. A white cross with curling Gothic extremities had been painted on it by an unskilled hand. While they waited his guide said something but McNab, leaning against the wall, was too spent to take it in.

'What nonsense! Am I the only doctor in Simla?'

The door opened suddenly with a crack of wood, the guide help up the lantern and handed the Doctor his bag. He stooped and passed inside.

He was greeted by Kingston. This was a surprise. McNab had assumed that it was Kingston he had been summoned to treat. He had even formed a strong impression of what the trouble might be and had been considering how best to deal with it.

'It's good of you to come so quickly, Doctor. Forgive me, you must be tired after your journey but . . . I'd not have called you if there'd been any alternative.'

The only light came from the lantern held up by the man at the door which projected a monstrous, swaying shadow of McNab's own head and shoulders into the hallway where they were standing. In here the smell of urine and curry was exchanged for a powerful smell of incense. McNab wrinkled his low-church nose with discomfort. Kingston had turned and was groping his way along the passage to another door. McNab followed, still preceded by his own gigantic shadow which flitted rapidly over musty wall-hangings or hanging garments and came to a halt on a facing wall. Kingston had stepped aside so that he could enter.

McNab was relieved to find that there was more light in this room. An oil-lamp burned on a table covered with books and papers and the remains of a meal, or several meals. A young man of about thirty in clerical dress was sitting on a straight-backed chair beside a fire of logs. A skeletal dog lay whining at his feet. The dog did not stir as McNab entered but the young man got to his feet and nodded. His neatly barbered head and thin, smoothly shaven cheeks lent him a somewhat saturnine air. He gazed expectantly at McNab but did not say anything. He appeared to be in the best of health. 'Surely they can't have summoned me to cure the dog!' thought McNab, but then he noticed that there was a bed in a dim alcove behind half-drawn curtains and upon it a figure was thrashing about restlessly.

'Doctor McNab, this is Mr Armitage, the Bishop's secretary. He heard that my curate Mr Forsythe was taken ill during my absence and kindly came to enquire.' There was a hint of irony in Kingston's voice, as if to cast doubt on the Bishop's interest in his curate's welfare.

Although Kingston should have been no less tired than McNab after his journey, he seemed to have acquired a new air of energy and authority now that he was back in his own parish. 'This is a very determined man,' McNab thought suddenly, and wondered why he had not noticed it before. But McNab himself was too tired to worry any further about these clergymen and he said rather curtly: 'Where's the patient?' All this time the bony dog by the fire continued to whimper wretchedly. Kingston indicated the alcove.

The bearer who had guided McNab from the hotel stepped forward and drew back the curtain. The secretary, Armitage, brought the oil-lamp from the table and set it on a chest of drawers where its light fell on the recumbent figure of the Reverend Forsythe. He was lying on a charpoy in a pile of dirty blankets; other blankets lay on the floor where they had been thrown off by his violent movements. His face was pinched and livid and there were dark rings under his eyes. He looked to be an old man but was doubtless not as elderly as he appeared, perhaps in his sixties. The moans which issued constantly from between his chattering teeth set up a weird descant to the whimpering of the dog from the adjoining room. Although his eyes were open he seemed not to know where he was. McNab stooped to pick up one of his shaking hands and examined it: it was dead white, the nails blue. The pulse at the wrist was small and hard and quick. Forsythe was clearly in the cold stage of an intermittent fever.

'When did this begin?'

Kingston looked enquiringly at the bearer.

'One hour, Sahib.'

'And yesterday?'

'Same time happen, Sahib.'

McNab's eyes moved from the clergyman's pinched white face to a prayer book open beside him on a little table and from there to a large painted crucifix above the bed. He gave an involuntary start because it seemed to him that beyond the bed a white bird was hovering in the gloom. He peered at it for a long moment, unable to make out what it was, then he returned his gaze to Forsythe. Muscular tremors continued to shake his thin frame unceasingly.

'This man should be in hospital. Why was a doctor not called to him yesterday?'

Kingston shrugged helplessly but said nothing.

'Man, there must be any number of doctors in Simla!'

Again there was silence except for the steady whining of the dog next door.

'Someone who knows the station could tell you where he should be taken. Here, let me see his urine.'

A chamber-pot was produced. It was brimming, as McNab had expected, with clear, watery urine.

'Is there someone who can be trusted to care for him? For the moment there is nothing to be done.'

'I can take care of him, Doctor,' said Kingston.

'Nonsense, you should be in bed yourself,' replied McNab brusquely, glancing at Kingston's pallid face and sunken eyes. 'How about you, Mr Armitage? Can you watch over him till morning?'

'Alas . . .' murmured Armitage uncomfortably, tapping the tips of his fingers together. 'My other duties . . .'

'His bearer, then?'

'Between us we will see that he is looked after,' said Kingston stubbornly.

Again McNab peered into the darkness, trying to make out the nature of that white bird apparently hovering under the ceiling. After a moment he gave it up with a sigh. He felt dizzy and light-headed himself. Ever since he had left the hotel he had had the impression of being in a stifling dream. Making an effort to collect himself he undid the buckle of his bag and jerked it open. He said to Kingston: 'Sometime in the next hour his coldness will be replaced by a hot dry stage. Most likely he will complain of thirst and there will be vomiting and perhaps diarrhoea. You should give him tepid draughts which will help to induce vomiting if it does not come of its own accord. If his headache and fever become severe soak a towel in cold water and place it on his temples. Is that clear?'

Kingston nodded wearily and with an effort stifled a fit of coughing. 'They are all sick here, even the dog,' thought McNab with wonder. 'All but the Bishop's secretary-wallah who looks as if he is newly hatched from an egg.'

'The hot dry stage will last three or four hours and then he will begin sweating. He must be watched carefully so that you know when the sweating begins. It will begin here and here.' He indicated Forsythe's mastoid processes and the insides of his wrists. '*Immediately* moisture begins to appear you must give him a purgative. I'll mix it for ye before I leave. If he throws it up then it must be repeated until it's retained. Once it is retained

then ye may give him the pills I'll leave for ye . . . two when the
sweating begins and one every three hours after. I'll come again
in the morning.'

Kingston nodded and repeated the instructions. McNab took
the oil-lamp over to the table to prepare the pills and the
purgative, moving aside the dirty dishes in order to make
himself room.

'Here are the pills,' he said when he had finished. 'He'll need
more, but that will do until tomorrow.' He handed Kingston
four pills of quinine, each of three grains. It was his custom to
prescribe half a drachm in ten three-grain pills for an adult male,
twenty to twenty-five grains for a female.

Some of his colleagues made a distinction between the
European and Indian male: giving to the latter the same dose as
to the female European. He estimated that Forsythe would need
another eighteen grains, perhaps more. Even allowing for the
pallor resulting from the spasmodic constriction of the surface
arteries during the cold stage of the paroxysm he suspected that
Forsythe might be badly anaemiated. McNab had found time
and again that illnesses which he would normally have expected
to cure within a few days instead remained intractable over
weeks or months because the patient had already been in a
debilitated state. This was almost invariably the case with the
half-starved natives he had spent so much of his career treating.
It was more unusual to find a European in the same condition.

'I'll need someone to show me the way back up to the Mall, if
ye'd be so kind.'

The secretary, Armitage, who already had his own hat in his
hand, volunteered to accompany the Doctor: it was on his way,
he explained. Kingston raised his eyebrows and seemed about to
say something but thought better of it. McNab went to pick up
his own hat which he had left on a chair beside Forsythe's litter.
It seemed to him that Forsythe had lost some of his pallor; the
pulse, when he felt it, had become a little softer and fuller. Most
likely he was already passing into the hot stage. McNab had a
last look round the room, ill at ease. Over the years he had
developed an instinct which told him when the atmosphere of a
place was not of a kind that would favour a cure. As a younger

man he had tried to resist the promptings of this instinct but it had proved itself correct too often to be ignored. Then he had tried to isolate the causes of it; but these had proved elusive. Sometimes, it was true, one could point to physical sources, a lack of ventilation, the proximity of an open sewer and suchlike. But the instinct had also at times manifested itself for no such obvious reason when the patient lay in comfortable, agreeable surroundings, as if there were, in addition to the physical, a mental or a moral aspect to an illness. Often he had found that if you removed a patient, preferably to a more salubrious spot but if that were impossible then *anywhere*, his chances of recovery were greatly enhanced. Now, looking around this dim room he tried to locate the source of his uneasiness but could not. The crucifix over the bed, the whimpering dog, the dirty dishes on the table, that faint pervasive smell, the dirty blankets, even that mysterious white bird hovering under the ceiling . . . they all combined to tell him that this was a house in which illness would flourish. He shook his head wearily and picked up his bag. Armitage was waiting for him with a bearer of his own holding a lantern. Even the fetid air of the passage outside came as a relief to McNab as he emerged.

Armitage, too, seemed anxious to be away from that house for he set off at a pace which McNab could not equal and was obliged to wait for him at the first corner. As McNab limped up to him wondering how on earth he would ever manage, exhausted as he was, to climb the hill to the Mall, he suddenly noticed that Armitage was shaking and for a moment feared that the secretary, too, had been taken by a malarial fit. But of course that was nonsense. Armitage was shaking with laughter, one hand cupped to his mouth.

'Did you see it, Doctor?' he asked, gasping in a rather strained and affected way to indicate the extent of his mirth.

'See what, Mr Armitage?'

'Why, the bird! The bird hovering there under the ceiling. I'd been told it was there but if I hadn't seen it with my own eyes I'd never have . . . Well, one shouldn't laugh, one really shouldn't.'

'I saw the bird but what is its purpose?'

'That's what Forsythe has been planning to hang over the altar at Whit, a stuffed white bird, supposed to be a dove to represent the Holy Ghost, yes, a dove "in flying attitude" as Forsythe puts it, did you ever hear anything more ridiculous! And Kingston is prepared to let him get away with it, that is what is so amazing. I hear that Forsythe has also been thinking of making a hole in the church roof and dropping lighted tapers through it on to the congregation to symbolize the fire of Pentecost descending on the disciples! No wonder that there has been trouble in the parish. The parishioners fear they will end up roasted like suckling pigs, I shouldn't wonder!'

'Ah, so it was a dove?'

'A dove, yes, *meant* to be a dove. It looked to me more like a white hen "in flying attitude"! Well, I shall have to make a report, of course. One doesn't like to do it but it is my clear duty. His Lordship must be kept informed.' And for no apparent reason Armitage grinned slyly in the darkness.

McNab, longing for a rest but obliged to keep up with the young clergyman or run the risk of getting lost in the maze of little alleys, limped along very much out of sorts and eager for his bed. He had had more than enough of clerics for one day. And yet there was still a question faintly disturbing him at the back of his mind and finally he said: 'Mr Armitage, how did it come about that I was called to Mr Forsythe and not another physician?'

'Why, Dr McNab, it's not every doctor who'll turn out on a chilly night for a curate who's known to be half-mad and three-quarters the way to Rome. Or who would for the Reverend Sir, his incumbent, if it came to that . . .'

'Rubbish,' said McNab crossly. 'A physician does not pick and choose.'

'I'm not saying they might not have come *eventually* if they'd known he was really ill.'

'But you had heard, had you not, that the man had malaria and the Bishop had sent you to enquire?'

'The Bishop had sent me to enquire not after the health of the curate but after that of Mr Kingston. *That*, I can assure you, is a health about which His Lordship is *much* more profoundly concerned. Why? Because the Bishop can simply take a curate's licence away and be rid of him. It is not so easy to be rid of an incumbent!' And again Armitage grinned to himself in the darkness.

8

'The girl must be warned,' said McNab to his wife the following morning, 'that young men are not always to be trusted. I fear she is not sensible.'

'Emily may not be a sensible girl,' replied Miriam, 'but she will never find a husband unless she is sometimes allowed to speak with young men before she grows too old to be of interest to them. And with us she will meet no one because neither of us is very fond of company. Are you worried that Simla is such a dissolute place then, David?'

'No, no, but she is innocent and yet thinks she is experienced. She has already told me of the swarms of young suitors she has put in their place . . . aye, and old ones, too. You see, I wouldna like to send her home with a broken heart.'

'What d'you know of broken hearts?' laughed Miriam.

'Oh, we doctors know a lot of things,' replied McNab.

'Well then, I'll have a word with her later, it will do no harm. At any rate we are agreed that she should be allowed to accept this invitation.'

'Yes, we are agreed. Though I wish it were not from Mrs Forester. I fear she may be no more sensible than Emily.'

'Would you say that Emily is plain?' Miriam asked him presently.

'No, not plain exactly. She's a good healthy girl. Perhaps a little on the plump side from shipboard lethargy. It'll only take a few waltzes and a spot of archery at Annandale to take the fat off her. Then she'll be trim enough to snare some young fellow. Beside, it makes no difference, thin, fat, tall, short . . .

there's always someone's taste you appeal to, thanks be to God.'

When Miriam knocked on the door of Emily's room she found her holding a grey silk dress to herself in front of a long mirror and looking helpless and bewildered. The colours of her clothes all looked different here for some reason, and certainly different from the way she had imagined them. And many of them were seriously crumpled, too. She was not a person to make a fuss over trifles, she explained to Miriam, but really, looking at her clothes she felt close to tears. She needed *help*. She needed a *maid*. As it happened her father, Sir Hector, had foreseen from afar his daughter's problems and had thoughtfully made arrangements with an acquaintance in Bombay that a European woman in his service should attach herself to Emily during her visit to India and assist her with such problems as tresses and dresses which needed brushing and ironing respectively. Alas, this woman had been laid low with dysentery and had been unable to make the journey to the hills. What was she to do?

Miriam soothed her and said she would make arrangements with the hotel to provide somebody suitable. In the meantime Mrs Forester had invited Emily to see some of the sights with her that afternoon, followed by tea at her bungalow. Emily brightened immediately at this prospect and had another quick look at herself in the mirror, afraid that this was not one of her good days . . . but on the whole she was not dissatisfied.

'Emily, your uncle and I would both like you to be . . . well, circumspect in your acquaintances at the station. You know, in the hills people are not always to be taken seriously in what they say, particularly where romance is concerned.'

'Oh, Aunt Miriam, you needn't worry about *me*!' laughed Emily. 'I know what rascals men are.'

'Well then,' Miriam was unable to prevent herself smiling at this blunt reply although she wanted to be serious. 'And it may be . . .' she hesitated, 'well, that your new friend Mrs Forester, although delightful and charming in every way, is not the best example for a young lady newly arrived in Simla.'

'Oh, Aunt Miriam, I've been wanting to ask you, what d'you

think of her . . . and of him . . . and of *him* . . . and above all of *him*!
I'm simply dying to know everything about them and I'm sure
you must have heard *some*thing!'

It was true. Emily's desire to discuss the people they had met
had become so acute that she felt as if she would burst; if only
some of her friends from England had been with her what a
wonderful gossip they would have had about Mrs Forester and
the officers and the clergyman! As it was, it looked as if the
taciturn McNabs were prepared to let this glorious opportunity
for passionate discussion go completely to waste without even a
raised eyebrow.

'I'm not sure who all these "hims" refer to,' replied Miriam
smiling, 'but it doesn't particularly matter as I haven't heard
anything about them at all. And as for *her*, who must be Mrs
Forester, you know a good deal more about her than I do as you
travelled up part of the way in her landau.'

'But wait,' wailed Emily, for Miriam looked like slipping
away to her own room. 'You could at least tell me what you
think . . . and you must think *some*thing or you wouldn't have
said she might not be a good example . . . and Mr Lowrie clearly
thought there was something not right because he said
something about an "entanglement" and blankets and mosquito
nets, it sounded most odd to me, and I couldn't understand half
of what he said and, anyway, who was that grey-faced man who
brought her to the train in Saharanpur and . . . and . . . oh please
wait . . . what about Captain Hagan and they seemed to be
having a row, didn't they? when we stopped to picnic in the
glade and what do you think of Teddy Potter? Of course, he's
just a silly boy, really, but he *is* quite amusing and quite good
looking although I'm not sure I like men with curly hair, and
could it be that she ran away with another man? I feel a bit sorry
for little Jack, don't you? who never says anything except in a
whisper, and Mr Lowrie said something about her coming back
here to brazen it out . . . which does make one wonder . . . but if
she left her husband can it be that she'll go back to him and
everything will go on as before and she will be received
and nobody will mind?' Here Emily was obliged to pause for
breath.

Miriam shrugged. 'People will gossip, no doubt. Your uncle says sometimes that he is thinking of including gossip among his Indian diseases. Since you seem already in danger of catching it, Emily dear,' she added, smiling, 'I hope yours will only be a mild attack.' And with that she slipped away, leaving Emily with any number of questions still unasked, let alone answered. A most unsatisfactory state of affairs.

Miriam returned to her room just in time to discover her husband, bag in hand, on his way out to visit his patient of the night before.

'Can I believe my eyes?' she exclaimed. 'Is this my dear husband who was going to leave his cares behind in Krishnapur?'

'It seems that people grow sick everywhere,' replied McNab with his melancholy smile, 'even in Simla. But I promise to do no more than I must.'

'That is what you *say*, but can you be trusted? I'm afraid that McNab's Indian Medicine will never be finished unless you mend your ways.'

The McNabs had indeed come to Simla not only with the intention of recuperating in the mountain air but in the hope that the Doctor would at last be able to find time to write his treatise on Indian medicine. Moreover, the visit to Simla would provide an opportunity of visiting the important sanitarium for convalescent troops at Subáthu and perhaps also that at Dagshai. In addition, and most important of all, since military medical records were more detailed and reliable than civilian ones, McNab was anxious to get his hands on statistical information relating to the Army in India: this was naturally easier to find in India's summer capital than in a remote station like Krishnapur. Nor was McNab's medical treatise merely a husband's hobby of the kind that fond wives so often encourage in their menfolk. Rather it was an attempt to distil some order from the chaos of a life's work in medicine.

It would have been only partly true, however, to say that until now McNab had always lacked the time to write his treatise. After all, he had had time enough to accumulate those mountains of notes in Krishnapur for the white ants to make their supper of. The truth was also that as the years had gone by McNab had come to sense that there was another dimension to sickness than the one he had considered until now in his writings on specific diseases: this was a moral or a social dimension, he was uncertain even how to define it. If you had insisted that he explain to you what he meant and show you his evidence he would have had to admit that all it amounted to, this 'moral dimension', was a conviction based not on objective evidence of the kind he had hitherto always cherished, nor on experiments which could be repeated, not even on experiments of any kind, repeatable or not, but simply on an instinct that all things were one, that everything was connected, that an illness was merely one of many fruits of an underground plant in the community as a whole. The illnesses popped up, here and there like mushrooms, apparently individual growths but all in fact the fruit of the same plant.

But (you and I begin to bay at him derisively) what is this underground plant? What is its nature? How do you know it exists? What are its functions? What is your evidence? Why are you, who have always until now made such a fuss about being detached and scientific, now suddenly trying to palm off an 'underground plant' on us? Please tell us (if you can)! All McNab could answer to these questions, for of course he had a hundred times asked them of himself, was: 'I don't know . . . yet.' He could also add that while delving for his underground plant he had not ceased to take a scientific attitude to medicine. He believed the evidence, for example, that cholera was waterborne and was astonished to find that certain of his colleagues in India still refused to acknowledge it after all these years. Moreover, hypothesis is a necessary and respectable part of scientific enquiry and without it evidence is no more use than a scabbard without a sword. If he was inhibited from beginning his treatise it was simply by the conviction that just below the surface of what was evident in sickness there lay this moral or social or even spiritual aspect to it which, if he could grasp it, would permit him to understand medicine in a more fundamental way. He had only been half-joking when he had remarked to

Miriam that he was thinking of including gossip among his Indian diseases.

'Has the *dak* been?' asked Miriam, noticing that in the hand which was not holding his leather bag McNab was holding a sheet of paper. He handed it to her. 'Read it. It was handed in to the hotel a few minutes ago. It's signed "a Well-wisher".'

It was a printed sheet headed 'The Punjab Army Scripture Reader's Society' on which certain words had been underlined in ink.

> I need *no priest* save Him who is above,
> No altar but the heavenly mercy-seat,
> Through these there flows to me the pardoning love,
> And thus in holy peace my God I meet.

> I need *no vestments* save the linen white
> With which *my* high priest clothes my filthy soul,
> He shares with me His seamless raiment bright
> And I in him an thus complete and whole.

> I leave to *those* who love the gay parade
> *The gold, the purple and the scarlet dye,*
> Mine be the robe which cannot rend or fade,
> For ever fair in the eternal eye.

> I need *no blood* but that of Golgotha,
> *No sacrifice* save that which on the tree
> Was offered *once*, without defect or flaw,
> And which, unchanged, availeth still for me.

'A Well-wisher' was scrawled underneath in ink.

'It was addressed to me by name,' said McNab. 'I wonder whether every visitor receives one or whether I am especially favoured. I suspect that it may be connected with my visit to treat the Reverend Forsythe last night.'

Miriam merely shrugged her shoulders. At a time when religious tracts, verses and exhortations were flowing from Indian presses almost as freely as they were from those in

England she could see no particular importance in it. But to McNab himself, as he set off once more along the Mall, this time carrying his own bag and without a guide, the fact that it was addressed to him personally and came from an anonymous source, did seem to him unusual and even faintly sinister.

9

Elysium House, the summer residence of the Bishop of Simla, was a magnificent half-timbered building set in a handsome grove of oaks and deodars on the south-western flank of Elysium Hill. From its wide veranda you stepped out on to an acre of lawn, as smooth as glass; from the lawn you stepped on to nothing but fresh air, for the ground dropped away suddenly, as it is inclined to in Simla, presenting the Bishop with a spectacular view of the next ridge and the even more spectacular ridges beyond. Playing croquet with his Chaplain and Secretary and the handful of young curates he liked to assemble around him (the Bishop believed that there was no game like croquet for revealing what a man was made of), he could occasionally turn his eyes to nourish themselves upon this view and feel uplifted by a sense of its Creator. This mild whiff of eternity, however, did not usually distract the Bishop from his game for more than a moment: he could see no point in losing unless there was some good reason for doing so. As it happened this afternoon he was once again proving his superiority as two *jampans*, one containing the Reverend Kingston, the other Dr McNab, were carried up the drive of Elysium House by panting *jampanis*.

Dr McNab, as he found himself being carried up the Bishop's drive, once again suffered that slight sensation of being in a dream that had assailed him the night before on his visit to the priest-house. It was partly Simla that he was not yet used to: the very Englishness of it all, the men and women you saw striding about in their tweeds, the houses with their English names, Rose House, Oakdale, Meadowbank, the smell of damp grass and

bracken, while you had only to glance southwards from the
Simla ridge down to the yellow burning plain far below to know
that India was still there waiting and that this was only a make-
believe England hanging almost high enough above to escape
the reality of India . . . but not quite, not quite. The pleasure
which McNab had experienced during the first moments of his
arrival in Simla when he had smelled again the unfamiliar scents
of damp temperate vegetation had disappeared, leaving him ill at
ease but unable to say why, unless it were the dislocation
between the reality of this place and of the dusty plains he could
not help glimpsing now and again far below. He felt as if he were
an actor in a play set in a factitious England, a play in which all
the actors but himself knew their lines. The Bishop's half-
timbered house, as it came into sight, only confirmed this
impression; its Tudor air was familiar to McNab as the backcloth of a thousand attempts to portray Merrie England. He eyed
it suspiciously, almost expecting to see it shivering in the breeze.

Having visited his patient that morning and found him
calmer during the interval of remission between paroxysms he
had returned to Lowrie's Hotel to find the Reverend Armitage
waiting for him with an invitation from the Bishop to tea that
afternoon 'to reassure him about the health of poor Mr
Forsythe'. The Reverend Kingston would be there, too.
Armitage had dropped his confidential manner of the night
before and showed no trace of his sly exultation at the scene in
the priest-house. The Bishop, he explained carefully, was
naturally concerned for the elderly curate, given the frailty of his
physique. McNab had received this information with a raised
eyebrow but Armitage showed no sign of being aware that it
contradicted what he had said the night before. Now, in any
case, he would have an opportunity to make his own estimate of
the Bishop's concern. The progress of the *jampan* had come to a
halt on a flat area in front of the house and the few steps which
led up to it but the *jampanis* were still holding the conveyance
aloft on their shoulders to make it easier for him to climb out of
it. He did so stiffly, he was getting old. The Reverend Kingston
had already descended from the other *jampan*. Armitage, hands
joined over his stomach and head lowered as if into a stiff breeze,

hastened towards them. The pleasant clock-clock of wood on wood drifted over the neatly trimmed lawn.

The Bishop of Simla was a handsome, powerfully built man of about sixty, greatly liked and respected throughout his diocese for his forthright and jovial manner. How many schemes for the betterment of his hillside flocks had he not initiated in the few years which had elapsed since he had come to occupy the see of Simla! Orphans both native and European could thank him for their Christian education and even, in some cases, for their daily bread. Impoverished widows, deserted by their husbands at the cemetery gates and obliged to continue their journeys alone, had found their faltering steps supported by his strong hand. He was energetic, yes, sometimes people were astonished by that energy of his, but he was moderate, too. He knew how to keep things in perspective. He would neither sanction nor approve missionary adventures to certain fanatical Muslim tribes of the Inner Himalayas who would kill a Christian without compunction as an infidel the moment they sniffed one out (this lack of approval had not prevented one or two hare-brained young enthusiasts from disguising themselves as natives and having a go). He believed that there was a best way of doing everything and that included the spreading of the Word. And the best way was the balanced way. Martyrdom, he was accustomed to say to the little band of curates he liked to gather around him, was a necessary and commendable part of the Early Church, but what the Church needs nowadays is common sense, prayer and effective administration. Martyrdom we may safely leave to our Roman brothers if they find they have a taste for it. This sensible doctrine sometimes took his young curates by surprise.

'But surely my Lord' one of them would find occasion to ask sooner or later, 'without the enthusiasm and faith of the Early Church we will never make any headway in our efforts to bring the Gospel to India and to the world?'

'Enthusiasm and Faith certainly!' the Bishop would reply swiftly. 'Enthusiasm and Faith by all means, but tempered by common sense. Look at what the Crusades achieved, those great examples of Enthusiasm and Faith . . . virtually nothing. Now look on the other hand at what has been done in a less dramatic and, I grant you, less sublime manner by such humble organizations as the Overseas Missionary Society, the Bible Society, or the Additional Clergy Society, working quietly, effectively, and altogether without flinching from their gigantic task . . . why, a very great deal!' The Bishop would pause for a moment smiling at his curates, giving this argument a chance to sink in, and then placing a fatherly hand on the shoulder of one of the young men he would add: 'A Children's Crusade? That is what my Reverend young friend here would like to see without a doubt!' While the young man in question tried to deny any such ambition to the laughter of his comrades the Bishop would say, shaking his head: 'Touching, deeply touching by its innocence and Faith but otherwise, oh dear! What a lamentable waste of life and treasure which could have been better used!'

Armitage was now steering Kingston and McNab across the lawn to the little knot of men gathered around the croquet hoops. McNab's eyes were drawn not by the men but by the panorama of snow-capped mountain peaks against which they stood and which he knew belonged to the high Himalayas although in the clear, still air they seemed quite close at hand. While they were still at some little distance from the group a cheer went up from it and laughter. The Bishop, croquet mallet in hand, emerged to greet them, smiling. 'Forgive me, Mr Kingston, and you, too, Doctor . . . Doctor McNab, isn't it? . . . I had to show these young men of mine how they should play the game lest they should think that youth has all the advantages.' He handed his mallet to Armitage without taking his eyes off the Doctor's face; Armitage gave an involuntary little bow, almost a genuflexion, as he took the mallet and spirited it away. The Bishop, meanwhile, had taken McNab's hand in a firm grasp and not content with that had also taken hold of the Doctor's forearm and was squeezing it, at the same time gazing with warmth and sincerity into the Doctor's eyes. McNab, rendered uncomfortable by so much bonhomie, would have liked to withdraw his hand but was unable to do so because the Bishop, while he talked, refused to relinquish it. The hand which was squeezing his forearm, however, the Bishop did withdraw and place companionably on the shoulder of Kingston, but still without removing his sincere gaze from McNab's face. Kingston, too, looked as if he wanted to shrink away from that friendly touch. He looked strained and pale except for a high spot of colour burning on each cheek and it was clear that this visit was an ordeal for him, despite the Bishop's warmth.

'We are the fortunate ones, Doctor,' the Bishop was saying. 'It is easy for us to serve Our Lord in such a place. I'm afraid that those of us, like Mr Kingston, who must work in the hovels of the sickly and the wretched are called to a sterner test. Come. Let us see whether they have brought us some refreshments. I am anxious to hear what news you have of poor Mr Forsythe.'

As they moved on Kingston was taken by a sudden and serious fit of coughing. He took himself swiftly aside, however, to where he was partly screened by a splendid magenta rhododendron. The Bishop affected not to notice and went on conversing politely with McNab, asking the purpose of his visit to Simla and showing interest when he mentioned the work he hoped to do on his medical treatise. McNab had not intended to mention so private a matter but felt himself hypnotized by the strong personality of the Bishop into revealing more of himself than he would have wished. Kingston's strangled coughing followed them over the lawn until the Doctor wondered if he had better return and do something to assist him. 'This is absurd,' he thought. 'These church people are no concern of mine, they're perfect strangers. I've no business here at all.' And he decided to make an excuse and leave Kingston to his fate as soon as he decently could. But the Bishop's magnetic personality had neutralized his will to resist and the most he could do was to grumble to himself: 'He'd have me, too, trailing after him with a croquet mallet laughing at his jokes!'

Indeed, the curates, evidently having finished their game, were already drifting over the lawn to where the Bishop had installed himself and McNab at a long oak table on the veranda. While the *khitmutghar* supervised the serving of tea the young men, still chattering among themselves about the game they had just played, took seats at the table at a respectful distance from

the Bishop and McNab. Presently one of them said in a louder
voice: 'My Lord, we believe we've at last found a champion
capable of defeating you.'

'Do you, indeed? And who is this champion?'

'It's Mr Grenville, here. None of *us* can beat him and we've all
tried.'

'Well then, let him come forward and do battle, if Doctor
McNab does not object to having his tea disturbed!'

'Not at all,' murmured McNab, wondering what nonsense
this could be. In the meantime, the Reverend Grenville, a husky
young curate in his early twenties, had risen and seated himself
opposite the Bishop, smiling self-consciously. He placed his
elbow on the table in front of him with his forearm
perpendicular and the Bishop did the same. The two men locked
hands and on a signal from one of the curates each set about the
task of forcing the other's forearm down on to the table without
removing his own elbow from it. McNab watched, surprised
that a man of the Bishop's dignity should engage in such childish
games and at the same time intrigued, for it was clear to him
even before the two men with set lips and straining muscles
began to wrestle which of them would win. Although both men
were strongly built, the Reverend Grenville was a good deal
heavier and at least thirty years younger: the forearm which he
had placed on the table more resembled a leg of mutton and
when he flexed his muscles the black sleeve of his coat shrivelled
up into tight rings and looked as if it would burst. 'Well, how
then,' wondered McNab, 'do I know as surely as the night
follows day that the Bishop will prevail though he is the weaker?
The answer can only be that physical strength is in some way
connected with moral strength or strength of personality . . . or
can it be that physical strength may in some way be tapped and
channelled from a position of authority, such as the Bishop's vis-
à-vis this athletic young man?' To McNab it seemed that this
small piece of evidence linking the moral to the physical was
another indication that there could very well exist 'a moral
dimension' to a physical illness . . . and if it did not exactly prove
it (it was a long way from doing that) at least it fitted in quite
comfortably with his theory that illness was all one, its apparent

variety being merely the fruits of his 'underground plant' in the community.

Although the Bishop had once or twice had his hand forced almost to the table he had now, as McNab had foreseen, begun to prevail. His face was set into a mask of determination, but gradually it relaxed and grew calm. His eyes remained on the young man's face, gazing at him with a faintly interrogative air and showing no interest in the quivering hands between them. Though his opponent was labouring for breath the Bishop hardly seemed to breathe. Grenville had grown quite red in the face and drops of perspiration had gathered in his brows. In a moment he began to pant more noisily even than seemed quite necessary and McNab thought: 'Any moment now he will snap.' Hardly had the thought entered his head when the Bishop began without apparent effort to force Grenville's hand down on the table. With a final explosion of air the young man's resistance collapsed amid laughter and cheering from the other curates.

'My Lord, you're too much for me!' cried Grenville, laughing self-consciously.

'Nonsense,' laughed the Bishop. 'When you return to Mussoorie you must make them give you a bigger breakfast, is that not what he needs, Doctor? But one day I'm afraid one of you fellows will get the better of me, it is a law of Nature.' After a moment he added lightly: 'Ah here comes Mr Kingston, perhaps it will be him.'

The curates took this for a joke and there was laughter, for Kingston had now at last got over his fit of coughing in the rhododendrons and was hastening to join the party at the table, a puny and unimpressive figure with his somewhat stooping gait, his pale, gaunt face and the bony wrists which emerged from the too short sleeves of his coat which McNab noticed resembled a cassock a good deal more than it resembled the dress of the other clerics present.

The Bishop rose to greet him saying with a kindly smile: 'That is a bad cough, Mr Kingston. We were becoming concerned about you.' To the Doctor he said: 'I fear Mr Kingston does not look after himself as he should.'

'That could be,' said McNab.

'No doubt he works too hard.'

'Aye, it is possible,' agreed McNab. 'We canna always choose when to stop if other folk depend upon us.'

'You will have even more to do,' said the Bishop speaking at last directly to Kingston, 'now that poor Mr Forsythe is taken ill. Would you not like one of these young men as a curate to assist your ministry?'

'Thank you, my Lord, but God will see to it that I have the strength I need,' replied Kingston in a surprisingly strong and confident voice. 'Besides, Doctor McNab assures me that Mr Forsythe will not be incapacitated for more than a few days by his illness.'

McNab, who had assured Mr Kingston of no such thing, sighed at this and studied his fingernails but otherwise made no comment. Smiling faintly, the Bishop glanced from Kingston to the Doctor and back again.

'We have one or two matters to discuss,' he said in a more businesslike tone than he had used until now. 'Will you come to my study, please, where we may be quiet. You, too, Doctor, if you would be so kind.'

10

The Bishop's study was a large, airy room with a high ceiling ornamented with plaster fleur-de-lys picked out in gold. Tall, glass-fronted book-cases ran along the walls and the room was lit by leaded windows giving a view to the West towards the magnificent, snow-covered ranges which McNab had admired from the lawn. There was much heavy oak furniture, highly polished, and some teak panelling on which paintings in gilded plaster frames had been hung and which depicted scenes of an improving or affecting nature. Altogether it was very much the study that a bishop who had never left England might have expected to find himself granted. Mr Armitage, who had accompanied them, bringing up the rear of the party, showed

Kingston and McNab to chairs and then withdrew, silently closing the door after him.

'Mr Kingston, I think I'm correct in describing Dr McNab as a physician in whom you have confidence?'

'Yes, that is so, my Lord,' replied Kingston, surprised.

'In the last few months we have sent several physicians to your aid in whom you have *not* had confidence and have declined to see, as a result.'

'I doubted their power, my Lord, to cure someone who was not ill. Both the Reverend Forsythe and myself enjoyed perfect health at the time.'

'Would you agree that the Reverend Forsythe no longer does so?' enquired the Bishop rather sharply, irritated by Kingston's ironic tone.

'Certainly. The Doctor is treating him for intermittent fever. Otherwise he is as right as rain.'

'May I ask Dr McNab to give me in your presence his frank opinion of Mr Forsythe's physical and mental capacities?'

'By all means.'

'That is not possible,' said McNab. 'I have seen the gentleman last night for the first time and again this morning. I believe he will recover from the intermittent fever if he is cared for. As for the rest I canna say, until I see him healthy. Until now I have only seen him ill.'

The Bishop pondered this for a moment. 'You could not say whether you consider him to be in his right senses?'

McNab shook his head.

'I can assure you, my Lord,' said Kingston calmly, 'that Mr Forsythe . . .'

'I cannot accept your assurances,' broke in the Bishop irritably. 'In your absence from the station I have heard reports of all sorts of unseemly behaviour at Saint Saviour's. Is it sensible to drop lighted tapers on his congregation at Pentecost or plan to do so . . . Only a lunatic would think of it.'

'It is not perhaps very sensible, and yet it was a custom widespread in Christendom after the Reformation which he wished to emulate. A sign of enthusiasm for the traditions of the Church perhaps, but hardly of lunacy.'

'And the bird he wants to hang over the altar, the stuffed white bird "in flying attitude"?'

Kingston merely shrugged to indicate that he considered the bird a trivial matter. Despite his apparent calm, however, McNab noticed that he was constantly scratching at his bony wrists where red marks had appeared, perhaps of eczema.

'And the dog?'

'The dog, my Lord?'

'The dog which lives with you in your house,' said the Bishop impatiently. 'Is it not true that Mr Forsythe has been obliging it to fast during Lent?'

Kingston nodded. 'That is true, yes, but perhaps he was already becoming feverish when he thought of it.'

'Thank you, Mr Kingston,' said the Bishop in a milder tone and after a pause to consider he went on: 'You see, it is my duty to the Church which we both serve to decide whether it would be in the best interests of your parishioners were I to withdraw Mr Forsythe's licence. I am aware of his long and valuable service in India but he is elderly and frail and becoming at the least confused in his mind. That is something to be considered, however, when our friend, Dr McNab, has restored him to full health once more.' And he gave McNab, who had been rendered distinctly ill at ease by the inquisitorial nature of the interview, a friendly smile. He went on: 'Your flock at Saint Saviour's are the simplest of people, many of them native Christians or private soldiers from the barracks at Subáthu and Dagshai, or even ill-educated Europeans of the lower classes who have been brought up to the station as servants, and yet, Mr Kingston, I have had complaints laid before me that certain elaborate variations of ritual have crept into the Divine Service you provide for these plain people. No doubt . . .' He held up his hand as Kingston attempted to speak . . . 'No doubt much of this has occurred during your absence under the unhappy inspiration of your curate. I shall, therefore, be satisfied with your assurances that all such innovations, but in particular that of placing lighted candles on the Communion Table, will be discontinued immediately.'

'I'm afraid I am intruding on a private discussion,' said

McNab, getting to his feet with the intention of leaving, but neither man paid any attention to him and on second thoughts he sat down again. He was concerned for Kingston's health and could not think why until now he had taken it so lightly. Not only was the man most likely suffering from a serious illness, he was at this moment in a state of dangerous nervous excitement. His habitually pale face had been invaded by a deathly grey pallor such as McNab was more accustomed to see at a death-bed; the only colour was the red of his eyelids, doubtless also the result of eczema, which he had rubbed until they were raw; meanwhile, muscles were working like clockwork in his jaw and neck.

'I must respectfully decline to give this assurance, my Lord,' replied Kingston in a low voice. The Bishop was silent for a moment, thinking.

'And if, as your Diocesan, I lay my commands upon you to discontinue this practice of placing lighted candles on the Communion Table in broad daylight, a practice which you have introduced without any authority, do you intend to persist in setting me at defiance, despite the oath you have taken to obey your Diocesan in all things lawful and honest?'

'I object to the expression "setting you at defiance": I have the greatest respect both for you personally and for the office you hold in our Church. However, if I decline to obey this command it is because I believe that in issuing it you have unintentionally exceeded the limits of that authority which the Church has committed to her Bishops.'

'Ah, and how have I done that, Mr Kingston?' asked the Bishop with a humourless smile.

'By forbidding, sir, what the law of the Church distinctly authorizes, for the Rubric is our law in this matter and it very clearly authorizes "such ornaments of the Church, and of the ministers thereof, as were in use in the Church of England, by authority of Parliament, in the second year of Edward VI" . . . Now I've no doubt whatever that lights were generally used at the celebration of the Sacrament throughout the Church of England in that year. If I'm wrong in this belief I am, of course, subject to correction.'

'Mr Kingston,' said the Bishop in a somewhat conciliatory tone. 'I hoped . . . and continue to hope . . . that this difference between us may be settled in a sensible manner rather than with recourse to legal niceties. You know, I'm quite sure, that this question of lights on the altar has already been much argued about, notably in the case of St Paul's Knightsbridge, in 1855 where the judge of the Diocesan Court decided that lighted candles on the Communion Table are contrary to the law except when they are there for the purpose of giving necessary light. Leaving that judgement aside for the moment, I must say that it doesn't seem to me a good reason for lighting them today that they used to be lit before the Sacrament during Mass in England in Roman Catholic times or even, as you want to insist, during the short period of transition before the Reformation was fully settled in England and our Protestant Church well established. But, as I say, I don't want to enter into an arid legal dispute over the matter. I earnestly trust that on reflection you will see the extreme impropriety of an individual clergyman, on the authority of his own private judgement as to what he considers an admissible return to ancient usage, disregarding the distinct commands of those who are set over him in the Lord. There has been much agitation both at home in England and here in India over these matters of ceremonial and to what purpose? I'm afraid, to none. All we have achieved is to divert ourselves from our proper task which is the saving of souls . . .'

'But it is only by showing devotion and respect for the traditions of our Church,' interrupted Kingston with excitement, 'and to its central act of worship, the Sacrament, that with the help of Providence we can bring men to Salvation . . . These are traditions which have been handed down to us in a direct line from Christ to his Apostles and from them to the bishops of our Church, from one generation to the next, not mere trimmings which we can take or leave as we please! If since the Reformation such important traditions have been lost or have fallen into disuse it is a matter of the greatest importance that they should be restored.'

'Man, what a great way they have of wasting their time, these clergymen!' marvelled McNab, wishing now that he had left after all when he had been about to. But he could not help being a little bit interested, nevertheless, if not by the argument at least by the arguers. He noticed that the Bishop had looked quite disconcerted for a moment, perhaps at the thought that he was in a direct line of succession to the Apostles. It was clear, moreover, that he was increasingly losing patience with Kingston. His tone became brusque, almost brutal.

'Saint Saviour's is hardly the parish for such an experiment and I do not in the least see why you should not accept the decisions of the leaders of the Church. Besides, the candles are but one of many aspects of your conduct about which I have received complaints. Is it true that you have trained a choir of native boys to sing the Psalms and the responses and have dressed them in surplices?'

'Yes, it is true.'

'And that you have been having processions with a Crucifix, and kissing the Prayer Book and using wafer bread and making the sign of the Cross and I don't know what else you haven't been doing?'

Kingston this time remained silent.

'Only a madman,' said the Bishop testily, 'would persist in such tomfooleries.'

'My Lord,' replied Kingston, rising to his feet in anger. 'I'm not in the habit of being addressed in such terms as these!'

'Ah, forgive me,' murmured the Bishop, 'but you have caused me some exasperation.'

Kingston resumed his seat, quivering.

There was a long silence during which, very faintly, there came the sound of someone shouting in Hindustani, perhaps the Bishop's *khitmutghar* shouting at one of his sweepers. At length the Bishop said: 'Your parishioners are plain people. They are alarmed and disturbed by your ritual. They feel they are in danger of being turned into Roman Catholics without their knowledge. The Vestry Committee has asked me to intervene and that is why, for the sake of peace in your parish, I am asking you to moderate your behaviour and to submit obediently to those whom Our Lord has set over you in the Church. I cannot sanction any innovations or returns to old usages of the unreformed Church which I believe likely to break down the barriers which mark in the minds of simple people the distinction between our worship and that of Rome. I need not add that I strictly forbid you during your service from using any dress except the common surplice, university hood and black scarf with the black preaching gown.' The Bishop had risen and was resting both hands on the table behind which he had been seated. It was a signal to leave and both Kingston and McNab rose to their feet.

'I apologize, Doctor, for airing our private difficulties in your presence,' added the Bishop, 'but perhaps it is no bad thing to have an outside intelligence on hand to prevent us from becoming turned in on ourselves.'

'Aye, perhaps,' said the Doctor, convinced that the Bishop had intended him to be present all along for some reason of his own. They lingered for a moment at the door. The Bishop seemed anxious to say something but was unable to find the words. Kingston raised a shaking hand to rub his raw eyelids. Finally, the Bishop said in a tone not of reproof but of curiosity: 'Why will you not submit to my authority? Would it not be better?'

'It is a matter of conscience, my Lord.'

'Ah, yes, I see,' the Bishop replied. 'Of course.'

McNab had had more than his fill of religious matters and turned to go but Kingston said: 'Will you give me your blessing, my Lord?'

Again the Bishop appeared disconcerted for a moment and he stumbled a little over the blessing. Meanwhile, McNab had made himself scarce.

The *jampanis* all this while had been sitting in the shade of a magnificent blue cedar that flourished near the Bishop's gate. They rose when they saw the Doctor appear, followed a moment later by Kingston.

'You are sick, Mr Kingston,' McNab said to him. 'You must let me examine you shortly. I should have done it before this.'

'I am tired, that is all,' replied Kingston with a weak smile. 'Besides, I cannot afford to be ill except behind a closed door.

They are anxious to be rid of me from my living on health grounds . . . or any grounds.'

'That is a poor state of affairs indeed.'

At this moment a bearer hastened up with a note from the Bishop asking the Doctor if before he departed he would be so kind as to have a look at one of the young curates who was worried by a swollen gland in his neck. The Doctor clicked his tongue with annoyance but said he would come. Kingston climbed into his *jampan* and was lifted from the ground. 'Will you come to worship at Saint Saviour's on Sunday morning?' he asked.

'I'm not a very religious man, Mr Kingston,' replied the Doctor, 'but . . . aye, I'll come if you like.'

With that Kingston lifted his skeleton's hand and was carried away.

When he had examined the curate and prescribed a purgative (he was coming to the view that all these clergymen needed purgatives), he was not surprised to be asked to return to the Bishop's study for a few moments: the Bishop was anxious to have a word with him.

· 'Not too ill, I hope. No? Good. Inclined to worry a bit about himself, you know, living alone with natives a lot of the time at a remote station in the Mofussil. I like to have these young men to stay with me here from time to time. They miss their mothers, y'know. In any case it's good for them to have each other's company. It's healthy. They don't get odd ideas like poor Kingston who, by the way, is a sick man, is he not?'

'He has a bad cough, certainly.'

'No. I mean really sick.'

'Aye, perhaps . . . I havena had a chance to examine him yet. It might be his lungs, you know.'

The Bishop nodded, rubbing the palm of his hand over his luxuriantly whiskered cheeks. 'I would be personally grateful to you, Doctor, if you would examine him as soon as possible. He is very, very dear to us . . .' He added hastily: 'It may not have seemed like that but nevertheless . . . I'm afraid we have been remiss where Kingston is concerned. We have failed to gain his confidence. We have left him too much alone in the bazaar with that poor old fanatic Forsythe. It seems, Doctor, that you have some influence over Kingston ... it does you great credit for he is not an easy man to deal with. And now it seems that he is getting himself into grave difficulties in his parish. It is worrying. And if he continues with incense and his chanting there will be an explosion. In themselves these things are trivial, these signs of the Cross and genuflexions and wafer bread, they are harmless, but if people take them seriously and allow themselves to be provoked it becomes serious ... Doctor, could you use your influence to persuade him to abandon them before it is too late.'

'I know nothing of these religious matters,' McNab replied grimly. 'Medicine is my affair.'

'But you believe in God, don't you?' asked the Bishop, surprised.

McNab sighed. 'I think I do, sir. In my own way.'

The Bishop paused for thought. Then he brightened suddenly: 'This book of yours, I wonder whether it would be a help to you to put your questions to the Surgeon-General of the Army. He's a friend of mine. He'll be glad to see you. Here, let me write you a chit to take to him now while I think of it. Now you're quite sure you couldn't put in just a small word with Kingston about this foolishness, are you?'

I I

It had not taken Emily long to get over the feeling of discouragement she had felt that morning as, without a maid to help her, she had stood running her fingers through her tangled hair in front of the crumpled clothing which had tumbled out of her suitcase. It was true that her prettiest dresses still had not reached her, as is the way with pretty dresses when they are most urgently needed. No doubt a pair of bullocks was still labouring on the lower slopes with the trunk which contained them under the supervision of a native who was not fully aware of the importance of his mission. But now that there was something to look forward to, even if it was merely a little sight-seeing and a cup of tea in the company of Mrs Forester, the lack of her finery and of a maid to lay it out for her no longer seemed so dismaying. It often happens that one shifts the blame for a vague feeling of frustration from its true but intangible source to something more concrete and visible; in Emily's case this was the lack of a maid, whereas the real source of her discomfort was the belief that in the company of her uncle and aunt, wonderful and lovable though she found them in every way, she would find herself isolated in Simla from making friends of her own kind.

The fact was that Emily's mother had married a little above her rank in society when she had become the wife of Sir Hector Anderson from being plain Miss McNab (not plain in appearance, though, for she was a great beauty). It had not been a difficult feat for her to adapt herself, intelligent and cultured as she was, to her improved circumstances, particularly since she had no family of her own except her brother in India. It's the family which gives the game away in such a situation because while you, the social mountaineer, are scrambling upwards, securely roped to your husband and in-laws, *they* remain where they are, eating peas off their knives (itself by no means an easy feat when you come to think of it) or making whatever other social blunders come naturally to them. Not that Dr McNab ate peas off his knife, or was anything but presentable . . . it was simply that he was a *doctor*. A hundred years ago the social position of a doctor was better than, say, that of a grocer, but by no means what it is today. Hence Emily, brought up a Miss Anderson of Saltwater House, could not help but feel that when she was with the McNabs she suffered a slight but perceptible loss of rank. She felt that people saw her as Miss McNab instead of Miss Anderson. She saw her uncle and aunt as being a kind, cautious, respectable, but limited couple. They lacked that little touch of aristocratic *ampleur* in their attitude to life, it seemed to Emily. If you were a person of 'a good family' as Emily was, you benefited by a little extra freedom from the self-imposed constraints and prejudices of the *petite bourgeoisie*. Even now she could hardly keep her face straight when she thought of Miriam actually coming to *warn* her that men were not to be trusted! A girl growing up in Saltwater House knew *that* before she could walk, almost. And yet, the curious thing was that Miriam was also of 'a good family', so Emily had heard. While Miss McNab had been climbing Miriam had made an equal and opposite descent. And she had taken on the colour of her husband just as Emily's mother had done, but in her case a greyer colour. The McNabs had met under strained circumstances, Emily's mother had told her, in some battle or other with lots of flies about and without clothes on, which might account for it. Still, every now and again Emily had noticed some tiny indication which told her that fundamentally she and Miriam were both of the same kind, even though Miriam had done what she herself could never possibly do . . . marry beneath her. One thing, by the way, to be said for Teddy Potter was that he came from a family as good as Emily's, she had sensed it immediately, or even a little bit better. Could he even be related to those Potters from Chilcombe in Dorset her father had got to know in London? Mind you, Teddy was only a silly boy at heart and not to be taken seriously.

Mrs Forester's company might be lacking in certain respects but if Emily felt light-hearted as she climbed into her *jampan* outside Lowrie's Hotel and was whisked away on the shoulders of her smiling *jampanis* at a fast shuffle in the wake of Mrs Forester's *jampan* it was because, no matter what, at least she was now running with her own pack. It would be harsh to blame Emily for not having re-invented the class-stratified view of the world she had inherited from her parents along more egalitarian lines. (In any case, as Emily, light as a feather, went bobbing away on the strong brown shoulders of her *jampanis*, a few thousand miles away in London a familiar bearded leonine figure sucking a pencil turned a little in his seat in the British Museum to see the hands of the clock at the northern quarter of the Reading Room, and thought, 'Soon it will be closing time.')

Mrs Forester had not planned an elaborate excursion for Emily's first glimpse of Simla. There would be plenty of time for visits to the outlying beauty spots of the station once she was a

little acclimatized. For the moment they would content
themselves with the traditional circuit of Jakko Hill by way of
the Lakkar Bazaar, the recently established Mayo Orphanage
and the Lady's Mile. In the imperious and rather shrill tone
which she reserved for addressing the natives she ordered the
jampanis to stay as much together as possible so that she would
be able to point out to Emily the principal sights which lay on
their route, but having issued these instructions at the outset she
promptly appeared to forget about them for she sank back into
the shade of her *jampan* and allowed herself to be carried forward
speechless. Emily, seeing her in a pensive mood, did not like to
bother her with questions and had to do the best she could with
what she had already managed to glean' about Simla's
topography. Behind them as they made their way east along the
Mall lay Observatory Hill: she knew that because she had asked
Miriam where Viceregal Lodge was and it had been pointed out,
together with its neighbour, Summer Hill. They passed the Post
Office, a three-storey building fronted with carved wooden
verandas which made it look not like a post office at all; then
they came to a wide open space and a handsome church with a
clock-tower. A thickly wooded hill lay straight ahead as you
looked down the Mall. This, it appeared, was Jakko. They took
a fork to the left to pass around its northern flank and
immediately found themselves passing through a bazaar where a
score of Punjabi carpenters were at work, sawing, hammering,
planing in front of their open stalls: the sweet, heavy scent of
pine resin hung in the air. How fresh everything seemed up here
after the weary hours they had spent in the train.

Soon Emily because less interested in the scenery (take away
the 'eternal snows' that everyone made such a fuss about and it
would be rather like Scotland, she thought) and very much more
interested in the people she saw passing by. For what was taking
place was not the mere 'breath of fresh air' to while away the
afternoon which she had been led to expect, it was a parade of
fashionable people such as one might have seen on the Champs-
Elysées or Rotten Row. Just for a moment it struck her as a little
incongruous that here, buried deep in the mountains miles from
anywhere, people should be strutting and giving themselves airs

as if they were spending the summer in Marienbad or Deauville. Did they not realize, wondered Emily, that if someone caught them in a butterfly net and pinned them in a collector's case beside the real thing, that's to say, a *really* fashionable person caught last year in Deauville, not to mention Marienbad or Vichy, they would look like country bumpkins! Not that they looked all that different (well, some of them did for the passing parade contained a number of native princes fancifully dressed), it was simply that they were *here* instead of *there*. There was a geographical element to being fashionable that they were simply ignorant of! You can't be fashionable *any*where . . . if that were the case a shepherd on a hillside with nothing but sheep between him and the horizon might consider himself quite modish.

But this inner protest which rose in Emily's breast was really but a dying flicker of her London and Bath frame of mind. If people in India thought that Simla was fashionable enough for it to be worth their while to trick themselves out in silks and satins and feathers or to canter about on a thousand-rupee horse displaying a straight back and a handsome profile, then it was so. Fashion has this in common with religion: if you believe in it, it works. Moreover, Emily was not by nature a detached observer interested in the comparative strength of frenzies of fashion in this or that place. If she saw people being fashionable she wanted to join in, learn the rules and, if possible, be more so. That is why, after her first reaction of surprise and disdain, she wasted no further time before turning a critical and calculating eye over the faces and *toilettes* of the passing throng, paying particular attention to the dresses of the ladies. She was by no means displeased with what she saw: she believed that once her trunk had arrived she would not appear at a disadvantage. On the other hand there were signs that the elite here could tell the difference, that they were not exiled so far from the Champs-Elysées that when Emily opened her trunk they would escape the sensation of being out-classed. Although she did not know it, her trunk and several others at this moment were in danger of slithering out of a cart which had one wheel over a sheer thousand-foot precipice while the carter tried to explain to his bullocks that it would somehow be to their advantage to drag it back on to the road again.

It was just as well that Emily had that trunk full of elegant clothes because when it came to the matter of display in at least one respect she would not be able to compete. She had already noticed that Mrs Forester's *jampanis* were all neatly turned out in a livery of dark-brown cloth secured around the waist with a primrose-yellow cummerbund which matched the primrose turbans they wore around their heads, while her own were a motley selection hired by the Doctor on an *ad hoc* basis for the afternoon from the *chaudhri* at the *jampan* stand where the vehicle itself, a somewhat dilapidated one, had been hired. Not only were they not well turned out, they were not even well assorted as to size, one being bigger than average and another smaller. The result was that however they arranged themselves Emily found herself listing slightly. It is not at all easy to create the right impression if you are not quite on an even keel; she felt as someone would with a flat tyre in a motor parade today. But even Mrs Forester's elegant team of *jampanis* were outshone by certain of the other ladies and gentlemen of fashion: if the sober good taste of London and Paris obliged them to be restrained in their own clothes they did not feel similarly obliged when it came to their *jampanis*: scarlet, yellow ochre, even turquoise liveried *jampanis* met Emily's astonished gaze. 'Oh dear,' she thought as her own willing but ill-assorted scarecrows were once again overtaken at the shuffle and she felt herself pass under the lorgnette of a lady with a complexion like a dried-up apple. As this lady, lorgnette at the ready, went bobbing on ahead Emily was able to admire the salmon-pink tunics and knee-breeches of her retinue and, above all, the elegance of their white powdered wigs. It was just as she was watching the salmon-pink bottoms of this lady's two rear *jampanis* disappearing round the bend ahead that Emily noticed something significant.

It was a snub. Not just a snub either, but a snub administered to Mrs Forester. Mrs Forester's *jampanis*, better trained and in better condition, had pulled so far ahead of Emily's with their rhythmic swinging shuffle that they had been obliged to pause and wait for Emily's to catch up. It was at this moment that a

lady of about thirty, somewhat hawk-like in appearance,
approached from the opposite direction borne by a powder-blue
cortège with gold tassels on their shoulders, gold sporrans at
their stomachs and gold pom-poms on their berets. Mrs Forester
evidently knew the person being carried along by this glittering
team. She raised a hand and with a pretty smile and in her most
ingratiating voice she called: 'Good afternoon, Mrs
Cloreworthy!' The lady in question took a brief look at Mrs
Forester, an even briefer look at Emily who at that moment
happened to be listing more seriously than ever and was
wondering whether she might not end up capsizing ignom-
iniously into the road, and turned her face resolutely and quite
deliberately to look in another direction where, as ill-luck would
have it, one tattered mongrel had just mounted another and was
pumping vigorously, unaware that ladies were in the vicinity.
Mrs Forester flushed and tears glistened in her eyes. She, too,
began to look in another direction, as if she had never sought the
attention of Mrs Cloreworthy. She began to name hills for
Emily whose conveyance had at last limped up but did so
somewhat at random, it seemed to Emily (surely Prospect Hill
was not *there* but back the way they had come?), and more than
once contradicted herself by applying the same name to different
hills. From time to time she would acknowledge with a nod or a
smile the raised hat of a gentleman riding by on a magnificently
groomed horse. But she made no further attempt to greet the
ladies. Whenever one approached on the brilliant eight legs of
her *jampanis* Mrs Forester would become more than ever
engrossed in the geography lesson she was giving Emily. She
waved to no more ladies and no more ladies waved to her. But
hardly a gentleman passed by without greeting her. Indeed, by
the time she decided that it was time to turn for home, that they
would make the complete round of Jakko on another day, two
or three gentlemen (not all of them in their first youth but all
splendidly turned out) had trotted enough and preferred to
continue at a walk. Thus the ladies returned to Christ Church
with a gallant little escort of rather sporting old gentlemen,
some of whom even insisted on continuing with them when
they turned around the southern flank of Jakko towards Mrs

Forester's bungalow which lay near Barnes Court.

The latter part of the journey had been accomplished with the ladies' *jampans* carried side by side on Mrs Forester's orders so that they could talk ... or, as it turned out, so that she could talk and Emily could listen. Emily found something a bit odd about this, because though Mrs Forester continued to have an urgent desire to communicate, paying no heed to the gamey old gentlemen who occasionally ventured remarks and even leaning out of her *jampan* in order to reach Emily's ears the better, what she was actually saying appeared to be little better than nonsense, the first thing that came into her head. It was not long, though, before the truth dawned on Emily: it was only the appearance of being engrossed conversation that Mrs Forester was seeking. In fact she had been using her company to give herself face ever since the snub and perhaps, by seeming to be engrossed in conversation with *her,* to escape the risk of another. Perhaps indeed that had been Mrs Forester's only reason for inviting her? And now Emily began to wonder rather seriously what Mrs Forester's sin could have been that Mrs Cloreworthy and other ladies of fashion in Simla should treat her so. And what of her own position? Had she not unwittingly blighted her own social prospects by appearing in Mrs Forester's company?

When they reached the gates of Mrs Forester's bungalow, a delightful place nestling in a grove of deodars, the sporting old gentlemen dismounted in a further show of gallantry to help the ladies alight from their *jampans,* although with all their pulling and grunting and screwing in of monocles they made the task if anything more difficult. While Emily was being dragged out on to her feet by trembling blue-veined hands she felt what in any other circumstances she would have interpreted as an attempt to pinch her bottom through the stuff of her riding-coat. However, since there was no one within range but the two white-haired old gentlemen who had been helping her, one of whom bore a striking resemblance to her Grandfather Anderson, she assumed she must have been mistaken. This grandfatherly person smoothed his white moustaches and gave Emily a long peculiar stare. She stared back, surprised. Then he gave her a wink ... But no, it was probably just a facial grimace

or tic. Still, there was something a bit odd about the old boy, and
Emily was quite relieved that Mrs Forester did not invite them
in for tea, though they hung about as if they expected an
invitation.

1 2

Mrs Forester had appeared a little strained, perhaps, but
otherwise cheerful while she was bidding farewell to their
elderly escorts (one or two of whom still lingered muttering at
the gates and seemed far from pleased for some reason). But
once she had sent her *khitmutghar* for tea and closed the door of
her drawing room behind him she allowed herself to collapse
sobbing on to the sofa. Emily ran to her and put her arm round
her in concern. 'Mary, what is it?' she asked in alarm. 'Are you
not well?'

But Mrs Forester was too choked by sobs and hiccups to do
anything but cling to Emily and dampen her collar with tears.

'Mary, are you ill? Shall I send for a doctor?'

The sobbing continued and Mrs Forester kept her pretty face
hidden on Emily's breast but there was a slight negative shaking
of her head.

'Mary, you must tell me what's the matter. Is it because that
horrible woman being carried by powder-blue natives wouldn't
answer your wave?'

This time there was an affirmative nodding of the brown curls
which Emily was stroking.

'Oh, Mary, I wouldn't worry about *that*!' Emily comforted
her. 'What does it matter what such a dreadful woman does? I'm
sure nobody pays the least attention.'

A negative shake of the curls and a mumble against her
nipple.

'Others, too? I don't think so, really, Mary. I think it was just
that the other ladies happened to be looking in a different
direction . . .'

Mrs Forester did not seem to find this a comfort, indeed she howled.

'You mustn't worry what such silly people think!'

There was another mumble which Emily found hard to interpret.

'Quite high? I don't understand?'

Mrs Forester shook her head and raising her lips a little from Emily's breast she repeated: 'Quite right. They're quite right.'

'But . . . but surely not!' protested Emily. 'How *can* they be quite right to be so rude to someone?'

'Well, they are!'

'*I* don't think so, anyway,' declared Emily and went on rather sententiously: 'There's simply no excuse for not being polite to people who greet you.'

'Yes there is!' sobbed Mrs Forester in a new shower of tears. 'They have a reason!'

'Oh Mary, *really*! What reason can they possibly have?'

'It's because I've fallen!'

Emily froze and her hand involuntarily stopped stroking the pretty brown curls. She began to blush. Mrs Forester stopped crying for a moment and opened an eye to squint up at Emily, then she closed it and went on howling worse than ever.

There was a knock on the door and the *khitmutghar* entered, looking anxious and grave. He placed the tea-pot and cups on a table and withdrew silently, closing the door again after himself. Emily sat unable to move with Mrs Forester's face pressed against her.

'You're my only friend, Emily, and now you'll turn against me.'

'No, I won't,' protested Emily in a hollow voice.

'It's not as if I fell *badly*, you know. I just went away with someone for a few weeks.' With a few more sobs and a deep sigh Mrs Forester removed her face from Emily's breast and sat upright again. She took a handkerchief from her sleeve and dabbed her red eyes. Then, with a few sniffs, she poured out the tea. Emily was surprised by the speed with which Mrs Forester had got over her tears. She said in an encouraging tone: 'At least those gentlemen didn't seem to mind.'

'Those nasty old men,' said Mrs Forester bitterly. 'I hate
them! If they hear that a woman has fallen they gather around
her as if she were a bitch in heat!'

Emily was too shocked to speak. Everything was suddenly
plain to her. That old gentleman *had* tried to pinch her, just as if
she were a common trollop. And if he had felt himself permitted
to do such a thing to her it was because . . . because . . .

'Mary, how *dare* you take me out with you to be seen by
everyone! What about *my* reputation? Now you've ruined
everything . . . my whole life!' And it was Emily's turn to burst
into a fit of sobbing.

Mrs Forester looked sheepish and mumbled: 'I'm sorry,
Emily dear, I thought you knew . . .'

Perhaps she would have thought of something better to say in
her defence but at this moment the clatter of hooves and the
patter of *jampanis'* bare feet were heard outside accompanied by
cheerful cries. A party of young officers and ladies had come to
pay a visit.

Not everyone feels inclined to join a merry party so swiftly
after having decided that her life and reputation have been
ruined but Emily's tears had contained a lot more anger with
Mrs Forester for having taken advantage of her than real
conviction that things were quite as bad as she had said. It was
partly, too, that this was one of those occasions where Emily's
aristocratic *ampleur* came in handy. A situation like this which
might have meant despair for a girl of the *petite bourgeoisie* could
be shrugged off with disdain by a Miss Anderson of Bath. All
the same . . . all the same . . . it did not make things any easier.

At any rate, the fact that this party of young people who
seemed at first glance to be perfectly respectable and who must
know everything there was to be known about Mrs Forester's
dishonour had managed to overcome their abhorrence without
apparent difficulty was in itself distinctly encouraging. Besides,
it need not necessarily matter that her reputation had suffered in
the eyes of a few Simla prunes, provided there was no harm done
to it more generally in the station. The prunes would have found
something else to disapprove of, most likely, even if she had
avoided being seen in Mrs Forester's company. This brave and

independent way of thinking was one, thought Emily, of which her father would have approved. She could almost hear him say: 'Stout girl!'

By this time Emily's sobs, too, had become sniffs and sighs. After all, she did not want to make her eyes too red with weeping. Mrs Forester, who was at the window, had lifted a delicate finger to move the lace curtain aside an inch or two and was watching the arrival of her visitors. 'Ah,' she said over her shoulder, 'Captain Hagan is with them. It seems he has got over his fit of bad temper.'

The memory of what Mrs Forester had said about men gathering around a dishonoured woman like dogs around a bitch in heat returned unbidden to Emily's mind.

'Perhaps Lieutenant Potter will have come, too,' said Mrs Forester encouragingly, returning to the sofa, 'or another of your admirers.'

'I'm sure I don't care whether he has or not,' replied Emily. 'I must soon be returning to the hotel, in any case.'

'Oh, please stay and keep me company, Emily dear. I shall despair without you to comfort me.' But although she spoke of despair Mrs Forester had rallied remarkably. It was not simply that she had overcome her tears, her eyes were already sparkling with anticipation and hardly red at all. An ornate mirror beside her told Emily that this was not the case with her eyes, which still looked positively bleary. 'Anyone would think to look at us that I was the fallen woman and not *her*!'

At this moment the door opened and both ladies looked up expectantly, but it was only little Jack who was habitually brought in by his bearer at this hour, brushed and combed, to watch his mother taking her tea. After a quick glance at Emily he stood in front of his mother but with his eyes on her lap-dog asleep with an air of importance on a cushion at her side.

'Jackie darling! My darling little Jackie!' cried Mrs Forester, hugging him. He surrendered meekly to the hug which evidently he had expected but his eyes remained on the dog.

'Mama, can I play with your dog?'

'Of course you can, my little darling,' said Mrs Forester whose attention, however, was again on the door which was being opened with deference and ceremony by one of the bearers. Jack gently lifted the cushion from the sofa and sank with it to the floor: his bearer crept forward and sat on his heels behind the little boy. The little dog continued to sleep importantly on its cushion. A moment later and the sleeping dog, Jack, and his bearer had all disappeared somewhere behind the sofa and were no more to be seen.

Meanwhile the room was filling up with cheerful, noisy young men and women, none of whom Emily had seen before except Captain Hagan who bowed to her coldly and went to stand by the log fire with one elbow on the mantelpiece in a studied pose. By way of introduction Mrs Forester reeled off names but so quickly that Emily was unable to take them in: there was a Mrs Bright and a Mrs Laver and a Miss Scott and Lieutenants Evans, Todd, Ritchie, Sykes, Pollitt and several others, but by that time Mrs Forester had abandoned introductions and was calling shrilly for 'simkin'. This proved to be champagne. Very soon glasses were being clinked and toasts drunk . . . 'to Her Majesty, God bless her!', 'to India', 'to Mary, our jolly hostess!!' 'And where's Tommy, that old reprobate, don't tell me Mary left him stuck in the plains again?' demanded one of the lieutenants.

'Mum's the word where Tommy's concerned, isn't that right, Mary?' asked another.

Mrs Forester wagged a finger at them reprovingly.

'Go on, tell us where you left his bones to be picked by the vultures. Jaipur, wasn't it? Yes, I know it was Jaipur. Bet you anything I'm right.'

'His fate is written on my heart,' laughed Mrs Forester.

'Written where? I say, that's a good one. On her heart, she says. Depends where she keeps her heart, that's what I say, eh?'

Most of the gentlemen and perhaps even one or two of the ladies had already been drinking before they arrived and found themselves in a decidedly jolly mood, permitting themselves a familiarity of language and behaviour which was bound to seem offensive to someone as sober as Emily. This was not at all the way she had imagined that she would find society in India. She had expected to find herself dancing at formal balls with black-coated Government officials and red-coated officers but this . . . this was the atmosphere of a tavern! Meanwhile, two more bearers had entered carrying between them a heavy wooden case and followed by a saturnine gentleman still wearing a cloak and carrying a top hat as if he had just come from the opera. He was followed by a native page-boy carrying a crowbar. He nodded to the page-boy who set to work prising up the lid of the case which turned out to contain a dozen bottles of Moselle. Emily watched in dismay as bottles were snatched out of it. Hagan, too, elbow still on the mantelpiece, was watching the proceedings with gloomy disdain.

'Hello, I'm Lizzie Bright,' said someone beside her and taking her by the wrist dragged her down to sit on the sofa. 'Come and talk to us.'

There was already a gentleman sitting on that part of the sofa that Emily was being dragged down on to, a lanky officer with an immensely long neck which lay like a snake on the curving back of the sofa and ended in a gaunt face with a blond moustache and bulging blue eyes gazing directly up at the ceiling. He grunted wearily but consented to move along to give Emily room to sit down. She smiled apprehensively at her new acquaintance who seemed to be scarcely more than a child but nevertheless wore a large diamond wedding ring.

'I see you're looking at my ring,' she said, holding her hand up so that Emily could see it better. 'Guess how much it cost.'

'Oh, I couldn't.'

'Go on, try.'

'Well . . . two thousand rupees,' said Emily at a hazard.

'Five thousand! My husband got it in Calcutta. He says it's really worth twice as much. That's his way . . . he says "It's no use to us when we're dead." He doesn't care what he spends. Before we were married he'd already spent a *lakh* of rupees. I asked him on what? D'you know what he said?'

'Well, no . . .'

'He said: "Horses and houses, that's what I like." Horses and houses! And women, too, says I, because I really knew where that *lakh* of rupees went. D'you know what he said then?'

Emily shook her head.

'He laughed and said: "Maybe so, girl, but you're the one I like best."' And Mrs Bright hooted with laughter, her childish face pink with pleasure. 'He's had to go to Lahore but he said: "Lizzie, you take the children up to the Celestial Abode ... that's what he calls Simla, and I'll follow when I can." I made him promise, no native women. I wouldn't care for that. "Cross my heart," says he.'

'How many children have you?' asked Emily hurriedly, anxious to steer the conversation on to safer ground. Mrs Bright held up three fingers and said, looking around: 'Is your husband here? Which one is he?'

'I'm not yet married,' said Emily, a little bit taken aback at the thought that this girl so much younger than herself should already have three children. And looking around the room she saw that there were three or four other women in the room no older than Mrs Bright and all wearing wedding rings.

'Oh, I wouldn't worry,' Mrs Bright was saying consolingly, as if she had guessed Emily's thoughts. 'You'll soon find one up here. Simla's full of lonely bachelors,' and she hooted with laughter again. 'You could begin with this one,' she said indicating the long-necked officer beside them. 'Wake up, Charles, there's a pretty girl here who wants to marry you.'

'I'm not at all sure that I want to get married,' said Emily, offended by Mrs Bright's laughter. 'I'm quite happy as I am.'

But Mrs Bright paid no attention and said: 'I think he's most handsome and if you don't want him then I shall have him for myself. It's no fun up here unless you have at least one admirer.' Plucking a feather from her hat she began to tickle the prominent Adam's apple of the long-necked officer who, for his part, showed no sign of being aware of it. He continued to lie there as if in a stupor with his head on the back of the sofa gazing up at the ceiling.

'I'll find you a husband in no time, don't worry,' went on Mrs Bright over her shoulder without ceasing to torment the officer. 'You must come to our picnic at Annandale, that's the place for husbands.'

Emily looked unhappily at the floor, hoping that nobody else had overheard Mrs Bright's chatter. The afternoon which had begun so promisingly had turned into an ordeal. It was time that she left.

When she next looked up, however, she saw that Teddy Potter had come into the room accompanied by Woodleigh and Arkwright. The sight of him caused her a feeling of warmth and relief. It was not simply that here at last was somebody she knew, it was rather that amongst these strangers all of whom had husbands or wives or at least friends, Teddy· Potter belonged at least a little bit to her. And so, seeing him look up she smiled and waved at him quite openly to attract his attention. He saw her immediately and nodded and waved back but he showed no sign of coming over to her as she had expected he would. He went on with the conversation he was having . . . indeed, he had not for a moment stopped speaking while he waved to her. He now even turned his back while he went on talking to a girl whose age could not be more than eighteen though she, too, wore a wedding ring. She was a tall, grave girl with black hair, blue eyes and a fair complexion. Emily had noticed her earlier in that jocular company for her plain dress and earnest expression. But now of a sudden she was all dimples and coquettish smiles, listening with exaggerated interest to what Teddy was saying.

This was nearly too much for Emily. She really had to struggle with herself not to burst into tears. But somehow she managed it. If Sir Hector Anderson in faraway Bath had been present would he have said: 'Stout girl'? Yes, he would. And he would have been right too, for it is only in such minuscule acts of bravery as this that most of us ever have a chance to show our mettle.

Well, it might just have been possible to take a lenient view of Teddy Potter's indifference. After all, a gentleman does not immediately desert the person he is talking to the moment he spots somebody more interesting across the room. But presently he forsook his interlocutor in favour of an older woman, common-looking, with a red face, who simpered. In no time, arms folded on his chest, he was rocking back and forth in laughter at what she had to tell him. Emily had now decided that she must leave promptly rather than suffer any further humiliation. She would say goodbye to Mary Forester and have herself conveyed back to the hotel. At this moment, however, a sudden scuffle accompanied by angry shouting broke out. There was a sudden hush while everyone peered to see what the trouble was. Captain Hagan and a bleary-eyed, heavy-lidded young man were shouting at each other and shoving aggressively at each other's shoulders; they were both very red in the face with anger. A little earlier the heavy-lidded young man had been talking to Mrs Forester. Now Teddy Potter had seized his arms and was holding him back while some other gentleman did the same for Hagan. They continued to shout at each other upsettingly, however. It was impossible to say what the trouble was about. Mrs Forester, who seemed as little perturbed as if such shoving and shouting were a common occurrence in polite society, took hold of Captain Hagan by the wrist and led him aside to another room.

'She's gone to take the thorn out of his paw,' said Mrs Bright and hooted with laughter. Then she returned her attention to what she had been doing, which was picking salted cashew nuts out of a little silver dish and popping them one by one into the open mouth of the long-necked officer who continued to gaze at the ceiling. With each cashew nut his Adam's apple rose and fell. Mrs Bright by this time was sitting half on the arm of the sofa and half on his lap as if she were a harlot and not a respectable mother of three. And this was how Emily later remembered her upsetting introduction to Simla society . . . not by the scuffle between Hagan and the other man, nor even by Teddy Potter and his adoring married women, but by Mrs Bright and the cashew nuts and the Adam's apple.

As she was leaving Teddy Potter came up, smiling, and said: 'Miss Anderson, are you leaving already . . . and may I call you Emily?'

'I am leaving,' replied Emily coldly, 'and you may not.'

'Miss Anderson, then,' said Teddy, taken aback by the coldness of her tone. He smiled winningly, however, and placing a hand on her arm said: 'I won't *allow* you to leave.' But then, seeing by her expression that Emily was quite genuinely indignant at this gesture, he released her and stepped back with a shrug, looking upset.

Later, in the quiet and loneliness of her own room, Emily wondered whether she might not have been too hard on him and began to think of possible excuses for his behaviour to her and even to wish that she had given him a chance to redeem himself.

13

Doctor McNab had not forgotten his intention to examine the Reverend Kingston at the earliest opportunity. Therefore when he visited the priest-house on the evening of his visit to the Bishop's residence to see how the Reverend Forsythe was faring he expected to have the parson as well as the curate under his care. But Kingston was not at home when the Doctor called: the bearer said he had gone out among his parishioners. Nor was he to be found there on the following morning. McNab began to wonder whether Kingston might not be avoiding him deliberately in order to avoid his diagnosis. Moreover, McNab suffered a renewed concern for the Reverend Forsythe who was not responding to the quinine as well as he had hoped: the interval between paroxysms had grown no longer, the usual first sign that a patient was on the mend. He wanted to discuss with Kingston the possibility of having Forsythe removed from the priest-house. But there was a difficulty. He strongly suspected that neither Forsythe nor his parson had any money and McNab had discovered that for a European pauper who fell sick in Simla there was no alternative to a bed in the native ward at the Simla Dispensary. But perhaps the Bishop would intervene. 'I shall pay a visit late in the evening when Kingston has no excuse not to be present,' McNab decided and putting the matter out of his mind he settled down to work on his treatise.

At four o'clock, feeling drowsy, he decided to go for a walk before the chill of evening began to settle on the hills. Miriam and Emily had gone to investigate a bungalow that they had heard might be for rent, then to pay a visit to a Krishnapur acquaintance who was also passing the hot weather in Simla; so McNab took a cane and descended alone. As he was leaving the hotel, however, he heard his name called and turning recognized a small, portly figure who was approaching him with excitement. It was Mr Lowrie. McNab's heart sank at the sight of those bright, bulging eyes and curling moustaches but it was too late to pretend he had not heard Mr Lowrie's greeting so he stood his ground.

'Dr McNab, sir, I hope you are finding everything to your convenience and that Mrs McNab also and Miss . . . Miss . . .'

'Thank you, Lowrie, everything is perfectly satisfactory,' interrupted McNab rather curtly, preparing to go on his way. But Mr Lowrie was already standing in his path, smiling in a friendly fashion and tapping two fingers to his temple so the Doctor was obliged to linger a moment.

'You see, sir, my duties require my presence "up here" as well as "down there" . . . in Heaven, as it were, as well as . . . hm . . . in less fortunate regions, but usually only at weekends.'

'Indeed?' McNab raised a discouraging eyebrow.

'I refer, sir, not to my business activities but to my duties on the Vestry Committee of Saint Saviour's.'

'I see,' said McNab, tapping his cane.

'Sometimes it happens, Doctor,' went on Mr Lowrie hurriedly, 'that visitors to Simla during the season find it hard to get a pew at Christ Church for their families, particularly now that we ourselves are having our little spot of bother and so many of our congregation feel obliged to worship elsewhere . . . Perhaps, sir, I could be of assistance in this ah . . . regrettable . . . ah . . . I have friends, I might even call them . . . ah . . . colleagues at Christ Church who would see you snug, as it were, should you be desirous, sir, of attending the Sacrament there with your . . . your ladies.' And Mr Lowrie saluted briskly as he finished with a double tap of his fingers.

'That won't be necessary but thank you all the same,' said McNab, and again prepared to move off. But Mr Lowrie still had not finished with him. Licking his lips and smiling nervously he said: 'I have heard that you have been called to attend the curate of Saint Saviour's.'

'That is so, yes.'

'The incumbent, however, Mr Kingston, is in the best of health.' This was a statement not a question. Nevertheless, Mr Lowrie seemed to hope that it might shake loose some qualifying comment from McNab, who remained silent, however. 'You said so while at breakfast, ah, three days ago,' Mr Lowrie was obliged to add at length.

'To be precise, I said his health was as good as yours, Mr Lowrie.'

'Quite so, quite so,' agreed Mr Lowrie.

'Well then, I shall be on my way,' declared McNab rapping his cane purposefully against his shoe. Mr Lowrie became agitated. 'But you must be warned, Doctor,' he blurted suddenly, 'not to attend those two gentlemen or . . . or . . . hm, except perhaps in an emergency,' he added quickly seeing McNab's face darken. 'They are not popular with us. They are sowing dissension amongst us with their Romish innovations. They are filtering their poison into our . . . Please let me arrange a pew for you at Christ Church where you will have an excellent view of the Viceroy and his party, and where you will not be disturbed by unseemly . . .'

'I don't require either your advice or your assistance, Mr Lowrie,' said McNab, very angry. 'We shall be leaving your hotel tomorrow.' He had decided that if a bungalow could not be found it would be better to leave Simla altogether rather than to continue under Mr Lowrie's roof.

Mr Lowrie appeared taken aback. He bowed mutely. Again the Doctor started for the door. Before he had quite passed through it and out of earshot Mr Lowrie called after him: 'We have been most grateful for your custom, sir! All arrangements will be made! Perhaps you would like to know that there will be a lecture here shortly by a lay preacher well known in the hills. He is known as Bo'sun Smith, sir. His subject will be "Roman ritual, dangerous all round", should the subject be of interest to you, sir. All are welcome. At half past five. Thank you, sir, thank you . . .'

McNab found himself striding along the Mall in the welcome pine-scented air. He hoped that Miriam and Emily had been successful in their quest for a bungalow. That little encounter with Mr Lowrie had spoiled his walk. Romish ritual, dangerous all round.

Neither McNab nor Miriam were habitual church-goers, unusually for the time. In his youth McNab had discovered in himself only the faintest echo of response to the Christian story, even less to the Old Testament. These happenings at a distant point of history in a land which he had never visited had always seemed to him so remote as to deny him any correspondence with his own experience. He had known other people who had suffered Doubt . . . or had even, in some cases, embraced it with passion. But both those who suffered and those who embraced had this in common: they knew what their Faith would have amounted to if they *had* believed. In this respect McNab felt himself to be lacking. He considered himself to be in the position of a man at a concert who is tone deaf. All around him people sit rapt as they listen to sounds which to him are meaningless. Moreover, it might have been said of McNab that the scientific nature of his profession predisposed him to a rationalistic view of the world. However, he was not by any means one of those vociferous atheists or anticlerics who appear to derive as much satisfaction out of disbelieving as others do from their faith. He was decidedly cautious in this respect. It seemed to him, when he thought about it, quite remarkable that Christianity, which was composed, at least to his own objective eye, of many bizarre, alien, and even preposterous elements, should have the effect it did have on so many people. As a physician who had exercised his profession throughout the third quarter of the nineteenth century and a little beyond, and had stood by at births, funerals, and all the changes and chances of mortal men which lay between, McNab had been in a good position to see the power of faith. It was true, too, that McNab could scarcely be objective when he considered Christianity, having himself grown up in a culture permeated by it. His wife, Miriam, on the other hand, was a practising Christian who enjoyed singing hymns and laughed at McNab for his doubts and misgivings, calling him 'a poor Scottish bloodhound condemned by his own nose to sniff eternally for evidence of what everyone else took for granted'. He did sometimes accompany her to church, though rather infrequently.

Despite this inability to share in the faith of those around him he had not ceased to be intrigued by it and by the power of the spirit in general. A couple of years earlier while on leave in Delhi, he had been summoned to help with an epidemic of cholera at the ancient town of Hardwar in the United Provinces, a Hindu place of pilgrimage on the upper Ganges. Here the pilgrims came to the Hari-ka-charan, or bathing *ghat*, and to the adjoining temple of Gangadwara. The *charan* or foot-print of Vishnu on a stone in the upper wall of the *ghat* drew a crowd of a hundred thousand or more to this small town annually at the beginning of the Hindu solar year. In such overcrowded conditions an outbreak of cholera was almost inevitable. McNab and the physician from Dehra Dun who had asked for his help had done what they could but all the advantages had been in favour of the disease. The only way of containing it would have been to send the pilgrims home immediately and close down the *ghat*, which was out of the question. McNab had naturally seen many examples of religious fervour in the native population during the years he had spent in India. But he had never been so close to it before. He himself had felt frightened and uplifted without being able to say why: there was an almost palpable electricity in the air; although no longer young and obliged to work long hours without rest in the makeshift hospital on the river bank, he had felt a boundless energy, almost a sense of exaltation, a feeling quite foreign to his cautious and phlegmatic nature. One image in particular from that time had remained in his mind: it was of a small party of peasants arriving at Hardwar and singing in praise of Vishnu as they approached the river, having walked perhaps many miles with their few belongings. Now at the end of their journey their faces were transfigured with joy. Those faces were still in his mind as he walked, more slowly now, for he was getting on in years and only the desire to escape from Mr Lowrie had made him step out.

It was not that he was inclined after his experience at Hardwar to attribute a special quality to the Hindu creed which had given rise to the radiance in the faces of the peasants. What he knew of Hinduism seemed to him even more alien, outlandish and beyond his understanding than Christianity. But he was intrigued by faith itself and its power. He began to reconsider some of the other wonders he had seen in India: for example, the population of an entire village walking barefoot across a bed of red-hot cinders. Such events were so commonly witnessed by visitors to India that they no longer provoked any comment, being merely dismissed without further attempts to explain them, as hallucinations or tricks, part of the shimmering, colourful but fundamentally unreliable vaudeville of life in the East. But if McNab was too unimaginative and down to earth to soar away on the wings of faith on a Sunday morning with his fellow-Europeans he was also too down to earth not to believe his own eyes. He knew that he had witnessed something that ought not to be possible: people walking barefoot across red-hot embers without burning themselves. Even if he accused himself of having been distracted by the excessive heat in the vicinity of the bed of embers, or by the distortion of the heat waves and smoke arising from it, and ruled that this particular miracle could not be accepted, there were plenty of other examples of the power of faith. He had seen at close range a holy fanatic plunge a dagger through his hand and withdraw it: yet within a few moments the wound had closed, healed and disappeared. Well, you might argue, perhaps McNab had been mesmerized by a trickster. McNab, losing patience with you, would go down to the nearest river-bank and bring back to his study a holy man who had been sitting so long with his arm raised above his head that it could no longer be lowered without surgery, and he would make you put your fingertips on the man's shoulder to feel the shrunken tendons.

And it seemed to McNab that if the power of faith, of the spirit, or merely of the concentrated mind, could produce the least of these wonders in defiance of the physical world as the physician assumed it to be, then he would have to change his assumptions, or at least proceed with the utmost caution while he considered the matter.

He delved in his waistcoat pocket for his watch. It was time to turn back. The sooner he confessed to Miriam that he had arranged their departure from Lowrie's Hotel in a fit of exasperation with its proprietor the better. He hoped that Emily would not be too disappointed if they had to leave Simla for want of other accommodation; for himself it would be a relief. He felt uneasy here, as if beside the beautiful scenery, the prodigious vistas, the snow-capped mountains sparkling in the clear air, there lurked the malevolent presence of a disease he would be unable to control.

14

There were a number of *jampans* waiting outside the hotel when he returned and signs of unusual bustle. He realized at once that this must be on account of the lecture by Bo'sun Smith which was evidently being delivered at that moment, to judge by the sound of a strident voice and a resonant murmur, in the hotel's inner courtyard. McNab climbed the stairs to his room, reflecting that Mr Lowrie's invitation to attend the lecture had been superfluous: since their rooms gave on to the inner courtyard they would have to attend whether they liked to or not. He dropped his hat and cane on to a table and took a chair over to the open window.

The size of the gathering surprised him. The courtyard was not spacious but every corner of it had been packed with chairs, every one of which was occupied. Other people were standing at the back of the yard and at the sides, concentrating intently on the speaker who was standing on a platform improvised out of two tables placed side by side. He was a short, sturdy, deep-chested man with powerful fists which he beat one into the other for emphasis. His voice, however, did not quite seem to belong to him, for it was higher than one would have expected. The sound of it set McNab's teeth on edge. This presumably was Smith. Mr Lowrie stood beside the table, his face on a level with the speaker's knee and moving constantly back and forth from Smith to his audience nodding in agreement and occasionally grinning.

'Friends,' Smith was saying, 'some years ago the Americans were greatly alarmed by a report that cholera had broken out in New York and was spreading rapidly throughout the country. Day after day the newspapers published the numbers of deaths in the population. There was panic, friends, in that place. At its height some learned physicians of their government published a paper which proved that the epidemic was not the genuine Asiatic cholera at all and that hence the panic was unnecessary. Well now. Can you guess what the public thought of that? They laughed those clever doctors to scorn. The suffering patients, I can tell you, cared very little whether this was the kind of cholera which prevailed in Bengal or not, so long as it made them writhe in agonizing cramps and brought death to stare them in the face!

'Friends, for some years now the Christian public of India has been deeply agitated by the introduction of certain changes in the Church of England service at many stations. I do not have to tell you what those changes are. You have seen the like of 'em within a few hundred yards of this building. Time and again, friends, the Bishop of Calcutta has been importuned to arrest the innovations called Ritualistic. The Church over which he presides is torn and bleeding on account of the controversy.

'Friends, after a long silence this high dignitary has at last spoken . . . Yes, you have guessed it is of that fearless Christian warrior Bishop Milman that I speak . . .' Bo'sun Smith held up a hand to quell the ripple of laughter that his ironic tone had provoked. 'He has at last spoken. And to what effect, you wonder. Why, to no effect whatever. Like the American doctors and the cholera he attempts to deal with Ritualism without dealing with it at all. He has discovered that the Ritualism which prevails in England does not exist here in India at all. That is certainly an interesting discovery . . .'

Again there was laughter.

'. . . I should have thought that any man present would know where to find it within a few hundred yards of here and flourishing remarkably even though Bishop Milman says it does not exist.

'Well, friends, if the Bishop of Calcutta says it is not Ritualism then what is it? We have a right to know for are we not taxed to pay for it? There are many stations where the only choice for our soldiers is between a Romish priest and a Romanizing chaplain. We have known a chaplain preach in an empty church month after month, sometimes only three or four persons being present, wholly on account of *something* . . . let the Bishop call it what he may . . . of something called by the decent Protestant worshippers of that station *Ritualism*!'

Bo'sun Smith had raised his voice to a shriek on this last word and a deep murmur arose from his audience.

'We have heard not of a chaplain but a priest . . . he is to be found not far from here . . . preaching against, yes, and almost ridiculing the only pious soldiers in his congregation because they prayed extempore and tried to explain the New Testament to one another without his priestly aid. And yet such a man is paid five hundred rupees per mensem from our taxes by the Government. He is paid for all manner of Romish mummery! He is paid for dressing singing-boys in surplices! He is paid for intoning unintelligible words to empty benches. I believe that if the most bigoted, most hostile, uncompromising Non-conformist in the country were to choose a method of hurrying forward the abolition of Government support of religion in India he could not devise a better plan than to allow such a state of affairs to continue.

'One more word, friends, and then I'm done. I know you want to hear what Doctor Bateman has to say. Before I leave you I want you to cast your minds back many years to a time before many of you came out to India . . . to the year 1838 when the Protestant Church had a more doughty champion and a less tepid leader than I fear it has today, I refer to that great Bishop of Calcutta, Bishop Wilson. Friends, on July 6th of that year he delivered a most important Charge which he dedicated to the Bishops of Madras and Bombay. This Charge was delivered to the assembled clergy in Calcutta and in it he conceived that the greatest dangers threatening the Church arose from the publication of *The Tracts for the Times* and the ritualistic movement which it spawned. Do you know, friends, what he said the year before this Charge was delivered? I give you his words. He said: "I am disgusted to indignation at the folly of some at home in swallowing the gross Popery of Newman and his coadjutors. Why, the foot of Satan is not even concealed. That 'tradition sermon' ought to be burnt. Such drivelling, such magnifying of uncertain petty matters, such evaporating of the authority of Scripture, such nibbling at all the baits of Popery! Mark my words, if some of these men do not leave our Church and join the Apostasy of Rome." I need not tell you that his prediction was swiftly proved correct. Thank you.'

Bo'sun Smith got down from the table to a burst of applause and chatter from the audience. McNab looked around, for Miriam had come into the room a little while earlier and had been standing in silence by the doorway listening to the speaker. She came forward now, asking: 'What is this excitement? Has Mr Lowrie turned his hotel into a church?'

'I fear it is on account of our friend, Mr Kingston. His congregation, or a part of it, has some objection to the way in which he conducts his service. I think that is the heart of it.'

Below in the courtyard preparations were being made for another speaker. Mr Lowrie, with the help of Bo'sun Smith, was attempting to get his fat little legs up on to the table but was having difficulty. A chair was brought forward to facilitate matters. The sight of Mr Lowrie reminded McNab of his impulsive decision to quit the hotel and he told Miriam what he had done.

'It is as well then that I have found a bungalow for us,' replied Miriam with a smile, 'or our visit to Simla would have been brief indeed. But David, you look quite disappointed! Do you really want to return to Krishnapur so soon? The worst of the hot weather is still to come.'

'No, no. You have done the best thing. We'll be well enough off in a bungalow where there will be no one to bother us.'

Below in the courtyard the chatter of the audience grew suddenly quiet. Mr Lowrie, his face flushed with excitement and perspiring freely, was holding up a hand for silence. 'Ladies and gentlemen, we have heard what our friend Bo'sun Smith has had to say. Some of you . . . ah, one or two of you may be wondering if we aren't making a bit too much of these bits of ritual. That's why our friend Doctor Bateman would like a word on the question of Symbols in Worship . . . Ah, thank you!'

Dr Bateman was very small and neat with gleaming black hair, a pale face and glittering eye-glasses. He sprang up on to the table without the least assistance and began speaking eagerly without preamble as if he were in danger of being whisked away again before he had time to finish. He was hard to understand he spoke so fast. McNab had to strain to make out what he was saying. He was asking his audience to think of a church as a pile of symbols. Its height spoke to the worshippers of 'the high and lofty one that inhabiteth eternity', its ground-plan was a cross to speak of the Redeemer, its three towers, its three porches, its three aisles told them of the glory of the Eternal Trinity; its Mystic Rose called on them 'in the power of the Divine Majesty to worship the unity'; its crypt underneath told of the dark house where all go down into silence, into the land where all things are forgotten, till the material body is raised a spiritual body. A thousand lesser things on walls and windows made the church a prodigious hieroglyphic monument which no one could read but the priests . . . and even they soon forgot its meanings.

'And what was the result of all this architectural symbolism?' cried Dr Bateman in a voice that throbbed and echoed around the courtyard. 'Ladies and gentlemen, the height and the space became so vast that these churches failed to answer the purposes for which all sacred edifices ought to be built, namely, the audible offering of prayer and the audible preaching of the Gospel. They were built more to gratify man's pride than to extol God's glory, more to impose on the senses than to awaken the soul. They were places where the altar was raised and the pulpit set on one side. They were in fact the birth places of most of the adulterations of a pure service which we see at present reviving among us. How could prayers be heard unless wafted through the long aisles by intonation and organ strains? The ear could not always be reached, well then, the eye must be appealed to. And was not a gorgeous ritual, moreover, in harmony with everything about them? And thus the Church became an opera-house . . . the service – a *spectacle*, the priests – performers . . . and the worshippers, why, they became mere lookers-on!'

'I'm afraid he will have a seizure if he continues like this,' remarked McNab to his wife in an undertone.

Trembling and blinking with passion Dr Bateman continued: 'This opera-house needed a focus, ladies and gentlemen. What better then than to turn the plain table of the early Christians into an *altar*? In no time Ritualism began to bestow her treasures around it and deck it out with sacerdotal glory. She set up a cross, an ornament that had not been seen on it in three hundred years! And as the symbol soon passes into effigy she then set up that often-abused emblem . . . the crucifix. Then followed holy gates, folding doors, mystic veils . . . to keep the laity at a distance, to shroud the altar from the vulgar gaze, to make it more awe-inspiring by its distance and obscurity. If these ornaments signify nothing, they ought not to be there . . . if something true, they *need* not be there . . . if something false, they *must* not be there! What a Babel of childish contradictions! A chancel, a "holy of holies" with a wall across it, when Christ has "broken down the middle wall of partition" . . . with gates when Christ has "opened unto us the gate of everlasting life" which no priest on earth shall shut against us . . . with a veil which they sometimes draw over its ornaments when Christ as He passed from the Cross rent the temple-veil "in twain, from the top to the bottom"!

'Ladies and gentlemen, you may now see all the Pagan rites of genuflexions, luminaries and incense reproduced in your Christian churches . . . candles lighted while the one magnificent and universal symbol of God and His Word, the light of heaven, is streaming in through the windows. You may now see congregations parading the House of the Lord like awkward squadrons of lamplighters with tapers in their hands supposed to symbolize the lamps with which the ransomed shall go forth to meet the Bridegroom. But in the name of the first Father of our Faith, away with such symbolism which stultifies the truth! For there on the black edge of the grave, where the righteous shall awake in the smile of the resurrection morning, they shall emerge from the long dormitories of the dust "with their loins girded about, and their lights burning" . . . there in the Heaven which you strive in vain to shadow out and symbolize "they need no candle, neither the light of the sun, for the Lord God giveth them light".

'Ladies and gentlemen,' shrieked Dr Bateman swaying about on the table so precariously that several of those standing around it raised hands to steady him or to protect themselves in case he fell, 'in the name of the Truth, go to the chandlers for your illumination. Ours is a brighter and a costlier candle, kindled afresh by the fiery martyr-tongue of Latimer when he said, "Be of good cheer, Master Ridley, we shall this day light a candle in England which shall never be put out!"'

With that Dr Bateman fell back swooning into the powerful arms of Bo'sun Smith, aided by Mr Lowrie and others nearby, and the meeting broke up.

McNab closed the window and went to sit down near Miriam. His face wore its habitual expression of melancholy patience.

'Well, aren't you going to tell me what you think?' asked Miriam.

McNab shook his head, however. 'In religious matters I look to you for guidance, my dear. As you know, medicine is my affair.' And that was all he had to say.

Presently Emily came in and they went down together to supper.

15

The dining room of Lowrie's Hotel was unusually busy that evening, perhaps because a number of the people who had come to hear the lecture had decided to stay and dine on the premises. But even though they were a little late in arriving the McNabs' table had been reserved for them and they did not have to wait. McNab had a brief look round, curious to see at closer range the faces of those who had been attending the lecture. But although while in the courtyard it had seemed as if every member of the audience must be recognizably stamped by some special light of vehemence or excitement, now that they were outside it, it was quite impossible to distinguish those who had been present from those who had not. McNab could only recognize one or two faces in addition to Bo'sun Smith and Dr Bateman who were dining together under the solicitous eye of Mr Lowrie.

'Isn't that young Potter?' he said, seeing another face he recognized at the far side of the room. 'And what was the other chap called?'

Emily said nothing. Her spirits had been heavy since the afternoon at Mrs Forester's: she had felt unattractive, unloved, and had suffered sharp pangs of homesickness as one tends to when things aren't going well. She had already noticed Teddy Potter and his friend Woodleigh sitting with a third officer she did not know. By now Potter had seen them and was coming over to speak to them. She felt that his eyes were on her as he approached and she lowered her own mournfully to her plate, determined to ignore him as much as she could.

Teddy Potter was brimming with cheerfulness, however. He explained that he and his companions had been passing the hotel and had noticed the great assembly of horses and *jampans* that had collected in front of it. They had therefore come in for supper, assuming that there must be a ball or some other big *tamasha* taking place, only to learn that it was all for some religious lecture. Miriam smiled at him, McNab eyed him with an air of good-humoured resignation, Emily grimaced at the salt-cellar. Potter lingered for a moment after this explanation, suddenly at a loss for a topic. Then he said suddenly: 'You see that officer sitting now with Woodleigh? You know, one of us must dine with him every evening, otherwise he would eat nothing and starve himself to death. It's a most extraordinary thing.'

The McNabs peered curiously at the officer who would starve to death without a dining-companion and even Emily could not resist glancing at him. He was a mild, bewildered-looking man in his forties wearing thick spectacles. He also had a very copious reddish moustache which puffed out from under his nostrils on each side like a fox's tail. He was gazing in mournful silence at an empty glass. While they watched, indeed, Woodleigh nudged him and nodded at the plate of soup in front of him. The officer obediently raised the spoon to his lips and took a mouthful before returning to his contemplation of the wine-glass.

'It's a rather rum business,' went on Potter, 'but it's because he's fallen in love. I'm afraid the ladies won't approve but the fact is he's gone and fallen in love with a native girl, a chambermaid in one of the other hotels. And she has with him, too. They're mad about each other and spend every minute together except when she has to work. He's wretched because he has no money which would allow her to stop being a chambermaid. What little he has he spends on buying her trinkets. It's the oddest thing!'

'He doesn't look very happy,' said Miriam, smiling. And the others smiled, too, even McNab, because there was something amusing about this officer who had fallen so deeply in love that he had to be reminded to eat by his friends though what this was exactly it was hard to say, unless it were his melancholy appearance.

'It wasn't until he fell off his horse from weakness that anyone noticed he'd stopped eating. He says he's not interested in food any more.'

On Woodleigh's direction the lovelorn officer picked up a piece of buttered chapati and began to masticate it slowly, his eyes lost in the wine-glass.

'Well, I suppose I must go and take my turn with him,' Teddy Potter said at length, and Emily again felt his eyes on her but continued to gaze absently at the other table. 'Shall we see you at Christ Church tomorrow, sir?' added Potter addressing McNab. 'We must get there early because Captain Hagan wants a pew where he can be seen by the *Lat Sahib* and the Commander-in-Chief, so Woodleigh says at any rate. Perhaps we shall all catch the General's eye and be promoted! Shall we keep you a place?'

McNab explained that he had already promised the Reverend Kingston that he would attend the morning service at Saint

Saviour's. 'Which reminds me,' he added, looking at his watch, 'that I must go and attend to my patients.'

'I thought you had only one patient,' said Miriam as Teddy Potter retired to his own table.

'I hope that is the case but I canna say it is what I expect.'

Presently the Doctor set out, accompanied by one of the hotel bearers. It was a fine night and a little warmer than it had been of late. The sun, though it had already sunk beneath Summer Hill, had left the sky stained with pink and gold in its wake and against it the hills stood out still clearly silhouetted in delicately varied shades of grey. A feeling of great peace unexpectedly settled on McNab's soul. Sounds came to him from far away on the still, clear air. Voices of young couples calling, perhaps on their way out to watch the moon rise over the outlying hills of Mashobra and Mahasu from the northern slopes of Jakko. And he thought: 'How wonderful it is to be young!' And he was quite annoyed for a moment to remember that he was old . . . on the other hand, he thought of poor Emily, the yearning, the boredom, the heartache. As he turned from the bright dusk of the Mall to plunge into the shadows of the bazaar, he said to himself: 'No, no. Things are better as they are.'

There seemed to be a light burning in one window of the church as he passed under it but looking back from a few paces further on he could no longer see it. Perhaps it had been merely a last reflected glow of the sky. A few moments later he had negotiated the narrow passage outside the priest-house and was tugging at the bell-rope. 'You may go back to the hotel,' he told the bearer. 'Here, hold up the lantern a moment.'

The bearer did so, illuminating the low door itself. The white Gothic cross which had been painted on it was now unrecognizable: the wood had been ripped and gouged by some sharp instrument.

'Sahib, many *badmash* in bazaar,' said the bearer hoping for a tip. 'I wait for Sahib.'

'Rubbish, man.' McNab gave him a few paese and turned to the door. As it opened a strangled cry came from just inside, a weird, unnatural sound. The bearer hung back in alarm, ready to bolt, and even McNab felt a sudden chill at that unearthly sound.

Then he stepped forward and with lowered head entered the
door: he had recognized the man in the shadows who had
opened it. It was the tall imbecile native who had attached
himself to the Reverend Kingston at Kalka and was evidently
still living here with him.

'What? Have they left you to look after my patient?' McNab
grumbled to himself as he groped his way towards the lighted
door down the passage. The Reverend Forsythe lay on his bed
asleep, covered by a dirty blanket. He looked very feeble and
aged in the dim light but at this hour McNab had expected to
find him in a paroxysm and he was cheered in consequence. It
appeared that the quinine was having an effect at last. McNab
lightly put a finger on Forsythe's wrist to feel his pulse but did
not wake him. As he stood looking down at the silver half-
hunter in his palm and counting he was aware of the white bird
hovering above him in the shadows 'in flying attitude'.

'Where is the Reverend Kingston?' he asked the imbecile
bearer as he prepared to leave, not expecting the man to
understand. Whether or not the man did understand he
suddenly began to groan and gibber with excitement, grimacing
at the Doctor with such distress that McNab regretted his
question immediately and wasted no time in stepping out into
the dark passage and making his way towards the bazaar. But he
heard footsteps behind him and turning saw that the imbecile
was following him. 'Go home!' he said. But the man only
gibbered and grasping his sleeve began to tug at it. 'What d'you
want?' By now they were standing only a few paces from the
church itself and presently McNab realized that the man was
trying to lead him in that direction. 'Very well,' he said and
allowed himself to be guided, marvelling that will and
intelligence, rising like bubbles, should succeed in finding their
way to the surface through such a silt of disability.

He was led to a side door to the church which stood half-
open. Here the imbecile stopped and began to writhe in a
frenzied attempt to speak.

'Yes, thank you, I understand,' McNab reassured him and
entered confident that he would find Kingston.

He found himself standing not in the church itself but in what he supposed must be the vestry. The Reverend Kingston sat at a table beneath an oil-lamp. He was wearing metal-rimmed spectacles and working with a needle and thread on a white cotton surplice which lay on the table before him. He stirred as the Doctor came in and peered to see who it was, but did not rise. He looked more hollow-cheeked than ever in the shadows cast by the lamp. 'Ah, you have found me, Doctor,' he said. 'Forgive me, I had hoped to be back at the priest-house before this. Mr Forsythe is a little better, is he not?'

'He is a little better but you are a little worse if I am not mistaken,' said McNab gently. 'In any event I have come to ascertain.'

The Doctor could not recall having been in a vestry before and looked around curiously. There was a knee-hole desk in one corner with an ink-pot and a bundle of pens: a register and a few papers lay on it. There was a pendulum clock without a glass on the wall above it showing the time to be half past nine which might well be correct, but the pendulum hung still and a spider had constructed a handsome web between the hands. There were several cupboards and shelves against the outer wall and a washbasin of the reversible sort with an earthenware pitcher standing in it; against the wall furthest from the outside door was another door, above which a notice said 'Silence': a row of pegs in pairs ran up to it from each of which hung a cassock or a surplice.

'Those are for the choir to which the Bishop has such an objection,' remarked Kingston noticing the direction of McNab's gaze. He added with a smile: 'If he objected on practical grounds I would have to agree with him. Small boys are destructive creatures and take a delight in tearing their surplices. Besides, here we have but a single vestry for the needs of priest, choir, and churchwardens.'

'Must you do that work yourself?' enquired McNab inspecting Dr Wickham Legg's 'Churchman's Oxford Calendar' with a dubious air. It had only just occurred to him that there must be a great deal of practical as well as spiritual and pastoral work to be done.

'In happier times there is a sacristan who supervises the

vestments and looks after various other matters. He is a good-tempered and devout, but unfortunately weak man, who has let himself be frightened away by the churchwardens. So for the moment I must see to everything myself.'

McNab, still on his tour of inspection, had come to a tall, narrow cupboard standing open, whose contents he found puzzling for a moment. There was a tin box labelled *Gum Olibanum* and beside it two smaller boxes, one labelled *Gum Benzoin*, the other *Cascarilla Bark*. From them came a strong, sweet smell which caused McNab to wrinkle his low-church nose uncomfortably.

'Man, you are not well enough to look after a parish by yourself,' he remarked, picking the lid off a brown earthenware jar and peering at its contents. 'That is the truth of the matter.' Unable to see what the jar contained he picked up a small pair of tongs which lay beside it, delved in the jar, captured some of the substance and held it up for inspection. He dropped it back and replaced the lid. 'Why do you need charcoal, if I may ask?'

'To burn in the censer,' replied Kingston. 'What you are looking at is the thurifer's cupboard, Doctor. That is another source of irritation to the Bishop. You will see the censer hanging beside it from a nail.'

'I fear you mean to make things difficult for yourself, Mr Kingston.'

'I've never understood why some people allow themselves to become enraged by the smell of incense when they are prepared to tolerate the most disagreeable perfumes on their wives. It is curious.'

'Mr Kingston, the Bishop asked me if I would try to persuade you to remove from your service whatever it is that is causing excitement to your parishioners. I declined. Not being a religious man myself I do not understand what is at issue. However, this business has an ugly side, has it not? Someone has taken a chisel to the cross painted on your door.'

Kingston shrugged. 'One of the saddest things in India is to see our own British troops, the representatives on this heathen continent of our Christian nation, rolling about drunk in the bazaars. They come up from the sanitarium at Subáthu at the mercy of whatever mischief occurs to them.'

'Is it not more serious, Mr Kingston? This evening there was a meeting at Lowrie's Hotel. There were signs of great indignation and vehemence. It is alarming to see people in such a state.'

Kingston got to his feet and took the surplice to hang it on one of the row of hooks. Then he returned, removing his spectacles and pinching the bridge of his nose with a weary gesture.

'It is always possible to rouse an English rabble with a cry of "No Popery". I suppose it was Dr Bateman or Smith? And Lowrie himself, perhaps? Put simply, Doctor, the difference between us is this: they would have a service based only on the preaching of the Gospel . . . I myself, however, and those clergy and laymen who believe that the true traditions of the Church of England passed down to us from the Reformation and ultimately from the Apostles themselves may not be so lightly discarded, consider the Holy Communion to be the great central act of worship, communicating to us those priceless blessings which flow from the Incarnation, Passion, Death, Resurrection and Ascension of our Blessed Lord. Do you understand?'

'Aye,' McNab nodded gloomily.

'We believe that for our worship of the Eucharist to be seemly we must obey the traditions of our Church.'

'But Lowrie and your churchwardens and parishioners consider that these traditions which include, I suppose, the burning of incense, are turning them into Roman Catholics against their will? Is that it? And where, if I may ask, does the Bishop stand?'

'That is something you must ask the Bishop. But you heard him describe some of these traditions as foolishness.' Kingston sighed and was silent for a moment. Then he said: 'He does not share the violent antipathy to them of my churchwardens. I believe he considers them trivial but a source of nuisance in his administration of the diocese. I do not mean to criticize him but it appears that he is more interested in good works than in the saving of souls which is our prime responsibility.'

Silence fell. A dog could be heard barking faintly at a distance. The oil-lamp flickered. Kingston's head had sunk to his breast, almost as if he were falling asleep. Dr McNab himself felt a great weariness invade him. He roused himself.

'Well, I came to examine you. Kindly remove your shirt.'

'I must warn you, Doctor,' said Kingston with a smile, undoing buttons at his neck, 'that I have prayed that to you, too, Our Lord may show Himself.'

'Aye,' said McNab. Opening his bag and peering into it with a grimace, he removed his stethoscope. 'I thought that you might.' He remained standing there gazing sightlessly at this instrument for a few moments longer, lost in thought. Then, approaching the clergyman, he said grimly: 'You must prepare yourself for bad news. Mr Kingston, I believe you to have phthisis though I hope I am wrong. At any rate, let us see whether you have.'

'I am in God's hands, Doctor,' replied Kingston firmly though he had grown paler.

16

At that time it was widely believed in the medical profession that certain characteristics might predispose a person to contract phthisis or pulmonary consumption, as tuberculosis used to be called. Among them there was a certain formation of the body marked by a long neck, prominent shoulders and a narrow chest. If Dr McNab had happened to hold this belief the mere sight of the Reverend Kingston's naked neck, chest and shoulders might have given him added cause to think the clergyman consumptive even before he had begun to examine him. His neck was exceedingly long, his frail shoulders stuck out awkwardly, and his chest, constricted beneath the collar-bone, seemed to splay out at the diaphragm. Moreover, there were other signs of potential vulnerability in his appearance: a thin upper lip, a fine clear skin, delicate complexion and fine dark chestnut hair (admittedly, it was claimed that black hair, dark eyes and a sallow complexion were also indications). Given that such people were predisposed and at greater risk, what were the causes which excited or generated the illness? Previous attacks of pneumonia, catarrh, asthma, scrofula, syphilis, variola, rubeola; the dust to which certain artificers were exposed, such as needle-pointers, stone-cutters, pearl-button-makers, milliners, etc; irritating fumes.

In Italy and by a few medical men in our own country, pulmonary consumption was believed to be contagious. The opinion, however, rested on very slender grounds; and the strongest argument in favour of it, namely the occasional death by consumption of a husband and wife, lost its force when it was borne in mind that in the case of a disease which destroyed so large a fraction of the adult population, such coincidences might not infrequently occur.

Dr McNab had retained an open mind on the question, though it interested him. By comparison with physicians in Europe he had seen few cases of phthisis and was therefore in a poor position to decide whether there was anything to be said for either theory. Experience had taught him however to embrace warmly only those theories of which he himself had seen clear evidence. There was one other indication where bodily appearance was concerned and, picking up Kingston's hand and studying it, turning it over and back, he saw that in this respect, too, he fitted the description: he had long slender fingers with large ends and filbert nails.

'Have any of your parents or grandparents suffered from consumption or from scrofula?'

'No, Doctor. Not that I know of,' replied the Reverend Kingston meekly. The tone of condescending authority which a few moments earlier had been used by the parson speaking to a layman (and one besieged by Doubt at that) had now passed from one man to the other, neatly reversing their roles. McNab was unaccustomed to being condescended to by clerics and, now speaking as doctor to patient, could not help savouring the change a little.

Meanwhile he had begun tapping with his fingertips the

upper part of the clergyman's chest. He expected to find, and found, a dullness on percussion over the clavicles on both sides, but more pronounced on the right side. There was a similar dullness between the scapulae. At the same time he noticed again how deeply hollowed were the supra-clavicular areas. Increasingly convinced that Kingston was consumptive he continued to explore, now using his stethoscope, the clergyman's bony pink and white chest on which only the faintest shadow of fine hair was to be seen; he asked him to take a deep breath. The act of doing so excited Kingston's cough and he became convulsed. McNab withdrew a little, his face expressionless. He had heard an ominous click and bubbling sound which suggested that the illness was already well advanced.

'Here, spit in the basin, please, so that I may examine the sputa.'

Although by now convinced of the parson's condition McNab continued for a little while to use his stethoscope, partly to allow Kingston to settle after his fit of coughing but principally out of scientific curiosity. The diagnosis of phthisis in its early stages was difficult because so easily confused with other less serious ailments. Attempts had been made to classify the variety of morbid sounds that one might hear while listening to the chest of a consumptive: the incipient disease might be heralded by slight clicks, by mucous, sub-mucous, and sibilant rhonchus, slight, crepitant rhonchus (that's to say, a rattle or *râle*), or even by increased resonance of the voice (indeed, this had been in McNab's mind when he had asked Kingston about the resonance of his voice, on the occasion of their first meeting in the train). But such sounds might well be produced merely by minor bronchial conditions. As the disease progressed, however, the sounds became more distinctive though no less varied and might include cavernous respiration, cavernous rhonchus, amphoric resonance, metallic tinkling, that ominous clicking and bubbling which McNab had just heard, pectori-loquy (the sound of the patient's voice heard through the stethoscope) and, though rarely, the distinct sound of fluid in motion on succussion (the shaking of the patient's thorax). It was also common in phthisis to hear the heart's beat with peculiar distinctness over the entire chest. Naturally, certain of these sounds were inclined to shade into each other and their classification might be uncertain, but what they amounted to, severally or together, was a sound which to the physician's experienced ear betrayed the disease.

'Thank you. You may put on your shirt.'

What McNab found most perplexing was that Kingston, though the illness appeared to be well established, should have retained sufficient energy to continue his ministry.

'Have you found yourself short of breath, Mr Kingston?'

'Yes.'

'Shooting pains in the chest?'

'Yes.' Now that his air of authority had deserted him he looked so vulnerable that McNab felt sorry for him suddenly, though he had not expected to, and thought with disgust: 'It must be a harsh God who would leave His minister to learn his fate in such a way . . . alone with his shoddy ecclesiastical paraphernalia in this wretched place and with his parishioners baying for his blood. But doubtless they have some explanation for it.'

Kingston added: 'You asked me in the train whether I had had headaches and I said, "No". I'm afraid that was not the truth.'

McNab nodded; he was quite accustomed to not being answered truthfully when he asked about symptoms.

'Have you noticed unusual feelings of coldness or that you perspire more easily?'

'Perspiration, yes. I have also suffered from diarrhoea but perhaps that is not connected, it is so common in India.'

'May I see your tongue, please?'

Kingston stuck out his tongue which was white.

'Have you always been so thin, Mr Kingston, or have you lost weight?'

'I've lost a little weight. With these parish difficulties I find it hard to eat.'

'Quite so,' agreed McNab, getting up to inspect the sputa in the basin. 'Will you be so kind as to reserve a little urine so that I may see it tomorrow when I come to visit Mr Forsythe?'

'I should be grateful, Doctor, if you would keep this illness from the Bishop for the time being.'

'Certainly,' nodded McNab, looking at the sputa which were opaque and muco-purulent: there was no sign of blood or tissue and they could have resulted merely from bronchitis.

'Have you spat blood?'

'Not recently, Doctor . . . but yes, some days ago. But a very little, hardly to be noticed.'

Kingston had resumed his seat. He shook his head, exhausted and bewildered, perhaps on the verge of breaking down. His illness was a secret he had had to carry alone for too long. McNab had seen this many times: the very bravery and self-control which a man or woman displayed when obliged to face the fear of suffering and death by themselves made the release of feeling all the more overwhelming once there was someone to confide in. Kingston's chin had sunk to his chest bringing his chestnut curls closer to the lamp. McNab noticed how dusty they were: most likely the clergyman had little time or energy to spare for washing his hair.

'It is certain, then?' Though the tone was weary his voice was quite strong. 'I know you will not attempt to hide the truth from me, Doctor. It is what I prefer.'

'I'm afraid it is . . . nearly certain,' replied McNab. He added: 'Although the illness is most serious, fatal consequences are not inevitable in every case. In your own case where there is no apparent hereditary predisposition, little sign of hectic fever or increased debility and emaciation, one might be very cautiously optimistic.'

'God has sent this to me as a trial!' cried Kingston suddenly in a muffled tone as if he had not heard McNab's attempt to reassure him.

'There is a little hope, Mr Kingston, only if you pay the greatest attention to your general health and diet. Warm clothing. Avoid exposure to wet and cold. A diet chiefly or entirely of vegetable food and without any stimulants. Above all, I should say it is of the greatest importance that you resign your living which makes quite unreasonable demands on your strength. In any case I should recommend you not to remain in Simla for the rainy, misty weather which will shortly begin. A sea voyage or the seaside would be best.'

'It is impossible . . .' Kingston was interrupted by a long stifling fit of coughing and rose to spit in the basin once more. In the few days since McNab had first seen him he had passed from a dry cough to one with abundant sputa. McNab, therefore, now seated at the table, was writing a prescription for tartar-emetic to be taken every morning in half-grain doses followed by warm camomile tea, the purpose being to assist the coughing up of mucus and, it might be, the detaching of tuberculous matter from the walls of the suppurating cavity. And yet even as he wrote he knew that it was quite useless, that any beneficial effects would be trivial. And he felt again that dull affliction, somewhere between anger and resignation, which he had experienced throughout his life in medicine when faced with an illness over which his knowledge and experience held no sway.

'It is impossible,' repeated Kingston who had at last regained his breath, 'that I should either resign my living or leave my parish. D'you not see what has happened?' he went on with sudden intensity, his eyes glinting in the lamplight. 'God has been pleased to send me this illness to test my resolution at the most critical moment of my life. Why else would it have come at the very moment when I am fighting to restore to our Church those traditions of which three centuries of laxity and ignorance have robbed it . . . at *the very moment?*'

'Rubbish, man,' said McNab tersely.

'It is a test of faith!' cried Kingston. 'You do not understand such things, it is in such a way that the Almighty works. It is only through such an ordeal that a man may prove himself.'

'Nonsense! It is a coincidence, merely. Or more likely you have worn yourself out and damaged your constitution in quarrelling with your parishioners and have fallen ill as a result. And now you will make yourself worse.'

But Kingston was not even listening. He had begun to walk about the vestry in an agitated way, breathing noisily and with difficulty. On the inside wall which the vestry shared with the church itself there hung a small crucifix, perhaps of ivory or of a light-coloured wood, it was impossible to say in the dim light. Kingston sank to his knees in front of this crucifix and murmured: 'I have been weak..I have prayed that this burden might be taken from me. Let me accept, Lord, without wavering whatever suffering You in Your infinite wisdom have seen fit to bestow on me!' He stumbled to his feet again and continued pacing agitatedly this way and that. McNab replaced his stethoscope and closed his bag with a snap.

'Have you any money, Mr Kingston, if I may ask?'

The clergyman stopped in his tracks and was silent for a moment. 'Of course, forgive me, you require payment for your services.' He scratched his head.

'By no means. But it is likely that in due course you will need to be cared for in hospital.'

McNab, who had earlier made enquiries on behalf of the Reverend Forsythe, had discovered that there was only the Simla Dispensary to supply the medical needs of the sick poor: this was an old tumbledown building with beds for some thirty native inpatients. The poor European who could not afford the expense of being cared for privately must make the best of a bed in the native ward. McNab now suddenly remembered that a reference had been made by Bo'sun Smith to the five hundred rupees a month that the clergyman was paid. Or was that merely the Army chaplain? There was little evidence of five hundred rupees about the Reverend Kingston.

'I have a little saved,' the clergyman said. 'I am not sure that it would be enough.' After a moment he added with a bleak smile: 'Perhaps I would not need very much.'

'Well, we needna worry for the present,' said McNab and, with a final admonition to Kingston that he should do everything to rest and conserve his strength, he took his leave feeling more than ever doubtful that there was anything he could do for his patient.

17

Mrs Forester's little dog, Garibaldi, was these days wearing a muzzle: something that was inclined to shorten his temper, already short by nature. But with a muzzle it is impossible to bite people who do not treat you correctly so he was obliged to put up with this humiliation without even such a modest satisfaction. McNab had first noticed that Garibaldi was wearing a muzzle when he happened to see Mrs Forester emerging from Phelps's dress-shop carrying that small but important animal in her arms while an assistant followed with her parcel. He had thought no more about it until presently he noticed another muzzled dog. And soon he saw another, and another. Could this be some absurd new fashion? he wondered, or was there a more serious reason for it? Noticing that the shopkeeper from whom he bought his tobacco also sold a variety of leather goods such as wallets and pouches and hip-flask holders and that this enterprising man now had dog muzzles on display in addition, he asked the reason.

'Have you not heard, sir, that there is rabies in the station?' exclaimed the shopkeeper in surprise. 'They don't seem able to get to the bottom of it and so people take what precautions they can.'

'You mean there has been an actual case of rabies here?' enquired McNab dubiously. 'I've heard nothing of it.'

'It appears that three or four poor folk have been bitten and now must wait, expecting the worst, to see whether they carry the poison inside them,' said the shopkeeper, adding: 'Perhaps you have a dog yourself, sir, and would like to inspect our range ... All most solidly stitched, sir, as you can see, and designed to afford the least discomfort to "a dear friend", if I may put it so, sir.'

McNab declined the muzzle on the grounds that he had no dog.

'Perhaps, sir, I could interest you then in a pair of ankle-protectors of our own design and guaranteed proof against even the most savage bite. We have sold many of them, sir, they are most popular. The ankle is the part of the body most at risk, sir, as I'm sure you know. Gentlemen may wear them beneath the trouser-leg quite hidden from view.'

'No thank you. I shall risk it for the present.'

'As you please, sir, though I gather the death from rabies is a most unpleasant one. As you see, I wear protectors myself and would not be without them.' The shopkeeper lifted a trouser-leg a few inches to reveal a protected ankle. He added in a confidential tone: 'I believe it is no betrayal of confidences to say that more than one pair has been delivered to Prospect Hill, I'll say no more.' And with solemn dignity he winked at McNab. 'The *Lat Sahib*, sir, and his ADCs are no more immune to a sudden bite than other men, I'll say no more.'

'Have they not killed the rabid animal?'

'In one or two cases, yes, I believe they have, sir, but it appears that it is always too late . . . there is already another animal infected and on the prowl. It is sad indeed for the station. If this goes on Mussoorie and Nainital will soon have all our business. Darjeeling is already attempting to divert our visitors from Calcutta and Bengal, so it is said.' The shopkeeper had been rummaging deftly in a box on the counter and now raised both hands in surprise and dismay. 'It appears there is only one remaining pair in your size, sir, and it will undoubtedly take several days before new orders can be filled. They go so fast! Would it not be wise, sir, to seize this rare opportunity rather than . . .? Well, just as you please, sir.'

Later, McNab mentioned this supposed outbreak of rabies to Miriam and asked whether she had heard anything of it. She had heard it discussed, certainly, she replied. It was on everybody's lips. But none of her acquaintances, who were few, in any case, had first-hand knowledge of someone who had been bitten. It was said that some of the more timorous ladies in the station would no longer take a step outside on their own two legs but insisted on being carried everywhere by *jampanis*.

'Such was the case already,' said McNab dryly, 'they have simply found another reason for it.'

The following day was Sunday. McNab was escorting Miriam and Emily along the Mall on the first part of their journey to morning service at Saint Saviour's when they were overtaken by the Viceregal couple being driven to Christ Church in an open landau with a half a dozen ADCs, all wearing dark frock-coats, cantering behind them. McNab could not help noticing the interest and longing with which Emily watched the Viceregal party go by and, as they themselves turned off the Mall and down into the narrow, stifling alleys of the bazaar, he regretted not having made arrangements for the ladies to go to Christ Church with the young officers. By this time their trunks had successfully completed the perilous journey up from the plains and Emily had gone to some pains to look her best. A few pins had been required at the last moment for unaccountably her clothes seemed to have shrunk a little in transit. McNab was afraid that these efforts would be wasted on the Reverend Kingston's congregation of private soldiers and native Christians from the bazaar.

But as they emerged into the open space in front of the church they saw a *jampan* arriving and Emily exclaimed: 'Is that not Mrs Forester?' She had recognized the chocolate livery and primrose cummerbunds of her *jampanis*. And a moment later she picked out Captain Hagan trotting behind the *jampan* on horseback holding a frightened-looking little Jack on the saddle-mount in front of him while the boy's bearer scampered behind as best he could. The McNabs approached to greet them and Mrs Forester gave Emily a kiss, taking care not to disarrange her own *toilette*, whispering: 'Emily dear, I was so afraid you were upset with me.' Mrs Forester had chosen to worship at Saint Saviour's rather than to risk another painful snub from Mrs Claworth and her like. Captain Hagan had evidently abandoned his hopes of catching the eye of the Commander-in-Chief at Christ Church in favour of accompanying her. Having dismounted and without a backward look left his *sais* to deal with the horse, he bowed in his usual cold manner to the McNabs and stifled a yawn.

As they made to enter the church itself McNab noticed that a large crowd of men had assembled around the main door of the church which stood open. These men were Europeans and dressed some in private's uniform, some in civilian clothes, some in a mixture of both. One or two carried their arms in slings, others grasped crutches or walking-sticks. But what was most curious was that they stood there in complete silence, immobile, their faces expressionless. There was something about those ranks of closed faces that conveyed a strong air of hostility.

'There's something amiss here, I'm afraid,' said McNab to Miriam as they passed through these silent ranks and entered the church which, despite the crowd outside, proved to be almost empty except for a handful of natives dressed in European clothes and one or two isolated white faces. 'Ah, here comes Lowrie,' he added as the hotelier who had been on his knees but watchful in a pew nearby hurried forward to greet them, tapping his brow with two fingers as he came. 'I had hoped that you might reconsider, sir,' he said to McNab in a reverend whisper. 'That is to say . . . Christ Church might have been more suitable for the ladies. *Here* we cannot say *what* will happen . . . I've tried to reason with him but, no! He turns a deaf ear. He's there now in the vestry saying something in Latin, if you please, and decking himself out in a chasuble gorgeous enough for the Pope himself. But they won't stand for it, Doctor, you've seen 'em, the way they look. They want their pure service back, that's what they want, not this Romish play-acting . . . They'll tear him limb from limb, sir. There'll be an explosion, Doctor, when they see the singing-boys in skirts he has lined up there.' Mr Lowrie gestured contemptuously towards the choir-stalls where a dozen choir-boys of varying ages but all of them native were watching him apprehensively. 'Mind you, he must pay 'em out of his own pocket because the churchwardens won't stand for it . . .'

'Would you be so kind as to show us to a pew, Mr Lowrie?' interrupted McNab, afraid that Lowrie's reverend whisper might continue for some time. At the same time there was something disturbing about those men outside: what was their purpose in standing there?

Bowing, Mr Lowrie conducted them to the pew directly in

front of his own. 'Ah,' he muttered, reaching over to the
Doctor's ear, 'I expect she has come here thinking that she will
get herself *confessed*. That'll be the next thing, I shouldn't be
surprised!' With that, he went to conduct Mrs Forester and
Captain Hagan to a nearby pew. McNab sank to his knees if not
to pray, at least to consider the possibility of prayer. But though
he could no longer see them he could still feel the hostile
pressure of those silent men outside. A barefoot native boy in a
dhoti climbed nimbly to the organ loft at the end of the chancel
and began to pump a bellows for a white-haired bespectacled
native who sat at a harmonium. He twisted around on his stool
for a moment and then the first wheezing strains began to issue
from the instrument. The crowd outside showed no sign of
wanting to enter for the service but there were a few late-
comers, one or two of whom bowed to the altar as they crossed
the main aisle. There was a clatter of boots: a large man and a
small man entered together. McNab recognized Bo'sun Smith
and Dr Bateman, the latter neat and gleaming as ever. They went
to sit alone in separate pews at some distance from each other.
Dr Bateman knelt to pray. Having done so he stood up suddenly
and in a loud voice he addressed Mr Lowrie across the aisle.
'Churchwarden, I call upon you to take note of any irregularities!' This was so unexpected that even the organ music
faltered and there was a moment of shocked silence before it
took up again.

The main doors had been closed – the bell was still ringing –
but now they suddenly burst open. McNab looked up, afraid
that the crowd outside might have decided to enter at last, but it
was Potter, Woodleigh and Arkwright, accompanied by the
bewildered-looking officer who was too much in love to eat.
The healthy, good-humoured faces of these young men seemed
to cause a sudden breeze of fresh air to blow through the church.
Potter smiled and waved at the McNabs and Emily as they
crossed the aisle and, without waiting for Mr Lowrie to conduct
them, installed themselves in the pew just in front of Hagan and
Mrs Forester.

The wheezing, aimless chords which the harmonium had
been playing at last became more purposeful and the

congregation stood and began to sing or murmur a psalm. Turning, McNab saw the verger, an elderly Indian with drooping white moustaches, pacing up the chancel from the west. He was followed by an even older Indian with a bald freckled scalp dressed in cassock and surplice: this man, although he was bent crooked with age and appeared to McNab's experienced eye to be suffering from arthritis of the hip, was nevertheless carrying a large brass cross somewhat tarnished, mounted on yellowed ivory. He in turn was followed by two native youths each carrying a candle. The thurifer with the censer followed, accompanied by the boat-bearer, both very dark-skinned Dravidians. Then at last came Kingston, his pallor quite shocking by comparison. His hands, almost hidden by their ample sleeves, were joined in front of him, his eyes were on the ground, his lips moved silently. Seeing him now in church for the first time McNab was surprised that the somewhat clumsy, poorly co-ordinated, physically weak Kingston should manage to radiate such a strong sense of authority and presence and wondered whether it was the man himself or whether, wearing the magnificently embroidered green silk chasuble which Kingston wore, any man would have appeared as impressive. Kingston's fleshless face and red-rimmed eyelids, the green tinge that his white skin had taken from the chasuble, made him look like a saint or martyr by El Greco. All this time a single bell continued to toll. The little procession approached the altar. Dr Bateman, standing in the front row, removed his spectacles and polished them with intensity: his myopic eyes, blinking helplessly, appeared very naked until he had replaced his spectacles which he did just in time to see Kingston arrive at the foot of the altar and make a quick genuflexion, bowing his head at the same time. The torchbearers set down the candles on each side of the altar. The verger broke off from the group and padded away wearily down a side aisle coughing noisily. The elderly Indian set down the cross with trembling hands and propped it against the north wall . . . he, too, appeared spent from his efforts. The thurifer and boat-bearer remained behind Kingston who, going up to the altar with hands joined in silent prayer, bent forward and kissed it reverendly.

Bateman turned and nodded significantly across the aisle at Bo'sun Smith as if to say: 'Note that! Altar-kissing!'

The thurifer and boat-bearer followed and stood behind Kingston while he prayed. Now the elderly bald Indian taking a deep breath, started forward again, leaving the brass cross where it was propped against the wall. He shuffled up to the thurifer and taking the spoon from the boat-bearer, opened the lid of the incense boat, and spooned some incense into the censer, not without the difficulty caused by a shaking hand. Kingston, having turned to the right, blessed the incense and then took the censer from the thurifer, holding it up by the ring in his left hand and gripping it by the chains near the lid with his right. He then censed the altar in the middle so that an aromatic blue cloud hung in the still air; next he turned to the south end of the altar and swung the censer again. Here he had to pause, convulsed by a silent fit of coughing.

'Romish mummery!' declared Dr Bateman in a distinct and audible tone.

'See, it is choking him!' came Mr Lowrie's voice in a penetrating whisper from behind McNab's back. Kingston had recovered, however, and swung the censer at the north end of the altar, before returning to the south end where the elderly Indian stood waiting to take the censer from him; he took it and censed Kingston, who again became convulsed. All this time the single bell continued to toll above.

There was a pause while Kingston fought for breath. Teddy Potter turned round with a friendly half-smile for the McNabs, his eyes resting a little longer on Emily. Then he turned to face the altar again. Emily had dropped her eyes mournfully to the prayer book in her gloved hand.

Kingston, standing alone at the altar with his back to the congregation, began to recite the Lord's Prayer in an audible tone and as he did so the bell above at last fell silent. 'Amen,' said the congregation when he had finished. Kingston said the Collect for Purity.

'Cock-a-doodle-doo!' called a voice outside the building, followed by laughter and shouts of 'Down with Puseyites!' 'Down with Popery!'

Kingston, very pale, appeared oblivious to the noise from outside. Remaining at the altar but turning towards the congregation he began to recite on a note the Ten Commandments. After each Commandment the choir sang the Kyrie. This was evidently what the crowd outside had been listening and waiting for. As the singing began a great din of caterwauling broke out, shouting and screaming, grunting and coughing. The choirboys faltered, looking apprehensive, but Kingston continued to intone the Commandments.

'This is a Roman travesty!' declared Dr Bateman in a high voice.

'Be quiet or I'll throw you out!' shouted Captain Hagan suddenly, glaring across the aisle at Dr Bateman. Dr Bateman appeared taken aback for a moment, peering resentfully at Hagan whom he had not noticed until this moment. To add to the confusion, whenever the choir attempted to sing the Kyrie, Bo'sun Smith and Dr Bateman, aided by Mr Lowrie and his wife, boomed in a speaking tone 'Lord, have mercy upon us, and incline our hearts to keep this law,' attempting to erase the impression of a sung note by the choir. As for the congregation, some sang, some spoke, but most merely moved their lips, bewildered.

'This is disgraceful,' whispered Mr Lowrie with a suppressed chortle of excitement. Meanwhile there was more activity around the altar for the two native boys who were acting as torch-bearers had taken up their candles and advanced to the chancel steps where they stood facing each other. The elderly Indian doddered up the aisle with a veil on his shoulders, his left hand holding the stem of the chalice wrapped in one end of the veil to his chin, his right hand holding the other end over the burse. The two torch-bearers met him when he reached the chancel gates and moved ahead of him to the sanctuary step, where they stood, holding up their candles for the old man to pass between them and set the sacred vessels on a table to the right, covering them with the veil. 'Friends, this is an opera!' boomed Bo'sun Smith instead of his 'Lord, have mercy . . .' The old man had to pause then for a few moments, panting, before taking up the burse and setting it on the altar. All this time

Kingston and the choir had been struggling to make themselves heard against the monotone from Bo'sun Smith and Dr Bateman and the catcalls, whistles and farmyard noises from outside the church. When the choir, manifestly demoralized by the noise from outside, had sung the last Kyrie, Kingston turned back to the altar and began the Collect for the Queen. 'Almighty and everlasting God, we are taught by the holy Word, that the hearts of Kings are in thy rule and governance, and that thou dost dispose and turn them as it seemeth best to thy godly wisdom: We humbly beseech thee so to dispose and govern the heart of Victoria thy Servant, our Queen and Governor, that, in all her thoughts, words and works, she may ever seek thy honour and glory, and study to preserve thy people committed to her charge, in wealth, peace, and godliness: Grant this, O merciful Father, for thy dear Son's sake, Jesus Christ our Lord. Amen.'

This Collect had a sobering effect, not only on the restive members of the congregation but on the noisy mob outside who appeared to have some means of following the progress of the service within. They remained quiet, too, during the Epistle and the Gospel both of which Kingston read in a normal speaking tone. McNab dared to hope that the interruptions were now over.

18

Dr McNab's hope that the service would continue without further interruption seemed as if it might well be realized. There were a few shouts of 'No Popery!' from outside, however, as Kingston began to sing the Creed; Bo'sun Smith and Dr Bateman ostentatiously declined to follow the example of the choir in turning east and repeated the words as loudly as they could in speaking tone. When the Creed was finished Kingston crumpled to his knees at the altar with his head in his hands. McNab watched him with concern, uncertain from the clergyman's attitude whether it was one of devotion or collapse. But presently Kingston struggled to his feet again.

There was a pause in the proceedings. Even the hecklers outside had fallen silent for the moment. Kingston was whispering some instruction to one of the native boys in the choir; the boy in question was looking uncertainly at the congregation. Kingston, too, studied the congregation and particularly that part of it on the left-hand side of the aisle; he whispered some more instructions and the boy nodded doubtfully; slipping from his place in the choir-stalls he made his way down the side aisle to where Hagan and Mrs Forester were sitting. He leaned over and whispered something to them: they looked at each other, perplexed. Hagan frowned with anger, Mrs Forester blushed furiously and dropped her head into her exquisitely gloved hand.

In the meantime Kingston had climbed the steps to the pulpit and was surveying his sparse, partly hostile congregation with a remote, almost indifferent air. He was shaken by a long fit of coughing and averted his face to spit copiously into a handkerchief. There was silence again while he recovered his breath. Then he began to preach on the nature of the ministry, taking at his text Galatians vi, verse 14: 'But God forbid that I should glory, save in the cross of our Lord Jesus Christ by whom the world is crucified unto me, and I unto the world.' There were, he said, many different conceptions of the ministry. Not all the members of his parish shared his own conception of it, they had made that all too clear. There were arguments about what a minister should or should not do. No doubt many of these convictions were strongly and sincerely held. But a great evil might be bred out of these festering arguments and like a contagious disease over which we have no control spread rapidly throughout the parish and the Church itself. 'This very morning,' exclaimed Kingston, his voice suddenly increasing in resonance and power so that it rang about the walls of the empty building, 'we have heard blasphemy and abuse shouted within the walls of this, God's house, as if it were a drinking-shop in the bazaar. We have heard a most scandalous outcry against the solemn and traditional forms of worship of our Church.

Brethren . . .' Kingston paused for a few moments to suck in air
. . . 'there is another text, from the same chapter in Galatians,
with which I know you are familiar: "Be not deceived, God is
not mocked: for whatsoever a man soweth that shall he reap."'
Kingston paused for a moment with his eyes closed and then
repeated very quietly, so quietly that one had to strain one's ears
to catch his words: '"Be not deceived, God is not mocked."'

Despite himself McNab found that he was captivated by what
he knew to be a trick of oratory. That Kingston should display a
gift as a speaker was unexpected; that he should use it with such
power in his present circumstances was altogether remarkable,
at least to McNab who had listened to his lungs. A moment later
and the voice was ringing out again, strong and vibrant,
demanding to be listened to . . . as the Church is, so must her
ministers be . . . what they will wear, what they will do, a custom
here, a tradition there, discarding this or that because it does not
agree with their opinions . . . No! Her ministers may *not* pick and
choose without thereby diminishing the Church, nor may *any*
member of the Church, for the Church has come down to us in
an unbroken line of succession from the Apostles, bringing with
it its sacred traditions, its most holy rites.

'Why do you come to church?' thundered Kingston in a voice
that rattled the window-panes and caused even Dr Bateman to
assume a cowed air. 'You do not come here in order that your
minister should support your faith with rational arguments or
moving oratory, you come here in order to receive *Grace!* It is by
participating in holy mysteries and sacraments of the Church
that you fulfil your duties as a Christian and receive the precious
gift of Grace in return, not by argument or clever reasoning, not
by some form of service which through laxity, ignorance or
caprice has lost many of those traditions enjoined upon us by the
rubrics of the Prayer Book at the time of the Reformation, no,
brethren, not even by good works among the people, by caring
for the poor, the sick and the helpless, however worthy such
actions may be in themselves. No, there is only one way to
salvation. Let those who are willing to risk everlasting
damnation choose some other! Let them . . . if they will . . . by
blasphemy and abuse and mockery attempt to come between

God Almighty and those who attempt faithfully to worship Him. I tell you . . .' Kingston's voice again rose until it rang and echoed under the roof timbers . . . 'I tell you, "Be not deceived: God is not mocked: for whatsoever a man soweth that shall he reap!"' He turned to the east, muttered, 'In the name of God the Father, God the Son, God the . . .' and groped his way coughing, quivering, half-strangled by his prodigious effort, down the pulpit steps.

'Ha!' ejaculated Dr Bateman, his spectacles glinting oddly. He looked around self-consciously.

Kingston, having steadied himself at the foot of the pulpit steps and patted his brow with a handkerchief he had extracted with difficulty from within his vestments, now made his way to stand at the middle of the altar. He took a deep breath and on a note said: 'Whatsoever ye would that men should do unto you, even so do unto them; for this is the Law and the Prophets.' While he was doing so there were renewed shouts of 'Down with the Puseyites!' from outside, accompanied by hooting and cackling.

A long hymn began: it was evidently one which both Miriam and Emily recognized for they sang with a will. McNab gazed sightlessly at the page of his hymn book, his lips moving imperceptibly while his mind wandered to other matters. He was no longer afraid now that there would be a serious disturbance at the church. He was roused from his reverie by a discreet throat-clearing: it was Mr Lowrie carrying an embroidered green bag for the collection. McNab passed it along to the ladies who had prepared themselves for this contingency while he searched his own pockets for a coin. Mr Lowrie proceeded with dignity and importance to the next pew.

The elderly Indian who had been taking a breather in the choir-stalls now shuffled out to the chancel gates with a large wooden plate held in his quivering hands, waiting there for Mr Lowrie to complete the collection and have a few whispered words with Dr Bateman. When Mr Lowrie had placed the bag on his plate, the Indian took the alms to the altar and handed them to Kingston who raised them reverently, and set them down on the altar. Next the clerk took the chalice and the paten and handed them to Kingston who placed them on the altar, raised them slightly before arranging the paten in front of the chalice. Meanwhile the thurifer had reappeared with the censer.

The hymn had come to an end by now and the harmonium had fallen silent. The shouting had also died down. Had the crowd perhaps dispersed? McNab was wondering. He was answered by a renewed burst of cheering and hilarity at something that had happened outside. There was clapping, a gruff bawling of men's voices, more shouts of 'No Popery!'

Kingston had taken the censer and was censing the oblations. He first made three signs of the Cross with the censer over them, then swung the censer round them three times and gave another swing on each side of them. 'Can incense really be necessary for a man's salvation?' mused McNab, thinking of the sermon.

The elderly Indian clerk had once more approached Kingston at the south side of the altar. They bowed to each other. He took the censer and censed Kingston, who was once again convulsed. He sank to his knees, heaving.

'Disgraceful,' said Dr Bateman.

'See, it sticks in his papish lungs!' whispered Mr Lowrie gleefully to his wife. McNab, too, clicked his tongue but on medical grounds, thinking: 'He'll finish himself off in no time like this.' The thurifer had taken the censer and was swinging it over the choir, first on one side then on the other, so that a blue haze hung in the chancel and over the altar.

The shouting, cheering and bawling outside grew to a crescendo. Hagan and Teddy Potter exchanged a word, their faces serious, perhaps wondering whether to expect a rough-house. Suddenly the door opened with a bang. A gale of laughter and shouting blew into the church accompanied by a terrified squealing. The door slammed shut again almost immediately, diminishing the noise from outside. But the high-pitched squealing continued. It came now from one side, now from another. The congregation strained to see what it was. Kingston had left the altar at the commotion and started towards the chancel gates. As he did so a small pink pig, squealing with panic, sped up the chancel steps, past him, veered in front of the altar and darted under the feet of the choir who uttered cries of alarm. An older boy with a dark down of moustache on his upper lip dived for the pig to try and catch it as it shot from the other end of the choir-stalls but the pig was too quick and a moment later it was galloping down the centre aisle in search of a way to escape, shrilling as it went. The congregation watched it go, shocked into immobility. Again the door opened and this time a man was shoved inside amid laughter and a cry of 'Go and catch it!' The door clattered shut. It was Kingston's imbecile bearer; he was twisting his neck and looking horribly agitated. He started after the pig with his clumsy, unco-ordinated movements. At this moment the pig, swerving to elude the clutches of Woodleigh and Arkwright who had at last left their pew in pursuit, collided heavily with a table bearing hymn books, upsetting it. The pig disappeared under an avalanche of books. The bearer, blundering into the overturned table, lost his uncertain footing and fell into the pile of books, rapping his head with a terrible thud against a pew door. He lay still where he had fallen.

Kingston was leaning drunkenly against the pulpit steps, his face grey. 'God is not mocked,' he said in a whisper. The service was abandoned.

19

The officers were considered, particularly by Emily, to have emerged very well from this disgraceful affair at Saint Saviour's. Even Captain Hagan, about whom Emily knew nothing except that he was inclined to be moody and quarrelsome and always striking attitudes, displayed an unexpected gift of firmness in the crisis. Why, even the officer who was so much in love he could not remember to eat mastered himself sufficiently to forget his emotional preoccupations and assist in leading clergy, choir, and faithful to safety while Captain Hagan gave a tongue-lashing to the mob assembled outside, calling them a disgrace to the Indian Army. The mob listened to him in sullen silence . . . they had been looking forward to pelting and heckling a Romanizing minister and his singing-boys, some of them had even brought rotten eggs for the purpose (it's unsettling to have a potent missile in the palm of your hand and to find yourself suddenly deprived of a target), and were not prepared to be met by an angry and contemptuous officer who might, for all they knew, have some means of identifying them individually and, who could say? perhaps even of having their sick-certificates revoked. The crowd was not entirely composed of soldiers, however, and there were still a few cries of 'No Popery!' and 'Down with the Puseyites' from amongst the private citizens of the Parish who had assembled to protest against the ritualistic leanings of their incumbent. But now their cries sounded lame and achieved no answering echo. The wind goes out of a crowd as it does out of a sail, and then it hangs as limp as any piece of canvas. The crowd began to disperse except for the diehards and as for them, not even the Archangel Gabriel could have persuaded them to move along until they had hissed and booed their hatred. The mob felt somewhat cheated, they felt that one day they would have their revenge, but in the meantime they had caused a Romish service to be abandoned and that was not half bad.

Yes, it was lucky, when you came to think about it, that the officers had changed their minds about going to Christ Church to catch the eyes of the Viceroy and Commander-in-Chief. It meant that Potter and Arkwright could stand guard over the ladies and see they came to no harm while Dr McNab attended to the Reverend Kingston's half-witted bearer who lay senseless on the hymn books where he had been smitten. He revived presently and seemed none the worse once his scattered brains had been assembled with the help of a cold sponge and a whiff of sal volatile. Dr McNab was more concerned for Kingston himself who for a long time sat on the chancel steps and seemed too spent to move. 'You must lie down for the rest of the day,' he told him, resolving at the same time to ask Miriam later whether there might be room in the bungalow to accommodate the clergyman for a few days. Kingston shook his head but otherwise made no reply. After a while he returned to the altar to bring the discontinued service to as seemly a conclusion as he might.

For Emily, at least, this lamentable affair had one good result: she found herself for a few moments alone with Teddy Potter while the McNabs were occupied elsewhere and Arkwright wandered away to immerse himself in a prayer book with exaggerated interest.

'I think you are displeased with me, Miss Anderson, and yet I don't know why.' Teddy's tone was respectful and even contrite, though he professed not to know why contrition should be expected of him. And why should it, indeed? His only sin was that he had lingered chatting with other young women, unaware that Emily's imagination, galloping on as usual far ahead of the reality, had snatched him up on to her saddle and made off with him, hoofbeats drumming, as a prize of her very own. He could hardly be blamed for not behaving towards the new proprietor of his heart in a way that acknowledged the change of ownership when he had still to learn of it. Still, the mere thought of those simpering, wedding-ringed wife-children caused Emily's brow to darken again and for a moment it seemed that she might be just as cold to Teddy as she had been before.

'I've no reason to be displeased with you, Lieutenant Potter. Why should I have?' she said in a neutral, or even encouraging tone. 'It seemed to me that you were not friendly towards me at Mrs Forester's but preferred the company of those young married ladies. And they are all remarkably pretty, I must admit, and might turn any young man's head.'

'But, Miss Anderson . . .'

Emily held up her hand to interrupt him. 'I've decided that you may call me Emily after all,' she said magnanimously. 'Proceed.'

'Emily, it certainly never entered my head . . . I mean, the last thing I would have wanted was to seem unfriendly to you. It never occurred to me that you might think that . . . Gracious!' And Teddy mimed the mopping of his brow and put on a specially penitent air. He was good at mime and seeing him suddenly transformed from a young officer full of bounce to a poor hang-dog bank-clerk sort of fellow seemed very droll to Emily. She had to raise her gloved hand to conceal a chuckle which would have been far from suitable, given that they were standing in church. Over Teddy's shoulder Emily caught Arkwright's eye for a second. He had a disgusted look. He dropped his gaze hurriedly to the open book in front of him but Emily had seen his expression and wondered whether it was because he disapproved of their lovemaking.

'But you do find them rather pretty, you must admit,' said Emily, looking around to see where Mrs Forester was and at the same time recalling that before the sudden irruption of the pig a choirboy had been sent with a message to her and Captain Hagan.

Teddy had been in the middle of protesting in his most droll and extravagant manner that far from finding the wife-children pretty it seemed to him that the delightful pink pig which had just brought the service to such an unfortunate close was in many respects to be preferred for its grace and charm of manner and even for its conversation, and that in any case, no other young lady could possibly hold a candle to a certain Miss Anderson of his acquaintance, the very sight of whom made him want to kneel in veneration . . . Here, in the middle of the aisle where they were standing, Teddy started to kneel in front of her.

'Teddy! Stop it! People will see you,' whispered Emily in alarm, at the same time trying to conceal her giggles. She had to grasp his arm to prevent him sinking to the tiled floor. 'We're in church!'

'Oh, all right,' grinned Teddy.

Emily took a quick look around to make sure nobody had seen him. Arkwright continued to frown steadfastly at his prayer book. Near the door the imbecile bearer was being helped up from his couch of hymn books and led away by a member of the choir. Mrs Forester sat in a pew with little Jack beside her, waiting for Captain Hagan to return from dispersing the mob. Dr McNab and Miriam stood conversing in low tones beside the pulpit.

Emily asked Teddy if he knew what the message was that the Reverend Kingston had sent to Hagan and Mrs Forester in the middle of the service which had caused them to look so disturbed. Teddy's playful manner disappeared immediately. He even looked a little embarrassed, which was unusual for him. 'Well, I'm not *sure*,' he said hesitantly, 'but I think it may have been, well . . . Mind you, it may not have been that at all,' he added uncomfortably.

'May not have been *what*, though?'

'I think it was to say that he would refuse to communicate them because they were . . . you know, evil livers and that sort of thing.' Teddy scratched his chin and then added hurriedly: 'But I'm sure it's all a misunderstanding. An awful lot of dreadful *gup* flies about the bazaar, you know. It's the servants in India, Emily, they spread all sort of fanciful tales.'

Two Appreciations and
a Personal Memoir

AS DOES THE BISHOP

John Spurling

The Heath Government's attempt to discipline over-competitive trade unionists by means of the National Industrial Relations Court was scrapped by the incoming Labour Government in 1974. Exactly a century earlier the new Disraeli Government of 1874 set up an equally ill-conceived Court for dealing with clergymen accused of irregularities in church ritual. The Public Worship Regulation Act, unlike the Industrial Relations Act, is still on the statute-book, but it was a dead-letter and the judge of its Court unemployed within about a decade. It is hard for most of us · even those for whom the mere mention of trade unions threatens apoplexy – to imagine a society which felt so strongly about public worship within the Church of England that respected members of it were prepared to break up church services on account of the use of candles, incense and choir surplices (let alone such esoteric questions as 'the Eastward Position', the definition of kneeling or the colour of vestments) and later to sanction the imprisonment of refractory clerics. Yet it happened, in London, and our great-grandfathers or their fathers might well have written intemperate letters to the papers about it.

When J. G. Farrell, having written three novels with contemporary settings, turned to historical settings, it was no doubt largely because the passage of time puts inverted commas around issues which once seemed of vital importance and allows the novelist to observe human behaviour more coolly and clearly, from a seat in the gods. This was no sudden change of attitude on Farrell's part. From the first page of his first novel he was aware of the long perspective:

> It was early morning and the Earth was revolving at a terrifying speed ... Sayer was watching an old man and a dog walk slowly along the street ... A woman who was passing in

the other direction stopped to pat it and exchange a word with the old man . . . And the world continued to revolve with terrifying speed as it circled the sun. Considering the speed of its revolution, the old man and the woman were doing very well to keep their balance. The dog was standing squarely on four legs and so deserved less credit.

The rest of *A Man From Elsewhere* (1963) is unlike the later novels. After this first page Farrell drops both the long perspective and the suggestion of humour. One would hardly guess that the same person had written *A Man From Elsewhere* and the last, unfinished novel about a clergyman suffering for his High Church convictions. Yet there is a consistency of theme.

The plot of *A Man From Elsewhere* revolves round a dying writer called Sinclair Regan, once a Communist but now an equally fanatical individualist, who is about to receive a Catholic prize for his best-selling novels. Before Regan dies his old comrade Gerhardt, now the editor of a Communist journal, hopes to dig up unpleasant facts from Regan's past in order to discredit both him and the Church for the greater benefit of international Communism. Regan himself, moribund but still game for a fight, has actually invited Gerhardt for a last visit, but Gerhardt declines. Instead he sends one of his staff, the novel's hero, Sayer, with instructions to interrogate Regan, his household and the local villagers and discover the truth about Regan's rumoured collaboration with the Germans during the Second World War. There is a girl in the case, too, Regan's supposed daughter Gretchen, who finally makes it impossible for Sayer to complete his mission.

The story, almost needless to say, takes place in France. It is a distinctly period piece of the late fifties, complete with Algerian and Cold War noises off, indebted to Sartre and to French post-war films (even the photograph of Farrell on the back of the book's jacket makes him look like a young Frenchman), and it is not surprising that he would have preferred it to be forgotten. Nevertheless, the theme – the cockfight between Regan and Gerhardt and the effect of this clash of rigid and irreconcilable convictions on all the more fluid, more impressionable personalities caught in the middle – continued to smoulder. In treating it at this first attempt Farrell was hampered both by his own earnestness and that of the period. Gerhardt and Regan are melodramatic figures and Sayer himself, placed in an unreal position, is more of an existentialist model than a person. By the time, more than fifteen years later, Farrell came back to another story of irreconcilable convictions, he had taught himself how to fan it into flame.

He got rid of serious-minded melodrama at once. His second novel, *The Lung* (1965), is a black comedy based on his own experience as a polio victim. The novel is seen entirely through the eyes of its hero, Martin Sands, who is motivated when we first meet him by an irresistible craving for alcohol and a slightly milder one for women. The aggressive, threatening circumstances of the world and its powerful interests have become, inevitably through such eyes, a blurred background of silly or insufficiently loving people (especially Sands's ex-wife), out of which, like a thunderbolt from Jove, the crippling disease suddenly emerges to strike our man almost dead. Farrell must by this stage have read Malcolm Lowry's *Under the Volcano* (which always remained one of his favourite books), since in the early chapters, before he catches polio, the drunken, divorced, cynical Sands bears such a resemblance to Lowry's Consul. However, unlike the Consul (that latter-day Faust), Sands is essentially a comic figure and Farrell's triumph is to keep him so through all the vicissitudes of his gradual cure in a private hospital.

Most of the immediate comedy arises from the reawakening of Sands's two driving appetites in the wholly unsuitable context of the hospital, so that, for example, while he is still immured in the Iron Lung he persuades one of the nurses (his ex-stepdaughter, as it happens) to pour whisky down his feeding-tube; and later, when he is still scarcely able to walk, drags himself to the swimming-pool after lights out and there makes love to her. But behind these particular acts of indiscipline the real division between the benevolent but rigidly organized society represented by the hospital staff and Sands is that they want to return him, cured, to the world, while he sees nothing in the world worth returning to except the temporary expedients of drink and sex. Farrell does not really take sides on this issue, which is odd considering that, ostensibly, everything is seen from Sands's point of view. He is not the narrator, but the narration sometimes shifts into the first person to accommodate his interior monologue:

> I could never have been happy living happily in a suburb and watching my children grow up around me. I had to do something great and desperate so that when I entered a room people would nudge each other and say: that's Martin Sands. So that people would love me in spite of my indifference. The trouble is, the disaster is that it's not easy to find a vehicle for one's ambitions.

Without disputing Sands's pessimism, Farrell points up his egotism and, as it were behind his back, treats the hospital staff with considerable respect. Whereas the doctor attending the dying Regan in *A Man From Elsewhere* is a rather feeble, lackey-like creature, Dr Baker in *The Lung* is a fine, upstanding figure whose angry rebuke to Sands is not mocked, indeed leaves the hero temporarily deflated:

> 'Why do you have to behave like a spoiled child all the time! It's time you became an adult.'

On the other hand the book ends very much in Sands's frame of mind as he leaves the hospital wondering whether or not to marry his ex-stepdaughter and live happily ever after. It was probably in many ways a faithful retrospect of Farrell's own ambivalent feelings at the time of his encounter with the Iron Lung: grateful for the help given him; envious still of those to whom all the ordinary, taken-for-granted options were still available (he had been playing rugby for his college when the disease caught him); half-proud, half-resentful that he himself, picked out at random by a single stroke of bad luck, was from then on (to himself if not very noticeably to others) a cripple and an outsider.

But the most remarkable thing about *The Lung* is the way that its factual elements are transmuted so smoothly into comic fantasy. At one point he can describe exactly what it is like to be put into an Iron Lung or to be taken by the physiotherapist for one's first remedial swim in the hospital pool; at another, with equal precision, the elaborate preparations and grotesque contortions necessary to a crippled patient when attempting to grasp a reluctant nurse's hand on the bedcover, let alone when administering when he calls the *coup de grâce* beside that same remedial pool. This close attention to detail, which starting soberly in fact can later be made to yield episodes of pure surrealism, is brought to a fine art in the three historical novels. One thinks of the overgrown conservatory in *Troubles*, of what happens to the Residency furniture in *The Siege of Krishnapur*, of the orang-utan and the naked girl doing her keep-fit exercises in *The Singapore Grip* — there are innumerable other examples. Farrell's mature comedy embraced activities, things and animals quite as much as people. His treatment of dogs is especially interesting. He saw them in the same light as Lowry did, not as dear, faithful pets, but squalid, even faintly sinister creatures which attach themselves to people purely for the dogs' own convenience and protection. Dogs, after all, as he noted in the opening to *A Man From Elsewhere*, are better equipped than humans for keeping a firm grip on the surface of a revolving globe. One of the funniest passages in *The Hill Station* is the Simla shopkeeper's attempt to sell Dr McNab a pair of ankle-protectors against the bites of rabid dogs. But Farrell's notes make it clear that this joke was intended to turn sour: Mrs Forester's little boy Jack was to catch rabies and die of it.

The slapstick surrealism in this last, unfinished, novel was mostly still to come, because it needed working up to. Forsythe's white bird hanging in the priest-house is never brought to its apotheosis, the pig released into the church service was only a start. Observe Farrell in his Indian Diary listing the contents of a Maharajah's palace; observe what he does with them in *The Siege of Krishnapur*. It was *The Lung* which first unlocked all these treasures.

The hero of Farrell's third novel, *A Girl in the Head* (1967), is the spitting image of Sands, except that he is not crippled physically (though he certainly is emotionally) and has acquired a somewhat Nabokovian background as the last survivor of a titled Polish family. By the time we meet him he is washed up in an English south-coast resort called Maidenhair and married -- for the same reason as an ugly, smelly dog called Bonzo has attached itself to him, in order to have a roof over his head -- into the seedily respectable family Dongeon, proud of their Huguenot extraction. Count Boris Slattery is driven, like Sands, by fairly voracious appetites for drink and sex, in that order, and like Sands has seen through life:

> Of course, I realize that it's nonsense to think of one's life as a meaningless detail rapidly receding into a mass of other meaningless details. But I confess that the thought has occurred to me from time to time.

There is a repeat performance of Sands's difficult act of sex, this time in a small boat-house with an under-age prostitute, while an old man keeps watch outside in case the owner of the boat-house should return too early from lunch. The difficulty does not arise, of course, from the hero being crippled but purely from the circumstances, the act being performed in a newly varnished rowing-boat, which not only rocks alarmingly but, like the girl's bottom, retains evidence of their encounter. There is also a sympathetic doctor, who again makes the solipsistic hero look and feel rather small. Boris is horrified at being shown a group of cripples exercising in the hospital gymnasium. The doctor tells him:

> 'When *you* look at those people you don't see *them*, you see great dramas of suffering and pain and heroism and God knows what else . . . But that's all nonsense, perfectly irrelevant. I expect you noticed that most of these patients were young people paralysed in some way or other. Well, it's merely that they have in some respect aged all of a sudden. Part of the machinery has gone out of action. And that's all there is to it. Nothing else.'

*

Boris is unconvinced. The world is all black.

> 'I used to be rather like you,' the doctor said vaguely, looking somewhat bored. 'All misery is invented.' After a moment he turned back to Boris and smiled. 'Happiness, too, I daresay.'

A Girl in the Head was not well reviewed and one can see why. In spite of some good passages of comedy with the Dongeons it was written too much from the head and lacks *The Lung*'s basis in real experience. There is a whole strand concerning the girl of the title and an impossibly romantic young man called Alessandro riding a white horse and wearing a scarlet cloak which, though it is partly used to cast Boris in the role of voyeur and thus complete his misery, is frankly embarrassing and unlike anything else in the rest of Farrell's *oeuvre*. Perhaps he had been reading Iris Murdoch as well as Nabokov. But in general the stakes are too low. Boris is intermittently entertaining, but the earth has not come up and hit him as it has Sands and his pessimism seems merely wilful. Farrell was too serious a person himself to be able to take such a butterfly misanthrope seriously. All the same, in a letter dated 1967 to his friend G. M. Arthurson, who had taught him French at school, Farrell wrote that he was perplexed by the bad reviews

> as I consider this book as by far my best. Hardly anyone, even the people who liked the book, had any sympathy for Boris and his predicament. Well, apart from his appalling defects of character, pride, dishonesty, self-centredness and so on, I couldn't help thinking that Boris was significant in some way . . .

His ultimate significance was that he did not appear again. Instead of trying to convince the present of its own bitter and ludicrous insignificance, Farrell turned his attention to the half-forgotten but well-recorded troubles of the past. He no longer needed to strive for comic effect or set an anti-hero on a collision course with the rest of society. Time, distance and facts did all that for him and on a far grander scale. His problems now were to marshal, to compose and develop his swarming detail and, most important of all, to reconcile the long view of the narrator up in the gods with the short view of the characters down there in the thick of it.

Troubles (1970), although it looks at first like a complete break with the earlier work, is actually a transitional novel. Its setting is certainly historical – Ireland between 1919 and 1921 – but recent enough for everything, including the outlook of the characters, to be moderately familiar, at least to people of Farrell's generation, whose fathers could have been teenage visitors to the Majestic Hotel in Kilnalough. The world depicted – mostly shabby gentlefolk in unpromising if not quite distressed circumstances – is essentially that of the Dongeons. The two Dongeon grannies have multiplied into any number of halt, deaf and ailing old permanent residents. Dongeon *père*, much enlarged and developed into a full-length portrait of the British upper-middle-class stag at bay, has become the Hotel's proprietor, Edward Spencer. Maurice Dongeon, the unspeakable young cad of *A Girl in the Head*, is Ripon, the ditto of *Troubles*; and Flower Dongeon, Boris's wilting wife, is Angela, whose early death saves the protagonist of *Troubles*, Major Brendan Archer, from being married himself. *Troubles* contains more than its fair share of dogs (cats too) and also its 'wise' doctor, the sour and decaying old Ryan, whose stoical, 'scientific' view of life echoes that of the doctor in *A Girl in the Head*:

'People are insubstantial. They really do not last . . . A doctor should know. People never last.'

The great improvements are: firstly, the invention of the palatial, crumbling Hotel as both backcloth and plot device for the full unfolding of the Dongeon/Spencer characteristics; secondly, the malevolent presence, just off-stage, of the Sinn Feiners, with their rooted objection to all that the Dongeons/Spencers, even if only half-consciously, stand for; and thirdly, the character of the central figure. The Major, though the constant use of his rank instead of his name reminds one that

Farrell had not lost his enthusiasm for *Under the Volcano*, is nothing like the Consul and hardly at all like the Consul's progeny, Martin Sands or Boris Slattery. There is more than a touch of Chekhov in the Major and even perhaps a trace of Dostoyevsky's Idiot – Sarah, the crippled and 'cruel' girl he is in love with, treats him on one occasion to a distinctly Dostoyevskian tirade. But really he is the first truly Farrellian hero, one of the most sympathetic heroes in fiction.

At once diffident and passive and, when the need arises, energetic and competent, the Major contrives to belong equally to the grotesquely comic foreground of the Hotel and its occupants and to the not at all comic background of the Great War (from which he emerged shell-shocked and apparently engaged to Angela) and the activities of the Black and Tans and the Sinn Feiners (whose victim he becomes at the end of the book). He is a Quixote without being a fool and a Galahad without being a prig. He suffers from nerves, bad dreams, embarrassment, love, envy, apathy, slightly blimpish opinions, likes and dislikes, fear, melancholy -- a gamut of the minor emotions – without ever becoming overwhelmed or chained down by any of them. This is, of course, the secret of his charm as well as of the book's success. The Major acts as an extraordinarily subtle sounding-board for everything that happens, absurd, lugubrious, laughable, pitiable, gruesome or merely irritating. He is the outsider turned temporarily insider, but with no axe to grind. He did not make this enclosed world, he doesn't endorse or condemn it, he just happens to be there. Like the novelist or the reader he can leave at any moment and go back to England. He doesn't choose to, perhaps because he is in love, but more likely because there is always something happening or about to happen, some further deterioration in the Hotel, some change in relationships, somebody new arriving, somebody old taking leave of his or her senses. The Major's virtues, in keeping with his emotions, are the minor ones of tolerance and decency, but in the context of the eternal blood-feud between England and Ireland, they turn into major ones.

There is no one quite like the Major in *The Siege of Krishnapur* (1973). There does not need to be, since, supported by the

Major's accommodating character, Farrell had found in writing *Troubles* that he was increasingly at ease in his newly expanded and distanced fictional world. From time to time he was even able to leave the shelter of the Major's presence altogether and venture independently into the minds and actions of other characters. The Major's place as anchorman is taken in *Krishnapur* by two characters, the Collector and Fleury, but the real ringmaster is now the novelist himself, coming and going from his safe seat in the late twentieth century to this heroic scene of blood and thunder, closely based on the fact of the Indian Mutiny, yet in Farrell's hands metamorphosed into comedy and even farce. As other admirers of *Krishnapur* have noted, it sometimes seems almost as if Blandings Castle and its household have been carried eastwards and set down on the site of Lucknow. The Collector certainly has an air of Lord Emsworth, except that he believes in Progress instead of the divine rights of the landed aristocracy and collects inventions from the Great Exhibition instead of prizes for his pig. True, the Collector's manservant Vokins is a poor specimen of his profession and would hardly command the respect of the servants' hall at Blandings, but he is described in Wodehousian terms:

> Vokins lacked the broader view. He tended only to see the prospect of the Death of Vokins. Although some of the Collectors' guests might have been hard put to it to think of what a man of Vokins's class had to lose, to Vokins it was very clear what he had to lose: namely his life. He was not at all anxious to leave his skin on the Indian plains; he wanted to take it back to the slums of Soho or wherever it came from.

Fleury and Harry in different circumstances would not be manning a brass cannon and blowing off the heads of advancing sepoys, but repelling with equally desperate ingenuity the assault of some ferocious aunt. Their responses to the siren Lucy and to Harry's sister, the sweetly respectable Louise, are precisely the same, even *in extremis*, as they would have been at Blandings. This is perhaps to make *Krishnapur* sound trivial, but at the very heart of Farrell's mature fiction is his discovery of the importance of not being earnest. Characters may be earnest, but not authors, at least not the authors of novels about the British ruling classes.

The Second World War was full of Emsworths and Woosters, translated in stern reality from Blandings to the edge of the abyss, blundering, obsessed, ludicrous, heroic. Farrell's last completed novel, *The Singapore Grip* (1978), shows them in that very situation and in those terms. When the unhappy General Percival, hopelessly organizing the impossible defence of Singapore against the Japanese, hears the sound of somebody sawing wood he becomes jumpy and irritable. Farrell has already introduced us to Percival's notion that Fate is busy sawing away each step of a ladder just before he, Percival, puts his foot on it. It is again a Wodehousian conceit, but it could apply perfectly well to the later stages of *Macbeth*. Shakespeare would have used the image grimly, even savagely, as if it were freshly conceived; Farrell after Wodehouse presents it ironically, derisively underlining its banality. But it is still a grim image. Percival is not trivialized by it; he is given his true place, somewhere between Wodehouse and Shakespeare. From a seat in the gods the British in their short-lived Empire – in Ireland, in India or in Malaya at those particular moments of disintegration – look tragic; but when you get down amongst them, the thing is a farce. In all three of his completed historical novels Farrell sets the scene for tragedy in his beautiful, slow passages of topographical introduction – Hardy, as it were, on Egdon Heath. The mood changes abruptly as soon as his characters come on, yet for all their antics one is never allowed entirely to lose the mood of that first stately approach. The two moods interact: farce is edged with black; tragedy is seen to be incompatible with the day-to-day lives of people for whom respectability and the done thing act as an extraordinarily elastic and adaptable cocoon against reality.

Yet to call it farce is to suggest a travesty which Farrell was very far from intending or creating. The events are often farcical, but the persons are not, or mostly not. In *Krishnapur* there remain one or two clockwork mice, such as the Padre and the Magistrate (very entertaining clockwork mice, certainly), whose characteristics and obsessions serve solely to keep them on the move in the interests of particular scenes or the action as a whole. In *Singapore* only the doctor, will his over-repetitive anxiety about inviting the Blacketts back to dinner, is mechanical in this way. There are no such characters in *The Hill Station*. The more he worked on and delved into the characteristics of the Dongeon/Spencer brigade, the more independent dignity Farrell allowed them; not of course the dignity of being in the right or of being exactly what they saw themselves as, but complexity and opacity, the dignities of thought and emotion beneath a stereotypical surface. The Collector in *Krishnapur* and Walter Blackett in *Singapore* are later versions of Edward Spencer, a fine rounded portrait, as I have already suggested, but of somebody alien. The Collector is partly absurd, partly heroic in his outward aspect (as how should a standard Victorian type with a simple belief in Progress not seem to post-imperial eyes?), but we are also able to feel what it is like to be him. In Farrell's Indian Diary there is a sketch of an ex-administrator of the Raj composed in just the same way from a combination of Farrell's sharp eye for outward absurdity and his instinctive sympathy for the person inside. Walter Blackett is a still more complex example, for he is in large measure the villain of *Singapore*, representing the whole self-seeking and materialistic side of the Empire and of the class which exploited it for their own advantage at others' expense. Yet Blackett is sympathetic. He is given the same sort of scope for seeing the action in his own terms as only authorially approved of characters such as Sands or Boris are given in the early novels. Of course there was a limit to Farrell's tolerance in this direction, especially since his political views became more radical latterly. The young Dongeons and Spencers are not very likable, but they are treated with a certain indulgence, due to their negligibility. The portraits of Joan and Monty Blackett, on the other hand, are stinging indictments of gilded self-interest.

Farrell's new ability to inhabit more and more of his characters – it is significant that the Major, reappearing in *Singapore*, now takes, if not quite a back-pew, certainly only one of several front seats – was accompanied by a new skill at matching the inner and outer actions of the story. There is no outer world in *The Lung* or *A Girl in the Head*, only flashbacks to Sands's and Boris's pasts. In *Troubles* the outer world is either deliberately shadowy or conveyed rather too crudely by the bald insertion of paragraphs from contemporary newspapers. In *Krishnapur* and *Singapore* the outer world and Farrell's fictional world coalesce. In *Singapore* especially – a triumph of the organization and fictional assimilation of massive amounts of documentary material – one feels that for the first time Farrell has arrived exactly where he wants to be. Now he is telling not just a story, but history itself, from inside and outside.

Of the writers who had done this before, three, I think, were of special importance to him: Richard Hughes, Thomas Mann and Stendhal. Stendhal must have been an early influence: G. M. Arthurson remembers the schoolboy Farrell delivering a talk on Stendhal, although he was not in the syllabus. What Farrell thought about Stendhal then or later has not been recorded, but he surely admired the easy, gossipy manner of Stendhal's narrative, his mastery of the long-shot and the close-up; certainly he shared Stendhal's view of the shapelessness and messiness of history when one is actually involved in it (compare the battles in *Singapore* with Stendhal's Waterloo or, on a smaller scale, Fleury's and the giant Sikh's duel to the death in *Krishnapur* with Fabrizio's 'unlucky encounter' in *La Chartreuse de Parme*); and he presumably recognized in Fabrizio the prototype of his own fresh-faced, open-hearted, idealistic heroes, Fleury in *Krishnapur* and Matthew in *Singapore*. Farrell's earlier heroes, incidentally, are all middle aged or nearly.

Mann would have taught him not to be afraid of detail, even copious detail, and how to animate it and integrate it with the larger movements of the novel by lodging it in particular characters. The Collector's passion for the Great Exhibition and Walter Blackett's deep interest (in both senses) in the rubber trade are obvious examples; while the medical details of cholera in *Krishnapur* and of tuberculosis in *The Hill Station* are direct tributes to *The Magic Mountain*, a book, like *Under the Volcano*, which he was always trying to persuade friends to read. Mann gave him the courage to be weighty, to build up slowly, to dwell on things, to allow his characters long speeches even at the risk of being boring: all this under the wonderful covering of a consistent irony which converts big things into small and small into big, so that nothing escapes the novelist's control.

Yet Farrell lacks Stendhal's and Mann's callousness. Perhaps that is too strong a word. Better say that for him, as not for them, a kind of unscheduled compassion in the author breaks through the irony. He knows as well as they that compassion is only another human foible, that it belongs to the inside of history not the outside, intrinsic to the Matthews and Majors in the same way as hopes for the success of the League of Nations or to be loved in return by a *princess lointaine*, but irrelevant to the outside, where scientific or semi-scientific causes and effects prevail. All the same and in spite of his deep-seated pessimism (which one might simply call a sense of reality), he objects to the inevitable disaster (for individual human beings) of time and history, would like to deny it and in a way does so with the gentle domestic endings of his three historical novels and by twice resuscitating his favourite characters, the Major in *Singapore* and Dr McNab in *The Hill Station*. This flying in the face of history, this -- by Mann's and Stendhal's standards – sentimentality is also evident in Richard Hughes's novels. Farrell knew Hughes and enormously admired his work. He borrowed from him certain tricks of storytelling, especially a conversational immediacy suggested by stops and starts in the narration or *faux-naif* exclamations, as if the storyteller were seeing the thing happen there and then before his eyes. He even lifted from Hughes certain conjunctive words and phrases, such as 'presently', 'for' (as in 'But no – for they got up') and 'just then', which have a slightly old-world, fireside, nannyish cosiness. Of course Mann also uses devices of this sort, in a heavier manner, rolling his eyeballs, as it were, the while. But Hughes is no ironist. Even where he brings in actual historical events and personages, as in the fine scenes describing Hitler and the Munich Putsch in *The Fox in the Attic*, he views them from inside history, undistanced.

Farrell, I think, was torn. In the midst of achieving the

magnificent double scale (historical and human) of *Singapore*, he perhaps envied Hughes's resolutely human scale.

> In human affairs things tend inevitably to go wrong. Things are slightly worse at any given moment than at any preceding moment.

The truth of Ehrendorf's Second Law is, as the narrator points out, rubbing his hands, 'demonstrated on a remarkably generous scale' in *Singapore*. Yet the worse they get, the more Farrell abandons irony for straightforward description, as if he were himself, like the Major and Matthew fighting their fires, trying to counter the uncontrollable tendency of history, once unleashed, to reduce everything human to ashes. The scene in the Chinese dying-house, just over half-way through the book, is treated ironically in spite of its horror. The later scenes of devastation and desperation are not. The book works, just as he intended it to, in long-shot and close-up, but I wonder if he had entirely bargained for what he ended up with. It is one thing for a Sands or a Boris to complain of the worthlessness of life, from inside the house, as it were. It is quite another for the truth of what they believe to be demonstrated from outside by the novelist in the role of history putting his boot on the house and, however understandingly, mocking its occupants as he does so. Neither Mann nor Stendhal shrinks from that – the ending of *Chartreuse* is wilfully cruel, beyond the call of history even – but Farrell does. His irony becomes muted and intermittent; at the end he half-pulls his favourite characters out from under history's boot and leaves it possible that they will survive that particular catastrophe. As for Ehrendorf himself, the framer of the Second Law, we are allowed to suppose that he escapes altogether, achieving a triumphantly domestic ending across a London breakfast table from Kate (the only nice Blackett).

Farrell had thought for some time of returning to Dr McNab's later career after his escape from Krishnapur and the vindication of his modern ideas about cholera. It was surely not just a weariness with size and massive documentation which led him, after he had finished *Singapore*, to start writing a

comparatively plain tale from the hills. He very much needed a
predominantly human scale. This may seem an odd comment in
view of the fact that *The Hill Station* is Farrell's first novel with a
religious subject. Nor was it just the one religious subject – the
battle between Ritualists and the rest – which appears in this
fragment. According to Farrell's notes, McNab was going to
tangle with Hindu religion too, in the shape of a fakir living on
the top of Jakko, the mountain behind Simla. Not only that. Ten
years after the date Farrell chose for this novel (1871), Simla was
visited by Madame Blavatsky, who established the Simla
Eclectic Theosophical Society. Madame Blavatsky appears
prominently in one set of Farrell's notes and there is a batch of
filing-cards containing research material about her, so it seems
that at some stage she was inended to figure in this novel.

But the very fact that religion was to have been the main
burden of *The Hill Station* argues its human scale. Farrell, as is
evident from all his previous novels, regarded religion in the
same light as any other optimistic opiate. Where it is established
religion, where it is used for essentially materialistic purposes, to
underpin society, as in the marriage services ('physically one of
the most punishing ever invented') in *The Lung* or *A Girl in the
Head*, or competitively, as in the separate Protestant and
Catholic burials in *Krishnapur*, Farrell takes pleasure in ridiculing
it. There is a brief passage in *Troubles*, during the interview
between the Major and Father O'Byrne over the death of a
young Sinn Feiner, when ridicule turns to disgust:

> At length he [the priest] lifted his eyes from the Major's face
> to the crucifix on the wall. To the Major the steadiness of this
> gaze on the crucifix seemed blind, inhuman, fanatical. The
> yellowish naked body, the straining ribs, the rolling eyes and
> parted lips, the languorously draped arms and long trailing
> fingers, the feet crossed to economize on nails, the cherry
> splash of blood from the side . . .

And the Major, most uncharacteristically, loses his temper with
the priest and goes out slamming the door. But where religion is
something to cling to, a spar in life's shipwreck, as it is for the

Padre in *Krishnapur* or the semi-lunatic Exmoore in *The Lung*, Farrell tempers his ridicule with sympathy. He seems to view it as a more pathetic version of the Collector's belief in Progress or Fleury's and Matthew's faith in human nature. Exmoore, as it happens, clings to the ritual aspect of religion (he is an ex-priest) and the Rev. Kingston in *The Hill Station* is obviously a developed version of him. It is therefore not so much the nature of what Kingston believes that matters as the fact that, compared to the Bishop, his belief is the only important thing in his life. The beliefs and the sincerity or otherwise of the fakir and Madame Blavatsky would no doubt have complicated and enriched this fundamental opposition of substance and form, one of the ironies being, of course, that Kingston's substance consists of the forms of ritual.

Nevertheless, there is a new element. McNab is one of Farrell's 'wise' doctors (the first being Dr Baker in *The Lung*) and represents in *Krishnapur* a kind of stalwart if gruff sanity based on experience, unselfish care for other people and open-minded expertise. Farrell gives Conrad's *Nostromo* rather a poor review in his Indian Diary, but he thought a lot of *Heart of Darkness*. When Marlow in Conrad's story is steaming up river to rescue Kurtz from the jungle, he finds a little book left at an abandoned trading-post by another benighted white man. It is called 'An Inquiry into some Points of Seamanship':

> Not a very enthralling book; but at the first glance you could see there a singleness of intention, an honest concern for the right way of going to work, which made these humble pages, thought out so many years ago, luminous with another than a professional light. The simple old sailor, with his talk of chains and purchases, made me forget the jungle and the pilgrims [white traders] in a delicious sensation of having come upon something unmistakably real.

What this book is for Marlow and Conrad in the heart of the intangible horrors of the Congo, its scenery, its savages and its colonizers alike, McNab and his medical expertise are for Farrell in both his Indian novels. The disquisitions on disease and its

cure may read like extracts from *The Magic Mountain*, but they are
there for the opposite purpose: to dispel mists and evil
circumstances, not to contribute to them.

The new element in *The Hill Station* is that McNab has become
infected with a belief; not in religion as such but in something
that lies behind the observable facts of medicine. There is no
way of telling how much of a will o' the wisp this was meant to
prove, whether or not McNab's intuition would have been
substantiated by his meetings (there were to be at least two) with
the fakir, only perhaps to be devalued completely by an
encounter with Madame Blavatsky. Farrell left a note summing
up the general content of his novel in four sections. The first
three read as follows:

1 Kingston's stubborn defence of Ritualism . . . and
martyrdom. At loggerheads with Vestry, Bishop, congregation, etc.
2 The Indian Ramakrishna angle on religion.
3 McNab as anchor man . . . supposed to be writing on
medicine actually investigating religion.

It is clear at least that the cross-current of human belief (however
ironized by the distance of time) were in this novel to take the
place of overwhelming historical circumstances as the motive
force of the story and one can already see in the half that is
written the pleasure Farrell was finding in this backwater with
its quaint storms in teacups. *The Hill Station* was his own hill
station after the hot, grim firefighting of *Krishnapur* and *Singapore*.

The new work, however, was not to be as light and escapist as
all that. The last item on Farrell's summary is:

4 The significance of Emily's love-affair. The young
officers, leaping also to the defence of Kingston, treat
everything as a game or competition . . . AS DOES THE BISHOP

Something of the defence of Kingston is already there in the
fragment, but to judge from the notes there was to be a second
and even more disgraceful church service in which peashooters

were used from the gallery, prayer-books thrown, windows smashed, dogs released and a pitched battle fought with the choir (supported presumably by the gallant officers) at the chancel gates. Most of this actually happened at St George's-in-the-East, Stepney, in 1859. Farrell simply shipped it to Simla together with Bo'sun Smith (a real person), elements of Bishop Tait, Bishop of London and later Archbishop of Canterbury during the heyday of anti-Ritualism, and much curious material from Michael Reynolds's biography (*Martyr of Ritualism*) of the Rev. A. H. Mackonochie, Vicar of St Alban's, Holborn.

As for the games and competitions, there was to have been a scene —surely an extended one, occupying more than one chapter – at the Annandale Races. Here is one of Farrell's notes:

> The races at Annandale, the race ball and the fancy fair: which takes place between the first and second days of races. Pretty women in stalls. Potatoes in buckets at the gallop. Flower show, dog show, cricket and croquet. Poem. Rain. Men under rug. Treasure hunt. A rider and horse both killed.

And here are some fuller details from Farrell's file-cards:

> A large dell shaded by pine and fir with a semi-circular amphitheatre of hill sand and a level spot of a few acres below . . . half the pretty women in Simla are established in their stalls, selling wares for less than nothing. And still further in the wood a most spacious tent to which butlers and khitmutghars run with champagne, hams and patties.

> Egg and spoon races at Annandale. 'The Shepherd's Race': a sheep is tied to a long pole in the centre of Annandale; couples race to it and sing 'Ba, ba, black sheep, have you any wool?' The sheep, alarmed at being made so much of by the gymkhana folk, bleats for all it is worth. The competitors then proceed to divine what reply it has made, write down their answers and race back to the starting point. The first couple to arrive back with the correct answer wins the prize.

*

The Simla races began today and weather caused anxiety. Capt. Burn, starving for weeks to reach the proper weight . . . When there has been rain the ground gets so slippery that sharp turns on the racecourse are positively dangerous. Riders are nervous. During the second race a tremendous storm and Capt. Burn won it in a downpour. The spectators all crowded into the stand and watched with amusement the jockeys, grooms and natives who had no shelter. The cloths on the refreshment tables had turned blue with the rain and a large party of men walked about under a long rug they had taken up from the ground.

A wonderful treasure hunt with instructions so well chosen that many seats were vacant at the final supper and some of the searchers with their partners did not reach the hill top till early morning.

The old racecourse was really the hard road that ran round the outside of the gardens and pleasure ground. It had a steep and dangerous descent through the village with an extremely sharp turn immediately behind the old volunteer rifle butts. At the race meeting a rider and horse went over the wall at this angle and both were killed.

It is some measure of Farrell's unique quality that one can imagine so vividly, almost as if it had been written, what he would have done with all this, yet be unable to imagine anyone else writing it. Amongst all the delights and excitements of Annandale, Emily's affair with Lieutenant Potter would no doubt have blossomed. But what was its 'significance'? That it was just another treasure hunt? Would she have offered him an 'invitation to a picnic of pegs', mentioned in the notes and explained by a poem which Farrell copied out?

> *Her Invitation to Him*
> Under the deodars up on the hill,
> Come to my picnic, dear Sir, if you will,
> Come to my picnic, a picnic of pegs,
> On pony, in rickshaw, or on your own legs.

A picnic of tea where they meet by the score
Is an obviously, stupidly out-of-date bore.
Mine is a picnic which shan't exceed two,
Myself on the one part and – shall it be you?

But we up on Jakko, among the old apes
With extract of barley and juice of the grapes
We'll talk of philosophy, science and art,
Music, theosophy, things of the heart.

Whether or not, it would not have turned out well for her, since Lieutenant Potter was to leave her in the lurch. As Farrell's chilling note has it:

Emily sees Potter going through his arrow-pulling for another girl. Later she feeds him peanuts almost sitting in his lap.

One can outline the rest of Mrs Forester's story from the notes: her little boy catching rabies would seem to her a judgment on her sin; she would be discovered in the act of confessing to and being absolved by Kingston, causing a further outcry from the anti-Ritualists; and she would elope with Captain Hagan. There was to be, as the poem suggests, a troupe of monkeys up the hill with the fakir; and an operation on Dr Bateman's throat, presumably damaged by too much public ranting, was to be performed by Dr McNab with a penknife. Finally Kingston, having taken refuge in the McNabs' new bungalow, was to renounce his living at the earnest request of the apparently dying Bishop and leave Simla, only to die himself; whereupon

The Bishop, recovered, is playing croquet again. Another curate-challenger. McNab does not wait, he knows how it will end.

'As does the Bishop', in capitals and underlined, is the key to that theme in Farrell's writing which stems from his first novel.

In *A Man From Elsewhere* a 'Bishop' (Gerhardt the Communist) and an apostate (Regan) wrestle for mastery, compete for no good reason except competition's sake and in doing so are meant to stand for the greater, equally purposeless, competition between the Soviet bloc and the West. Once one has spotted the theme one can see it lurking in all Farrell's work. Sands and Boris are both refugees from competition and for this reason life has no meaning for them. When Sands, against all the odds of his physical handicaps, succeeds in winning the competition for the pretty nurse, his interest in life is briefly restored. The Major, shocked almost into saintliness by the deadly competition in the trenches, is drawn by mistake and simply because he happens to be British into the game of murder between the Black and Tans and the Sinn Feiners.

The theme is less immediately evident in *The Siege of Krishnapur*. Indeed Farrell himself, ending the book through the eyes of the Collector, seems still unsure of what exactly constitutes history's malevolence towards human beings:

> Perhaps, by the very end of his life, in 1880, he had come to believe that a people, a nation does not create itself according to its own best ideas, but is shaped by other forces, of which it has little knowledge.

Yet knowledge is the only hope, as the Collector also recognizes:

> 'Ah, yes, McNab,' said the Collector thoughtfully. 'He was the best of us all. The only one who knew what he was doing.'

By the time he came to writing *Singapore*, Farrell reckoned he knew what those forces were. He represented them with the most circumstantial detail in Walter Blackett and his blind, wholly selfish commercialism. For all their good intentions and even good actions, the British Empire and the race and class which ran it shaped their own destruction. How could they have done otherwise? Competition is built into human beings, from their mating habits to their recreations to their personal and national relationships to their religious and political creeds. Was Marxism the solution? The 'familiar bearded leonine figure' makes a sudden parenthetical appearance in *The Hill Station*, but only as an ironic comment on Emily's blinkered view of class, not as the prophet of a world freed from economic competition. The Ramakrishna angle? Was that going to be the opening in the clouds for McNab? Not, I think, on Farrell's earth. 'As does the Bishop' is his ironic, disarmingly mild but devastating equivalent for Conrad's 'the horror, the horror'.

THINGS FALL APART

Margaret Drabble

One of the most noticeable features of J. G. Farrell's style is its curious obliquity, all the more curious when allied, at least in the later novels, to a strong narrative drive and to a narrator who addresses the reader directly and at times intimately. The action, even when taking place inside the heads of the characters, or when, as often, violent and bizarre, seems to happen at a strange remove from the reader, with the effect that we become simultaneously involved and disengaged, held at a distance and yet impelled to read on because we do, after all, care about the fate of the protagonists, however indifferent they seem at times to be to it themselves, and however passively they accept it.

Few serious modern novels have as powerful a plot as *The Siege of Krishnapur*, or involve incidents as dramatic; it moves to a thrilling climax, defying one to lay it aside before the end, and yet the tone is predominantly ironic, its appeal does not rest on vulgar suspense, and it constantly raises questions about the relationship of past events to the present and indeed the future. The comedy is serious, and although there are moments of mock-epic and mock-heroic, we remain convinced that Farrell is deeply engaged with his subject matter, which is serious enough – nothing less than the nature of colonialism, the end of an Empire, and the end of an ideology. Comedy and irony are in themselves distancing techniques, and it is interesting to note that Farrell himself was disturbed by a criticism that *Krishnapur* was too funny for its theme; he took this to heart while writing *The Singapore Grip* but nevertheless its most profound and dark moments mingle with scenes of surreal farce – indeed some of its darkest moments *are* surreal farce.

A favourite Farrell device is to accompany his (or his characters') more solemn reflections with a pathetic and ludicrous physical activity, or to create between his characters crossed purposes of such complexity that the effect is of high comedy: Matthew Webb, trying to explain his thoughts about Geneva and the role of the League of Nations over the Blacketts' dinner table, is constantly interrupted by comments on the menu (a dark tide of fish in vinegar and peppercorns, followed by roast beef at which the gourmet Dupigny sneers, followed by bread-and-butter pudding of which Dupigny surprisingly approves), by the pointless interjections of the other guests, and even by his own hunger, for he, accustomed to wartime rationing, finds the beef delicious, and takes time off from thoughts of Geneva to wonder if he will be offered some more. What chance has serious discussion when counterpointed with sentences like this?

> 'Did someone mention Geneva?' asked Brooke-Popham, who, at first busy with a large helping of fish, had now got the better of it and was free to enter the conversation.

There are many other fine examples of this kind of counter-point: Fleury, in *Krishnapur*, in the heat of battle, and in the act of drawing his sabre from a dead sepoy's back, is pursued relentlessly by the Padre, intent on expounding his argument for the existence of God drawn from Supreme Design.

> 'Think how apt fins are to water, wings to air . . .' exclaimed the Padre . . . Fleury stared at the Padre, too harrowed and exhausted to speak. Could it not be, he wondered vaguely, trembling on the brink of an idea that would have made him famous, that somehow or other fish designed their own eyes?

This is entirely characteristic: even in the extremes of physical danger, Farrell's characters continue to think, to speculate, to try to justify their own picture of the world. Or take Matthew Webb's visit to a Singapore brothel with Monty Blackett, confronted by a row of unattractive prostitutes (one of them a schoolgirl puzzling over her Latin homework and pondering 'the mysterious workings of the occidental mind'): Matthew continues to lecture the bored Monty on Geneva and Manchuria instead of choosing a girl, as, later in the book, in the middle of fighting a raging fire, he attempts to convert his old friend

Ehrendorf to his view that people could and should use co-
operation instead of self-interest as the basis of their behaviour.

> 'So many people already do!' he exclaimed, but Ehrendorf,
> who was not as accustomed to fire-fighting as Matthew,
> looked too distressed to reply.

('Distressed' is a favourite Farrell understatement, often
employed at moments of high drama.) Or Matthew again, in one
of the novel's most harrowing scenes, in which he visits a
Chinese dying-house with Vera Chiang to find himself
harangued in turn by a dying old man about the European
swindling of smallholders in the rubber trade (a harangue
substantiated, again characteristically, by documentary evidence
in the form of a yellowing cutting from *The Planter*, 1930):
Matthew defends himself from this attack by dismissing the old
man as a 'poor old blighter':

> 'What a disagreeable old codger,' he thought, taken aback by
> this list of complaints. 'You'd think that at death's door he'd
> have better things to think about.'

This comic undercutting is not merely a sugaring of the pill,
though it does serve to enliven otherwise unpalatable chunks
of thoroughly researched information. It is integral to the
work.

The effect of distance is compounded in many ways, some of
them apparently trivial, but nonetheless significant. For
instance, Farrell has a peculiar fondness for inverted commas,
and puts a good many phrases between them, picking them out,
as it were, for ironic inspection. Sarah, in *Troubles*, writes that
her fingers are 'dropping off' from the cold. Vera Chiang
employs them too, though for different reasons, as all her
English phrases – 'kicking the bucket', 'snaps', 'nose in a book'
– are carefully isolated for our attention, as is, in *Troubles*, the
phrase 'senile old codger' which Edward habitually applies to
Dr Ryan. The effect is to make the English language itself look
quaintly fossilized, like the Empire that created it. Even when

commas are not employed, their effect lingers, as when Walter Blackett reflects that the life of his old partner Webb

> was surely a tragedy worthy of that . . . what was his name? . . . that French blighter . . . yes, Balzac, that was it.

But even more conspicuously, Farrell uses inverted commas in a manner rare since the widespread infiltration of the stream-of-consciousness technique – to enclose his characters' thoughts. With the Major, in *Troubles*, the practice is habitual. While staring at Edward in the bath, he wonders.

> 'How could any young woman possibly be interested in *that*?' he wondered glumly,

or (in an interestingly similar situation, having glimpsed a maid naked by a wash basin) –

> Later, lying in bed, he mused: 'She could have been a lady for all the difference there was . . . Of course without clothes on everybody looks the same. They look just like we do.'

The effect here is of a curious dislocation between thought and language, as though the words of the thought can't quite catch the painful complexity without an undue formality. This contributes to the sense of stiffness with which many of the characters manipulate their ideas in bewildering circumstances, as though trying to cling to some sense of order in a rapidly dissolving world. The Major does not understand himself or his own situation, is not even sure why he is in Ireland at all, is easily duped, imposed upon and taken by surprise; against all the evidence he attempts quixotically to believe that others are as pure of heart as he is himself. No wonder his thoughts are confused. He takes refuge from his fears that his reason has become unhinged (entirely understandable to the reader) by formulations that are often wildly inappropriate; his last thought before losing consciousness as he stands buried to the neck in sand before an oncoming tide proves as wide of the mark as most of his speculations – 'Soon Sarah will come and dig me out,' he thinks, but of course she does no such thing. In the same desperate way people cling to hope and convention in Ireland, Krishnapur and Singapore: bridge parties and dinner parties continue to be held, tea parties (even when there is only hot water to drink) survive, Walter Blackett unflinchingly and in the face of obvious disaster continues to construct Blackett and Webb's Jubilee celebration floats as the Japanese pour towards him as relentlessly as the tide of change had poured towards the Major. There is an air of mingled futility and heroism: real life flows on outside the tiny temporary barriers of inverted commas and tea parties, at the mercy of those 'other forces' which the Collector suspects, at the end of *The Siege of Krishnapur*, to be more powerful than even the best ideas.

The powerlessness of the characters, the gaping distance between their expressed intentions and the actual course of events, is also stressed by the role which Farrell assigns to objects, by a pervasive implication that they have a recalcitrant autonomy. Dogs, as John Spurling points out, tend to manipulate their reluctant owners, and buildings – notably the decaying Majestic Hotel of *Troubles* – also have a life of their own, which no amount of human endeavour can control. The giant M of its very name falls on an old lady's tea-table, a piece of stucco the size of a man nearly squashes a long-haired dachshund. Ivy rampages round its outer walls, creepers force their way in and dislodge the furniture. Swimming pools revert to nature in both *Troubles* and *The Singapore Grip*, and in the streets of Singapore abandoned fire-hoses writhe like snakes. Telephones also become animated, and a brilliantly evocative sentence describes them in the Operations Room in Singapore as 'shrilling in little herds, all together like frogs in a pond'. Walter Blackett's dignity is completely undermined by a small spot of egg on his chin during a crucial interview. Thus are people at the mercy of things. Pieces of mid-Victorian furniture and decor are used as ammunition in *Krishnapur*, and though it was the Collector's idea thus to employ them, even he is shocked by the devastation they cause. 'How terrible . . . I mean, I had no idea anything like that would happen,' he says, as he surveys a scene

of carnage in which a surviving sepoy tries to remove a silver
fork from one of his lungs.

People are themselves reduced to objects by Farrell's bizarre
imagery. In the opening sequence of *A Girl in the Head* its hero
Boris suffers a mild heart attack while carrying a parcel of
potatoes; someone collects them and arranges them 'on the
stretcher round his recumbent body, rather as if he had been a
side of beef on its way to the oven'. When Edward in *Troubles*
shoots a Sinn Feiner, 'the dreadful thought occurred to the
Major that Edward had now gone completely insane and was
looking for a place on the wall to mount' him amidst the existing
array of stags, antelopes and zebra.

Indeed, one character is described with extreme obliquity
almost wholly in terms of things. Angela, the Major's fiancée,
and the occasion of his arrival at the Majestic, makes hardly any
direct appearances, and the Major, baffled by the secrecy
surrounding her withdrawal, is reduced to watching trays of
food as they go up and down from her room.

> . . . coming down, the meat and vegetables might be
> somewhat disarranged, mixed up together, one might
> suppose, by a listless hand. And a fork might be lying on the
> plate, though the knife was rarely touched; most often, on the
> way down, it lay beside the plate, clean and shining as it had
> been on the way up. Similarly, the apple on the tray usually
> made the return journey with its skin unflawed . . . One day,
> however, he noticed a raw apple travelling upstairs that
> looked so fresh and shining that it might even have been an
> early arrival of the new season's crop. On the way down it
> was still there on the tray but one despairing bite had been
> taken out of it. He could see the marks of small teeth that had
> clipped a shallow oval furrow from its side, the exposed
> white flesh already beginning to oxidize and turn brown, like
> an old photograph or love-letter. He was extremely moved
> by this single bite and wanted to say something.

Shortly afterwards the shadowy Angela dies, and we see our last
of her through the remains of her wardrobe – a heavy afternoon

dress of velvet embossed with chrysanthemums, a moleskin cape and muff, a silk jersey afternoon dress with a belt of gold cord – which her father Edward hands on to her reluctant twin sisters. Angela is distanced indeed, and gone forever.

Yet even Angela had once been lively and talkative, and possessed of enough energy to persuade the Major that he ought to consider himself engaged to her, though he remains uncertain how this has come about. And Angela leads us to another area in which Farrell employs a considerable amount of obliquity – his treatment of women and sex.

It cannot be a coincidence that three Farrell protagonists – Boris, the Major, and Matthew Webb – find themselves or risk finding themselves trapped in marriages that they have not themselves initiated. In Farrell's work, men tend to be passive rather than active participants in the sexual game. There are several portraits of predatory females – the twins, Angela by innuendo, the 'fallen' Lucy Hughes, and the appalling Joan Blackett. Sarah has much more spirit than the Major, and is far less inhibited. Vera Chiang seduces Matthew Webb: he succumbs, though willingly, to her advances. Through most of the novels runs the sense that women are not at all the quiet womanly pure creatures of Victorian mythology and romantic love; they are dangerous trouble-makers, capricious and destructive. (Walter Blackett thinking of Joan: 'A great deal of thought must be given to your daughter's marriage. Otherwise she will simply slink off like a cat on a dark night and get herself fertilized under a bush by God knows whom!') When the fifteen-year-old Viola starts to flirt with the Major, his instinct is to back away at once. Of the female characters, only Kate Blackett is treated with indulgence, and allowed a glimpse of what a harmonious companionable relationship with a man could be – and not only is she well under the danger age, she is also offset by her predatory and alarmingly bold friend Melanie, who forces Matthew against his better judgment to take both girls to see a highly unsuitable film. So Farrell's portrayal of sexual love is not wholly favourable. Even the sane and intelligent Ehrendorf makes a fool of himself over Joan Blackett.

One of the explanations for this lies in Farrell's highly

developed sense of the ridiculous, which tends as Lady Chatterley found to inhibit passion (though in her case only temporarily). But there are also moments when the ludicrous intensifies into the repulsive. In *A Girl in the Head* the beautiful and inaccessible girl of the title is contrasted with some less attractive women, including Lady Jane of the circus, whose huge naked breast peers round her shoulder at Boris 'like a bulging featureless face', and underage June Furlough whose 'pubic hair looked like a wad of steel wool'. Nastiest of all is the description in *Troubles* of the experience of one of the Auxiliaries at the Majestic. The memory of it flashes unbidden into his mind when he realizes that one of the twins, by now thoroughly drunk, is intent on seducing him:

> The truth was that Mortimer, though determined to put the best possible face on it in front of Matthews (to whom he had once in a moment of weakness confided the description of one or two fictitious conquests), was distinctly alarmed by the turn events had taken and was secretly wondering what he was in for . . . that is to say, he already *knew* more or less what he was in for, having had (or almost had) a thoroughly nauseating experience in a brothel in France, one of those 'reserved for officers' (one shuddered to think what those reserved for other ranks had been like). Even now, chatting garrulously on the stairs about Jack Hobbs hitting long-hops over the pavilion, he had only to close his eyes to see glittering-ringed fingers parting thick white curtains of fat to invite him into some appalling darkness.

The macabre scene continues with an account of the attempts of Matthews and Mortimer to undress the by now helpless twins (one of whom is referred to as 'a parcel' done up with string): Mortimer, relieved to find that his twin is at least not fat, finds himself thinking

> 'Really . . . girls seem to be perfectly splendid little creatures!'
> But at this moment his hand, which had been hovering in the darkness over her ribs, swooped down to land by misfortune

on Faith's ample bosom – which fled silkily in all directions, quivering like a beef jelly.

At this point, he passes out; shortly afterwards Matthews in the next room has his skull fractured by Charity wielding a champagne bottle.

An equally bizarre scene takes place in *Krishnapur*, again possessing only an oblique relationship to sexual passion or indeed even to sexual intercourse. The beautiful (though 'fallen') Lucy Hughes is engaged in one of her polite little hot-water tea parties when the Residence is invaded by a great dark cloud of cockchafers, which make straight for her.

Poor Lucy! Her nerves had already been in a bad enough state. She leapt to her feet with a cry which was instantly stifled by a mouthful of insects. She beat at her face, her bosom, her stomach, her hips, with hands which looked as if they were dripping with damson jam. Her hair was crawling with insects; they clung to her eyebrows and eyelashes, were sucked into her nostrils and swarmed into the crevices and cornices of her ears, into all the narrow loops and whorls, they poured in a dark river down the back of her dress between her shoulder-blades and down the front between her breasts. No wonder the poor girl found herself tearing away her clothes with frenzied fingers as she felt them pullulating beneath her chemise; this was no time to worry about modesty. Her muslin dress, her petticoats, chemise and underlinen were all discarded in a trice and there she stood, stark naked but as black and glistening as an African slave-girl. How those flying bugs loved Lucy's white skin!

The gallant Harry and Fleury, both chivalric young Victorian gentlemen, neither of whom has ever seen a naked woman before, come to her rescue, scraping the bugs from her with the boards of a bible, revealing a body which bears a marked resemblance to the naked statues from which they had gathered their notions of the female form:

*

The only significant difference between Lucy and a statue was that Lucy had pubic hair; this caused them a bit of a surprise at first. It was not something that had ever occurred to them as possible, likely, or even desirable.

'D'you think this is *supposed* to be here?' asked Harry, who had spent a moment or two scraping at it ineffectually with his board. Because the hair, too, was black it was hard to be sure that it was not simply matted and dried insects.

'That's odd,' said Fleury, peering at it with interest; he had never seen anything like it on a statue. 'Better leave it, anyway, for the time being. We can always come back to it later when we've done the rest.'

This is comedy, certainly, and largely at the expense of the two young men and their defective education (Farrell must have been familiar with the theory that Ruskin's revulsion from his wife Effie arose from his discovery that she had pubic hair, a peculiarity which he appeared to fear unique), but there is an uneasiness beyond comedy lurking somewhere behind it. Lucy's beauty is described in curiously ambiguous terms, as though it is being held at a very safe distance, and made to appear slightly ridiculous in the process: one of her breasts is 'revealed to be the shape of a plump carp', a startling and unlikely simile. The same breasts, at the close of the novel and the end of the siege, show through a rent in her dress 'sadly deflated by hunger . . . no longer like plump carp (they were more like plaice or Dover sole).' This is one way of putting sexual attraction in its place.

The physical manoeuvres of sex are described in considerable detail in all the novels, and are usually made ludicrous. Even a simple action like the holding of hands is rendered at once surprising, faintly sinister and faintly aggressive. Joan Blackett takes Matthew's hand in the dark of a tropical garden, as he worries about fruit bats:

He was so absorbed in this speculation that when, presently, he felt something slip into his hand he jumped, thinking it might be a 'flying snake'. But it was only Joan's soft fingers . . .

A few sentences later,

> Not content with the damp, inert clasp of two palms, Joan's
> fingers had become active, alternately squeezing his own and
> trying to burrow into the hollow of his palm.

And yet surprisingly these hand-squeezings are described as
'delicious', and not necessarily ironically. When, later in the
novel, Matthew is seduced by Vera Chiang, the scene is
characteristically comic in tone, and full of obstacles. She is
slippery, 'like a bar of soap in the bath tub', and when he after
much difficulty manages to undress,

> a dense cloud of white dust rose from his loins and hung
> glimmering in the lamplight. Vera looked surprised at so
> much dust, wondering whether his private parts might not be
> covered in cobwebs too. But Matthew hurriedly explained
> that it was just talcum from his evening bath.

Soap and talcum: an interesting conjunction of ideas. Surprise,
embarrassment covered by a note of clinical detachment – again,
familiar ingredients, as is the intellectual and discursive aspect of
the affair which follows when Vera insists on giving Matthew a
course in oriental sexual terminology before settling down to
anything more practical.

It could be argued that all these illustrations add up to a
hostility towards women, an inability to see them as anything
other than decorative or dangerous objects, and no doubt there
are feminist critics who would so argue. But the overall
impression is not of hostility but of bewilderment. Farrell's
characters are genuinely surprised, so lamentable and crippling
has been their upbringing, to find that the colonel's lady and
Judy O'Grady are sisters not only under the skin but in the skin,
for skin is what they have never seen. But sexuality is only one of
a number of baffling problems. There are few writers who have
made such pervasive use of the emotion of bewilderment.
Confused, puzzled, surprised, doubtful, uncertain, hesitating,
depressed – these are words that appear with haunting

regularity. The typical Farrell man is baffled by politics, by economics, by history itself, which cannot be made to fit his preconceived notions. His response is at first eager, vulnerable, naïve. Yet he is honourably and honestly, if a little hopelessly, engaged in an attempt to understand, to fit the incomprehensible parts together. The Major, in *Troubles*, had fought in the Great War

> believing . . . that the cause *had* been a just one and that throughout the world the great civilizing power of the British Empire had been at stake

(a view clearly not shared by the author): yet during the course of the novel, though he does little more heroic than entertain old ladies with his customary courtesy, he learns to appreciate the plight of the starving and desperate Irish, and to feel a sympathy for them that the stubborn and truly fossilized Edward never approaches. (It is interesting to note that both Edward and the equally inflexible Walter Blackett are burdened with useless and cowardly sons, Ripon and Monty, neither of them in any way fit or willing to take up the burden of Empire, a sure indication of the end of a line.) Similarly the Collector, though he conducts himself and his campaign throughout (and successfully, as it happens) on the most rigid principles of inherited disciplines, wavers at the end, relinquishing, we are led to believe, his faith in Progress and the inevitable civilizing power of the British Empire. Matthew Webb, in *Singapore*, is allowed a more hopeful denouement: in the companionship of fire-fighting he finds a real embodiment of his ideal of disinterested co-operation between people, and there is a suggestion that though Singapore and all it represents may fall, and though the Walter Blacketts of this world will never receive a new idea, change is nevertheless possible, and not only, as Ehrendorf predicts, for the worse. In fact, I think one may detect, between the last two finished novels, a growth not exactly of hope – for *Singapore* is far from optimistic – but of compassion and purpose. Compare, for instance, the treatment of the non-British characters in these books. It has been objected, and with some reason, that the sepoys are never shown as people at all, but merely as cannon fodder, and comic fodder at that, and that their cause is given only the most frivolous explanation, seen, as it were, through British eyes. In *Singapore*, however, Farrell makes a heroic and memorable attempt to portray and understand not only the Japanese, but also the lives of the millions of poor, oppressed, displaced and dying whose destruction came about through no fault of their own, who were swept away by the tides of commercial interest and war. One of the most haunting moments in the whole book, a moment worthy of a great epic writer, is the description of the last moments of an insignificant old man in Chinatown:

> In one cubicle, not much bigger than a large wardrobe, an elderly Chinese wharf-coolie lies awake beside a window covered with wire-netting. Beside him, close to his head, is the shrine for the worship of his ancestors with bunches of red and white candles strung together by their wicks. It was here beside him that his wife died and sometimes, in the early hours, she returns to be with him for a little while. But tonight she has not come and so, presently, he slips out of his cubicle and down the stairs, stepping over sleeping forms, to visit the privy outside. As he returns, stepping into the looming shadow of the tenement, there is a white flash and the darkness drains like a liquid out of everything he can see. The building seems to hang over him for a moment and then slowly dissolves, engulfing him. Later, when official estimates are made of this first raid on Singapore (sixty-one killed, one hundred and thirty-three injured), there will be no mention of this old man for the simple reason that he, in common with so many others, has left no trace of ever having existed either in this part of the world or in any other.

This is very fine, and fine in a manner that earlier works did not attempt. The white flash presages Hiroshima, and there is no irony here.

Finally, it seems to me that his last three finished novels are at heart political, and that his own attitude is neither as detached nor as neutral as it may at first glance appear. All the distancing is directed towards one end – the revelation of the absurdity and injustice of things as they are, and the need for radical change. How much faith he had in the possibility of change is another question. John Spurling suggests that Farrell's final mood was one of resigned horror at the inbuilt competitive nature of man – a cynical attitude not far from Dupigny's in *Singapore*, who sees nations simply as organisms destined to devour one another – but there is a good deal of Matthew Webb in Farrell as well (I was particularly interested to note from Malcolm Dean's memoir that he had himself been engaged in fire-fighting in Canada) – and I find in the work a delicate balance of the two attitudes. Farrell combined a sense of the pointless absurdity of man with a real and increasing compassion for characters caught up in decay and confusion, so that, though they may be the puppets of history, they are not merely puppets. Kindness, gentleness, concern for others – these are enduring values, in which British gentlemen like the Major do not hold a monopoly (witness Matthew's delight at finding a non-European doctor, a 'lonely philanthropist', devoting all his spare time and money to the inmates of a dying-house). There is a hope for the future, and the final chapter of *The Singapore Grip* has, despite its hesitations, a friendly warmth: the narrator has become 'pleasant, kindly and humorous' like Kate herself in her final manifestation.

Perhaps I could conclude with a personal memory, which seems to sum up much of his character both as a writer and as a man. We and several other friends were off to Brighton for the day, and assembled on Victoria Station, where he presented me with a book – appropriately, N. Mandelstam's *Hope against Hope*, which we'd been talking about the week before. And for the rest of the day he continued to apologize for having so thoughtlessly burdened me with a gift. 'Oh do let me carry it!' he would cry, every now and then, as though the weight of a paperback book might crush me. 'How thoughtless I am!' How thoughtless, I hope this memory makes clear.

A PERSONAL MEMOIR

Malcolm Dean

Appropriately, it is his storytelling that stands out most vividly in my memories of Jim. I know of no other person who could tell a story so well or who would be urged so strenuously by friends to retell a tale even though everyone round the table had heard it several times before. Paradoxically, for a shy and private man, he not only told the stories brilliantly but also quite clearly enjoyed providing the performance. That was part of their charm: observing the pleasure which the entertainer himself received.

Jim was at his best in his own home where he never had large gatherings, not just because he intensely disliked them but also because there was scarcely room to accommodate more than eight people in any of his last three London homes. At other people's parties he was something of a Cinderella often making embarrassed and apologetic excuses as early as 10 p.m. before bicycling back home. In his own burrow, however, it was rarely much earlier than 2 a.m. that his close friends would start to leave and only then reluctantly but with that warm feeling which six hours of close companionship create.

For his last nine years in London, home was a tiny, cramped, Knightsbridge flat where he wrote his last two novels. It consisted of just two rooms: one a bathroom which he had painted red and was crammed with crates of fine wine bought in Sotheby's sales. Even the narrow gaps on either side of the lavatory contained half bottles of good claret, and after the success of his last two novels, he would sometimes treat himself to one of these when he was dining alone. His other room was where he slept, worked and entertained. There was just enough room for a double bed, a large table and an assortment of chairs which allowed eight people to be seated for dinner. Yet, for all its tight ground space, the flat did not feel confined. As part of the ground floor of what at one time had been an imposing Victorian home, his flat had an exceptionally high ceiling and the main room had french windows leading out on to a small private patio and communal garden.

His cooking was done in a minuscule kitchen cut off from the main room by a thin partition wall. Dinner in his own home was never hurried. There were always four courses. Always, after his Booker prize, good wine. Most of this was bought at Sotheby's fine wine sales from which he would come back with some real coups. One of his few really rich friends was full of admiration for the shrewdness with which he selected and stocked his cellar. He was certainly shrewd – as the present publisher, who had to negotiate directly with him for his last two novels after he had got rid of his agent, would testify – but it was not always shrewdness which sent him to Sotheby's. Occasionally, when his writing was not going well, a Sotheby sale was Jim's form of 'displacement activity'. He would rush off with relish. By the end, he had so much wine that even the high ceilings of Egerton Gardens were unable to provide enough rack space to accommodate all his purchases.

He was as serious a cook as he was a writer. His cookery lessons began a couple of years after Oxford when a generous acquaintance from university, who was already making plenty of money, invited Jim, who had no money and was struggling to write a second novel, to have a free room in his large apartment. His new flatmate was a homosexual – which Jim was not – who had decided if he was not going to get married he had better learn to cook. Jim confessed that until then – the mid 1960s – he had always thought cooking beyond the competence of men. But although introduced to the art in London – 'I was determined if he could do it, so could I' – it really blossomed in New York, where he went on a Harkness Fellowship awarded for his writing in 1965. It was where we first met and was a good place to develop the art of cooking because of all the ethnic food shops. His kitchen bible remained to the end the cookery books of the American writer, Julia Child. He concentrated at first on French cuisine but became much bolder later and as the research trips for his novels began taking him overseas, first to India and then to South East Asia, he added both Indian and Chinese dishes to his repertoire. One example of Jim's perfectionist streak was his first dinner party on returning to London from India where he had been completing the research for *Krishnapur*. It was tandoori chicken and was superb. He later confessed that he had cooked it four times that week to make sure it would be right on the night.

Dinner at Jim's began soon after the guests arrived. The dishes would appear on the table almost unseen because he was a master at setting up dialogues and, having knitted his guests together, he would retire to the kitchen to put the finishing touches to the next course. It was no easy matter getting into the kitchen. Just inside its entrance was a child's wardrobe. He kept his only two suits in it but unfortunately for the unwary, the wardrobe's door was loose and its latch broken. Visitors who tried to walk into the kitchen almost invariably bumped into the door. Once in, there were other problems if they had dishes they were trying to clear away. There was almost nowhere to put anything down. Everything seemed to be balanced on something else in a most precarious manner. His herb tray, for example, rested on the drinking glasses. Perched above it, on an equally insecure base, was a fluorescent lamp rigged with Heath Robinson ingenuity to a clock so that the herbs could have light twenty-four hours a day. Almost unbelievably, I can never remember anything collapsing. An equally bizarre touch was that the walls of the kitchen were lined with ordinary baking foil and glistened like silver. The cooking was carried out in a tiny gas oven and on two rings. Yet out of this muddle emerged the best meals I have tasted in London.

What arrived for the main course would depend on whether he was writing or researching. If he was researching, one could expect all manner of creative dishes. If he was writing it was more often than not a superb piece of lamb cooked in the French style: *gigot à la moutarde*. He had cooked it so often that it was no effort. Guests would rave but he would privately grumble about it being boring but that his imagination must be reserved for his book rather than his cooking. Of his two arts, he would pretend to prefer cooking for the obvious reason that the rewards were so much more immediate. But like most writers, his happiest periods were when the writing was going well. His sense of well-being and satisfaction in these periods was clear to all.

He was an extremely disciplined writer and although he had his difficult periods he did not suffer from 'blockages' in the conventional sense of not being able to write at all. Once he had finished the bulk of his research for a novel, which would take him more than a year in the British Museum and other archives, he would write most days even during the difficult periods. At times he would complain that he had turned himself into a 'writing machine'. His day followed a strict routine. Most of his writing was done in the morning, which is one reason why he would leave other people's parties early. In the afternoons he would go for walks in London's parks or, in the early stages of writing, supplement his research with visits to the British Museum Reading Room. He compared himself to a clockwork mouse which gradually ran down during the day. His favourite day was Sunday when the telephone did not ring and he could work uninterrupted. For all his self-discipline, he still found it difficult to resist the pull of his friends. 'Too much wassail', he would wail down the telephone but still accept late invitations to dinner. He disliked talking about his novels and would place a plain sheet of paper on the unfinished manuscript of his latest work which, when there were only a few coming to dinner, would be left at the end of his table.

It was only with the arrival of the main course that people who did not know Jim might notice part of his physical disability, the result of polio, which struck at the end of his first term at Oxford. It left him with severely weakened muscles from the waist up. His diaphragm no longer worked properly and his shoulder muscles and right arm were particularly restricted but he cleverly disguised his disability and was fiercely independent. All manner of new techniques had to be learned to do such fundamental physical functions as breathing, for which he developed new muscles, and belching. All sorts of other techniques had to be devised for everyday tasks like getting out of bed, putting on clothes or, as visitors to his flat might notice, carving meat. His shoulder muscles were not strong enough to provide the sawing action which most people use to carve meat or to cut bread, so Jim devised a new routine using the weight of his body to provide the power for the knife. Why it was particularly noticeable was that he placed one hand over the other. But with the exception of this exercise, which he was always ready to do but would sometimes leave to others, it was difficult for a visitor to notice anything except the prematurely silver hair.

Polio, obviously, was a traumatic turning-point in his life but the manner in which it changed his personality was undoubtedly not as sweeping as Jim pretended to his friends. As Jim would have it, there were two separate, distinct and totally different J. G. Farrells – pre- and post-polio. I only met the post-polio Farrell but pre-polio Jim, according to Jim, was an insensitive, unthinking, hearty, rugby-loving, public-school philistine. For those of us who did not know him then, the idea of the philistine being turned overnight into the sensitive plant which we did know, was totally unreal although there was more truth in it than some of us would accept. Physically, he had been a strong person. The pictures of him prior to polio, his friends who knew him then and his family confirm this. The pictures show a well-built, almost overweight man with a barrel-like chest and a ruggedness which explains why he played in the centre for his school's first team at rugby. His only physical defect before polio, according to his parents, was a large nose which had been broken five times. But the philistine part of his pre-polio days was grossly exaggerated by the post-polio Farrell. It was a Jim-like exaggeration.

Friends and facts point to J. G. Farrell already being a sensitive person some time before polio struck. One Oxford contemporary, who became a friend in Jim's first term, remembers his gentleness and reluctance to throw his weight around even when he was a robust Brasenose freshman. Photographs of him in the Canadian Arctic, where he worked on the DEW line before going to Oxford, show a muscular man but with a pensive and anxious expression on his face. And some time before he reached Oxford, he had developed a beautiful script. Calligraphy is hardly an art an insensitive person would have chosen. Typically, he struggled hard to recapture the skill with his weakened wrists after polio and although he regained a standard much higher than most, he remained dissatisfied with the product, which was one reason why he typed most of his personal letters.

What polio did do, obviously, was to heighten certain character traits which were already there and deny him any chance of developing other, more physical parts, of his personality. The sardonic side of his wit, which his Oxford friends had noted even in the first term, was presumably sharpened as a means of self-defence and the introspection, which the disease fostered if not caused, no doubt helped extend his sensitivity. Less time for physical exercise meant more time for books. He would 'meet books', as one friend put it, as others meet people. He had little time for material possessions but he cherished old books, like the Victorian guide which he had discovered, providing advice and tips on how to go to India, or the bound nineteenth-century volumes of the *British Medical Journal*, which he picked up from a barrow only to find they contained the blow-by-blow battle within the medical world on the causes of cholera, which he later made use of in *Krishnapur*. Once discovered, the finds had to be shared. He sent me away with the *BMJ* volumes just as he insisted, once he had been introduced to Trotsky's autobiography and Solzhenitsyn's *First Circle*, that I must also 'meet them'. Jim was not an easily excitable man but writing he admired, like Trotsky's and Solzhenitsyn's, would break his thin cynical veneer and make him unashamedly enthusiastic.

If polio prevented him from playing rugby, he remained an enthusiastic rugby follower. I even lured him to Twickenham twice but he decided that he preferred to watch the internationals on television where he could see the replays. He grumbled away in the corner of the ground, plaintively asking me every time a try was scored whether I could arrange a replay. He also had to stop playing cricket, which he had previously enjoyed but at which he had not excelled, leaving bicycling and walking his main physical pursuits. His legs were unaffected by the disease and he could walk for miles although this was done mostly in London's parks. We did spend two long weekends walking in the Lake District. Unaware of his vulnerability to colds because of the difficulties he had in coughing, I led a fourteen-hour walk through mist and rain on the first weekend climbing Scafell and three other peaks on the same day. He ended by far the freshest of four. And it was on the following day that the widest smile I ever saw pass across his face, occurred: when walking downhill behind the other three, I slipped unceremoniously on to my bottom just as Jim looked around, 'Ahah . . . look at our fallen leader . . .' he cried with glee.

His mother's main memory of him during his polio period was his steely determination while in the iron lung to survive; but survival, not surprisingly, did produce a deep depression during his convalescence. On occasions, in our fifteen years of friendship, he suffered depression but it is difficult to know how much they could be traced back to polio. Certainly the depressive periods were not excessive and even in a depression his humour never disappeared. His voice, which never had much variation in pitch, would drawl with even more feigned weariness but he would still be ready to tell some doleful joke or make some wry and derogatory crack against his visitor.

What polio also did was to switch Jim's studies at Oxford from Law to French, because having missed two terms he was required to start from scratch on his return and he decided that French was more interesting. This undoubtedly widened his literary education but he suffered the disadvantage on his return of joining a group considerably younger than himself as national service was coming to an end. He was not drafted himself but he had already spent one academic year teaching in Dublin, another year working in the Canadian Arctic before his polio made him miss a third year. He lived, at Oxford, in an uneasy position between the students of two academic years.

How much of his hesitancy was due to polio is difficult to say but he was always loath to act in an authoritative manner. This sometimes caused confusion particularly in restaurants where with his instinctive generosity he would often insist on being the host. It was difficult to sort out his politics, which made him identify with the waitresses, from his character, which so wanted to withdraw from an authoritative role, that collecting and giving the orders was never straightforward. As well as being hesitant in manner he was hesitant in speech except when telling stories. His normal conversation was littered wth 'ums' and 'ers', 'sort ofs' and 'kind ofs'. He was also diffident when invited to join trips like those to the Lakes, but once persuaded would thoroughly enjoy himself. There was a similar wariness when talk at his dinner table turned to personal feelings. Even with a group of close friends he was usually reticent and would slide out of the probing questions of his experienced journalist friends with a clever joke or a sly poke at the questioner.

Faced with an intellectual question there was no problem. There would be 'ers' and 'ums' but Jim would be eager to engage with the questioner and visibly enjoy the exchanges. He was a genuine intellectual in that he was fascinated by ideas, determined to understand them and free from any trace of pretentiousness. Like a university student, he would become absorbed in the issue under immediate study. When, for example, at the beginning of his research for *The Singapore Grip* he decided to look at the Empire from an economic vantage point – something he had avoided with both *Troubles* and *Krishnapur* – he steeped himself in the subject by borrowing long-forgotten economics textbooks from my shelves and even more daunting original Marx and Engels texts from others. His joy, at the discovery of a self-taught Marxist doctor at the home of a mutual friend, was infectious and though their hour-long dialogue over the meaning of surplus labour may sound affected in cold print, the sincerity with which each side struggled with the other's arguments and the genuine excitement they generated in each other with their ideas, removed any thoughts of affectation for onlookers. But all this makes Jim sound far too solemn. He would wince at the image. He could not stand the over-serious and had a wonderfully witty way of putting serious people into perspective. Of one earnest American friend, he noted wearily: 'He's a nice chap but he will relate everything back to Beethoven or Proust.'

Much of his humour was spontaneous. It flowed so easily he

was almost ashamed of it. Fortunately, however, it remained irrepressible. To one girl-friend, for example, who asked what the 'G' in J. G. Farrell stood for, he launched into a wonderful, absurd and, for a moment, believable story about having eccentric Edwardian parents who wanted to name all their children after fruit – Robert Raspberry the eldest son, followed by James Grapefruit . . . A prime ingredient of his humour was exaggeration. He would fasten on to certain salient characteristics of people, refine and exaggerate them so that their quirks became quite absurd. If you had not met the person this only made you all the more eager to do so. An American girl-friend, for example, was awaited with keen anticipation by his English friends after they had been told about her inability to throw away the *New York Times*. This part was true. She did in fact have several years' supply in her apartment. But as Jim described it, the whole flat had been furnished with the newspapers, great blocks of back numbers being used to build solid sofas, easy chairs and tables. With close friends he would play verbal games: for example collecting pronunciations which told you more about the people than what they said. One of his categories in this game was people who pronounced socialists as though they all came from the Seychelles – 'seychellists'.

Teasing friends was another element. Any cliché which passed one's lips would be pounced on and one would be mercilessly mocked with it. Years after I foolishly used the phrase in an unguarded moment, he was still introducing me to new people as 'This is Malcolm . . . he was educated in "the university of life".' Similarly, solecisms, misnomers and malapropisms were rarely allowed to pass. The misused words would be caught, repeated with mock incredulity, and the offender asked if he really meant what he had said. Since he was just as ready to mock himself as others, his teasing rarely caused offence.

It was in his stories that his gift for mockery was fully turned on to himself. But before the storytelling would begin at his dinner parties, the cheese would arrive. It was always bought from Harrods. Jim's instincts were deeply offended by the shop with its emphasis on expense, its love of luxury and the preposterous status which shopping there was meant to bestow. Even so, he would still slink through a back door to the store's food counters to buy his bread, a large slice of Brie and sometimes his meat and vegetables, which were of a much higher quality than in any of his other local shops. 'Life is full of compromises,' he would sigh, when mocked about giving his custom to an emporium which was the embodiment of wealth, class and snobbery. Jim intensely disliked the middle-class image. Part of his antipathy to the image was political and part personal. In his first ten years as a novelist there was no problem. He had no money. Indeed, when he returned to London after writing his first novel in France, he lived in a greenhouse. Inevitably this episode became embellished with Jim-like exaggerations. Those of us who did not know him then have a clear picture of Jim, the single-minded young novelist, huddled in his garden greenhouse. One of the few people who did visit him there reveals that it was in fact attached to a house and was more like a conservatory. Huddle, however, he had to in winter because the heater was small and inadequate. Jim was still short of money on his return from America but he preferred to stick to writing rather than supplement his income with literary reviewing. He furnished a seedy hotel room in Notting Hill from bits and bobs he found abandoned. It was at this time he picked up a chair with a loose leg which inspired the wonderful scene in *Krishnapur* where the Collector is discouraged from holding strong convictions because of a wonky, three-legged oak throne on which he was in the habit of sitting. Every time the Collector leaned forward with enthusiasm, he only narrowly avoided being plunged to the floor.

Acquisitiveness was not part of Jim's character. When I asked him during an interview for the *Guardian* about scenes in *Krishnapur* and *The Singapore Grip*, in which the characters were lumbered with unnecessary belongings, he answered prophetically: 'I didn't invent either example. It's just something that happens. During the Indian mutiny, Cawnpore was made almost indefensible by pianos and stuffed owls and other bric-à-brac. It's human nature. I don't mean to sound

superior. If Kensington were besieged tomorrow I wouldn't
want to leave my own stuffed owls behind. But I do have a
feeling that as human beings property, materialism, is our
undoing.' And yet, for all his personal frugality and asceticism,
Jim was the first to recognize that there was also an aristocratic
dimension to his London life. Jim would have called it high-
class hermitship. He did not have to suffer the London tube or
traffic jams to get to work. Radio Three and his record player
provided him with fine music. He was able to walk through
London's parks most afternoons. There was good food, good
wine and good conversation always available. Poets, painters
and writers came regularly to his house and invited him to
theirs. The British Library provided him with all the books he
needed.

It was easy, in these circumstances, to be an armchair socialist.
But Jim was more than this. He never joined a political party but
long before he borrowed my economic textbooks he talked of
the need for more redistribution of wealth and greater equality.
The most surprising part of his outburst against capitalism at the
presentation of the Booker prize was not his criticism of the
multi-national corporation but the fact that he was ready to
make a public stand. Jim was not a media man. He shrank from
public exposure. It was only Tony Godwin, his editor at
Weidenfeld, who persuaded him of the need to give newspaper
interviews. Up to that time, despite *Troubles* having won the
1970 Faber Memorial Prize awarded by critics from the three
serious Sunday papers, Jim had still not been interviewed on
any Fleet Street feature page. The first was an interview, which
I wrote in the *Guardian* in September 1973, and to which he
agreed reluctantly. His criticism of Booker McConnell at the
presentation of the £5000 prize two months later inevitably
attracted more newspaper attention but his remarks were not
made to further J. G. Farrell's career but because he genuinely
felt the company should be paying its overseas employees higher
wages.

The Booker prize (for *The Siege of Krishnapur*) was the second
major turning-point in Jim's career. It gave him the public
recognition which, unlike some of his contemporaries, he

would never have been able to achieve by media manipulation. For all his confidence in his talent, Jim needed this recognition. It gave him much more self-confidence, made him more secure, and turned him into an even nicer man. He became more tolerant of the intellectually nervous and less scathing about people on the literary fringe. He was sucked in further by the literary circuit but he refused to lose touch with any of his old friends.

Some appreciations at the time of his death noted the apparent paradox of a solitary man having so many friends. Yet, the two sides were more complementary than they might seem. While he needed his friends as a break from the solitude, he needed the solitude to recharge the emotional energy required in maintaining links with so many close friends. Most of those friends will have their own list of favourite stories told by Jim. Like a favourite walk, the old stories were never quite the same in the retracing. There were subtle changes and new nuances depending on who was round the dinner table. Guests would still be at the table because there was nowhere else to go in the Egerton Gardens flat. When, late in the evening, the storyteller was persuaded to tell one of his tales, it was clear that it had been lovingly polished and improved over the years. Unlike the 'ums' and 'ers' in his normal conversation, the storyteller only paused in his storytelling if a pause would improve the effects. The stories were as bizarre, ridiculous and funny as those in his books. Listening to them was like reading his books. Part of the humour, as John Spurling noted in his *Observer* obituary, was that although Jim was the central character he was always cast as a somewhat baffled, well-meaning fall guy. 'How was I to know . . .?' was a common rhetorical question. My own favourite stories included the one about the burglar, who got stuck outside Jim's hotel window, having shinned up a drainpipe and been unable to go further up or down; his stint in the Canadian Arctic as a fireman on the DEW line where he was caught taking photographs of a fire – 'It looked so beautiful against the snow' – rather than fighting it; and a mushroom-hunt in a Dordogne wood with the headmaster of a French school, where Jim was a trainee teacher, and the headmaster's French wife, who was intent on seducing him.

Why, when he had so many friends in London, did he move to Ireland? One reason was the greater help his homeland provided for writers with fluctuating incomes. Jim was born in England (in 1935) but had links with Ireland on both sides of his family. His parents returned to Ireland after the Second World War, though they continued to send Jim to Rossall, his Lancashire public school. Another and more crucial reason for his return was the desire to see his friends in a setting other than round a dinner table. Like most single metropolitan people, nine out of ten times Jim saw a friend it was at a dinner party. He had become tired of the format and wanted a country place to which his friends could come and stay. His belated financial success allowed him to buy just such a place. He found a lovely old farmhouse on the beautiful Sheep's Head peninsula on the isolated West Coast of Ireland. It even had a barn which he was going to convert to accommodate his friends. During the four months he spent in his new home his affection for his new life continued to grow. In one of his last letters to arrive, he confessed he had never been as happy. In other letters he described cows getting into the cabbages, baby hares nibbling the leaves of his celeriac and fishing expeditions from the rocks below his house. In the last letter he sent to me in late July he wrote: 'An old grandpa seal wallows thirty yards away watching me fish, with the air of someone who thinks he might know a better way of doing it.'

And then, one day in early August 1979, while fishing from his favourite rocks, he was swept out to sea by a wave. A family who were picnicking on the peninsula saw the accident but were too far away to help. Jim's body was washed ashore later the same month on the other side of Bantry Bay. He was buried in Ireland. His death stunned all his friends. It was difficult to believe we would never again enjoy his wit, warmth and humour. Many of us met frequently in the weeks which immediately followed to give each other support. Even Jim in his most affected cynical mood would have been moved. For he was the least cynical of men. Beneath the camouflage was a kindness and compassion which was generously bestowed on any of his friends in trouble. Derek Mahon, the poet, wrote the most fitting epitaph: 'Jim Farrell has laid down his pen but the books remain. The books and the memory of a lovable man.' Most people remind you of other people you know. Jim just reminded you of Jim.

Indian Diary

The main feeling I have after my first twenty-four hours here in India is one of great security due, I think, to the lack of aggressiveness in the people. The most aggressive person I have seen so far is Heidi, one of the two Swiss Air-India girls, and she was merely scolding the waiter for the leathery chicken he produced at the South End Hotel dinner table. Her father, a stout and stolid Swiss gentleman, produced a Swiss army penknife – one of the red kind with a cross on it – and began to hack away gloomily. The other girl, Katria, chatters non-stop and is proud of herself for knowing things about India and being able to fix things up. I must say that without her I should have been lost in the struggle of arrival; without her ordering me around as if I were a child, a sensation reinforced by her arriving promptly at twelve to shake hands formally and wish me happy birthday. (I had mentioned my birthday in one of the simple-minded conversations that we managed across the aisle.)

On the 'plane from London I had found myself sitting next to Anders Sandvig, reluctantly conversing across the hedge of seats with a print-struck American girl; he had been a war correspondent in Vietnam and was on his way back there at the behest of the South Vietnamese government to look at the Vietnamization of the war.

Landing from the 'plane in Bombay I got a breath of that smoky, rubbishy smell that I remember from the poor parts of Morocco, Puerto Rico and Mexico, and from some of the French bidonvilles. But in Bombay it seems to be all over the city, except perhaps in the magnificent Victorian-oriented Taj Mahal. A large extension to it was going beside it and a swimming pool was being excavated at the expense of how many graceful arches I was unable to tell; the work had reached as far as the main reception desk which now teeters on the edge of a dusty chasm; the liveried flunkeys pretend not to notice. The work is being done in a primitive way with wooden scaffolding and women labourers carrying bricks on their heads in baskets. Overfed tourists from the West will splash in the result of their labours in a month or two, but I doubt if they even resent it.

People everywhere, one has never seen anything like it; they crowd on the roads and in the streets, only wealth gives you a little peace: you can withdraw to the Taj Mahal for tea or sit in the first class on the train. The streets are constantly crammed in Bombay: perhaps one's sense of security comes from the numbers as much as anything. Indians, unlike Arabs, don't stare at you or pester you. Any advances made by money-changers are very discreet. Beggars and street-salesmen rarely insist. One sees horrors quite frequently, in the course of a few moments: an Anglo-Saxon hippy in a dhoti, arms covered in scabs, stoned out of his mind, really in extremis. He staggered past me in a street of dirt and cripples and abject misery not far from Victoria Station. You constantly find yourself looking at naked children, babies squatting in the dust. What hope have they? A kitten lay on the pavement in the hot sun, so thin I thought it was merely a skin at first. I was as horrified when I saw that it was still breathing as I was by the children, even more perhaps. By the Church Gate Station a girl was stretched, very dark, naked to the waist, one arm outstretched. In the Tea Lounge of the Taj Mahal a group of young Indians talking very loud and possessively about Europe. The pavement dwellers have wooden frames strung with string or canvas to sleep on. People organize themselves even in this misery.

Towards about five o'clock, however, there was a moment of peace. I had left the Taj Mahal and had gone to sprawl on the stone bench by the Gateway to India waiting for it to be time to eat the next meal (the only structural element in my day). There were a lot of people, rich and poor, some utterly in rags, sitting there enjoying the cool evening sunlight, or strolling. Number of couples, the girls in lovely saris: how wonderfully feminine they look: one has no idea, seeing the occasionally frostbitten begum in Knightsbridge or a too pale English girl, how good they can look in the right setting. What was good about this moment was the harmony of everything – even some hippies sleeping on the marble floor didn't seem out of place. A bespectacled gentleman sitting on the stone beside me was reading *Power* by Bertrand Russell. INDIRA, THOU ART SOCIALISM. The slogans for the coming election have a picturesque element. Another reads: EAST, WEST, JAN SANGH IS BEST.

It's very easy to be a sahib in India, it seems. Servants are automatically deferential even to the most bizarre whims, which they seem to accept without surprise. Moreover, I wish my eye were better able to see the *differences* between them. I see things without understanding them. It took me ages to realize that what appeared to be splashes of blood all over the pavements of Bombay was merely people spitting betel juice.

25 January
A cloud of birds circles over the Towers of Silence where the Parsis expose their dead to be eaten by vultures. The birds circling are mainly kites, I think; the bigger vultures can be seen heaving themselves in and out of trees which hide the racks on which the bodies are stretched. In the park it is very pleasant; Indian families stroll in the evening sunshine. In England or America a huge crowd would have formed and someone would be selling tickets.

'Livva little hot, sippa Gold Spot', says an advertisement for a mineral on the buses.
TRUTH IS BEAUTY, JAN SANGH FOR DUTY.

Jaipur, 30 January
What looks strangely like a vulture is perched in a tree about a hundred yards away, watching me as I write . . . but no, it has left the tree and moved to another; it is only a kite. From the train, however, I did see vultures gathered around the skeleton of some animal. We had passed too quickly to inspect it more closely. Green parrots with red beaks quarrel and fly from one tree to another. It is very pleasant in the garden of the Jaimahal Palace Hotel: the weather is cold, crisp, sunny and perfect. Here and there in the garden turbanned Rajasthani gardeners squat with their chins on their knees working at the beds. An Indian lady passes. An old gardener with a white moustache offers her a red flower and steps back deferentially. It very much resembles an English garden in summer except that there are not so many

varieties of flowers. There are marigolds in beds, some red and white flowers that look rather like storks; also a little bed of pansies, not looking very content. Beside that there are green sculptured hedges, rather sparse in places, rather crude representations of peacocks, bodies too fat and tails too short and stumpy. The lawn is very successful, a little coarser than an English one but green. A woman is working here too, head and shoulders covered in a yellow shawl, ankles just visible and revealing thick silver anklets. She carries cut grass or weeds in a basket on her shoulders.

On the train journey, first class and sleeper, I feel I must have eaten about a bucket of dust. Like almost everything in India, bar one or two European hotels, only a token attempt had been made to clean it. Going to the restaurant car I passed a sweeper brushing his way along with the ubiquitous handless broom of twigs. A job reminiscent of the walrus and the carpenter. Indians do seem uncouth to the European. I shared the compartment with fat Mr Jain, a vegetarian with swollen lips of the kind known as 'sensual', mouth and teeth red-stained from betel juice, who punctuated the dark hours with snores and farts and hawkings – all Indians appear to do this. Yesterday morning an American family was taking breakfast with their guide who, in mid-conversation gave vent to an elaborate hawking and clearing of the passages: they regarded their cornflakes expressionlessly. Mr Jain was not a bad fellow, shared his bananas and biscuits with us. Gave his views on Mrs Gandhi (confused) and on other topics (also confused, or perhaps it was because his English, though fluent, was incomprehensible, a situation made worse by the fact that his mouth was often full). The other occupants of the train were Mrs Bhangabai, a very old, fat little lady being escorted to Delhi by her very nice and friendly son-in-law (I estimate). She sat dumpily cross-legged (as did the others) for most of the journey. He was very gentle and loving with her. Indians, with whom I had become disaffected in Bombay, made a better impression in the train.

Yesterday morning I wandered around the City Palace in Jaipur: it was more the impression of the elegant mogul building with its towers and carved marble lace windows in the clear sunlight, rather like Marrakesh, that struck me, than the beauty of any particular thing; a fountain made simply of tiny holes drilled in marble, heavy brass doors, marble and red-painted (dull) plaster everywhere. The bazaar here is full of life and not so depressing as in Bombay, though there are still plenty of destitute people: these tend to huddle in dusty encampments and waste ground. Outside the gates of this splendid hotel there is one of those dusty encampments under the trees. There are always countless young children amongst them and one sees, I think, more women than men, perhaps because the men are away trying to get food. I visited the city yesterday in a cycle rickshaw, seven miles, up a steep hill which didn't stop him, though it did slow him down.

A fortunate meeting with a Parsi girl, Roshan Lala, who took me to see the Amber Palace in the afternoon in her business rented car: here for a textiles firm. After that we went to see the cremation ground of the Maharajahs not far away, guided by a white-haired little old man who chattered enthusiastically to Roshan about the place. She is fat, friendly and without complexes, and from Bombay; strange to think that she is likely to end as a meal for the vultures in the Towers of Silence. Inevitably we talked about this: she said that the men who work as porters of the corpses are regarded as pariahs, other Parsis don't like to associate with them. It must be an extraordinarily grisly business. The young people are rebelling. Corpses are set out only twice a day, about seven fifteen and again in the afternoon. It only takes about half an hour for one to be cleared, apparently. I was somewhat surprised when Roshan, an educated girl, told me of the faith she placed in the astrological predictions made for her: she would refuse to get married perhaps during the coming four-year inauspicious period. Her father had recently died of cancer. I didn't ask if the vultures had got him. She told me a number of odd facts, among which: for the first year after marriage Hindu women wear a cup-shaped pendant hollow side out. On the first anniversary they turn it in. Parsis regard shells and peacocks as unlucky.

We saw a Rajasthani wedding procession: a band and the groom dressed up in elaborate turban riding on a horse. There were many other things that I should have asked, but didn't have time for. She said that she thought I looked a sad and lonely person. Amber Palace, incidentally, somewhat resembled the City Palace but in a much more spectacular location. We declined the thirty-rupee ride up on the elephant. Elephants are occasionally to be seen in the street, working elephants, and also camels, more common.

Agra, 4 February

An encounter with a sinister fortune-teller with strangely piercing eyes, a turban with a jewel and a feather and only one front tooth. He kept whipping out soiled testimonials from Americans and asking me to read them . . . offering to tell me the name of my mother for ten rupees and suchlike. He said as a sort of trailer of the coming feature that three ladies were interested in me, one foreign . . . that there were some difficulties coming but they would be overcome. I told him I didn't want to know the future. When I finally escaped his clutches he was quite angry and spat . . . but perhaps purely for bronchial reasons.

After a nightmarish day's journey . . . the last three or four hours anyway . . . in a third-class carriage full of young children, one of whom shat on the floor to the unconcern of its parents who flung it out of the window . . . a splendid, long and somewhat hectic ride on a bicycle tonga from the Fort Station. It was cold and I only had a thin pullover, but after the dullness of the railway carriage, the bazaar at night seemed fantastically full of life and excitement. To Laurie's Hotel, the old-established place to stay in Agra, a room with an enormously high ceiling, the lavatory failed to flush hard enough but *hot* water poured in when one pulled the chain, steam rising around one's bottom. I pulled the chain again, more determinedly. No more water came, but a fat lizard crept out from behind the cistern.

These green parrots always making a great row, chasing one another around and shrieking; their flight somewhat resembles that of swallows. Laurie's Hotel is a little island of English peace, if one leaves aside the people offering to sell you Indian junk licensed by the hotel (at Jaipur they were much more determined), surrounded by walls and trees on all sides; beyond lies the poverty and filth of the bazaar; one only notices in the morning when the rubbishy smoke drifts over and hangs in the moist air. At the gate, however, one is met by a swarm of bicycle tongas, one followed me for about twenty minutes trying to persuade me to take a ride. In the dining room, a bygone England prevails; a horde of waiters dressed up in elaborate cummerbunds and turbans. A pudding at lunch that was familiar, is it called Queen's pudding . . . creamed rice and jam and egg-white, baked . . . or something like that.

Yesterday at Fatehpur Sikri, the Red Fort, and the Taj Mahal (much more impressive than I had expected), an American couple in their fifties, high school teachers from Oregon on a sabbatical year's round-the-world trip . . . they reeled off the name of one continent after another as we had lunch (an excellent shahi korma in the Kwality) . . . so that the effect was nonsensical. They looked interesting from a distance but turned out to be not too intelligent. A round-the-world trip is the ultimate in travel without a purpose: but there's something valiant about it. A pity this couple with their rucksacks and cameras weren't more interesting. He reminded me of Ed Klein for some reason. She kept making simplistic remarks about Indians.

While waiting for the tourists to arrive on the Taj Express from Delhi so that the bus would fill up and go, I sat in a little park. On a lawn a few feet away a figure wrapped in some canvas was lying, one bare brown foot protruded. It was early morning. He had evidently slept there (after dark in winter it must be cold). What I suddenly realized was that I hadn't noticed him. I'd seen him, been vaguely aware of the fact that there was someone there, and discarded the matter as not sufficiently interesting to think about consciously. It's amazing how quickly one shuts off areas of vision. Even the children now hardly engage my attention as they play in the dust. It's an acceptance that this is the way things are. One must be thankful that not everyone accepts this. Katherine Mayo didn't; nor, come to that, does Malcolm.*

*Malcolm Dean, leader-writer for the *Guardian*.

There are so many people about everywhere, crowds of them; just one of these beggars, maimed or half-blind children peddling their deformities would cause a sensation in London. Here, one's attention is so rapidly diverted to another sight it almost lacks reality.

India is full of German tourists, mostly middle aged, comparatively few British. The Germans come and go in great busloads.

The dogs are dreadfully thin and mangy. The only fat and healthy dog is one belonging to someone at the hotel: its name-disc merely refers to it as DOG. The others obviously just wander around living as best they can, like the people. They don't appear to *belong* to anyone: they appear to be tolerated in the same way as cows and tourists. With total equanimity.

It occurred to me today that people here don't actually *look* unhappy. People in England, including Indians, look much more desperate.

New Delhi's elaborate lay-out is not made for the person who likes to walk everywhere. A 'conspicuous' example of town-planning is what the guide-book calls it: the impression one gets of New Delhi is of great emptiness after other Indian cities; I suppose that makes it exotic in Indian terms. There are pleasant fountains playing here and there at road covergences . . . but all the same there is a provincial air to it: Connaught Place, the centre, should be magnificent; instead it is somewhat seedy, lined with tiny shops selling dubious tourist junk, or dirty-windowed offices of rash-looking commercial enterprises. There are virtually no good shops and scarcely any good restaurants. Yesterday I wandered through the bazaar in old Delhi; narrow streets more crammed with human and animal life than I've yet seen. The contrast is shocking. Passing the Oberoi Intercontinental I noticed that not more than fifty yards from it is a ruined little house with an onion roof that might have once been a temple, white-washed; an old woman was crouched over a little pile of blazing twigs . . . an old man could be faintly discerned inside the open door.

A visit to the zoo to see the white tigers: rather more irritable-looking animals than Bengal tigers and they appear to have light-blue eyes.

While waiting for the train in Agra I got into conversation with a little old man who said he used to work in the canteen for the British Army. He had been obliged as a Hindu to leave Lahore on partition. He kept saying how happy he had been during the British time and mentioned the name of a general and of a Sgt. Roberts. His wife had died in 1956 and after that, although he had never done so before, he took to smoking and drinking: he missed her very badly. He told me he was a member of the Lions and showed me his lapel button. He was born in 1901: 'a self-made man' he informed me. Both his parents had died young but he had matriculated. We were separated in the struggle for seats in the third class. All the way to Delhi I sat on a providentially disposed tin box of an official nature. A Sikh and numerous other people stood for the three-and-a-half-hour journey; towards the end of it a ragged and dirty boy of about fourteen sang a song (I believe about Kali) in a sweet and powerful voice, accompanying himself by clicking castanet-wise a couple of shells. I saw no sign of him trying to collect money. I enjoyed the song. For the greater part of the journey, in order to forget the physical hardships, I read, interested but dubious, Paul Scott's *Day of the Scorpion*.

This afternoon (7 February) after my visit to the white tigers I slept for a while and woke feeling bored and discouraged. After a meal (makchau murga) I felt somewhat better and walked home.

On the whole New Delhi made a poor impression, in spite of its imperial town-planning. It has a seedy provincial air; the centre, Connaught Place, where all the roads converge in what one expects to be a climactic urban excitement, is dirty and peeling, areas of the pavement give way to dust; beneath the imperious arcades tiny and mean shops attempt to sell junk to insufficient tourists; touts prowl everywhere at the behest of moneychangers; beggars abound; a one-legged child, a boy, chased me for several yards at an extraordinary speed with his crablike gait . . . however, the desolation of the beggars on the

steps of the Jarna Masjid in Old Delhi is beyond description. I
feel a stranger everywhere in India but nowhere more so than in
Delhi.

A dinner-party at the Bhagats' friends: first of all Bhagat's car
picks me up and whisks me to his house a few minutes' drive
away: servants are bowing and holding open doors – that of the
car, the front door, door to the sitting room; so that, without
any of the customary pauses I find myself inside in a flash.
However, there's no one in the sitting room which is decorated
and furnished wth astonishing vulgarity and opulence in a
European manner: thick royal blue carpet, china dogs, a few
dreadful paintings in a 'modern' style. Bhagat enters and sits on
the couch beside me, perhaps so he won't have to look at me,
which he doesn't appear to like doing, out of a sort of shyness.
He is older than I expect and for an Indian, very unlimber, has
trouble getting out of chairs and so forth. A conversation limps,
partly because he addresses the air in front of him in long
conversational sorties, only at the end of which does he turn to
me. I find this off-putting. The bearer hovering around is asked
to furnish some gin and soda for me. A child with a pretty, dusky
nurse comes in to say goodnight. The kid fools around a bit,
Bhagat relating to it a shade better than to me. I stare with
discouragement at the pretty ayah who looks a bit more fun to
be with than Bhagat. Finally, spoiled up to its eyebrows, the kid
is got rid of. Mrs, done up like a Knightsbridge dame, comes in
and we set off. Bhagat tells me he also keeps houses in Calcutta
and Bombay; I forget whether he said Madras too.

The party itself a very Western one, except for the ubiquitous
servants: they are constantly at your elbow bowing over some
dish they are offering you. Both Bhagat and our host, a young
ex-Navy chap now with the Ford Foundation, seem to choose
old and servile men of diminutive stature as servants. There is an
air of decorous jollity about the party; the hostess is fat and
bouncy in a sort of sub-English way. I talk to an Indian Army
officer, who enlarges on the sins of Pakistan and doesn't care for
me very much, I suspect. Ditto another, more intelligent chap
with an elaborately un-Indian English accent, who works for a
British firm. Many educated Indians have chips on their

shoulders about the British, I fear. The host, however, is an elaborately sincere fellow who wants to be a painter: one or two of his latest paintings aren't too bad. The food wasn't bad; delicious chocolate ice-cream to finish. In my direction the hostess whipped out a book by some other visiting author and read a couple of lines referring to herself and husband. Chuckles all round. We faded into the night with my hypocritically good-natured grin chiselled on to my features. It would serve me right if the wind changed and it remained forever on my face.

Old Delhi station, ill-lit, unbelievably crowded, is like an illustration of Bedlam Jail. I stand there for an hour by my luggage waiting for the train. It's almost too dim to read. When the train does come, people trying to get seats in the third class board it in motion and scramble in through the windows. I thank heaven for the first class as the thought of fighting that mob all night after a rootless day roaming New Delhi and trying to pass time is too much.

In Dehra Dun it's a bit colder; it's pretty though; the air and the sunlight are very clear. A man with a spear sits beside the entrance to the Bank of Baroda. In the children's park, a fat boy with an air rifle keeps shooting squirrels and birds.

One other thing that struck me about Delhi, the appalling recklessness of the driving, worse even than Bombay: people drive constantly to make others give way. The endless horn-sounding swiftly gets on your nerves. Dehra has a pretty main street winding uphill, wide, flanked by some of the best shops I've seen in India (the standard is not very high). While I sat in the children's park, from a nearby establishment I could hear the sounds of a school sports day. A master was conducting the show by means of a loudspeaker. I heard him asking 'house captains' to report at such and such a place. All this punctuated by boys' treble cheering. Another odd legacy of the British . . . like early morning tea, or was that an Indian invention copied by us?

15 February
My sleeping self seems a lot less sanguine than my waking self; for the last few days I've been aware of waking out of feelings of

sadness and loss or absence. This morning I was dreaming that we were giving a splendid party in a luxurious house; that Margaret* arrived feeling she hadn't been invited, she was dirty and wanted to take a bath. I handed her a towel and tried to tell her that she *was* wanted. Somehow the sadness persisted.

For the past few days I've been feeling that being a tourist in India one gets very little from the country – apart from the voyeuring of superficial curiosities and horrors. In Delhi an Austrian hippy came up to me with a story about having got there too late to cash travellers' cheques (it's never too late to cash travellers' cheques in Delhi), and said he was hungry, asking for a rupee. I gave it to him but afterwards was annoyed with myself, thinking that it would have been so much better to give it to one of the really destitute Indians . . . whose pleas I am constantly resisting. The fact was that I gave him the rupee (not a huge sum) because I recognized a fraternity with him as a fellow-European. The fact that it was unscrupulous of him to play at being an Indian and use his European-ness to scrounge money made it no better. The only morally satisfactory conclusion would have been for him then to turn the rupee over to an Indian beggar. I fear that this did not occur, however.

At lunch in Dehra Dun a mouse scampers under my chair and continues on a tour of the restaurant. No one seems to mind.

In the same restaurant in the morning taking coffee, an elderly rather sad-looking Englishman dressed the way Englishmen no longer dress: thick flannel trousers with elaborate turn-ups and a green tweed jacket. An Indian who he knew came in and in passing, said in a friendly way, 'How are you? Are you enjoying your retirement?' He nodded his assent but he didn't look as if he was.

An extraordinary scene at the next table: an Indian businessman telling off a subordinate – a regional representative who had evidently failed to show up to meet him, for the second time in six weeks . . . Prevarications, excuses, pleas for forgiveness . . . the superior's ire was not assuaged – 'You are

*Margaret Dobbs, whose name is borrowed for a character in *Troubles*: 'The gay and charming Mrs Margaret Dobbs'.

bigger guilty than last time because crime is bigger – what am I
to say to Bombay; you tell me what I must say . . .' etc. In the end
he strode out of the restaurant: his junior followed crumpling a
handkerchief.

Large, fat, red-faced, perspiring priests in white organizing
the sports at St Joseph's Academy: one of them runs part of the
race with his small brown charges and shouts, 'Take that tennis
ball on out of that or you'll lose it!' in a rich Irish accent. Also,
standing by, a youth (European) in his late teens, superbly
togged out in athletic kit, spiked running shoes etc, but with no
one his age to compete with. Recollections of my own mis-spent
adolescence.

17 February

Visit to Ramgarh to see Sir Edmund Gibson.* In appearance
rather blimp-like, stout, red-faced with a stubble white
moustache, blue eyes. He suffers from congestion of the lungs
brought on by his heart condition. Coughing, while we were
having lunch, he turned a most alarming puce colour . . . for a
moment I wondered whether he wasn't going to do his number
. . . He is eighty-five. He told me that he had been keeping a diary
since he was eight (which would be 1893 by my reckoning), and
that the first entry is 'Had sausages for breakfast.' He was very
nervous and hard to communicate with at first, kept calling his
servant Lalit to bring him this, that or the other. He couldn't
find his matches or he wanted some beer or a pill. Part of his
distress may have been due to the fact that the wife of his driver
had committed suicide the night before. But I think he is
naturally a nervous person. After lunch, served beneath a stuffed
and mounted tiger's head, he relaxed considerably. Having
changed out of his suit (worn to Dehra Dun to keep the moths
out) may have helped him to relax also. He said he thought he

* John Spurling's great-uncle. Born in 1886, he joined the Indian Civil
Service in 1910 and was British Resident, first in Gwalior then in the
States of W. India, during the thirties and early forties. After his
retirement he continued to live in India, and died there in 1974. There
are references later in this passage to John and Hilary Spurling.

had been short-changed with the tiger . . . the one he had shot had been bigger. His house looked like a stage set for a colonial man circa 1920. In the dining room a portrait of King George V (QE2 in the sitting room). There was also a picture of a very fat rajah he had once had to deal with. He was obviously in some distress in respect to the meal being served and kept up a dismayed commentary. 'Heaven knows what you're getting. Lord knows what they think this is . . . curried eggs by the look of it and what on earth is this supposed to be (salad) and these glasses aren't for champagne you know. No idea what they're doing there.' (They were for pudding.) He showed me his sitting room and bedroom, laughing about all the pictures he has up on his wall, 'most of them crooked' which he didn't think John would approve of – 'but if I like something I put it up.' There was something rather sad about his bed neatly turned down in that very bachelor-like room – everything rough and masculine, dark leather or wood, slightly grimy. I wish I could remember more of the details of his room: I am so self-conscious I never notice things as I ought to. There were books everywhere, mainly in bookshelves against the white ants. He was pleased when I remarked on how peaceful it was. Snatching a framed silver photograph of a lady and baby off a bureau, he told me that that was John.

After lunch he took me down to look at his farm; he'd recently bought a new pair of bullocks that were eating peacefully out of a tub. We sat under the shade of a guava tree surveying his domain which stretches as far as the river, a tributary of the Ganges. A plume of blue smoke rising a little distance away marked the funeral pyre of his driver's wife who had recently given birth to twins. He showed me potato fields and seemed dismayed that none had yet appeared. He could hardly walk any distance because he became breathless. He showed me three lychee trees and sent me off to have a look at some pots where they were brewing up the ingredients for pan. The pots were placed in slots in a long hollowed-out ridge containing fire, bubbling away with chips of a dark reddish wood; the liquid was a mauve colour. When boiled it was placed in a pit for a week and then spread out to set in slats, if I understood the process correctly. He said he had about fifty cattle because he never sold any but just let them die of old age. On the way back up we passed his primary school – a score or so of children sitting in a clearing by a blackboard – two teachers. There were also his dogs, two large and fine animals who dashed to chase a monkey at one point – the monkey fled up a tree. From time to time he would call a servant to bring him a biscuit which he would then throw to one of the dogs.

The whole impression was a rather feudal one: he seemed very much concerned with the lives of his various 'retainers' as he called them . . . stopped to ask who some children belonged to. There was a young man, Martin, the son of (I think) the cook who had been educated at his expense at St Joseph's in Dehra Dun and was thought to some extent to have been adopted by him – he denied it though he said he kept them all. He drove me back in the car, at high speed, until I asked him to moderate it. Also in the car was the old grandfather (eighty-five) who took the opportunity – while Martin was out of the car for a moment – of trying to hit me for Rs.5. He evidently had had some experience of dunning Europeans because he worked up to it quite artfully. Asked me if I came from England, then told me his son had died of a heart attack, then another son in Calcutta had excited similarly, then told me he had a bad foot so he couldn't walk, then whipped out a piece of paper with the name of some nostrum on it, a prescription from the doctor which only cost Rs. 5, he averred. I suggested he ask Sir Edmund for it. He lapsed into silence when Martin got back into into the car.

There was evidently a drama going on because the servant, presumably Lalit, had fertilized the elder daughter of the cook with twins and although he had married her the cook was refusing to have anything more to do with him. She had thrown her daughter out without even letting her get her clothes. Sir Edmund seemed to think it was a good marriage though he was Gorkha and she a Christian . . . but said that the cook was a wicked woman.

Sir Edmund also expressed dismay over the length of Prince Charles's hair and enquired about John's, but he was remarkably un-blimplike in his opinions. He seemed gloomy about the prospects of getting back to England. As I was getting into the car to depart I noticed his fingernails were bitten down. He told me to give his love to John and Hilary and added, 'I do love them very much.' He said he didn't suppose he would see them again. Earlier he had said that he always used to buy his clothes in England. He needed a new hat: the one he had had two holes in it.

He is a very shy person but towards the end I did get the impression that he liked me and was glad that I had come. He asked me for the name of my last book and I told him I would send him a copy.

I forgot to mention that he kept going in to get things to show me: a postcard of Malawi sent by John's brother: a monochrome of a few palm trees and a beach that he enthused over.

Hardwar, 18 February

The town seems to be built up along the river: the main street runs for a long way parallel to it, a mile or two perhaps. Along the river there's an impression of light and freshness. The river flows quite swiftly between well-made cement steps: for once, in India, the water looks clean. On the lowest steps there are chains for the bathers to hang on to, and chains and trapezes dangle from the bridges – in case someone gets swept away they can grab at them as they shoot under. No doubt this is more likely to happen when the river is in full spate. Only one side of the river, that with the main bathing ghat, is built up . . . with some nice-looking houses built on to the river's edge . . . bathing steps run all along the other side which is open and park-like. Various fakirs and gurus live there in little houses, the size of dog kennels, made out of sacks. Some are asleep, others are talking, more than one is smoking a cigarette: many of them are sitting alone under trees; one of them has his face covered in white ash and devotional marks painted on his forehead. Sometimes the hair is busy and 'afro' . . . others braided into little ropes and orange tinted. An old woman was bathing, naked to the waist; few women bathe. I only saw two or three in all. The most affecting thing was a band of peasants chanting some song (pilgrims, I suppose) with a refrain, after immersion to judge by their wet hair. They had a tremendous appearance of joyful faith. I saw two or three other groups like this. I only saw one European, a bearded bloke, all day. Large fish gather by the Harki Pauri, the main bathing ghat and beggars abound there, some of them legless, scooting about on little trolleys.

There are also chaps scanning the bottom using pieces of glass to see below the surface, presumably looking for coins or jewels. There's a general air of fête in the sunshine: people bathing, a small naked boy crying as his father smilingly splashes water over him; a group of men dressing begin to sing, not very seriously. There's even a group playing cards. Cows wander about, eating rubbish, and unfortunate mangy skinny dogs . . . many fine-looking men in saffron robes, often with begging bowls. People with completely shaven heads except for the little tassel of hair at the crown. The pilgrims carry baskets on bamboo poles over their shoulders – these baskets are immersed and decorated with silk ribands and framed pictures of gods. They didn't seem to contain anything; I couldn't make out the purpose. A stall sells flowers to float down the river in boats made of leaves. The marigolds are collected in a stunning golden bank . . . and there are red flowers too, perhaps roses. There are children all over the place, eyes made up with kohl. A stall sells what I take to be kum-kum, little mounds of powder of varying reds and orange, together with half-crown-sized containers. There are also the usual stalls selling food and drink. Soon after I arrived there, an old chap dunned me for a rupee, for charity, for which he gave me a receipt. He wanted more and wasn't impressed when I told him I wasn't rich, as he had a right not to be. I had lunch of vegetable pakoras in a little restaurant in the main street, plus a cup of sweetened tea.

On the way back to Dehra Dun in the third class, a violent argument pro and con Indira Gandhi broke out. On arrival I saw that the contestants were both white-haired men: they smiled and joked with each other at the end and departed the best of friends in spite of their hard words.

19 February

From an early hour the servants hammer on my door on various pretexts since they know I am leaving and I probably represent the only chance the poor devils will have for some time of making an extra rupee. I thought of rewarding them in inverse ratio to their place in the caste system. I started off giving Rs. 5 to the sweeper (in addition to the odd rupees I've been showering on him), Rs. 3 to the dirty and dishevelled lad with an incipient moustache who trudges in with a frightful breakfast most mornings: this was ungenerous but seeing him grab the toast with his dirty hands from the serving plate to put it on mine reawakened my hygiene complexes which have been lying dormant the past few days. Shortly after, he reappeared with a one rupee note which was torn and which he wanted replacing. The white sahib in me simmering with the tension of getting my departure organized, and so I shooed the poor fellow away. When the main bearer in his black jacket started hammering on the door I indulged in a fit of pique and he retired chastened. Later in the day, back from Mussoorie to collect my chattels I relented and gave him Rs. 5. The misery of these chaps' lives can be judged by their gratitude for these microscopic sums.

The buses to Mussoorie were on strike, a fact which took some time to sink in. Finally I found taxi-drivers rounding people up and so shared a ride for Rs. 4 with five others. Unfortunately this was the first cloudy day since I'd been in India and wasn't able to see the views in all their magnificence. Nonetheless, Mussoorie is an extraordinary place, built on mountain tops and with a staggering panorama almost everywhere you look. This is very much the closed season so the streets were sparsely inhabited. A lot of Tibetan-like people: I passed some splendid-looking shaven-headed monks in cherry robes, one of them spinning a brass wheel as he walked – we smiled at each other. I was sitting by the roadside by then, reading the *Hindustan Times* so that I could throw it away with a clear conscience. After lunch in the local Kwality I climbed Gun Hill (having read Ruskin Bond's piece about it). From there more striking views. I also spied an English cemetery which I went down to investigate. I hadn't much time by then so it was only a cursory inspection. The oldest graves I saw were from the late 1860s. Some of the graves had had the lead leaf of their inscriptions picked off. Many young people, girls in their twenties, no doubt young wives in sickly condition, sent up from the plains who didn't make it. Quite a few children. One thirteen-year-old boy accidentally shot. Even if I had had more time I'm not sure that I would have stayed much longer. Gravestones don't tell you nearly enough about people -- only enough to depress you. I also stared at the splendid closed-up mansion of the Maharajah of Kapurthala: a small castle of stone with red pipes and, like many of the buildings here, a red corrugated-iron roof, as I recall.

All went smoothly. I boarded the train in Dehra Dun noting that I had the compartment to myself until Hardwar. I just had time to finish *Nostromo*. Quite a good read but basically so unreal and fatuous. All the characters idealized out of all recognition. No doubt it is an ambitious and prophetic novel: as in *Heart of Darkness* (but more so), Conrad was trying to get to grips with colonialism and capitalism, but the characters are cardboard cut-outs: it must have been a terribly taxing book to write, for the very reason that only briefly (the passage where Nostromo and Decoud are drifting in the dark gulf) does it get off the ground.

By Hardwar I was stretched in Shiv's* invaluable sleeping bag, awaiting developments. The platform at Hardwar was crammed with pilgrims each with baskets strung on a bamboo pole decked in orange or purple or multi-coloured silk and jingling with bells and mirrors. All of peasant appearance, they hurried panic-stricken from one end of the platform to the other trying to find room in a train that was evidently crammed. Some of them, whom I felt most sorry for, just stood as if completely overwhelmed with their gear on their shoulders. When we finally pulled out there were still many of them left on the platform. My companion turned out to be a very friendly and talkative man in his fifties, Mr Hira Lal Chaturvedia, the P.A. to the Home Minister of Uttar Pradesh who was in the next compartment and who had been electioneering. From time to time his bodyguard, a friendly non-English-speaking fellow

*Shiv Chirimar, then living in London.

with a gun and a shoulder strap studded with cartridges, came in. This morning while Chaturvedia and I were gossiping over tea in a simple-minded trans-continental manner (difference between our countries, etc), he sat cross-legged on the seat opposite and said his prayers, eyes closed, lips moving and hands devoutly joined. After that he gave me a cigarette.

20 February

At the Carlton Hotel in Lucknow – a magnificent old Victorian oriental building with immensely high ceilings and long cloistered walks outside the rooms – I have a room with a million mosquitoes. I am about to spend my first night under a mosquito net. A lizard is stationed on the ceiling waiting for developments.

The little boys in Lucknow all seem to be trained to say 'Good morning, Sahib,' as I pass.

The hotel has a supply of books lent by the British Council. I have seized a splendid one by Elizabeth Bowen, *The Last September* set in Ireland at the time of *Troubles*.*

It's amazing, or not amazing, how quickly one comes to accept the omnipresent servants in India and to expect all sorts of minor jobs to be done for one. In the Bowen novel someone goes off to pick raspberries. I have just caught myself wondering why she didn't send the servant.

21 February

The things I didn't notice, walking through Lucknow this morning:

Water-buffalo being tormented by crows alighting on their backs, they shrug their heads laboriously, an image of impotence, one of them forges slowly along in the river. A man ironing with a huge toy-boat-shaped iron, presumably full of cinders. The dhobis flailing away at stones, standing up to their calves in water. This morning the *Sunday Pioneer* had a story with

---

*Elizabeth Bowen particularly admired *Troubles* and gave it a glowing review in *Europa*: 'a major work made deceptive as to its size by apparent involvement with what is minor'.

the headline SOYBEAN CONFERENCE PARALYSED – a candidate for the most boring headline.

I walked around the Residency, having taken a great deal of time to find it. I spotted the iron bridge first of all, over which Polehampton drove on his way to the Residency. Now it is virtually disused as another bigger bridge has been built beside it carrying what looks like an arterial road. A couple of greenish yellow monkeys sat on it and at the Residency end there was a pestilential bustle, flies everywhere and evil-smelling open drains. In the graveyard of the church beside the Residency I came upon Polehampton's grave beside that of Henry Lawrence, as I remember Mrs Polehampton describing it. The stone has been somewhat damaged (how?) but I could make out the inscription she chose: 'Enter thou into the Joy of the Lord'. Mention is also made of their dead infant boy. In the cemetery I noticed an Indian chap sketching: he approached after a while and told me he studied at the College of Art. There was something about him, a tense sort of self-importance, that I recognized from other young men of artistic ambitions and which I found antipathetic. Presently he showed me one of his sketches, incongruously a portrait of President Johnson. Somehow it seemed fitting that he should have chosen LBJ even so. He started suggesting things, a visit to the Martinière, giving me some of his photographs. I declined, sensing difficulties, and faded off.

In the afternoon, a bagpipe band in dark-red uniforms, dark-blue trousers (some regimental outfit I suppose) came and played in the magnificent garden of the Carlton Hotel. The contrast they made against the green of the grass – I was watching from the arcaded veranda above – was very striking. They were playing for some function, I couldn't make out whether it was a wedding . . . a great number of tea-tables had been arrayed on the lawn with specially-placed red chairs at the focal point. It resembled the Sunday afternoon affair I saw in Jaipur when I glimpsed the lady with four arms standing in the shrubbery. Thinking of that incident, why didn't I stop and look more closely? I think it was because I was walking with one of the bearers to collect my luggage and felt it would be a loss of dignity to moderate my pace. 'Oh, mortal men, mortal men.'

In the evening as I was going into the dining room I exchanged smiles with an elderly gentleman and on an impulse asked if he minded me joining him. He said of course not, and bought me a beer. It turned out that he was from Nepal, son of a former prime minister dislodged in a palace revolution. I gave him a brief curriculum of my vitae. Thus we were exchanging confidences hotly when some friends of his appeared . . . four ladies to be exact. There was some hesitation and difficulty and then we all moved to another table. I found myself conversing with two of the ladies, fortunately the younger two, BAs of recent hatching from Lucknow University. One of them, a Miss Hamid, if I got her name, once briefly met Z——[name illegible in manuscript]. She nourishes ambitions of 'writing'. Very pretty and very young. Her companion, less pretty, was very charming too. They said I should meet the young intelligentsia of Lucknow.

22 February

This morning at breakfast the waiter standing behind my chair suddenly stepped forward to tell me he had a headache. No doubt a question-mark formed over my head. However, I recovered from my surprise and told him to come to my room for some aspirin. He did so. I gave him the tablets. He staggered away theatrically, lurching and clutching his brow. I hope at any rate that it was theatrical. I had noticed vaguely before how thin he was. His face is little more than a skull with some black beard on it. I wouldn't be surprised to hear that there was more wrong than just a headache.

At lunch he came up to me, wreathed in smiles, fully recovered. I've been thinking of using this incident in 'Difficulties' [an early title for *The Siege of Krishnapur*], substituting whatever the Victorians used for headaches, sal volatile, perhaps, or laudanum.

24 February

The 'writer' and her friend have not reappeared. However, I have had some further conversations with Mr Mussoorie, of

a vaguely unsatisfactory nature. Last night we touched on
religion; it had become evident that he was a vegetarian, and I
told him of my interest in Ramakrishna. He told me some odd
things to support his belief in the rebirth cycle. There was a dog
who once every two weeks, at the full moon and total absence of
moon, when Hindus fast, would fast also. Also of another dog
that was observed putting dust on its face and refusing meat
with indignation, as if refusing temptation. I responded to these
stories with caution. Encouraged, he invited me to his room for
a whisky, which failed to materialize as it turned out to be a 'dry'
day. Talking of astrology, he mentioned some chap he visits
who has made several accurate predictions, including one that
Miss Hamid would be asked for in marriage on the same day she
passed her exams. Sure enough the Maharajah of somewhere or
other came forward and so they are affianced. This morning
while wandering along I saw a poster at the corner of
Hazratgunj advertising a cabaret with 'Daringly Luscious Lola'.

One constantly sees extraordinary sights as one wanders the
streets. This afternoon my feeling of unquiet stomach and
general ennui drove me to the station: on the way there I saw a
man wheeling a minuscule water-buffalo on the back of his
bicycle – it was sitting in a basket on some straw. The mother,
unattached, walked behind through thick traffic of bicycles,
rickshaws and occasional cars and lorries. She fell behind,
however, and the baby began to gaze back anxiously so she had
to break into a canter to catch up again. On the way back I
passed a knot of people gazing at a woman sitting on the
pavement – a member of the 'backward classes' to judge by her
appearance. Beside her sat a girl of five or six. In front of her she
had a bowl of half-charred and scorched lizards and beside them
a number of half-alive lizards. These she would pick up and
gesticulate with from time to time as she harangued the crowd. I
wish I knew what she was saying: presumably magic of some
sort.

This morning, after going to see the colossal and imposing
Imam Bara on the far side of the Residency I walked back past
the iron bridge and along the River Gomati. A large, rather
blonder than usual, water-buffalo was flaked out on the sand. I

thought it was dead because there were crows standing all over
it and pecking. But one of them suddenly pecked inside the
nostril and it sat up, causing the birds to disperse. After that it
stared blearily round.

All day I've been feeling defeated by India, thinking of
reasons why this should be so. Being a tourist anywhere puts
you in a false and useless position. No doubt it would have been
better if I'd just chosen one place and gone to live there. As it is,
the only way I can keep my spirits up in one servant-infested
hotel after another is by moving on at regular intervals, which
gives one a Flying Dutchman sensation. A more fundamental
reason is my inability to get involved in things, in spite of heroic
attempts. So much of the 'mystery' of India and its 'wonder' is
connected with religion. I find it next to impossible to lend
myself to religious enthusiasm and consequently tend only to
see the misery. Aesthetically shoddiness, and hordes of people
prevail. And the hygiene barrier is still not surmounted . . . the
dogs in Lucknow·are more pitiful than I've seen anywhere.
There was a dreadful, utterly furless creature hopping along in
the botanical garden yesterday. Only the birds seem to do well
here – vultures sweeping into a palm-tree and squabbling
yesterday evening or drifting so high that they are mere specks.
It seems absurd, though, that the dogs should make a bigger
impression than the human beings; a young man in Dehra Dun
for example, who I first saw lying on the ground with flies
packed on his eyes . . . later he was sitting up in a dazed way,
dressed in sacking of some kind. By comparison one comes to
hate the fat businessmen one sees in hotels.

1 March

After a night spent fighting off mosquitoes during which I failed
to sleep a wink, I was out of bed at six to join the boat-load of
tourists on the Ganga. The sun was just rising as we went down
to the water. Many Hindus splashing away, rubbing themselves
with mustard oil to keep out the cold: women, mainly old,
bathing in a separate enclosure, equally visible from the water
however. They don't seem to mind tourists peering at them. A
lot of them are no doubt tourists, or at least visitors, themselves.

The guide tells us that Benares people prefer to go across to the outer bank for privacy. The worshippers cup water in their hands to the rising sun, facing it. The river is completely built up on the west side because the worshippers face east. All the time resonant chanting ... of the name of God ... echoes over the water and the ghats and there is a ringing of bells. We pass the house of the superintendent of the burning ghat looming over the water: on the cornice are two brightly-painted tigers about to pounce, signifying the constant imminence of death. A fire has just been lit on the burning ghat: a woman shrouded in white ... this means, I think, that she is unmarried or a widow ... a woman whose husband is still living wears red. The feet rather gruesomely stick out of the pyre about halfway up. The chief mourner has his head shaved and is stripped to the waist, bustling around with a few others. There are great piles of wood waiting for corpses. Later from the bus I saw a couple of peasants carrying what looked like a body into town, on a mattress on their heads.

After the trip on the river (during which a hippy on a houseboat was pointed out to us by the guide and we all stared dutifully at this bizarre creature, who was merely an ordinary-looking girl hanging up some clothes) we walked up through some incredibly narrow streets, past the golden temple and various other temples ... the way was crowded with cows and pilgrims and sadhus. Many of these holy men are of a commercial frame of mind and try to daub tourists with kum-kum and sell them various other things. Later in the morning at the Durga temple a demanding priest bounded up and garlanded us all with marigolds. I gave him ungenerously thirty paise. The guide actually turned out to be a very impressive person: he spoke very well about Hinduism when we later visited the Shiva temple at the Hindu university. Going in the worshippers reached up and rang a bell. Beside a phallic black stone set in oval tapering white marble sat a priest. The stone was decked in flowers and water continually dripped on to it from a brass receptacle to symbolize I'm not sure what – the passing of life, the fact that a Hindu's life should be devoted to God moment by moment? Three musicians sat and played drums and sang with

ecstatic enthusiasm and good cheer smiling at people going by;
they sat on the floor, all of marble, very little decoration but
shrines also to Kali, all black as her name indicates, and another
couple, I forget who. Worshippers come up, close their eyes and
murmur a prayer and making some sort of devotional sign and
an offering to the priest I believe. Great wax beehives had been
built on the spire of the temple, shaped like baskets.

In the afternoon we visited the Buddhist temple at Sarnath on
the site of the Buddha's first sermon. A great golden Buddha,
beside it a little old priest with spectacles sat cross-legged talking
to a devotee. Thence to the palace of the Maharajah of Benares: a
peeling collection of buildings with some magnificent rooms
over the Ganges. Like the Maharajah of Jaipur he has an
armoury with a collection of exotic weapons – spear pistols that
discharge a shot at the same time as stabbing you. Great knives
that by working a spring open out into four blades. Plus the
usual caparisons for elephants, howdahs of various descriptions,
a plain one for hunting, elaborate ones for other occasions . . .
together with all the attendant elephant gear – triangular caps to
go over the elephant's head, richly embroidered rugs, harnesses
and parasols. There were also torches: a long silver pole with a
cup on the end for oil-soaked cotton or a pole with a five-spiked
silver disc on the end. Blazing rags were stuck on the spikes. The
Maharajah also had lights for different moods: a blue-glassed
lamp for sleeping, a green one for waking, etc., and a whole
variety of velvet cushions, one to go under each joint, ankle,
knee, etc. While he slept the servant stood by to slip cushions
under joints if he moved. Also an astrological clock. A great dial
several feet across with apertures for moving bands, giving solar
time, conjunctions of the planets and so forth, numbers in
Hindi. Above the Maharajah's bed a great embroidered punkah
with gold tassels and a gilt rope, I think it measured about eight
feet by two. In the armoury there were also immensely long
flint-lock rifles, pistols with several barrels and a dagger
attached. Also numerous odds and ends: ostrich eggs, a marble
fireplace inlaid with flowers cut from semi-precious stones,
painted glass windows, rich Kashmir silk vestments and gilt-
embroidered caps with feathers, rich carpets, an iron ring with

interior spikes, hinged, with a chain attached for securing an elephant who misbehaves. Any number of pieces of carved ivory, flowers, trees and so forth. (My rajah might be sitting in the middle of all this gloomily eating a boiled egg and reading Blackwood's Magazine.) Four nailed spikes for throwing on the ground in front of the enemy also. Not to forget chairs made of antlers, tables of rhinoceros feet and something or other made of boar tusks.

Afternoon spent at the burning ghat, after a heavier lunch than I had intended of chicken masala, 'pease' pullao (for some reason they always add an 'e') and 'raita' and nan. I was walking bloatedly back to the hotel when I was hailed by one of a million rickshaw drivers who said he had taken me to the Kwality the day before. This decided me to get into his vehicle and head off towards the river. We had a puncture on the way and he transferred me to a colleague's vehicle. My doubts as to how to proceed on arrival were settled by letting myself be kidnapped by a young and sensitive student. We wound through the usual maze of narrow streets, squeezing past cows and an occasional water-buffalo (this morning I saw two with their heads locked together – two men had to unjam them) not to mention the usual crowds of people.

The scene at the ghat was a pretty casual one. I sat down on some steps for about an hour watching . . . there were about half a dozen pyres going . . . mostly in an advanced stage . . . while I was there a couple of women's corpses in coloured shrouds were brought down on green bamboo stretchers, dunked in the river and parked to wait their turn. There was no wailing or any signs of distress . . . a few peasants also sitting on the steps . . . I suppose I was ten yards away from the nearest fire . . . some of the corpses burning were of paupers and were being burned by men who worked there, who picked away at the fires with bamboo staves, constantly stirring them up and trying to get the unconsumed parts to burn. The outside bits tended to burn least quickly, the feet and the head; a couple of feet stuck out for some time, toes rather splayed, nails paler than the dark skin (the feet of a not young man I should say) while the middle portion of the body burned, the shin-bones showed very white, the skin having burned off quickly and there being little flesh to carbonize; presently the attendant turned one of the legs over – it was when it went right over against the natural articulation of the joint that the body really stopped being a person for me and became an object. Soon after the pyre had been lit the chief mourner, dressed in a white dhoti, head shaved, threw sandalwood powder on to the corpse and something else, perhaps some thick paste of some kind. In a narrow little alley behind the burning ghats holy men sat . . . . I saw them later eating. While I was watching the fires one of the holy men came down to collect embers from some of the more thoroughly reduced fires in a shallow pan; this was to do their cooking on. One of them was heating up a thick round bread of some kind. They picked the pan up with a stick. From time to time (twice anyway) I heard a dull report from one of the half-consumed bodies. Also the white ribs showed plainly for a moment, as the cloth and skin burnt away. When the bodies were consumed down to small pieces the attendant picked the charred lump, unrecognizable as any particular organ, up with two sticks and manoeuvred it into the river; it went in with a hiss of steam. One of the bodies was consumed down to a couple of pieces the size of (I'm trying to think of a non-edible object: apples, sausages, etc., seem indelicate) . . . of coca cola bottles and threw them in: they appeared to sink. One of the more solid hulks oozed a lot of liquid as it was turned over and the old man tending it was having great trouble getting it burned. I left before he had got it finished. When the remnant had been thrown into the river, the mourner got a round jar (earthenware) of water from the river and threw it over the fire, repeating it until it was doused, and then, with it full, throwing it over his shoulder on to the fire, where it smashed rather dramatically.

The chap with me told me that corpses came from all over the country, usually by car (rich people) so in the afternoon there would be many fires. I saw a chap later with one on a stretcher (they're tied on and look very insubstantial) on the back of a cycle rickshaw. He also said they came by water, though none did while I was there. He told me that corpses of babies, holy men, people who died of snake bite or smallpox are not burned but are taken out, tied to a stone and sunk in the river. There wasn't the slightest trace of ceremony about the scene (apart from the various rituals that were followed); three or four wretched crippled dogs lay about basking in the sun, peasants sat around hugging their knees; cows wandered up and down the steps browsing on odds and ends of vegetable matter that they found – paper, cardboard – and one of them even inspected one of the waiting corpses (but found nothing to eat) on which sparrows played too. One man with his son seemed a bit uncertain how to go about it and someone standing by shouted instructions – it was all very natural and matter-of-fact.

Nobody paid any attention to me, fortunately. Boats sailed by, including a vociferous wedding-party in a large boat being propelled by a number of oars sprouting from odd parts – for a while this overloaded vessel was going round in a circle on its own axis while music played merrily. Smoke sometimes blew in our eyes and for a while it was quite warm, particularly as the steps against which I was sitting were in the sun. There were no women present. Some of the larger pieces of body must drift around just beside the bank as not much effort was made to hurl them far in; there were several boats moored in the way as well. All this, which sounded distinctly gruesome to me yesterday when someone described it to me, now doesn't seem at all so. I think this is because a dead body being burned is so completely an object; which is consumed so quickly (they say three to four hours but it loses any recognizable quality very quickly) that one sees people, bodies and so on in a completely different light. It all seems extremely natural in some odd way.

Glimpsed in the streets of Benares, a pavement dentist with an array of pliers and pincers spread out on a dirty cloth in front of him, and three or four 'plates' with a tooth or two stuck in them; he seemed to be busy taking an impression of a patient's mouth. Also glimpsed a cage full of forty or fifty shivering little birds; an old man having his back rubbed with a rubber-ended stick; a very fat man doing exercises on the steps of the main bathing ghat standing with one arm and then the other against a concrete pillar; a party of nuns with a woman's body on a bamboo stretcher on their shoulders, jogging through the narrow streets, broad red marks on their foreheads, chanting words to the effect that 'Rama is Truth'... they turned a corner in front of me and vanished towards the burning ghat. I was escorted around by a highly strung young man wearing a lavender silk shirt who independently picked up the Australian I've been talking to, Robert Metherall. He steered us both, individually, into a silk factory... neither of us succumbed to the temptation of buying anything however.

Benares is a pleasant town but the streets here seem to be more crowded than any I've seen anywhere. Met and talked to a young English hippy who hangs around the Tourist Bungalow but sleeps at the station. He says he has no money but it doesn't worry him, he eats better now than he did before, people giving him food. 'Nod', he calls himself. A mild blond youth with glasses, not unintelligent. We talked a bit about Hinduism and Ramakrishna. He wants to join an ashram but was turned down in Pondicherry. His attitude to devotion seemed a bit muddled to me but he seemed to have a genuine desire for spiritual enlightenment. He had romanticized the Ganga in which he takes frequent dips. He has an off-putting mannerism of saying 'yeah' in the middle of sentences.

Coming out of the station I was idly inspecting some woven bags when a threadbare but respectably-dressed indian approaches and advises me to buy in the bazaar where they are cheaper. It's rare that an Indian approaches without an ulterior motive so I wait for it. He asks if I know anyone who could help him get work as a stenographer. He says he was turned down for a job by the British High Commission and says how, as a Christian (his name is Laurence Mitchell), the Hindus discriminate against him because Christians stood by the British. He wonders if they could have held something against him: this turns out to be a much-used cloth-backed letter purporting to be from a padre and saying that Mitchell had served ten years in gaol as a result of a misfortune: viz, having killed someone, a Hindu, in a train who wanted to throw away his Bible. Mitchell, it said, a trained boxer, had punched him in the solar plexus and it had killed him (this reminds me of the superstition among the British that Hindus cave in very easily if you punch them). It all seemed like the work of a fevered imagination to me, but who knows? In India anything is possible. After that had failed to excite my sympathy he produced a letter from, supposedly, some firm offering him a job which he couldn't take up for lack of the fare to get there. He offered to work for someone who could give him the money if I knew of any such person, suggesting car-washing and massage. Finally, he asked for money as he was 'giddy with hunger' . . . I didn't give him any, feeling that the performance was too smooth, the letter being cloth-backed and so on. Also I had just given Nod Rs. 3 for a meal and my generosity was exhausted.

Walking along the station platform a completely naked holy man carrying only a staff with a brass end like a window-rod and a metal water-jug with which he splashed some water on himself. His body was burned a uniform nut-brown colour. In this same place yesterday I saw a prisoner being marched along in leather-padded handcuffs with a rope tied round his middle, escorted by two policemen (or soldiers rather) one of them holding the end of the rope. He was a good-looking young chap.

6 March

Noted on return visit to the Maharajah's palace: You pass through an archway, not solid as it appears from outside, but hollow, two storeys high with a floor built half way up on each side and roofed over with rafters and plaster . . . all this space is crammed with wooden boards serving as beds and mattresses, some rolled up, others still with their owners reclining on them: all this small space taken up by the two hollowed-out towers seething with uniformed and armed soldiers. Thence you pass into an outer courtyard in the centre of which is a plot of grass and a derelict fountain, a hoopoe digging for food, old mattresses and pieces of iron, broken cartwheels lie about. On your left is the second archway into the Maharajah's apartments. On the right is a building in the European style, two-storeys level façade on the two outer sides with an inlet balcony between; shuttered windows, a deserted look. This has been described as 'a guest house' and 'the Prime Minister's house' respectively by different guides . . . there are low one-storey buildings on the other two sides, stables and storerooms perhaps, or servants' quarters. On the roof of one of these lower buildings near the archway, a peacock with its tail spread was revolving slowly, another picked its way across the grass. A peacock is the mount of Kartikeya, one of the sons of Shiva.

Coming through the second archway you notice immediately that the square is not quite rectangular, which gives a strangely jumbled appearance. Here the Maharajah has his elephant equipment, stables, armoury, and suchlike, beside his private apartments and the splendid main reception room. Here I had failed to notice the foaming chandeliers of Bohemian glass, the middle one being the most massive, ranges of crystal and curving-lipped glasses to protect the candles. The walls of this room are all of fragmented glass in flower-shaped wooden frames alternating with mirrors . . . stained glass above, say, twenty feet; green wooden shutters, some louvred in the French way, protect them outside. The effect is glittering and cathedral-like, both light and muted at the same time . . . a rich carpet and some ragged-looking tiger skins deck the floor. Primitive portraits of past maharajahs are all along one wall (the only one not glassed) and there is a European-style fireplace of marble inlaid with semi-precious stones such as lapis lazuli, agate, some (two shades) green and some dark blue, orange, yellow and red. (Peacocks strut on a dilapidated wall.) Over the mantelpiece is the Maharajah's crest in white plaster – two fish, head to tail, as I recall, and an elephant or two. Among objects noted: a giant fluted (corrugated) shell about a yard or more wide and a host of other shells and coral and sea-growths of one kind or another. The torches with five prongs are called mashala; rags would be soaked in mustard oil or linseed. A palanquin three poles fore and aft, a curving peak like the peak of a cricket cap, the sides done in designs of leaves, silver and gold plated . . . velvet inside. A display of duelling pistols, flintlock, varying in size with bell muzzles. A couch of teak with two very uncomfortable-looking lions as arm-rests. A revolving magazine sporting rifle made by Adams (c. 1850) with an eight-sided barrel . . . a few percussion-action rifles. A sporting rifle by Woodward in a case. Rifles with long barrels so you could rest the butt on the ground and reload from horseback. Swords of all shapes, convex, concave and wavy-bladed from Japan, Burma, Africa, with elaborately-carved hilts and scabbards . . . daggers with hilts of jade, marble and crystal. A flat cowpat-shaped turban made of coils with a feather of gold tinsel sprouting from the front. Jewelled punkahs. Miniature cannons of brass for mounting on camels' saddles, each as thick as a man's forearm.

Calcutta, 9–12 March

'Eating edibles brought from outside not permissible please' – a notice in the Indian coffee house.

First day spent entirely in the Salvation Army Hostel with volcanic diarrhoea, the worst I can remember. The first twinges became apparent on the train from Benares, a journey passed comfortably enough on a hard wooden three-tier sleeper in third. An hour after arrival in Calcutta I was as weak as a kitten. Next day I discovered that Shiv was in Calcutta and took a taxi out to his house in Alipore. In the afternoon we went to the Botanical Gardens on the other side of the river; to do this one has to cross Howrah Bridge, the station and a number of 'bas-fonds' which give the lie to the elegant and open areas of central Calcutta. All the same, I can't claim to have seen any worse-looking slums than I have already seen in Bombay and elsewhere. The gardens, great avenues of green, were almost deserted, except for the Army which was encamped there and kept preventing us from approaching the great banyan tree. After walking around we found a ferry to take us back across the river; it landed us in a Muslim district and since this was the day after Moharram festivities were still going full blast. People were beating drums and a great multi-coloured shield was revolving in the middle of a group. Other groups were watching young men, utterly stoned, having symbolic sword fights in which they took great waving slashes at each other. Later we went to Flory's for tea and ice cream. It smelled like Matti and Tissot's used to smell in Southport. In the evening we ate a pretty good meal in the Amber and thence to drink coffee at Trinca's, a pseudo nightclub, with an atrocious band of Anglo-Indians and ventriloquist with puppet: there was a faintly exotic flavour from hearing his tired act performed in an Indian accent. Also visited, after eating some delicious bhang, the Saturday Club, to which Shiv's brother belongs . . . it has only been admitting Indians for the last four years, they say. Having eaten bhang, this visit was possibly less nightmarish than it might have been sober, though dreadful anyway. We were lectured by an Indian lady for about half an hour of non-stop boasting about her husband's job and those of all her other relations: a really poisonous character. My mind was working so slowly I could think of no way of putting her down, though I should have liked to. However, the fact that Shiv and I simply sat there glassy-eyed and mute and then left abruptly, was no doubt sufficient. There was a deadly false Britishness about the other Indians I saw there. The place itself was magnificent: huge, with great rooms for billiards and so forth.

Sepoys wore, according to the water-colours of Atkinson in the Victoria Memorial, white caps and trousers and red tunics with white frogging.

Kathmandu, 13 March
Reading Mrs Gaskell, who is not one to miss an opportunity of putting on the sentimental screws, the griffin might be transfixed by the appalling notion that he too (see p. 121) will never again see his dear mother alive.

This diary is running down, in concert with my touristic energies. However, I keep seeing wonders no less frequently, if not more so.

14 March
This morning I rented a bicycle and cycled out to Bouddhanath to see the colossal stupa: a pleasant ride of seven miles or so; on the way I passed through a little village: even the poorest places have beautifully-carved wooden windows, some of them give the impression of lace, and eaves. A little further on I passed two men trudging into town with a splendid dead leopard slung on a pole by its feet. At one of the curio shops I bought a couple of Tibetan rings (Robert told me that Tibetans are having to sell off their effects to live). After that I paid an unexpected visit to

the Pashupatinath: an ancient gold-domed, silver-doored temple. I was vaguely exploring a road leading off down a hill when two little boys seized me and made off at a gallop, steering me towards the whole complex of interesting buildings . . . the poor house where a few old people lay around in distressed attitudes (but nothing like India!) . . . one of the little boys elected to watch my bike for fifty paise, the other to guide me. Although only eleven he was better at it than many adults I've come across . . . after a quick tour round he and his friend went off to the pictures which is what they wanted the money for. Memories of my own well-spent childhood. The great thing about Pashupatinath was that there was almost no one else about, except for a few of the inhabitants. The boy showed me the burning platforms where someone had been burned not long before; two or three people were searching in the shallow stream for the little piece of gold that is put in the dead person's mouth (but doesn't it melt and scatter?). Also a little farther upstream a family of monkeys were having a swim, splashing and chasing each other and actually swimming under water as well. They looked very funny when they decided to come out and dry themselves. Their hair was all plastered down and sticking out. They rolled about on the hot steps of the ghat for a while and then went to lie down.

There's another temple here with explicit painted wood carvings of erotic scenes, similar to the Nepalese one in Benares. I later discovered even more dramatic action scenes in the afternoon in one of the temples in the centre of Kathmandu . . . or two of them . . . in the Hanuman Dhoka there is an exquisitely carved man disrobing a woman . . . all the representations of Shiva here seem to show him with erect penis. Vaginae are also carved in great detail and sometimes coloured red for emphasis. After all this cultural and athletic activity (I forgot to mention that I saw a peasant during my morning promenade with a massive silver ring through his ear, not just the lobe, through the cartilaginous portion), I retired to eat buff momo (Tibetan dumplings) at Tashi's Trek Stop where all the hippies gather when they aren't at the Pie and Chai shop . . . I ate some delicious lemon meringue pie later. Buff steak tends to be tough but not disagreeable I discovered yesterday. I glimpsed a butcher's market in Calcutta through a thick haze of flies and really decided I should give up eating meat on this continent. A pile of buff horns lies on the little lane down to the Pie and Chai shop; there are a few vertebrae there too.

I should also say that I saw Everest from the 'plane. It looked somewhat lower than its companions for some reason. The flight tired me more than train journeys seem to. It was quite hot in Calcutta and as we drove around in the airline's bus picking up passengers at the posher hotels the moments of being parked motionless were roasting. It was Holi: shouting mobs of young men patrolled the streets while the foreigners cowered inside the door of the Salvation Army Hostel ('the red shithouse')... as we went through the streets towards the airport, the usual dense crowds of people, all stained crimson or blue, hair, face, clothes. No doubt it had already been going on since an early hour. Tired though I was, I took a walk through the streets (annoyed with myself because I hadn't been able to avail myself of the black market for my first £10) and in a rather narrow alley I saw a marvellous sight: two mountainous bulls fighting each other: that is, with their heads lowered, horn to horn and shoving for all they were worth ... from time to time one or other would gain the ascendancy, driving the other back a few paces and scattering the cheering crowd. Finally, one of them, I was unable to see which, must have acknowledged defeat and bolted because a great cheer went up and the scene of the combat moved rapidly off.

Sitting in the little park beside the Maidan I am approached by a Mr Ashoke Dey who gives me a grubby typewritten testimonial to read to the effect that he is quite conversant with the art of ear-cleaning. He stands by me while I read, flourishing a couple of instruments that resemble dividers ... or do I mean compasses? Anyway, he grabs my ear in a most alarming manner and seems reluctant to let go. In some place, I think it was Benares, I was besieged by people wanting to massage me.

A bad cold has had me staggering around in a daze for the last couple of days. A pile of used tissues litters the floor of my room.

I read Mrs Gaskell's *Cranford* and *Emma*. Of the two, I enjoyed the latter more though her height of mind becomes a bit sickly if you consume too much. I couldn't make out whether she deliberately telegraphs all her dénouements fifty pages ahead or whether we're supposed to be surprised.

A pleasant afternoon (18 March – this was someone's birthday in my youth, I'm sure. Hilary Kirwan's* perhaps) strolling out to the National Museum. They have one or two nice pieces . . . of Bhairava erect in metal . . . plus a shakti who at one stage appears to have fitted on, no doubt to another piece: the position of the limbs, soles turned out, is extraordinarily sensual . . . a picture of Queen Victoria as a young lady with rather bulging blue eyes and a vigorous and sharp look . . . on the whole there is nothing much that I could see of interest . . . the usual array of guns and so forth. On the way back I went round by the stupa at Swayambunath . . . where I was the other day as my cold and the rain were coming on concurrently . . . climbed around the back this time and sat for a while on a hillock by a monastery admiring the splendid view over the narrow strip of very green valley and the rising Himalayas. A service of some kind was going on in the Buddhist temple beside the stupa. Music, of a weird and ominous variety, beating of drums and blowing of great howling wind instruments with a suggestion of trumpet and chanting continually. I sat on my heels by the door and listened and watched. A dozen or so monks were sitting around and there were grains of rice left in front of them to suggest they might have been having a snack earlier. On the way home, in the village on the other side of the river I ran into the eldest of the boys from Tashi's Trek Shop. He greeted me like a long-lost friend and led me back by the hand . . . I bought him some chocolate pie at the Pie and Chai shop. With great tact he then bought us both a cigarette and a sweet in the bazaar on the way up. People are very sweet-natured here.

This morning I saw a dead water-buffalo at the side of the

*A friend from the time when Jim was living with his parents in Dublin.

road. A little crowd had formed round it. There was no sign of
what had done it in.

20 March
Cycled out to see the sleeping Vishnu at Budhanilkantha; a
rather hard ride going but not much pedalling on the way back.
The statue was very impressive: massive, lying on a bed of
snakes in a quite relaxed looking position in the middle of a tank.
There were a number of beggars, however, who made it difficult
to view the thing in comfort . . . they took the form of sadhus
and holy ladies with begging bowls. Usually sadhus don't insist
but this time I was pursued around the tank. I was anxious for
the bicycle which I had left outside untended with my lunch of
bananas and oranges: the bananas were poor, almost as inedible
as plantains, so perhaps it wouldn't have mattered very much if
someone had taken them. Coming back, the brightness of colour
in this particularly fertile part of the valley was extraordinary –
the fields bright green, the sky and the mountains bright blue. A
breeze was blowing which made it pleasantly fresh. On the way
back I turned aside to have a look at the water gardens at Balaju:
pleasant enough but scarcely worth a visit . . . fish in tanks and a
few thin fountains.

 I then took the road to Swayambunath and on my way back
into Kathmandu I stopped on the stout bridge, leaning myself
and bicycle against the wall, to watch a Buddhist funeral taking
place down on the bank beside the river. Some people were
standing around the pyre about five or six deep and it was
difficult to see at first what was going on: a number of people,
principal mourners, were kneeling, and prayers were being said:
half a dozen shaven-headed and saffron-robed monks were
standing there: some of the women also had shaven heads. All
one could see of the corpse was a bundle with a pile of flowers on
top. In due course the prayers came to an end and the mourners
stood up. Two women dressed in white advanced, wailing, I
think to sprinkle some water on the corpse's head: then they
retired to wash themselves in the river. Meanwhile, half a dozen
male mourners were stripping down to their underpants (two or
three wearing Y-fronts by the look of it) and going to the river

to bring water in their cupped hands to sprinkle on the corpse. Most of the observers had gone by this time, indeed, after the prayers the dealing with the body seemed to be merely a formality . . . the chief mourner went off behind the temple somewhere and came back with some blazing twigs to start the fire with, a cherry-robed monk threw a couple of cornet-shaped cartridges on the fire presumably containing some sweet-smelling material, but by this time the male mourners were drying themselves after a bathe in one or other of the miserable puddles that is all that's left of the river at this time of year . . . after they had climbed back into their clothes I saw them no more. The burning of the body was left to a couple of men.

I forgot to say that before the pyre was lit the main operator (one of the two men ultimately left to cope with the burning of the body) fumbled in the wrappings to produce the body's hands. I noticed that they lit the pyre about half way up . . . and as soon as the flames had begun to attack the cloth they did their best to remove it, poking it away with sticks, presumably so the corpse would burn better, the cloth being wet. In this way they uncovered a shaved head and a somewhat charred arm. They heaped straw on the body too to make it blaze better. I wondered whether they had some ulterior motive in the way they set about all this, such as the saving of wood. On the way back up to Kathmandu, I passed a group of men, I think at least a dozen, carrying an enormous dead cow upside down slung on an intricate arrangement of poles so that they could all get a shoulder under. I noticed how flies buzzed about the cow's eyes and upside down its udder sagged inwards. The men stopped to change shoulders and then went on again. No doubt they were taking it down to the river to burn it.

I forgot to record that I rattled up the twenty-two miles to Nagarkot in the back of a Land Rover in the dark: we started at about half past four, having been delayed by the non-appearance of the driver who was asleep, and an interminable collection of four or five other people from various hotels, then by the non-appearance of the guide who was also asleep. We finally got there, however, in time to see the sun rise from behind the High Himalayas, first lighting one peak then another and then finally appearing . . . a splendid sight, somewhat diminished by the touristic circumstances. We then had tea in the lodge up there (7,000 feet or so) where an oldish gentleman was playing with a baby monkey. Then rattled back via Bhadgaon, the bumps in the road were marginally less intolerable on the way back. I asked the guide if there was any religious significance in the erotic sculpture one sees in temples. He told me that one of the reasons for it (the other was to encourage procreation in a Buddhist unsexy society at a time when the kingdom was threatened by the Gorkhas) was as a lightning conductor; the goddess of lightning conductors being a virgin goddess it was thought that this sculpture would embarrass her and keep her away. On the subject of goddesses, he told me that the Living Goddess was chosen from the girls of Kathmandu, aged from three to five, that her body had to be flawless and a few other qualifications which I forget. She then remained the Living Goddess until puberty when another was selected (yes, she also had to sleep a night in a strange place without crying or being afraid). Due to the death of an earlier Living Goddess's husband, it was difficult for ex-Living Goddesses to find husbands. However, the guide told me that a friend of his was married to an ex-Living Goddess and was suffering no ill-effects.

Here (and elsewhere on the hippy circuit) one has brief and friendly but superficial encounters with a great number of people, many of them not particularly interesting. There's a narrowness of interest and, paradoxically, a conformity of behaviour about many of the proto-hippies, mainly American, that makes them dull dogs, in my view (they don't appear fascinated by me either, come to that). However, when Robert in Benares talked about someone being 'a real person' I knew immediately what he was talking about. Among the few who qualify among the people met here there is a Frenchman I talked to briefly in the 'Tibetan Dragon' who had cycled from Goa to Ceylon . . . he, like almost everyone here, takes a dim view of India. Indeed, Nepal is full of refugees from India.

2¾ March

Cycled out to the Chovar gorge where all the waters of the valley have their outlet: not very much at this time of year. With some misgivings, as massive black clouds were looming over the mountains, I cycled on three or four miles before turning back. Shortly after, while coasting down a hill at speed the back tyre burst and I was obliged to struggle back riding noisily and to the amazement of the locals, on the rim.

One sees and registers so much but it's hard to make it stick. I cycled out again early in the morning in the direction of Patan against the tide of workers and people going to market in Kathmandu: I peacefully inspected a couple of temples that I spotted from the street. One of them in particular was very fine with brightly-painted lions of a somewhat uncommon mould for Nepal and a group of small statues: Garuda, Vishnu, a fish. These temples are surrounded by prayer-wheels also. Is this what is meant by the blending of Hindu and Buddhist. John Habecker, on our way to the Pie and Chai shop, remarked on the stupa split by the bodh tree: I've noticed this in several places, in India too, I think. In the afternoon I went to the extreme end of the valley beyond Swayambunath where they are building a road. Women sitting by the roadside breaking stones with little hammers, sheltered by umbrellas. The dust on this road must have been a couple of inches thick in parts and every time a lorry passed there was a thick fog for some time. The road peters out into a track at the top of the valley but the view of green fields in the sun was again magnificent.

On the way back I happened to pass the burning place again and, without realizing it for a moment, found myself staring at a pyre from which a couple of perfectly serviceable looking feet crossed in a rather casual manner were protruding though the rest had been consumed. Later we passed a couple of live pigs being carried on poles, feet and snout trussed, on what I fear may not have been a very happy mission for them. In general, the smaller streets here all resemble farmyards. Pigs and hens wander about, the latter with broods of tiny chickens, not to mention cocks, bulls and cows. At night the hens seem to roost wherever they feel like, in shops and houses. During the day there are always scores of children, many unclothed, playing in the dust or mud. In some back streets they stretch badminton nets between the houses and play by the street light.

This evening I sold the blue cable [pullover] to a young Tibetan I met in the Dragon, having been pondering earlier whether it was worth taking home. I got Rs. 25 for it and a pair of socks, after some heated bargaining. I was very much inhibited in this by the fact that I didn't want him to pay much for it. I like to think of him striding about next winter looking like a Cornish fisherman in canary socks. Perhaps he will sell them, however. The pullover was somewhat too big for him, but he seemed pleased and it certainly was an improvement on his somewhat odd collection of clothes.

Finished *David Copperfield*: a very conditional surrender to its cosy charms.

The journey from Kathmandu turned into an odyssey which I survived better than might be expected, given general age and decrepitude. I sat in the very front of an ancient Mercedes bus apparently designed for discomfort for the long ride down through the hills: half-broiled by the heat of the engine, half-ecstatified by the panoramas. Up in the heights (8,000 feet or so) I ate an undelicious curry with my fingers. The trick is, I discovered from watching my companions, surreptitiously, to flick it in with your thumbnail.

Raxaul (which I kept thinking of as raxual) was hot and dusty. I overjoyed a rickshaw wallah by heaping loose Nepalese change into his hand. He shook hands before leaving.

In the train, a dull German and his Japanese wife: they were good company for the journey, however, as I was past doing anything more than assent to the German's travel anecdotes. A young and name-dropping Indian who claimed his family (he was called V. K. Parde) owned numerous mines, regaled me with stories about his emerald mines in Nepal and hobnobbing with the King, Crown Prince and Indira and suchlike. Whether he felt I was insufficiently impressed or whatever, he ran down progressively so that by the following morning (we all shared a spacious sleeping compartment on the train to Patna) we had lapsed into silence. There's a half-hour steamer voyage to cross the river before reaching Patna itself. This was pleasant in the early morning. The Indian, looking psychotic, hastened off up the steps without saying goodbye and was seen no more. He was a graduate of a Leeds mining school but I think that was only part of his problem. He was fat, with a thin sinister moustache and once or twice he stared fixedly at the Japanese girl. Poor fellow, no doubt he had problems but I couldn't help taking a dislike to him.

At Patna we waited for six hours for the strike-retarded train to come. It was very hot and I kept buying oranges. Indians formed up in listless crowds to watch us Europeans . . . a few vaguely hippy types . . . two or three Germans . . . an Australian engineer in grubby shorts with a badly infected and swollen foot, a Canadian and an American or two. We sat around panting and eating oranges while the Indians stared and scratched themselves and occasionally asked us for money. I chatted to a pretty Californian girl in Tibetan costume who had been in communes and in a Zen club and on macro. All this didn't make her noticeably different from any other nice, dull American college girl. Tibetans were her latest craze but she wasn't very interesting about them. She had been corresponding with some lamas, she told me. I'd love to know what the lamas make of it all. I should think a few question marks can be seen hovering over Himalayan monasteries these days.

When the train finally came the Germans and I got into a carriage with a nice young Army officer with whom we had a simple-minded conversation about how wonderful India . . . etc. At one stage while the train was standing in a station somewhere, he announced grandly from an upper berth: 'These are the fetters on the Nation's economy', indicating some unfortunates who were stretching their hands through the window for alms. I was attacked by a raging thirst and kept drinking tea from little flower-pots in the Hindu fashion.

Some religious festival was going on in Benares today. There was a procession this evening with some holy men on an illuminated float beside a garlanded picture of some bearded fellow. Also an elephant with its face painted carmine; a man was hurriedly drawing further designs on it in white chalk –

accentuating the eyes, etc. He did it very rapidly and added some words in Hindi. Meanwhile the elephant's sphincters bulged and released a few massive golden droppings the size of loaves. The crowds on the way to the ghat were thicker than I've seen anywhere and somehow in the humid heat and darkness the scene was very foreign and exciting. An old man with a beard, accompanied by a drummer and chorus was singing ecstatically and thrillingly under a canopy on the steps. On a dais beside them two or three yellow-robed holy men; one of them steadfastly reading a book. Many people watching but not joining in. Other things glimpsed: a bull dozing in the middle of a traffic jam undisturbed; a dwarf sitting cross-legged and apparently with no bone in his top leg because it was drooping over like a roll of dough. I saw him later, though, in a different position and the curve was permanent; a giant white bull, several inches bigger each way than the biggest I've seen.

2 April

Looking in the mirror of the Pointravel Hotel, Aurungabad, I decide that I look older and balder than when I started out on this trip, but perhaps it's only the hectic travelling of the last few days. From Benares to Satna, a long, boring and hot day in the train. Made the mistake of travelling first class with some giggling Indian businessmen . . . one in particular looked like a pig . . . who, though not unfriendly, got on my nerves. Third class from Jhansi to Jalgaon, fourteen hours, was an endurance test of another kind, particularly towards the end . . . the last two or three hours are always the hardest to get through. This time they coincided with the usual influx of peasants carrying bundles, babies, and sharp tin trunks. A trunk was shoved under my feet, a woman with a naked infant sat on it; another child half sat on my lap. No room to move in any direction and I'd already been sitting there for twelve hours. I did my best to read *Hard Times* by the very dim light . . . the one over me being kaput. Throughout the day it hadn't been so bad, however, except for the young chap opposite me who was suffering from a dreadful cough and hawked and spat endlessly out of the window. I occupied my day mainly buying cups of tea in the little flower pots they use and smash. In Satna and Jhansi I patronized the Railway Retiring Rooms: fortunately having one to myself on both occasions ... grimily adequate, pleasant to have a shower then and there ... All the Indians I've met since leaving Benares have been rather tiresome in some respect, with the exception of the very sweet-natured young man at the Bombay Lodge in Jalgaon. After becoming annoyed with the gharry driver who dragged me along to a luxurious hotel, after subsequently becoming annoyed with the fat proprietor who rudely questioned me and having, exhausted though I was after the marathon train journey, staggered petulantly off with my luggage into the hot and unfamiliar streets, it really had a miraculous quality that I should stumble on the Bombay Lodge and an adequate room to myself for Rs. 3.50. If there was a drawback it was the niceness of the two or three young men, a boy and an old servant who clustered around watching with sympathetic interest as I drank two coca colas and ate some mixture of curry-flavoured nuts and puffed rice they had got for me. Also I was dreadfully grimy and the washing conditions were primitive (two taps outside). The nice young man who worked in a bank took me out for a cup of tea afterwards and got the servant to take me to the Ajanta bus the following morning. Among the Indians encountered was a young chap, a nice fellow, I went round the caves with who kept saying 'Correct!' in places where 'I see' or 'Yes' would have been more appropriate. The guide would say something about one of the frescoes and the young man would bark 'Correct!' No doubt rather alarming for the guide. Also a departing Retiring Roommate, aged about fifty, who unsuccessfully tried to make me feel guilty about him missing his train because he had left his shirt in the bathroom and couldn't get in while I was having a shower. Having postulated all this, it then transpired that his train wasn't about to leave after all. Indeed he sat around talking for some time. Also a man who appeared the following morning, a railway official, dreadfully loquacious who insisted on praising the British for what they had taught India. He was enlarging on this in relentless detail when fortunately someone else distracted his attention for a moment and I was able to slink off. Also, an argumentative young engineer with a small foxy face and very big ears who nabbed me in the third-class compartment. We had a short and sharp difference of opinion about Louis Malle and the making of a film which shows India in a bad light. Although I resolutely defended Malle I fear that my arguments were opaque to him. He annoyed me enough for me not to bother about hurting his feelings.

Apart from the innumerable exquisite sculptures, the atmosphere at Khajuraho was very pleasant. I stayed in the Circuit House where, in the evening especially, there was a sweet smell of flowers, jasmine, I think. The fields round about, where they were reaping the harvest with bill-hooks, made me think of scenes in medieval paintings. I trudged out into the country to see the Jain temples and then three schoolboys, companionably defecating at the side of the road, without interrupting their labours, hailed me as I was passing and directed me through the village to see the other temples. The village too had the same medieval air . . . narrow, winding streets and hayricks in odd corners and so forth. A man in heavily clomping shoes (no socks) of the Mickey Mouse variety that the poorer people tend to wear, shooed away the boy who was guiding me and took over. I ignored him, however, and the boy presently reappeared in a surreptitious manner.